A young u...
A husband is...
Stirring times for...

THE STEEPWOOD

Scandals

VOLUME FOUR

When the debauched Marquis of Sywell won Steepwood
Abbey years ago at cards, it led to the death of the Earl
of Yardley. Now he's caused scandal again by marrying
a girl out of his class – and young enough to be his
granddaughter! After being married only a short time,
the Marchioness has disappeared, leaving no trace of her
whereabouts. There is every expectation that yet more
scandals will emerge, though no one yet knows just how
shocking they will be.

The four villages surrounding the Steepwood Abbey
estate are in turmoil, not only with the dire goings-on at
the Abbey, but also with their own affairs. Each of the
eight volumes in THE STEEPWOOD SCANDALS
contains two full novels that follow the mystery behind
the disappearance of the young woman, and the
individual romances of lovers connected in some way
with the intrigue.

THE STEEPWOOD
Scandals

*Regency drama, intrigue, mischief...
and marriage*

THE STEEPWOOD
Scandals

Volume 4

Sylvia Andrew & Paula Marshall

Harlequin Mills & Boon Limited, Eton House,
18-24 Paradise Road, Richmond, Surrey TW9 1SR

First published in Great Britain in 2001

THE STEEPWOOD SCANDALS © Harlequin Books S.A. 2007

An Unreasonable Match © Harlequin Books S.A. 2001
An Unconventional Duenna © Harlequin Books S.A. 2001

Special thanks and acknowledgement are given to
Sylvia Andrew and Paula Marshall for their contribution to
The Steepwood Scandals series.

ISBN-13: 978 0 263 85498 5
ISBN-10: 0 263 85498 1

052-0207

Printed and bound in Spain
by Litografia Rosés S.A., Barcelona

An Unreasonable Match
by
Sylvia Andrew

Sylvia Andrew taught modern languages for a number of years, ultimately becoming Vice-Principal of a sixth-form college. She lives in Somerset with two cats, a dog, and a husband who has a very necessary sense of humour, and a stern approach to punctuation. Sylvia has one daughter living in London and they share a lively interest in the theatre. She describes herself as an 'unrepentant romantic'.

Chapter One

1812

Feeling rather like a sheepdog in charge of a flock of very pretty lambs, Hester Perceval ushered her cousins out of Mr Hammond's draper's shop in the centre of Northampton. They were all in tearing spirits, exclaiming and laughing as they slipped on the snow-covered street, frantically clutching the parcels which they had adamantly refused to leave to be delivered the next day. Even Hester, normally so sober in public, found it impossible not to laugh at their antics, as she helped first one, then the other to negotiate the busy high street. The gentleman coming from the Receiving Office was enchanted by the picture of the four young ladies as they rounded the corner from Abington Street—rosy, animated faces framed in fur-lined hoods, youthfully slender figures in their warm pelisses, blue, wine-red, russet and green.

Just a few yards from the Peacock, Henrietta, the youngest of the cousins, slipped yet again and lost her balance. Hester managed to save her from falling, but dropped her own parcel in the snow as she did so. The gentleman hurried towards them and picked up the sadly sodden package. He held it for a moment, then said with a charming smile, 'I think the damage is superficial. Would you like it, or shall I hand it to the boy at the inn for treatment? I take it that you are making for the Peacock? Your servant is no doubt waiting for you there.'

Hester caught her breath in shock. A deep, drawling voice, a tall, elegant figure. Dungarran. Impossible to forget him, however often she may have wished to. Fortunately, the gentleman had apparently found it perfectly possible to forget her!

'Thank you, sir,' she said, keeping her head down. 'Our groom will be here in a few minutes. He has gone to fetch my brother from the Cambridge coach. We have a parlour bespoke in the Peacock, where we shall wait for him.' She turned to follow her cousins.

'Wait a moment!' He came round and stared hard at her. 'It's Miss Perceval, is it not? Hugo Perceval's sister! Well, well!' He looked at the three girls, standing in amazement behind Hester. 'Are these your sisters?'

'My cousins, Lord Dungarran.'

'But what am I thinking of! You shouldn't stand on the street in this weather. Come! You must allow me to escort you into the inn. We can talk inside.'

Hester hoped that her dislike of the idea did not

show on her face. It was impossible to refuse. He was right to express surprise, however disguised, at the lack of a maid or groom to attend them in such a busy town. It was certainly unheard of in London. And Dungarran, she thought bitterly, was the example *par excellence* of a London gentleman.

Inside the inn the landlord greeted her party with friendly respect. 'The parlour is ready, Miss Perceval, and I've laid out some pasties and pies in case you need something to keep you going. Shall I fetch some coffee or tea? Or would you like a drop of negus? It's cold enough outside, and shopping is thirsty work.'

'Thank you, Mr Watkins.' The innkeeper looked inquiringly at her escort. 'Lord Dungarran will join us until my brother arrives.'

'However, I'd like something stronger than negus, landlord. Have you a pint of good ale?'

'The best, my lord! Please to come this way.' He led them into a cheerful room, furnished with a table and cushioned settles, and warmed by a glowing fire. 'You'll be comfortable in here. We've sent the boy to Hammond's to have your parcel rewrapped, Miss Perceval. He should be back in a moment.'

Hester thanked him and he disappeared. There was slight pause, then she said coolly, 'Girls, I'd like to present a friend of Hugo's. Lord Dungarran, my cousins Miss Edwina Perceval, Miss Frederica and Miss Henrietta.' The girls curtsied rather solemnly. They all regarded their cousin Hugo with some awe, and this friend of his was just as impressive. The greatcoat he had removed on coming into the inn had no fewer than five capes, and one could see now that his indoor clothing—dark blue coat, a snowy, immaculately starched cravat, light-coloured buckskins—was in the first stare of fashion. They gazed at his tall figure and handsome looks, his short black hair and lazy grey eyes, with guarded admiration. However, they relaxed when Lord Dungarran smiled and said, 'I am charmed, ladies. Truly charmed. But I am consumed with curiosity, too. Tell me what is in those intriguing parcels which you are so reluctant to relinquish.'

The girls laughed and put their parcels down on one of the settles. At the same time they loosened their pelisses and took off their hoods. Hester slowly followed suit. Henrietta, the youngest and least shy, said eagerly, 'Muslins and silks. For dresses. We are all to have some new evening dresses, even me. Robina is coming out in the spring.'

Dungarran looked enquiringly at Hester. 'Robina is my eldest cousin,' she said colourlessly, not looking at him. 'She is not with us today. My aunt is taking her to London some time in March for her début in society.' She could feel the colour rising in her cheeks. Her own catastrophic début six years before had been witnessed by the gentleman standing before her. Indeed, he had been a key player and from the conscious look on his face he, too, was aware of awkwardness in the situation. Fortunately for her peace of mind the landlord reappeared with a tray laden with warm drinks and Dungarran's ale. By the time he had removed the covers from the food laid out on the table, adjured them to enjoy it, and gone out again, Hester had recovered her composure. Dungarran cleared his throat.

'Did you say Hugo has been in Cambridge, Miss Perceval? I thought he was in Gloucestershire with the Beaufort?'

'He is. We are meeting my other brother. My younger brother, Lowell. He should be here at any moment.'

Reminded of their favourite's imminent arrival, the girls went to look out of the window. Hester and Dungarran were left by the fire. Hester felt she must break the uncomfortable silence that followed.

'Are you staying in the district?' she asked stiffly. 'Althorp, perhaps?'

'Er…no. I was at my own place in Leicestershire, but the weather hasn't been good for hunting. I've decided to return to London. I've things to do there.'

Hester took a sip of her wine, and turned away to look at the girls. Why didn't Lowell come? It was impossible to sustain a casual conversation with this man. Yet it would be humiliating if he was reminded of the girl she had been six years ago—scornful of small talk, determined to discuss serious matters of state and politics, inept and unskilled in the manners of society… And, for a short while, stupidly in love with him. Her cheeks grew warm with shame and resentment at the memory of their last encounter. How she had hated him after that…!

'I hope the coach is not delayed by the weather. Would you like me to make enquiries?'

Hester pulled herself together and spoke as civilly as she could. 'Thank you, but we were early. It wasn't due before the hour. But please—you mustn't let us delay you. We are quite safe and comfortable here. The landlord is an old friend.'

'So I have observed. Very well, I shall finish my ale, and then be on my way.'

She was hard put to it to disguise her relief. Though the violent emotions of six years before had long been mastered and then forgotten, she still disliked and distrusted this man. She would be glad to see him go. Unfortunately, at that moment Henrietta scrambled from the window-seat and ran to the door, calling Lowell's name. Hester sighed. Dungarran would now be bound to stay a short while longer.

'But I think I know your brother already, Miss Perceval,' he said when she had introduced them. He turned to Lowell. 'I've seen you at White's with Hugo, but we didn't have an opportunity to speak. But tell me, are you still up at Cambridge?'

Lowell flushed with pleasure at this evidence that the great man had taken notice of him. 'No, I came down some time ago,' he replied. 'But I still have friends there. In fact I've just been arranging to share rooms with one of them when he comes to London in the spring. At the moment I'm living at Hugo's lodgings when I'm in town.'

'Why haven't we met more often?'

'Oh, Hugo's mode of life is a touch above mine, Lord Dungarran. We each go our own way.'

Dungarran nodded. 'All the same, we must meet again in London.'

In spite of her unease, Hester was amused at her brother's efforts to imitate the elegance of Dungarran's manner—Lowell was normally loudly self-confident, boisterous even. It was proof, if any were needed, of Dungarran's status in the closed world of London society. But the next moment she was horrified to hear her brother say somewhat shyly, 'Are you staying long in Northampton, sir? I am sure my family would be pleased to receive you at Abbot Quincey.'

She breathed again when she heard Dungarran expressing regret that he had to be on his way. 'I merely called in at the Receiving Office here. I had some enquiries to make. Miss Perceval, it was a pleasure to meet you again. Will you be joining your cousin in London for the Season?'

This harmless question roused a storm of protest in Hester's breast but she replied calmly. 'I am not sure, but I doubt it, Lord Dungarran. There's…there's always so much to occupy me at Abbot Quincey.' Then, she could not help adding, 'I'm sure you will be kind to Robina—she is very young.'

He gave her a sharp look then bowed, took smiling leave of the rest and left. Hester breathed a huge sigh of relief and prepared to gather her party together for the journey home.

Later, after they had deposited the three girls at the Vicarage in Abbot Quincey and were rolling up the drive to Perceval Hall, Lowell said, 'He's a great chap, Hester.'

'Please, Lowell, can we now leave the subject of Dungarran! Ever since we left Northampton the girls have talked of nothing but the polish of his address, the attraction of his looks, the elegance of his clothes, till I was sick of hearing his name. Surely there are more interesting topics of conversation?'

Lowell looked curiously at her. 'Come, it wasn't as bad as all that. I thought they talked quite as much about their shopping, and the dresses they were having made. What's wrong, Hes?'

Hester could not reply. The unexpected encounter with Dungarran had stirred up feelings she thought she had conquered years before. Anger and humiliation were choking her, six years' peaceful reconstruction of her pride and confidence were momentarily forgotten. Lowell waited patiently. He and Hester were very close. With just one year between them, they had always been allies, both fond of Hugo, their elder brother, but both somewhat in awe of him. It was natural enough—Hugo was five years older, a born leader, a touch autocratic, rather conscious of his position as the eldest of all the Perceval children, cousins included. When Hugo went off to London, the two younger ones had become even closer. Hester defended Lowell whenever one of his mad escapades had drawn his parents' wrath down on his head. And when Hester had come back from London in disgrace Lowell had been her chief support.

They were almost at the house before Hester said

finally, 'I'm sorry, Lowell. Seeing Dungarran again reminded me of London. It's wrong to allow myself to be so affected after all these years. I apologise.'

'There's no need for that. But since you mention London... What did you mean when you told him you weren't going there this year? Has Mama given in?'

'Not yet. But I'm still hoping.'

'I doubt she'll change her mind. And if she did, Papa would still have to be convinced. They seem set on giving you another Season, Hes.'

'It's absurd!' said Hester forcefully. 'There's only one reason for taking an unmarried daughter to London for the Season. And since I neither need nor want a husband, the whole exercise will be a waste of money—money the estate can ill afford!'

Lowell put a consoling hand on her arm. 'You might manage to persuade them—but if you don't, things will be different, you'll see. For a start, I'll be there!'

'Oh, that will make all the difference! If I had known the great Lowell Perceval was going to be in London this spring, I would never have argued with Mama. Not for a moment.'

'Hester!'

She smiled at him affectionately. 'I hope you'll have better things to do in London, Lowell, my love, than escort a spinster sister to dances she doesn't wish to attend, or soirées she'd rather die than be seen at! That would be no fun at all, not for you and not for me. No, we can only hope that I am able to change Mama's mind before April comes.'

Meanwhile Robert Dungarran was on the road to London. The weather remained inclement and it was proving a most unpleasant journey. Jolted and tossed as the chaise slipped on the ice and snow, and progress was reduced to walking pace, he had plenty of time to consider. The trip had altogether proved a disappointment. Hunting in the mist, rain and snow of Leicestershire had been dismal, and the society there even less attractive. His trip to Northampton had been a waste of time—he had learned nothing from the Receiving Office. However, it wasn't a matter of great importance, he could put it out of his mind. What was more annoying was the meeting with Hester Perceval... How strange that he hadn't recognised her! When he had first seen her coming round the corner with her cousins she had seemed a different creature altogether. Laughing, animated, capable. It had taken a minute or two to remember what a bore she had been—and the devilishly awkward circumstances of their last meeting... Still, if what she had said about not coming to town for the Season was right, he wouldn't have to see her again... How did Hugo, the most polished of men, and a damned amusing companion, come to have such a dull stick for a sister? Dungarran settled back more comfortably against the squabs and composed himself for sleep...

But sleep eluded him. Memories of Hester Perceval flitted about his mind like ghosts. She was very young, of course, about seventeen. Straight from school. Hugo hadn't wanted her to come to London so early, but the parents had insisted. When was it? 1805—the year of Trafalgar? No, Trafalgar had been the year before. It was 1806...

She had been so quiet at first, a watcher, an observer, with no conversation. They had all wondered what the devil her school had been about. Hugo had said proudly that she was a prize pupil, but the girl hadn't the slightest notion of how to behave in company. She had none of the usual female accomplishments, not even an elementary knowledge of dancing. Out of sympathy for Hugo he had done his best to teach her that, at least. None of the others had volunteered and Hugo had been desperate. Surprisingly enough, it wasn't all that bad. She could be amusing on occasion, and she picked things up quite quickly. You didn't have to tell her anything twice... Except when she refused to listen. He shook his head. She'd been a prize pupil, all right! Before long she had revealed herself as a prize, pigheaded, obstinate little know-all. She was finished after that, of course...

He shifted and made himself more comfortable. They would surely reach Dunstable soon, and then there would be only another day of this nightmare journey. He closed his eyes...

But the memories refused to go away... He hadn't been there when Hugo Perceval's little sister suddenly turned herself into some sort of crusader, bent on reforming the world. Trouble at Portsmouth had kept him out of the capital for a week or two. But when he got back, poor Lady Perceval was distraught, and Hugo was furious.

To begin with everyone was astonished at her impertinence. He grinned as he recalled Lady Scarsdale's outrage,

'Do you know, Robert, that…that *chit* of a girl had the effrontery to ask about the mill in Matlock! I'm sure I haven't the slightest idea what goes on up there, we only visit Derbyshire once or twice a year, and what Arkwright does with his mill is surely his own business. But this…this snip of seventeen—I don't know why I call her a snip, for she's taller than I am—this *pole* of a girl had the audacity to suggest that I *ought* to know how he treats his workers! What on earth is Lady Perceval thinking of, letting such a turniphead loose in society?'

Most of the younger members of the Ton, including himself, just laughed at Hester Perceval—it was impossible to take her seriously. Out of friendship for Hugo, and a sneaking sympathy for the girl, he had done his best to guide her into less stormy waters, but even he had given up in despair. She was bent on her own downfall, stubbornly refusing to listen to hints or even plain speaking. In the end most of the world simply avoided her company. And then had come the Great Scandal, and London had seen her no more.

Shouts and cries made him aware that they had drawn up before the Sugar Loaf in Dunstable. At last!

He got out and stretched himself. He would order a decent meal in a private parlour, have a good night's rest and be in Curzon Street well before dark tomorrow.

The first two of these were accomplished successfully, and Robert Dungarran set off the next day in a better mood. His comfortable home with its self-contained bachelor existence was within reach. But to his annoyance he was unable to rid his mind of the events which had led to Hester Perceval's banishment in 1806...

Society was bored, amused, offended by Miss Perceval, but in the end they had all been deeply shocked by the events at the Sutherlands' ball. He smiled cynically. The gossip hadn't done Canford any good, either, but he deserved what he had got. He should have known better than to complain to the world about a ruined coat after pressing his attentions on an unwilling girl less than a third his age. The man was dead now, but he had been no credit to himself or anyone else. But what, Robert Dungarran wondered, what would society have said if they had known what happened in the Duchess of Sutherland's library *after* the episode with Canford? No one did. No one but Hester Perceval and himself. Thinking back, he had perhaps been harsh with the girl, but encouraging her would have been even more unkind. He shifted uncomfortably, the scene six years before vivid in his mind's eye.

* * *

When Dungarran had arrived at the door of the library Canford had practically knocked him over as he stormed out, swearing vengeance. The noble earl was in a sorry state, his cravat, shirt and velvet coat soaked in wine. Apparently the girl had emptied a glass of the best Bordeaux over him. It looked more like the contents of a decanter. Inside the library he was met with a scene to send any young man of fashion running for cover. Hugo, who was usually calm in all circumstances, had lost his temper spectacularly. Hester, standing in the middle of the room, her bodice torn, and her hair halfway down her back, had been reduced by his words to hysterics. The situation was clearly desperate. When Hugo saw his friend standing in the door he had pleaded, 'Robert, would you take care of this sister of mine? I'll send my mother to her as soon as I can, but she can't leave the room in the state she's in, and I must go after Canford straight away to see what can be done to avoid a scandal.'

With the greatest possible reluctance, Robert, observing the state of both Percevals, had to agree. It was vital that Canford's tirade should be stemmed before too many people heard it, and the girl could not be left alone. Hugo hurried out and he and Hester were left in the room.

'Miss Perceval—'

Hester was now calm enough to speak between her sobs. 'It's all your fault!' she shouted. 'I would never have gone with that…that monster if you had been kinder.'

'Miss Perceval, let me fetch you something to calm you. I'm sorry—'

'I won't listen to your excuses! You all laughed at me, I heard you tonight with your friends! All laughing at me! You're no better than a fashion plate, a pasteboard figure without heart or mind! God might have given you brains, but lack of use has caused them to…to wither away! Don't speak to me! I don't want to hear your excuses!'

Robert Dungarran bowed. 'I was not aware that I had done anything to excuse. But I won't say another word, if that is what you wish.'

'Look at you!' she went on stormily. 'Elegantly empty! You don't care whose heart you break! Making me fall in love with you—'

'Oh no!' This was too much, even for a man of Robert Dungarran's equable temperament. 'That cannot be so. I have never given you the slightest reason to—'

'Of course you did! Why else would you spend so long teaching me to dance, taking me for drives, saying how pretty I looked, when I know very well I am not at all pretty? You are all the same, all of you. Just like Lord Canford—' She was working herself up into hysteria again. Robert had done the only thing possible. He had slapped her, not particularly gently. Eyes wide with shock, she had stared at him.

'You…you monster!' she stuttered. 'To hit a lady…'

'A lady!' he said derisively. 'You! Listen to me, Miss Perceval! You are as close to being a lady as I am to being the Great Cham of China! You are, in fact, an obstinate, conceited, ignorant child. My sympathies, such as they are, are with Hugo. How he came to have such a fool of a sister I cannot imagine. I am sorry the conversation you overheard tonight distressed you, but I would not retract one word from its message. You would do well to persuade your mother to take you away from London to somewhere where you can learn manners and sense in decent obscurity. And now, if you don't mind, I shall guard the door outside until your mother arrives.'

The chaise was passing Hyde Park. He was nearly home, thank God. It was as well. Remembering what he had said to Hester Perceval all those years ago was not a pleasant exercise. The girl had been an appalling nuisance, but he shouldn't have been quite so hard on her. He got out and stretched. Bates, his butler and steward in Curzon Street, was already outside the house, organising the footmen, paying off the chaise and generally being his usual supremely efficient self. It was time to forget Hester Perceval. With any luck he needn't meet her again.

Chapter Two

A few weeks after the trip to Northampton the weather had changed for the better. It was even quite warm. Hester Perceval paid her usual morning calls in Abbot Quincey village, then walked slowly back up the drive to the Hall, which was bathed in early spring sunshine. It was a lovely building of old rose brick decorated with a porch and pilasters of pale grey stone. A wide, graceful flight of steps in the same grey stone led up to its main entrance and two wings of rose brick curved gently to either side. Lawns and tall trees—chestnuts, oaks, ash and holly—sur-rounded it, though at this time of year most of the trees were bare. But there was a promise of spring in daffodils dancing along the drive, and in the faint haze of green in the hawthorn hedges on the edge of the park.

Hester gazed at it wistfully. Short of a miracle she would soon have to leave the Hall to spend two months or more in the capital. Lady Perceval, nor-mally the most understanding of mothers, had refused to abandon her plan to take her daughter to town in an effort to acquire a husband for her. It was ridiculous! She didn't want a husband—and what was more, she would be extremely surprised if she could find one. But however much she had pleaded, reasoned, even argued, it had been in vain. And now time was scarce. In a few weeks Sir James and Lady Perceval would leave for London, accompanied by their daughter, to take part in the annual carnival which called itself the London Season...Hester quickened her pace up the drive. She must make one last effort to bring her mother to see reason.

But half an hour later Hester was no nearer to success. Her mother was unshaken in her determination, and was growing quite upset by her daughter's obstinate refusal to accept her decision.

'You're a good, clever girl and your father and I love you dearly, Hester. Surely you don't believe that we wish to make you unhappy? Or that we haven't your best interests at heart?' Lady Perceval's voice trembled and her daughter quickly reassured her.

'Of course not, Mama! No one could ask for kinder or more generous parents. It's just... I really don't want another London Season. The last one was enough for me. And surely I'm old enough to know my own mind...'

'Exactly so. You'll be twenty-four in November, Hester! Twenty-four and not a single prospect in view. I did have hopes of Wyndham for you at one time, though he's hardly ever been at Bredington recently. But I hear he has found someone else. And now dear India is married, and Beatrice Roade, too—both very advantageously…'

'But I don't want a husband, Mama! Oh, I wish you would believe me. I could remain a perfectly happy spinster, leading my own life in my own way, if only you would let me.'

'My dear, I've heard all these arguments before, and I assure you yet again, that the only secure future for a woman is in marriage. Or would you prefer to be Hugo's pensioner, once your father and I are no longer here?'

'In no way! Hugo and I would be at odds before the month was out! But in any case that must be a very distant prospect. And I'm sure you could persuade Papa to settle a small amount of money on me instead of taking me to London—' Hester moved over to sit down on the sofa by her mother. She took her hand and looked pleadingly into her parent's unusually determined face. 'If he would give me just a small sum—enough to give me a very modest income—I should be happy to live by myself.'

'Alone?'

'With a maid or…or even a companion if you insisted.'

'Hester, I wouldn't even dream of passing on such a ridiculous notion to your father. And if I did he would laugh it out of court! It's our duty to see you safely married, and a London Season is the best way of doing it.' She looked appraisingly at her daughter. 'You could be quite a good-looking girl, if you would only make the effort. Your dowry, I know, is not large, but there must be someone somewhere who would want to marry you!'

This was too much for Hester's very ready sense of humour. Her mouth twitched as she said demurely, 'Why thank you, Mama! A widower, perhaps, with six children and a wooden leg? He might just be persuaded to take me on.'

'I didn't mean it that way, as you very well know. You are a wicked girl to tease me so. But an older man might be the answer?'

Hester was instantly serious again. 'No, Mama! I do not wish for a husband of any kind—old, young, widowed, single, decrepit, healthy… To put it absolutely plainly, I do not want to marry anyone.'

Lady Perceval looked helplessly at her daughter. 'But *why*, Hester?'

'Because I don't believe there's anyone in the world whom I could respect, and who would be willing to treat me in return as someone capable of rational thought! The polite world is singularly lacking in such men. At least it was six years ago, and I cannot suppose things have changed very much since then. In my experience gentlemen in London only want a pretty face to pay empty compliments to, a graceful partner to dance and flirt with, a…a mirror to tell them in return how witty, how handsome, how elegant they are. And I daresay when they eventually condescend to marry some poor girl, they will treat her like…like a piece of furniture—there to provide an heir and manage the household, while they go their selfish, masculine way, hunting, fishing, shooting and gambling into the night.'

'Hester! Stop, stop! That's quite enough of your nonsense. I won't allow you to say such things when your father is everything that is kind and considerate—you know he is! What other father would allow you to do very much as you please here in Abbot Quincey? Many another would have married you off to some country squire long before now. As it is, he has always respected your wish to live quietly with your books. He is even proud of your work in sorting your grandpapa's papers. He is taking us to London mainly because he honestly believes—as I do—that you would be happier with an establishment and family of your own. We wish to find a husband for you before it is too late.'

'Papa is an exceptional man, Mama, and I admit he has been very patient with me—'

'Well then,' said Lady Perceval, 'why don't you please him—and me—by overcoming your reluctance for another London Season?'

'That wouldn't guarantee a husband for me! Men don't find women like me attractive, Mama. I don't have to remind you of what happened six years ago—you were there.'

Lady Perceval shuddered. 'I was,' she replied with feeling.

'The so-called gentlemen made fun of me! I may have been inept and...and, yes, stupid! But they were so unkind! They made no effort to understand. They couldn't believe that a woman might want to ask questions or debate issues which went beyond the cut of a sleeve or who was whose latest flirt.' She frowned, then shrugged her shoulders and smiled wryly. 'I was foolish to try. The last thing they wanted to do was to be required to think.'

'I've always felt that a lot of the blame was mine, my dear. You were very young. Hugo always advised against taking you straight from Mrs Guarding's Academy into the fashionable world, and he was right. You weren't prepared for it.'

'Mrs Guarding is a wonderful woman. I...'

'I know about Mrs Guarding's advanced views on educating young women. She may be a wonderful teacher, but her ideas do not exactly prepare girls for success in society! You were stuffed full of half-digested notions of saving the world. Praiseworthy, no doubt, but hardly appropriate for the drawing-rooms of the Ton. And then the scandal with Lord Canford ruined everything—'

Hester shuddered. 'Please don't, Mama! If you only knew what that episode did to my self-esteem!'

'I do know! You didn't have a chance after that. I was never so shocked in all my life as when I heard how Canford had behaved at the Sutherlands' ball. Thank heaven Hugo was there to rescue you!'

'He may have saved me from Canford's attentions, but he didn't exactly spare my feelings afterwards—especially when the noble lord aired his grievance to anyone who cared to listen.' A giggle escaped her. 'Mind you, Canford had some cause. If he really be-lieved I had encouraged him, it must have come as a shock when I emptied the glass of wine over him. His coat was ruined. What he must have felt when Hugo came in and caught him chasing me round the room…!'

'I am surprised Canford had so much vitality. He must have been sixty if he was a day!'

'He had a quite remarkable turn of speed. And then Hugo got caught in Canford's walking stick and they both came down. Thank God neither was badly hurt. The scandal would have been even greater if such a prominent member of the aristocracy had been lamed for life by my brother! But Canford limped away quite nimbly in the end. Soaked in wine and cursing.' There was a pause. Then Hester added, 'Looking back now, it was a relief that you were more or less forced to bring me back to Northamptonshire afterwards… I had had enough of London, and Hugo had certainly had enough of me.'

'He was disappointed that his efforts to launch you had failed so disastrously. He suffered too, Hester.'

'My dear Mama, Hugo was far more concerned about his own dignity than he was about my reputation. I'd apparently let him down in front of…in front of…his friends.'

'I'm sure he had forgotten that Dungarran was there when he gave you such a dressing-down. He would never normally have done such a thing in front of anyone else.'

'You believe not?'

'I am sure he wouldn't. It was most unfortunate.

You haven't really been friends with him since, have you, my dear?'

'No. And he comes so seldom to Abbot Quincey now, that there's never an opportunity for us to put things right. Lowell is here quite often, but Hugo never comes.'

Lady Perceval said firmly, 'Hugo is like every other young man of his age—he enjoys life in society. He'll come when he is ready—you'll see. He's thirty in July, and that's when he always said he would settle down.'

'He was so unkind to me! But I miss him, all the same. We were good friends when we were young...' Hester got up, went to the window and gazed at the peaceful scene outside without really seeing it. There was a silence. Then she added bitterly, 'Is it so surprising that I never want to see London again?'

Lady Perceval sighed. 'I am sure things will be different now,' she said persuasively. 'Canford died two years ago. And memories are short.'

'Perhaps. But men still like pretty faces, and dainty, appealing ways in the young women they marry. They don't look for argument or debate. Well, I have never been either pretty or dainty. I'm too tall. And now I'm six years older and my bloom, such as it was, has faded. And, worst of all, though I've lost my passion to change the world, I still enjoy using the brains the Lord gave me in a good argument.' Hester came back to her mother and knelt down beside her. 'Oh Mama, I am convinced that I would never find a husband to please me. I'm perfectly content here in

Abbot Quincey. Please, please will you not speak to Papa?'

Lady Perceval shook her head. 'I would not at this moment even think of making the attempt. Not while there is still time for you to see how wrong you are. Listen to me, Hester,' she went on, gently taking both Hester's hands in hers and speaking very seriously. 'It may surprise you to learn that large numbers of women with considerable intelligence are clever enough to keep themselves and their husbands happy simply by disguising the fact! At seventeen you could be forgiven for not realising this, but not now, Hester. Not now. Look around you! The idea that it is impossible to find happiness in marriage is absurd! I have always been very happy with your dear Papa. And look at Beatrice Roade—a very clever, sensible girl—but since her marriage at Christmas she positively radiates happiness!'

'No one could possibly deny that. But she was lucky. She and Harry Ravensden are exactly right for each other—and Harry doesn't just put up with Mr Roade's eccentricities, he positively delights in them! No, there's no doubt about that marriage, I agree. But that does not change my mind, Mama!'

'And I shall not change mine, Hester. We are going to London for the coming Season.' There was a pause while she looked at her daughter's downcast face. Then her voice softened. 'If nothing has changed by the time we return from London, then we shall see what can be done.'

'Oh, thank you, Mama—'

'But first, you must give yourself another chance,' Lady Perceval said firmly. 'Is it a bargain? Will you promise me to keep an open mind? Will you try to mend fences with Hugo, and forget any grudges from the past? Will you do that?'

'I'll try, Mama,' Hester sighed, 'but it won't be easy.'

'There's my good girl! And now I expect you want to escape to that attic of yours for the rest of the morning, though I'm not at all sure it's good for you to spend so much time alone up there. Wait, Hester! Did you take Mrs Hardwick the eggs when you were in the village? Is she any better?'

'Not yet. But Dr Pettifer will come this afternoon. And the eggs were welcome. They had almost run out.'

'That's good. Off you go, then. You might spend some time reflecting on what I have said. Marriage is a woman's best chance of happiness.'

The way to her attic was long and took her past some of the most beautiful rooms in the house. The family lived in only a small section of the main block, together with a suite of rooms in the west wing occupied by Hester's grandmother. The Dowager Lady Perceval was away at the moment and the rest of the house was silent and unused, the furniture under holland covers, and pictures and ornaments packed away or even sold. Perceval Hall had been built in wealthier times, but Sanford Perceval, Hester's great-grandfather, had been a gambler and a wastrel.

Fortunately he died young, before he had entirely run through the handsome fortune left him by his father. The Percevals no longer owned the vast acres of former days, but they had managed to hold on to the Hall, and their name still counted for something. They were among the county's oldest and most respected landowners, and a Perceval could marry anyone. It was a pity, thought Hester, as she passed large, beautifully proportioned rooms and went up the handsome marble staircase, it was really very unfortunate, that since that London disaster she had been quite unable to imagine sharing her life with any man.

She came at length to her attic. This was her special place, her refuge. She had discovered it years ago, and had made it her own as soon as she found her grandfather's comfortable old chair, and a bureau stuffed full of his books and papers stored there. And when she had returned from London in disgrace, at odds with the world, and out of charity with her much admired elder brother, this was where she had taken refuge. Her parents believed that she was putting her grandfather's papers in order, possibly with a view to publication, and were happy to leave her to it. But, though that was how it had begun, it was far more than that.

For the last five years Hester, wary of exposing herself to yet more mockery for her 'unfeminine' studies, had lived a double life. In public she did what was expected of the daughter of a prominent local family. Though she was regarded as something of a recluse, she rode and walked, worked in the still-room, supported her mother in her charitable work, had frequently visited India Rushford before her marriage to Lord Isham. She was quite often seen in company with her other cousins at the Vicarage. But whenever she could she escaped to her attic. The work on the Perceval papers was nearly finished. But this was not all she did here. And she owed her new occupation to Lowell.

In an effort to rouse Hester from her depression and apathy six years before, Lowell had taken out a subscription for her to Mr Garimond's *Journal of the New Scientific and Philosophical Society*. The fact that the Society was exclusively for gentlemen was disregarded.

Even he could not have foreseen its effect. Hester read it eagerly, and then, greatly daring, sent in a short article on the use of mathematics in ciphers. Lowell had helped to keep her identity secret by delivering it in London himself. To her delight, the article was accepted and for some years now, with Lowell's help, Hester had been sending articles in quite regularly. She called herself 'Euclid', for Mr Garimond insisted that all his contributors used the names of famous mathematicians of the past.

For the past year or more Euclid had been engaged in a duel of wits with 'Zeno', the Journal's senior contributor. Zeno usually wrote scholarly articles on the philosophy of mathematics, but in response to something Hester had written in that first article he had set Euclid a cipher puzzle. He challenged 'him' to solve it before the month was out. This was now a regular feature, Mr Garimond acting as receiving office and umpire. Hester had just finished deciphering the latest, and it would soon go with Lowell to the Society's offices in London.

Lowell was waiting for her in her attic. 'Any luck? Have you managed to persuade Mama? I heard the discussion as I came up.'

'No,' Hester said in a resigned tone. 'I'm to be frizzed and primped and dressed up and paraded in London, somewhat long in the tooth, but apparently still hoping for a husband. Why, pray? So that some man can take me off home and assume he has the right to tell me how to act and what to think. I truly think the world is mad—to condemn, as it does, half of the human race to mindless nonentity. Things will change eventually I suppose—women won't tolerate it for ever. But it won't be in time to save me.'

'Hold on, old thing! Not all men are unreasonable—as you ought to know.' He spoke reproachfully. She went to him and hugged him.

'Oh, don't pay any attention to me, Lowell, I'm just totally out of humour at the idea of going to London again. I'm an ungrateful beast. You've been wonderful. I don't know what I would have done without you. But you wait and see! You're only twenty-two—still reasonably young. Another couple of years in society and you'll be like all the rest.'

'No, I won't,' he said stoutly. 'But people do change in six years, you know. Perhaps some of those fellows might look at you differently now.' Then he added casually, 'I know you have this prejudice about Dungarran, but he seemed very pleasant when we met him in Northampton. He's probably forgotten what happened six years ago.' When his sister remained silent he went on, 'Hester, he can't have been as bad as you think him. Why do you mind him so much? Or was there something more? Something you haven't told me.'

Hester's voice was muffled as she bent over the bureau, searching through her papers. 'Whatever could there be? He was one of Hugo's friends and he did what Hugo asked him. He was kind enough to me until it all went wrong.' She emerged from the bureau, somewhat flushed. 'Did you want something, Lowell?'

'Well, I came to hear Mama's verdict. And I wondered if you had anything for the *Journal*. I'm out for the rest of the day and off to London early tomorrow morning. Have you anything for Garimond? If so, I could deliver it on Friday.'

'Where are you going now?'

'To collect Henrietta from her dancing lesson. I expect I'll spend the rest of the day at the Vicarage.'

Hester suppressed a grin. Lowell had avoided his baby cousin like the plague only months ago, but he was now fascinated by her recent transformation into a very pretty young lady of fashion. She decided not to tease him, but said merely, 'I have something but it isn't quite ready yet. I'll leave it in your room.'

'What is it this time? Another article?'

'No, it's a new cipher they sent me, and I've finally

cracked it. I'm rather pleased with myself, it was quite difficult. You see this line—'

'Don't try to explain, Hes!' Lowell said hastily. 'I'll take your word for it. I wouldn't know where to begin.'

Hester looked at him in some amusement. 'Lowell, however do you convince Garimond that you're the author of these communications? You must meet him occasionally.'

'Never. He's a bit of a mysterious bird himself. But I don't claim to be the author. I just deliver the envelope to an elderly cove at the Society's office in St James's Square.'

'Lucky for us! It saves a few explanations—especially as you are so determined not to be another mathematician!'

'Lord, Hes, I wouldn't know how! But I'd give a lot to know what those clever codgers in St James's Square would say if they knew Euclid was a woman.'

'It would give them all an apoplectic fit! But do take care not to let it out, Lowell—I don't give a pin for their apoplectic fits, but it would mean an end to my fun, too.'

'I won't,' her brother said confidently. 'I like a bit of cloak-and-dagger work. When will the new stuff be ready?'

'It only wants a few corrections and then I'll write it out in my Euclid hand. I'll put it inside your overcoat before I go to bed.'

'Right-eeo.'

Lowell disappeared with a great deal of clattering

down the stairs. Hester shook her head, then smiled fondly. He was a good brother.

She sat down at the bureau, took out her papers and put on her grandfather's spectacles which she had found with his things, and which she now found useful for close work. They never left the attic. But after a few minutes she took them off again and sat back. She was finding it difficult to concentrate. It was Lowell's fault for mentioning Dungarran's name. That and the knowledge that she could not avoid seeing the man again in London... Lowell was right. She hadn't told him everything. There was one scene that no one knew of. No one but herself and Dungarran. It wasn't surprising that she had wished never to face him again. He had appeared to be so kind, so interested in her—until she had found him out. It had very nearly broken her heart to find that her idol had feet of such poor clay... And even then she had refused to accept it. Hester's eyes strayed to the tiny window, but what she saw was not the green fields and trees of Northamptonshire but the drawing-rooms and streets of London in 1806...

Hester Perceval's preparation for her début at seventeen was unusual. Her talents in the drawing-room were no more than adequate, but Mrs Guarding, a woman with advanced views on the education of women, had taken great pride in Hester's gift for languages and her agile mind. She had encouraged Hester to believe that an intelligent, informed woman could create interest in badly needed reforms, bring the rich, particularly those in London and the south, to appreciate the difficulties of the poor in the north.

An older and wiser Hester now knew better. Mrs Guarding was usually the most astute of women, but in Hester's case her enthusiasm had overcome her judgement. Social change has been brought about by intelligent women. But such women have been mature, sophisticated matrons with an established position, women of tact and experience who know their world, not naïve seventeen-year-olds with a strong sense of mission and no idea how to handle it.

All had gone well for the first few weeks after Hester's arrival in London in the spring of 1806. Her adored brother Hugo was ready to look after her and introduce her to his circle of friends, all of them prominent in the Ton. Feminine enough to enjoy the pretty dresses her mother had provided for her, she accepted with pleased surprise the compliments the gentlemen paid her on her appearance. Fascinated by life in the metropolis, at first she spoke little and observed much. She soon came to the conclusion that Mrs Guarding was right. Though society had been kind to her, it was all too frivolous, too uncaring. As soon as she had found her feet, she would start her campaign...

Meanwhile it was very pleasant to be looked after by Hugo's friends. It took a little time for her to become accustomed to their languid drawls, their refusal to take anything seriously, but it was flattering to a girl not yet eighteen to be attended by some of the most eligible young men in society. Even Dungarran, famous for his reluctance to put himself out for any-one—'Too fatiguin'!' was his favourite phrase—spent time teaching her the dance steps she had ignored at Mrs Guarding's. Elegant, handsome, with dark hair and cool grey eyes, he spoke less than the others, seldom paying her the pretty compliments she came to expect, but this did him no harm in Hester's opinion. There was an occasional glimmer of amusement in his eyes which intrigued her, but it was usually quickly replaced by his normal, indifferent courtesy. Though he evaded all her attempts at serious conversation, Hester was certain that behind the idle man of fashion there was an intelligence, an intellect she could respect. Inevitably, sadly, she was soon on the way to falling in love with him. She found herself listening for his lazy drawl, searching the crowds for a sight of his tall figure, always so immaculately dressed, rivalling Hugo in his calm self-possession. But though he was instantly welcome wherever he went, invited to every function, he was not always to be found. He seemed to come and go very much as he pleased. And as time went on he became even more elusive. Without him, life in London soon became very boring to Hester.

After a month, finding most conversations, even the compliments, tediously repetitive, she began her campaign. She would interrupt a frivolous discussion on the newest fashion for a collar, or Beau Brummell's latest *bon mot*, in order to comment on the condition of the workers in the north, or the passage of a bill for reform through Parliament. This was met with blank stares. When invited out for a drive she took to lecturing her companion on the greater role women could, and would, play in public life, or expressing a desire to be taken to the poorer districts of London in order to observe living conditions there. Needless to say, no one ever took her, but even the request caused the lifting of eyebrows...

Her mother saw what was happening but found herself powerless to stop it. Her remonstrances, her pleas to Hester to stop trying to reform society until she was better informed of its manners and customs, fell on deaf ears. Hugo warned her, his closer friends did their best to deflect her, but Hester remained obstinately idealistic, stubbornly sure that intelligent discussion could solve the problems of the world... The result was inevitable. Society began to ignore, then neglect her. The flow of compliments, the invitations to drive or ride, dried up quite suddenly as Miss Perceval was pronounced guilty of the worst sin of all. She was a bore. And not even a pretty one.

Chapter Three

At first Hester was puzzled rather than distressed. The young men around her had listened so charmingly. They had paid her such pretty compliments, taken such pleasure in her company. What was wrong? Why didn't they want to listen to her?

The awakening was painful. Alone, as she so often was, on a balcony overlooking one of the rooms in the Duchess of Sutherland's mansion, half hidden by long curtains, she heard a burst of laughter from below and then voices.

'I don't believe it! You must be making it up, Brummell! Are you trying to tell us that Hester Perceval actually took Addington to task on the question of Catholic emancipation? Addington!'

'My dear chap, every word of it is true, I swear.' Hester looked cautiously over the balcony. Seven or eight young gentlemen were gathered underneath. She drew quickly back.

'Oh God!' There was despair in Hugo's voice. 'What has she done now? What did he say?'

George Brummell was a born mimic. Addington's self-important tones were captured perfectly. 'My dear Miss Perceval, how you can think I would discuss policies of His Majesty's Government with an impertinent chit of a girl I cannot imagine. And why the devil you should see fit to mention such a subject in Lady O'Connell's drawing-room has me even more at a loss.'

Shouts of laughter, and applause. Then Hester strained forward as she heard Robert Dungarran's drawl.

'Poor girl! I know that blistering tone of Addington's.'

'Come, come, Robert! Little Miss Cure-all deserved the set-down. She's an impudent ninny. What have politics to do with a woman? Their little brains simply aren't up to it!'

'Do tell me, George—are yours?'

More laughter, and the good-natured reply. 'I've never tried t' fathom them—even if my health permitted me to try. Fatiguin' things, politics. All the same, Hugo, isn't it time you did something about the girl?'

'Quite right, Brummell!' The interruption came from Tom Beckenwaite. 'Dammit, when I'm with a woman I don't want to think—that's not what they're for!' He gave a low laugh, which was followed by a chorus of ribald remarks. Hester was shocked. She had always regarded Lord Beckenwaite as a true gentleman. A fool, but a gentlemanly fool. He spoke again.

'The fact is, Hugo, old dear, you are wasting your time. Your little sister is incurable. And unmarriageable. Demme, there's a limit to what a fellow can stand! I'm as ready as the next man to do a friend a favour, but your sister is demned hard work, and that's not something I look for. She never stops talkin'! Ridin', drivin', dancin'—it's all the same! Talk, talk, talk!'

'Hugo—' Hester leaned forward again. This was Dungarran speaking. She smiled in anticipation. He would defend her against these asses. He seldom spoke but when he did it was always to the point. They would listen to him. His drawl was more pronounced than ever. 'Hugo, I'm sorry to say it, but it's time you did something!'

'Not you too, Robert!' Hugo said resignedly.

'Have a word with Lady Perceval, old chap. Your wretched sister's behaviour is doing neither herself, nor anyone else, much good. She is too young, and much too foolish for life here. Get your mother to take her back to Nottingham, or Northampton or wherever it is you all come from. Perhaps the country air will blow away some of her silly notions. Bring her back when she's learned how to behave. But, please, not before.'

Hugo said stiffly, 'She never used to be like this, and I'm sorry for it. I don't know what my mother was thinking of, bringing her to London with her head full of such nonsense.'

'It's not nonsense, exactly. Just absurd coming from your sister.' Dungarran again. 'It would be better suited to a graybeard with a corporation than a child out of the schoolroom. A girl into the bargain.'

'I don't know what to say to you all. She's my sister and I love her, I suppose. But believe me, when I asked you all to give her a good start to the Season I never imagined it would be such hard work. You've been Trojans.'

'Well, from now on, dear boy, your sister can lecture someone else. This Trojan is retiring to his tent. Wounded in the course of duty, you might say. Shall we look for the card-room?' A chorus of agreement faded as they went away, leaving Hester sitting in her chair staring into space. How could they talk of her like that! How dare they! Shallow, stupid… It was as if a veil had been ripped from her eyes. She could now see that their smiles had been sly, their compliments mere flattery, their attentions empty… She drew in a shuddering breath. They were all fools! Every one of them! Fashionable fools with no more brain than a pea! Heartless, brainless fools!…

'You're looking serious, my dear. Are you alone?'

She looked up. An elderly gentleman was gazing at her in concern. His face was vaguely familiar.

'Sir…' she stammered. 'You must excuse me. I…I am a little…a little…' Her voice faded.

'My dear girl, you are clearly upset. How fortunate that I happened on your hiding place. Come. You shall have something to restore you, and then I shall take you back to your Mama. Or…' He eyed her speculatively. 'Perhaps you would tell me more of the very interesting reforms in the north you've been studying?'

Hester looked at him in surprise. 'I've talked to you before? I'm afraid…'

'No, but I was there when you were talking about them to Lady Castle. I found them quite absorbing. May I know more?'

This was balm to Hester's wounded pride. Here was a man of mature years, obviously distinguished, who, far from laughing at her, respected her views enough to want to hear more! What a contrast to those…fribbles of Hugo's, especially Dungarran! Here was someone who really appreciated her.

They talked for a moment or two, and never since she came to London had Hester had such an attentive listener. After a moment he winced as a burst of music came from below, and said, 'I hardly dare suggest it, but we would be more private in the library. Of course, if you don't care for the idea we could continue to sit here…'

The temptation to sit there on the balcony, to be seen by people who did not appreciate her as they ought, was very strong. But he went on, 'The Duchess has a splendid selection of books on the subject…?'

Books! She hadn't seen a book in weeks! Hester smiled and nodded with enthusiasm. She was too shy to ask him his name, but he clearly knew her family. There could be nothing wrong in accepting the invitation from such a very distinguished-looking old man. The cane he used to support him was of ebony with a silver-chased top. His coat was of blue velvet and the ribbon and diamonds of some sort of order was pinned to its front. His white hair was tied back in the old-fashioned way with a velvet ribbon. He was altogether the epitome of august respectability. Filled with pride at having attracted the attention of such a man, she accepted the arm he offered and let him guide her through the doors and on into the library. He led her to a sofa by the window. On a table next to it was a decanter filled with wine, and some glasses.

'Sit down, Miss Perceval. Will you have some wine?'

'I'm not sure… Why did you shut the door?'

'Do you not find the noise outside disturbing? You are young, of course. Your hearing is more acute than mine. Would you like me to open it again?'

'Oh no!'

'Good! Let me pour you some wine.' He smiled at her reassuringly in a grandfatherly way.

'Th…thank you.' Hester smiled nervously at him. He handed her a large glass of wine at which she gazed apprehensively, then came round and sat down beside her.

'Now, tell me why you think the north needs special attention. Are things there so very different from the south?'

'Oh, they are!' Relieved, Hester launched into a description of conditions in the manufacturing towns. She was flattered by the attention the gentleman was paying to her words, and failed to notice at first how very close to her he was sitting, his arm along the back of the sofa. It seemed very warm in the room, and she was relieved when he got up and walked over to one of the bookcases. But her relief was short-lived. When he returned with a heavy volume, he sat even more closely, his thigh pressing against hers.

'We shall look at this together,' he said with a smile, and opened the page at a spectacularly un-dressed lady...

Even today, six years later, she could still feel the shock. She had sat paralysed for a moment, and Canford had taken the opportunity to turn her head to his... His lips came down on hers with brutal force, his tongue forcing its way into her mouth. One hand clutched the front of her bodice... With a scream of outrage and horror she had leapt away, snatched up her glass of wine, which was still very full, and emp-tied it over him. She made for the door.

Canford was beside himself with rage. 'My coat! Look at my coat, you damned little vixen!' he snarled, picking up his stick and lifting it threateningly as he chased after her. She managed to unlock the door be-fore he reached her, but then he grabbed her hair and wrenched it painfully as he pulled her back.

She screamed again, whereupon the door burst open, knocking her aside, and Hugo rushed in. What happened next was a blur, but it ended with Canford and her brother crashing to the floor together. It was a dangerous moment, luckily interrupted by the arri-val of Robert Dungarran.

'Canford! Hugo!'

Canford, recalled to sanity by Dungarran's intervention, got up, glared at Hugo, and stormed out, swearing vengeance on all concerned.

Hugo then turned to her. After making sure she was unharmed, he lost his temper with her—comprehensively. The general drift was that he had finished with her. She had ruined not only herself, but the rest of the family in the eyes of the Ton. After a few other, similarly amiable sentiments, he had gone out after Canford to see, he snapped, whether he could limit the damage she had caused. She had been left, ashamed and humiliated, alone with Dungarran.

Hester preferred not to think of what had followed—the recriminations, the accusations, her stupid declaration of love, and his contemptuous rejection of her. If she was to meet Dungarran in April with any degree of equanimity she must put that scene out of her mind. Forget it completely.

Hester picked up the pen, put on her glasses and returned to work. This was what was important, what would be important in the future. She finished her copying and sealed the papers up. Recently Garimond had insisted that every precaution should be taken to keep her work from prying eyes. She always complied, though she couldn't see a reason for it. Men were basically very childish with their secrets and their ciphers. The messages Zeno had sent her recently had all been to do with Romans marching into Gaul, and transport over the Alps. Did he regard himself as a latter-day Caesar? Some of it didn't even make sense. But he was clever! His ciphers had always been devilishly ingenious, even the simpler ones he used for his covering letters… These were never published, of course.

Hester gave a little laugh. Who would think that Hester Perceval, spinster and recluse, would dare to conduct a secret correspondence with an unknown gentleman? Even parents as indulgent as hers would be shocked beyond measure at it. But Zeno could hardly be regarded as a danger, even by the strictest guardians, for, in the nature of things, she and Zeno would, regrettably, never meet! Though she felt a surprising sense of kinship with him, an astonishing similarity of humour and ideas, she could never reveal her true identity. The shock would probably kill the elderly gentleman, who sat in his club in St James, painstakingly writing his articles, and inventing the most tortuous, the most diabolically difficult ciphers—all for a woman to solve!

Hester's eyes wandered over her attic and stopped at a dusty cupboard in the corner. Should she open it? Inside was the manuscript of *The Wicked Marquis*, a ridiculous novel she had written in fury after her return in the summer of 1806. Her pen might well have been dipped in vitriol, so corrosive had been the caricatures of her unsuspecting victims. No, it was better left locked away where no one else could read it. She would otherwise face ruinous actions for libel! One day she would destroy it. But writing *The Wicked Marquis* had undoubtedly helped her recovery. Through its absurdities she had learned to laugh not only at society, but also at herself at seventeen—naïve, arrogant, so sure that she could change the world… She smiled as she thought of the absurd plot based on tales told by the servants of the local villain, the Marquis of Sywell—the orgies in the chapel, the deflowering of local maidens, the mysterious disappearance of the Marchioness… She had surrounded him with vain, empty-headed young men with ridiculous names, caricatures of the men she had met in London—even Hugo had not escaped. The Marquis of Rapeall, Sir Hugely Perfect, Viscount Windyhead—he had hardly deserved her malice, he had been scarcely older than herself—Lord Baconwit, the dandy Beau Broombrain and—Lord Dunthinkin.

Which brought her back to Dungarran. Hester straightened her shoulders and lifted her chin. At seventeen she had gone to London expecting the world to fall at her feet. At twenty-four she expected very little—merely to get through the Season with as little trouble as possible. Then she would return and continue her relationship with the only man she respected—Zeno. He was the man for her.

Lady Perceval was delighted when her daughter agreed to accompany them to London without further protest. She launched into a frenzy of discussions with the local dressmakers—already working at full capacity on Robina Perceval's wardrobe. The house was swamped in samples and pattern books. It soon became clear that they would unfortunately not get to town in time for Sophia Cleeve's come-out ball. This was held in March, and it was the middle of April before Sir James brought his wife and daughter to the house Hugo had found for them off Berkeley Square.

'Very pleasant!' pronounced Lady Perceval, looking round her as the family entered the spacious salon on the first floor. 'How clever of you, Hugo dear, to find such a pleasant house in such a convenient situation. Hester, do you not agree?'

Mindful of her promise, Hester smiled at her brother and offered her cheek. 'I would expect nothing less,' she said, as he kissed it. 'I'm glad to see you, brother. You're looking well—and very elegant.'

'I was delighted to hear you had agreed to come, Hester. I think we can do better this time, don't you?'

Hester sighed. 'I'll try, Hugo. I'll try. I can at least promise not to make a nuisance of myself.'

'We'll do better than that,' he promised, smiling down at her with a glint in his eye. Her heart warmed to him. When Hugo forgot he was a nonpareil with a position to uphold, there was no one kinder or more affectionate. The older brother she had loved was still there, underneath the man of fashion.

Lowell came bounding up the stairs, falling over some valises on the way, and the mood of family unity was disturbed.

'I'm sorry, Mama, Papa,' he gasped. 'I meant to be here when you arrived.'

'Ma'am,' said Hugo impatiently, turning to his mother. 'Ma'am, I wish you would persuade your younger son to be less…less noisy! It's like having a Great Dane in the drawing-room!'

Sir James laughed. 'Let him be, Hugo! He'll learn. How are you, my boy?'

'Well, sir, very well. I find London greatly to my taste—especially since I moved out of Sir Hugely Perfect's rooms. Sharing with Gaines is much more fun.'

Hester's start of surprise fortunately went unnoticed as Sir James said disapprovingly, 'What was that you said? Sir Hugely Perfect? That is not amusing, Lowell. It doesn't do to call your brother names.'

'Oh, I'm not alone, sir! That's how he is known here in London.'

'Sir Hugely Perfect?' Lady Perceval went over to her son. 'Hugo! How unkind! Are you really called so?'

The colour had risen in Hugo's cheeks, but he shrugged his shoulders and laughed. 'Not by everyone, only Lowell and his cronies. The rest of my acquaintance are not so childish.'

Hester cleared her throat. 'Where…where did such a name come from, Lowell? Mama is right. It isn't kind.'

'It's from a book,' Hugo answered for Lowell, who had hesitated. 'A piece of rubbish which came on the scene a month or two ago. But no one of any sense could possibly take it seriously.'

'A book?'

Lowell held his sister's eyes. 'A book called *The Wicked Marquis*. And Hugo is mistaken. It's not just my set. The whole of the beau-monde is talking about it.'

Lady Perceval was looking bewildered. '*Hugo?* A wicked marquis? What *are* you talking about, Lowell?'

'Hugo isn't the wicked marquis, Mama. He's just a character in the book. One of a great number.'

Hester said faintly, 'Mama, I should quite like to see my room. I feel sadly dishevelled, and…and I have a touch of the headache.'

'My poor child! I thought you seemed rather pale— we rose so early this morning, Hugo. I dare swear you were not even awake when we left Perceval Hall. Come, my dear!' At the door she paused. 'I hope to see you later, Hugo. Are you dining here?'

'Certainly! I couldn't neglect you all on your first evening in town. I must bring you up to date! Sophia Cleeve's ball was a huge success, by the way. No expense spared, naturally. And in her quiet way little Robina is doing very well.'

'Excellent! Excellent!' Sir James beamed with pleasure.

His wife was equally pleased. She left Hester and came back into the room to join Hugo and her husband. 'What a relief for her mother!' she exclaimed. 'Elizabeth was so worried at the expense of it all, but if Robina can make a reasonable match, the prospect for her sisters is vastly improved. She is, of course, a very pretty girl. Do you know who…?'

Hester seized her opportunity. She pulled Lowell out into the hall and pushed him into a side room, shutting the door firmly behind them. Then she turned.

'What have you done, Lowell?' she hissed.

'I don't know what you m—'

Hester gave her brother a most unladylike shake.

'Yes you do, you little toad! How did you find it? And what did you do with it?'

'Oh, you mean *The Wicked Marquis*? I sold it.'

'You *what*?'

'I sold it. I showed it to a friend of mine in Cambridge and he was as keen as mustard about it. He knew where to go to get it printed, and...'

'You...you sold it? For publication? You're trying to hoax me, Lowell—no respectable publisher would handle a thing like that!'

'Well, no. That's where old Marbury was so useful. He knew a fellow who dealt with the other kind.'

'Lowell!' Hester was horrified, but Lowell was too full of enthusiasm to notice.

He went on, 'It needed spicing up a bit for that kind of trade, of course, so I did that. I brought it up to date as well. I didn't do at all a bad job, either. The chap I sold it to was quite impressed.'

'You...you *traitor*, Lowell! How could you! How *dare* you!'

He looked injured. 'I thought you'd be pleased. It wasn't doing any good in that dusty old cupboard, and now it's a huge success. Don't listen to what Hugo says. It's not just my set—*everyone* is talking about it.'

'Oh God!' she said in despair, pacing up and down in a fever of anxiety. 'Oh, Lowell! How could you? We're ruined!'

'Nonsense! For one thing, no one knows who the author is—'

'But they're bound to find out! It wouldn't be difficult to work out who wrote it—all the people in it were the ones *I* knew. I'm surprised Hugo hasn't worked it out already.'

'That's where my bits came in,' said her brother proudly. 'I think you'll find that I've obscured the tracks enough.'

'I must see it—immediately. Tonight!'

'I don't think so, Hes. Gaines and I are off to Astley's tonight. Tomorrow.'

'You'll bring it tonight, you snake—'

'Hester!' Lady Perceval came into the room. 'I thought you had gone upstairs. Whatever are you doing here? And Lowell!'

'I... I...er... I have some messages for Lowell. From the Vicarage.'

'Henrietta, perhaps?' asked her mother with a significant smile. 'I won't ask what they are—you obviously want to deliver them in private. Lowell, shall we see you tonight?'

Her two children answered at the same time. 'Yes!' said Hester. 'No, unfortunately not,' said Lowell with an apologetic smile. Sir James, hearing this, was annoyed.

'What's this, sir? Your mother and I would have liked you to be here!'

'Sorry, Papa! It's Gaines. He's leaving town tomorrow. He has to go down to Devon for a few weeks. Tonight's the only night we can go and we've been promising ourselves this treat for ages. I'll be here tomorrow morning—about noon.'

With this his parents had to be content, though they were not best pleased. As they turned to go Hester, who had been thinking furiously, said, 'Mama, Lowell has suggested we go for a short walk. He thought that might relieve my headache better than lying in a stuffy room. I should dearly like to see where he lives. I know it isn't far. Just round the corner…almost.' She gave Lowell a sweet smile. Only he could sense the determination behind it.

'Well…'

'I'm sure he'll look after me, Mama. Won't you, Lowell?'

'Of course! If you're sure you want to…'

'I want to. May I, Mama?'

A few moments later Hester was accompanying Lowell to Half Moon Street. After a silence she said, 'You haven't told me yet how you discovered it.'

Lowell had had time to reflect on Hester's reaction. He had genuinely thought that it was a wonderful jest to have her book published, but now he was no longer so sure. It was a long time since he had seen Hester in such a rage.

'I… I was waiting for you in the attic. This was some time ago, Hes. You were a long time coming. So…so I explored. The key was on top of the cupboard, and…and…'

'You opened it. And stole the manuscript.'

'Don't say that! I read it on the spot. It isn't very long, as you know. If you had come in then I daresay

I shouldn't have done anything with it. But you were held up in the village or something, so I had plenty of time to finish it. I couldn't stop laughing. It was brilliant!'

'Laughing!' Hester exclaimed bitterly.

'Well, I daresay you didn't feel like laughing when you wrote it. But your caricatures were hilarious to an outsider. And one or two of them hit the nail right on the head. That's why it's such a wild success. All London is laughing. I don't know why you're taking it so badly, Hester!'

'Lowell! If it ever comes out that I wrote the thing then I am dished—completely. For ever! London won't laugh then. They'll hunt me out of town.'

'They won't find out. I told you, I altered it to disguise your part. And…and…'

'Continue, little brother,' said Hester ominously when Lowell hesitated.

'Well, I put things in it that a respectable girl couldn't possibly know about. You'd mentioned some of Sywell's escapades—you remember that party no one would talk about, until I got old Silas to tell? And the business with Abel Bardon's daughters? You didn't know the details—no one would tell you, of course, so you'd used your imagination. Well, I just added a few of the real facts. No one could possibly believe you knew anything about those.'

Hester stopped and put her hands over her face. 'Lowell, this is the worst thing you have ever done to me. I can't bear it!' she said.

Lowell took her arm, aware of the curious glances

directed at them both. He said in a low voice, 'The situation isn't nearly as bad as you think, Hester. Look! We're nearly at my place—come in and I'll give you something—a glass of wine, perhaps? Gaines has some first-class burgundy.'

Hester allowed herself to be shepherded into the small house in Half Moon Street where Lowell had his rooms. 'I'd like to drown you in it. But I'll have some water, or possibly some tea. Not wine.'

'I say, Hester! That's not fair! I did it for a lark!'

'That's what you always say, Lowell! But this is no lark!' Her brother's air of injured innocence, rather like that of a hurt puppy, was having its usual effect. Hester was never able to stay angry with Lowell for long. But when she looked at the book which Lowell put into her hands a few minutes later she exploded again.

'This is disgusting!'

'Well, yes. They did spread themselves on the cover. The Marquis is being really astonishingly wicked.' As Lowell looked at it he started to grin appreciatively. 'I don't know how the devil he managed that position, though.'

'Lowell!! You shouldn't be showing me this…this filth! You shouldn't even be mentioning such things to me! Oh Lord! I can't believe this is happening to me. Not another disaster, not again!' Hester was distraught. She walked up and down the room in agitation.

'Oh come, Hester! I may have spiced the novel up a little—'

'A little! If this is anything to go by…'

'A lot, then. But you can't go all prunes and prisms on me. After all, you thought it all up. I only embellished it.'

'Oh no!'

'And the cover is the worst thing about it. It's really not so lurid inside. Read it and see for yourself. I promise you, it will make you laugh.'

'I shall do nothing of the sort!' She stopped short. Then she wailed, 'I shall have to read the confounded thing! Tonight, if possible. I must see what you've done to it. Lowell, I shall never forgive you for this, never! Here, take the book and wrap it up—properly, mind! I don't want it to come undone before I can hide it in my room.'

Lowell was now so anxious to please that he wrapped the offending book into a small parcel and handed it over. 'I'll escort you back,' he said contritely.

'No! I don't want your company! I'm used to walking alone, and it's only a step.'

'But I must—'

'Lowell,' said Hester with awful calm. 'Don't argue with me. I shall scream if I have to say another word to you! I need to walk back to Bruton Street *alone*! I just might be able to speak to you tomorrow, but don't count on it.' She turned and left him standing on the door step. He waited irresolutely, then shrugged his shoulders and went in.

Hester walked swiftly back up towards Berkeley Square. She was seething with an explosive mixture of anger and apprehension. How dare Lowell do such an outrageous thing! What would become of her— and her family—if London ever found her out? The parcel in her hand seemed to burn through to her fingers; she wanted to drop it, but dared not let it go. She reached the top of Half Moon Street and turned in the direction of Berkeley Square, head down, still clutching her parcel—and collided with a tall gentleman who was coming towards her. She dropped her parcel and with a gasp of dismay bent down to pick it up. A hand came out to prevent her.

'You must allow me,' said a deep, drawling voice.

Hester groaned inwardly. Fate was always against her on such occasions. It was inevitable that out of all the gentlemen in society she should meet *this* one, just when she least wanted to. She summoned up her courage. 'Lord Dungarran!' she exclaimed. 'How…how…pleasant to meet you again!'

Chapter Four

Surprise, a fleeting expression of resignation, and then a faint hint of reproof—Hester saw all of these cross Dungarran's face before he resumed his normal calm.

'Miss Perceval. What an unexpected pleasure!'

The words were conventional, and were not supported by any warmth in his voice. Hester's eyes dropped. He must not be allowed to see the panic into which Lowell's revelations had thrown her. Not this man.

'Thank you for coming once again to my rescue, sir,' she said stiffly and held out her hand for the parcel.

He smiled briefly, but did not hand it over. 'At least it isn't wet.' His eyes surveyed the street. 'But...are you once again in need of an escort, Miss Perceval?'

'Not in the slightest. I am making for Berkeley Square. It isn't far.'

'All the same,' he said decidedly, 'I will accompany you.' He offered her his arm.

'It really isn't necessary, Lord Dungarran. If you will give me my parcel I am perfectly able to walk the few yards to the square.'

He frowned. 'Miss Perceval, I have no wish to force my company on you, believe me. But you may be assured that if your parents or Hugo knew that you were walking the streets of London without a maid or footman they would be as…surprised as I am. It is bad enough in Northampton. In London it is un-heard of. Come!' He presented his arm again.

The colour rose in Hester's cheeks. There was so much she wanted to say, none of it polite. So she remained silent, her eyes fixed anxiously on the parcel which he still carried in his other hand. She was faintly surprised not to see signs of scorching on its wrappings. As they walked along Curzon Street he held it out and said, 'What is it this time, Miss Perceval? Not muslin or satin—it is too hard for that. Or should I not ask? It feels like a book.'

Hester swallowed and tried to smile. 'It…it is a book. Lowell has lent me a book of…of…poetry. B—ballads.'

'You like poetry?'

'I… I… No, I don't.'

She heard him give a slight sigh. Then he began again, patiently making conversation with someone, she thought resentfully, he would much rather not have to talk to at all. If he only knew the strain she was under to say even a word that was sensible!

'Have you been in London long, Miss Perceval?'

'No. We have just arrived.'

'Ah!'

They entered Berkeley Square in silence. He paused. 'You are fortunate in finding a suitable house in the square. They are much in demand. Which is it?'

She disengaged herself. 'We...we are staying in Bruton Street, in fact. A few yards farther on. But you have done enough, Lord Dungarran. Thank you. May I have my book?' He gave her a look and offered her his arm again.

Still in silence they crossed the square. To Hester's relief the entrance to the house was in sight. She began to thank him again, holding out her hand for the book. 'No, Miss Perceval. I shall see you to your door,' he said grimly, ignoring her attempts at farewell.

At the door he bowed and at last handed her the parcel. 'Goodbye, Miss Perceval. No doubt we shall see each other again.'

'I look forward to it already,' said Hester.

He narrowed his eyes at her tone, then added coldly, 'Meanwhile, I would remind you that it is unwise to go out alone in London—as I am sure Hugo would tell you if he were here.'

It was too much! Hester lifted her chin and said in a high voice, 'Lord Dungarran, I am grateful for your solicitude for someone who is, after all, the merest acquaintance. I assure you that I shall do my utmost in the future not to put you to any more trouble, however unnecessary. Goodbye.' She curtseyed and went in.

* * *

As Robert Dungarran retraced his steps towards Curzon Street a slight frown marred his handsome features. The years had apparently not improved Hester Perceval. She was still uncomfortable in society, inept in conversation, and obstinate in her opinions. It was to be hoped that Hugo would not call on him again for support in looking after his sister. He would have to refuse. He walked on a little, then paused in thought. For someone who had so little command of language her last remark had been remarkably polished. In two sentences she had thanked him, accused him of unwarranted interference, and made it clear that she would avoid him in the future! And now he thought of it, her 'I look forward to it already' had been delivered with a nice touch of irony. Was there more to Hester Perceval than at first appeared…? Impossible! He strode on.

Meanwhile Hester, still clutching her parcel, had scurried up two flights of stairs. She had managed to avoid the servants, who would have taken her pelisse and hat, and had arrived, breathless, in her bedchamber. It was a charming little room decorated in blue and pale yellow, with a window from which she could just see a corner of the gardens in the centre of Berkeley Square. It was growing dark outside. But Hester had no eyes for any of this. In haste she hid the book, still in its wrappings, among the papers she had brought with her. The servants would not interfere with those. Then she called for her maid and

quickly changed her dress for dinner. She eventually
arrived in the drawing-room just as her mother was
remarking on her absence.

'Ah, there you are, Hester! I was almost coming to
see what had happened to you. Did you enjoy your
walk with Lowell?'

'Yes, Mama. His rooms are very agreeable.'

'Did you meet the famous Mr Gaines?'

'No—I gather he is seldom in. In any case, Mama,
I shouldn't raise your hopes if I were you. I'm afraid
Mr Gaines is useless as a prospective husband. After
tonight he will be in Devon for most of the Season,
and I doubt I shall see him again.'

'Good gracious, Hester, nothing was further from
my mind. Did…did Lowell see you safely back?'

'Er…no, Mama. I left him at his rooms.'

'You can't have walked alone. And you didn't take
one of the footmen. Who was that with you at the
door?'

Her mother would be most upset to learn that she
had set out from Half Moon Street without an escort.
Hester said, 'Lord Dungarran kindly offered to accompany me.'

'Indeed? A very good friend of Hugo's. And a most
eligible *parti*.' She smiled benevolently at her daughter.

'Not as far as I am concerned, Mama.'

Lady Perceval gave a sigh of exasperation. 'Hester,
I am quite sure you need have no apprehension about
Hugo's friends. They have surely all forgotten the
events of six years ago. You must forget them, too.

Simply behave as if this were your first visit to London, and you will do very well.' She paused, then went on, 'Dungarran appeared to be most attentive...'

There was a pause during which Hester tried to think of something to say. Her mother went on, 'It is a great pity that you went out this afternoon straight from your journey. If I had not been so interested in what Hugo was telling us I would have made you change your dress. Your pelisse was sadly crushed. I cannot imagine what Dungarran thought of it.'

'Mama, Dungarran is interested neither in my dress, nor in my person. Please do not imagine differently.'

Lady Perceval ignored her. She went on, 'That dress looks very well, my dear. But I must have a word with your abigail. Your hair is not at all well arranged.'

Since she had allowed her maid a mere three minutes for the task Hester was not surprised. She looked down. She had no idea what she was wearing. The dress consisted of a straight slip with an overskirt and sleeves of dull green. There had been much discussion during its making about her lack of curves, which had resulted in a lavish use of lace round the top of the bodice. She sighed. It was difficult to be enthusiastic about clothes when one was tall and skinny. Her cousin Robina could look appealing in a kitchenmaid's sack apron—not that Aunt Elizabeth, whose notions of propriety were very strict, would ever allow her daughter to be seen in one.

'Hester?'

'Oh, I'm sorry, Mama! I was wool-gathering. You were saying?'

'When Hugo arrives we shall decide what events we shall attend. There are several cards already here, and others are sure to come. In addition, your father and I plan to hold a couple of soirées. Hugo will help us to draw up a guest list... We must make sure Dungarran's name is included.'

Hester was about to protest, then she decided to hold her peace. The noble lord was almost sure to find himself 'unable to attend'! Her thoughts wandered again. How boring it all was! And all for nothing. Her encounter this afternoon had brought home to her once again how unfitted she was for life in society. How uninterested she was in life in society! Worse still, she was racked with anxiety about the book. As soon as she could she would escape and read the thing this evening. It was not something she looked forward to.

Nothing occurred during the next week to change Hester's opinion of society. She dutifully attended dinners, parties, soirées, balls, where she exchanged platitudes, pretended an interest she didn't feel in the latest styles or the latest engagements—and danced. She even danced once or twice with Lord Dungarran. Much as she still disliked him, she had to admit he was an agreeable partner. Their steps fitted very well. She only wished that she could demonstrate how much she had changed from the 'obstinate, conceited, ignorant child' he had called her all those years ago.

But she found she could not do it. His patent indifference, and her own lingering dislike and resentment, were in the way. And, from what she had observed, he had not changed a great deal in the intervening years. He was still a creature of society, basically frivolous in his pursuits and interests. She was quite unable to think of a single thing to say that might interest him, other than conventionally polite exchanges. As a result they spent a lot of their time together in silence. He was always courteous, but his boredom was palpable. It was small consolation that he was apparently as little impressed with all the other ladies—even the Season's successes—who tried to engage his attention, to flirt with him. He was much more charming with them, but he remained as elusive as ever.

Talk of *The Wicked Marquis*, which was widespread, was also a source of unease. She had read the novel herself of course, the night after receiving it from Lowell, and had been somewhat relieved. It was indeed very funny, and, apart from one or two shockingly salacious episodes, not nearly as scandalous as its cover would suggest. What was more, Lowell's additions and alterations had made it virtually impossible to guess the authorship from internal evidence. But everyone in London had identified Lord Baconwit, Beau Broombrain, and the rest, and quotations from it were free and frequent. And, though no respectable lady could admit to having read such a dreadful novel, there was much gossip and laughter at the expense of Hester's unfortunate victims.

After a while Hester stopped wincing inwardly when *The Wicked Marquis* came into the conversation, and was able to smile with the rest, feel indeed a faint touch of pride in its success. She was even willing to listen to Lowell's apologies.

Ten days after her arrival in London Hester came in, bored and tired from a shopping expedition, to find Lowell waiting for her. They were alone. Lady Perceval had gone up to her room.

'Hester! Look at this!'

Hester took the sheet he was holding out and carried it to the brighter light near the window. Though she had brought her grandfather's glasses with her, she never used them in public. She read out its contents with a sigh of rapture.

'"Mr Garimond announces a forthcoming Lecture to be given by an Eminent Cambridge Mathematician"—I wonder who that could be?—"under the Auspices of The New Scientific and Philosophical Society". Look, Lowell! Look! It's on my subject! "Algebra, Numbers and Ciphers—A New Approach". Where, where? And when?' Hester was so excited she could hardly speak. Lowell took the paper from her trembling hand.

'It's being given next Wednesday, at the Society's headquarters in St James's Street.'

'I must go!'

'Well...' Lowell looked uncomfortable. 'There's a problem.'

'What is it?'

'It's not an open lecture, Hes.'

'Not open? What does that mean?'

'The meeting is for gentlemen only. No ladies admitted.'

'But...but I must go!'

Lowell regretfully shook his head. 'It's not possible.'

Hester grew pale with rage and disappointment. 'Oh what a *devilish* world this is! I could explode, Lowell! The thought that you who are...are as ignorant as a swan in mathematics...'

'Steady on, Hester! I *can* count!'

His sister ignored this feeble interruption and swept on, 'You, who refuse even to *try* to understand ciphers, you can go freely among some of the best minds in England today, while I have to keep back and suffocate in the drawing-rooms of society... I shall burst with frustration!' She strode about the room, muttering, 'It's too bad! Too bad! Indeed, it is too bad!'

Lowell watched this display with some awe. He had long known his sister's views on the lack of opportunity for women, but this was the strongest demonstration yet. She looked magnificent in her rage, eyes flashing blue fire, cheeks glowing... He had seen for himself how Dungarran and the others dismissed his sister as quiet, insignificant and boring. If they could only see her now—a veritable tigress...

'Hester...' he said tentatively.

'No, Lowell! I'm not fit for company at the moment, and Mama might come in at any moment. Tell her I've gone upstairs to read, will you?'

'You...you won't do anything silly?'

'What is there to do? I might chew a few sheets, or tear up a few carpets, but nothing *serious*, such as going out without an escort or omitting to curtsey to Lady Jersey. But I wish to heaven you had not shown me that advertisement!' She went out.

Lowell also regretted his rash action. He had brought it without thinking of the consequences, only that Hester would be interested in the mention of Garimond and the Society. It was true that she was having a hard time in London. He was impressed at the effort she had made to please her parents. Only he knew how much she feared reminding the world of the cocksure girl she had been six years before, and of her subsequent humiliation. Only he knew the trouble she took to make unexceptionable conversation—but as soon as she was with someone who could be regarded as remotely eligible, she became quiet and dull. If only the world knew his sister as he did—teasing, laughing, affectionate, with a puckish sense of humour, and a strong liking for the ridiculous!

As he walked back to Half Moon Street that night he was deep in thought. The result was that he was back in Bruton Street the next day to invite Hester to a walk. She was pale and heavy-eyed, and responded reluctantly when Lady Perceval urged her to take the air. But eventually she and Lowell set off towards the park.

'I'm glad you came—I want to talk to you in private, Hes. I've had an idea, but I'm not sure you'll like it.'

'What is it?' asked Hester listlessly.

'You'd like to go to that lecture, wouldn't you?'

'Oh, don't talk any more of that! I couldn't sleep last night for thinking of it. But I can't go, and there's an end.'

'How much would you give to be able to attend?'

'Don't be so absurd! I can't *bribe* my way into an exclusively masculine meeting! I wouldn't feel comfortable if I did. Please don't mention it again, Lowell. It's too upsetting.'

'I wasn't thinking of money or bribes. Supposing you could disguise yourself?'

'Disguise myself? As what? A man? That's even more ridiculous! I would be discovered within seconds. And what a scandal *that* would cause!'

'No, you wouldn't! Hes, do think about it! It would be such a lark. You're tall enough for a man—a boy, anyway. You're thin enough. And Gaines left quite a bit of his stuff behind. Between us we could find something to fit you. No one would ever know.'

'I can't believe you mean it, Lowell! You're mad! It's far too risky! I wouldn't dream of doing such a thing.'

Lowell shrugged his shoulders. 'In that case, there's no more to be said.'

They walked on into the park. Hester was the first to break the silence. 'Besides, I don't even know where the Society's offices are.'

'We'd go together.'

'And what would I say to Mama?'

'Well, I suppose you could confess that you were going to a meeting for men only, disguised as a boy,' Lowell said with heavy irony. 'On the other hand, you could simply say that you were out for the evening with me. Look Hester, you could raise objections till the cows come home, but you know they could all be overcome with a little courage.'

'A little courage! My heavens, Lowell, you have no notion of what you're asking!'

'I'm not asking anything for me. It's you I was thinking of.'

'Don't try to tell me you wouldn't enjoy it, all the same. It's just the sort of mad escapade you love.'

'It'd be one in the eye for Hugo, too,' Lowell said with some satisfaction. 'He's so...so correct. Sir Hugely Perfect is just the right name for him. I always want to do something outrageous when he's been lecturing me.'

'In this case, it wouldn't be you, it would be me! And if you think I would risk my name and reputation just because you want to get even with Hugo you are very much mistaken, little brother! What has he been saying to you now?'

'Told me off for riding my horse,' Lowell said sulkily.

'You mean galloping at full stretch along Pall Mall for a wager? I heard about that. He was right.'

'Oh, not you too, Hes!'

Hester smiled, then grew serious. 'Do you...do you

really think we could get away with it? I would so
love to go.'

'I'm sure of it.' Lowell's face brightened. 'Let's
make a plan!'

Hester laughed. This had always been Lowell's favourite saying when he was about to embark on some
reckless enterprise. Entering into the spirit of it, however, she demanded, 'Well then, what are the dan-
gers?... My figure.'

'Hidden under coat, waistcoat and a well-arranged
cravat.' Then he added with brotherly candour, 'Besides, there isn't much of it.'

Hester was too much a realist to be offended. 'My
voice.'

'Deep enough, but you needn't use it. You'd be
there to listen, not to talk.'

'What about my hair?'

'The front of your hair is short, anyway. We'll find
something to do with the rest.'

'Admittance to the premises—under whose name?'

'They won't ask. But the subscription is in Gaines's
name, so if they did we'd use that.'

Hester thought for a moment. 'It seems almost too
easy,' she said slowly.

'Easy as falling off a log,' said Lowell. 'Trust me!'

'The last time you fell off a log you broke your
collarbone. But... I think I will try it.'

The walkers in London's Hyde Park were suddenly
startled by Lowell's jubilant 'Yoicks!'

Quite often during the ensuing days Hester wondered if she had gone mad. But then she reminded

herself that she was about to enjoy a privilege normally denied to women, and her resolve held firm.
She and Lowell held a dress rehearsal the day before
the lecture, and when they had stopped laughing, she
had to agree that she made a convincing youth, especially when Lowell produced her glasses and made
her put them on.

'By Jupiter, Hes, you make a better-looking fellow
than most of my friends!'

'You exaggerate. But I'm not bad.'

She stood admiring herself in the mirror. They had
drawn her back hair into a knot, and hidden it under
the inordinately high stand-up collar affected by
young Mr Gaines. Her long legs were encased in yellow pantaloons, her upper half in a snowy shirt, an
awesomely embroidered waistcoat and a starched, in-
tricately folded cravat. Mr Gaines was inclined to
dandyism, and her coat of blue superfine had handsome buttons, impressive lapels and well-padded
shoulders.

'I hope it will be all right, Lowell,' she said suddenly. 'I don't like to think of the consequences if
we're found out.'

'We shan't be. Remember what I've told you—
lengthen your stride, don't talk at all unless you have
to, and keep your voice deep if you do. We'll take
care to stay at the back out of sight. We'll be as right
as rain, you'll see. Unless Hugo comes.'

'Oh good God! I never thought of that! I can't
do it!'

'Don't worry—he won't come,' Lowell said comfortably. 'He's taking Sophia Cleeve to Lady Sefton's soirée.'

'Then why did you say he might? Lowell, you are the world's worst tease!'

All went well the following evening. They were admitted without question to the Society's headquarters in St James's Street, though Lowell was asked to sign in an impressive-looking register. Then they followed others to a large room at the back. This had clearly been a ballroom when the house had been in private hands, but it was now used as a lecture hall, with rows of chairs, a platform at one end and a balcony at the other. Hester had to restrain herself from clutching Lowell's arm as they made their way to a seat at the back under the shelter of the overhanging balcony.

'Ideal!' whispered Lowell as they sat down. 'Now all you have to do is to keep mum.'

'I won't forget. But Lowell, what did you sign? You seemed to write two names. Gaines and what?'

Lowell looked uneasy. 'They asked if I had a pseudonym. So I put… I put your name.'

'*What?*'

'I wrote 'Euclid'. They were impressed. Don't worry! They were too busy to have a good look at us. Now hush, it's beginning. And remember! Not a word!'

The lecture that followed was all Hester could have wished. It confirmed what she already knew, it presented her with the result of others' researches, it gave her food for a great deal of future speculation and thought. And to be in such company, such an atmosphere, went to her head like champagne. She clapped with enthusiasm when the speaker was thanked by Mr Garimond, and when comments from the floor were invited it was all she could do not to shower him with questions. Remembering Lowell's warning, however, she stayed in her seat. But then some nameless idiot got up and dared to cast doubt on the usefulness or purpose of substitute numbers, disparaging the study of algebra and 'all that nonsense', and referring to the whole field as toys for adults with no practical application. This was too much. Forgetting all caution, she leapt up and demolished the pretentious arguments, quoting the words of eminent mathematicians from all ages, and pointing out the vital work of cryptographers in times of war. A round of applause greeted her words and many turned to see this talented young speaker.

Hester sat down to see Lowell staring at her in consternation. He whispered, 'Of all the mutton-headed things to do...! We'd better lope off as soon as we can, otherwise we're for it. Look, the chairman's going to speak. We can slip out when all eyes are on him.'

But it wasn't so easy. They had hardly got to the end of the row when, after a brief conference on the platform, Mr Garimond stood up.

'We believe the young man who has just spoken

to be one of our most gifted contributors. Am I right in thinking we have Euclid here? If so, our president, whom most of you know as Zeno, is eager to make his acquaintance.'

Hester stopped and turned, eager to see 'Zeno' at last. But to her dazed eyes the platform was filled with a tall, elegant figure. Dungarran, immaculate as ever, was standing at Garimond's side. 'No!' she whispered. 'No! He *can't* be!' She sat down suddenly in the empty chair at the end of the row. Dungarran appeared to be looking straight at her, and she cowered down behind the person in front.

Garimond went on, 'We should like young Euclid to come to the platform after these proceedings are over. And now…' He turned to other business.

Hester was still sitting in a daze when Lowell hauled her up by the sleeve. 'Come *on*, Hes! Unless you want to get caught here and now, we'd better get out. No one is looking at the moment. We can escape round the back of this pillar. Come *on*!'

Hester allowed herself to be dragged away. Her knees felt as if they were made of wax, and Lowell had to support her as they left the building. He spotted a hackney coach a few yards away and bundled her into it. They drove the short distance to Half Moon Street in silence. Having spoken so eloquently just a few minutes before Hester could not now say a word.

At Half Moon Street Lowell paid off the coachman, who cast a jaundiced eye over Hester and said gloomily, 'The lad's 'ad a bit too much from the look of 'im… Want any 'elp wiv cartin' 'im in?'

Lowell hastily refused and the coach drove off. Fortunately, Gaines's absence meant that there were fewer servants around to observe Lowell's efforts to get his sister safely hidden inside his room. It wasn't easy. Hester was still in a state of shock, and had to be led every inch of the way.

Once inside Lowell poured a glass of brandy and held it to her lips. She choked, and shuddered as the spirit went down, but it revived her.

'Lowell!' She took a deep breath. 'Lowell, I can't believe it!' she said, clutching his sleeve. 'Tell me it isn't true. Am I mad or was it indeed Dungarran on that platform?'

Lowell nodded slowly. 'I'm afraid he was, Hes.' He looked at her sympathetically. 'A bit of a shock, isn't it?'

Hester gave a gasping laugh. 'A *bit*! Dungarran as Zeno! It's impossible! He hasn't the brains.'

'Apparently he has.'

Hester felt as if her world had turned upside down. Her pride in her work, her delight in her exchanges with Zeno, her feeling of oneness with his mind—all these had been tossed into the air and now lay scattered around her. How could she reconcile all that with what she had learned tonight?

'Hes…' Lowell's voice seemed to come from a great distance. 'Hester, I don't want to worry you more than I have to, but it's time you went back to Bruton Street. Are you fit? Mama will be back soon.'

'Yes… Yes, of course.' She got up and went to the door.

'Wait! You can't go like that, Hester! What's wrong with you? You must change.'

'What? Oh, my clothes! Of course!' She looked round vaguely for her dress and the rest of her things.

'Are you sure you can manage?' Lowell looked so concerned that she made herself respond.

'Of course I can. Wait outside a minute or two. I'll call when I'm ready.'

Twenty minutes later Hester was back in the Bruton Street house. Her parents had not yet come in, and she was able to bid Lowell goodnight and go upstairs without encountering any of the family. Her maid exclaimed at the state of her hair, but Hester was too tired to listen, or to offer any explanation. In near silence she got ready for bed and when her mother came in she pretended to be asleep. The house gradually settled down for the night and Hester was left lying wide-eyed, alone with her thoughts.

They were not pleasant. She had learned to laugh both at herself and at those young men who had made her so unhappy six years before. It had taken time, but she had managed it. She had gradually forgotten the hurt and heartache they had caused, though her determination never to marry had remained undiminished. And, since coming to London again, she had found no reason to change her mind. She had comforted herself that she would go back to her attic when the Season was over and take up her secret work once again, her secret, totally satisfying relationship with a man called Zeno. She had basked in the knowledge that here was a man—however old, however distant—whom she admired, and who in turn admired her...

But tonight Dungarran, the heartless, shallow man of a frivolous society, someone whom she cordially disliked, for whom she certainly had little respect, had been revealed as Zeno, her hero and mentor. The world in which she had found such comfort, the world of the journal and Zeno, had been shattered. The only possible way to put the pieces back together again would be to change her view of Dungarran. Radically... The thought appalled her. She couldn't do it!

Her last and most despairing thought was that Zeno had been revealed as someone who knew Hester Perceval. Knew her already, and already despised her... Hester hid her face in her hands in despair.

Chapter Five

But as the night wore on hope started to grow once more. All was not lost. As long as Robert Dungarran remained ignorant of Euclid's identity, she and Zeno could continue their work together. It would not be easy to reconcile Dungarran, the indolent man of fashion and one of her cruellest critics, with the figure of Zeno, the serious mathematician and her treasured friend. But, if she were strong-minded enough, she could derive some ironic amusement from the situation—the respect Zeno and Euclid had for each other contrasted with the dislike and contempt felt between Robert Dungarran and Hester Perceval. Yes! It could work. That was how she would regard it—as a piquant, amusing situation. She must, if she were to survive.

By the time Friday dawned, Hester was, on the surface at least, almost her normal self again. When she found that her glasses were missing, she concluded that she had probably left them in her brother's rooms on the night of the lecture, and walked quite cheerfully round to Half Moon Street. It was, in any case, time to have a talk with Lowell.

Lowell was in, and glad to see her. 'I called at Bruton Street yesterday to see how you were. But the house was deserted.'

'We spent half the day with Aunt Elizabeth. Have you seen my glasses? I must have left them somewhere here the other night.' As they rummaged among the piles of books and newspapers she went on, 'You know, I think London has done Robina a lot of good. She's such a pretty thing, and now she actually appears to be coming out of her shell.'

'Good for her! Aunt Elizabeth is far too strict with all the girls!'

'If only she weren't such a perfectionist! Poor Robina is forever afraid of failing to live up to her mother's expectations. Ah! here they are!' She picked up her glasses and put them on without thinking. She continued, 'It's not that Aunt Elizabeth is unkind. Not at all. Did you know that she's thinking of inviting poor Deborah Staunton to live with them in Abbot Quincey?'

'Deborah! At the Vicarage! For God's sake, don't tell Hugo! He'd never come home if he heard that.' They both grinned. Lady Elizabeth's niece Deborah had a genius for getting into scrapes, and Hugo had been involved in one or two of them a couple of years back. He still hadn't forgiven her. He had sworn at the time that he would never come within a mile of the girl again! There was a short silence, then Hester said, 'Lowell, I've been thinking…'

Lowell instantly grew serious. 'About Dungarran?'

'Yes. I couldn't see straight on Wednesday night, but now I've had a chance to think it over. If we can only keep him from finding out that I'm Euclid, there's nothing to stop us carrying on as before. Is there?'

Lowell thought. 'You mean writing for the journal and the rest? I suppose not,' he said slowly. 'And it shouldn't be all that difficult to keep Euclid's identity a secret. Dungarran is most unlikely to spend a lot of time finding him, it's not his style. Besides, how could he do it? The only clue he might have is Gaines's name from the register, and Gaines is safely tucked away in Devon for the summer. He would have to go to some trouble to find out this address, and I can't see him doing that—it can't be all that important. No, Hes, I think you're safe.'

At that moment they heard a knock on the street door and a murmured discussion. A minute later the servant came to ask if Mr Perceval would see Lord Dungarran.

Hester looked at Lowell in consternation, and shook her head imploringly. But Lowell knew better. It was impossible to deny such an important visitor, impossible even to keep him waiting.

'Show Lord Dungarran in, Withers.' Then he turned to Hester and said rapidly, 'Be as female as you can, Hes. High voice, fluttery manner—you know! And for goodness' sake, take your glasses off!' Hester snatched off her spectacles just as Dungarran strolled in, ducking slightly as he came through the low door.

'Good afternoon, Perceval. I hope you don't mind my calling like this without warning.'

'Not at all, not at all,' said Lowell with a fair degree of calm. 'I believe you know my sister, sir.'

'Miss Perceval! Forgive me, I didn't see you there in the shadows. How d'y do?'

They exchanged the usual greeting and enquiries. Hester knew that, in common courtesy, she should offer to leave the gentlemen to it. But she was determined to stay. She sat down firmly by the window and smiled sweetly. 'Pay no attention to me,' she said airily. 'I shall return to Bruton Street in a few minutes, but meanwhile I shall sit here and gather my strength. The weather is so fatiguing, do you not think, Lord Dungarran? My brother was just about to offer me some lemonade. Weren't you, Lowell?'

'Why...y...yes!' Lowell put his head out of the door and talked to Withers.

Dungarran walked over to the bookcase and examined the titles there. Hester regarded him from her vantage point by the window. He looked his usual, calmly superior self, and yet how differently she now saw him! Somewhere behind that lazily fashionable façade, was Zeno, her respected ally and friend, a man whose mind she knew better than anyone else's. She savoured the notion. The feeling that she knew more about Robert Dungarran than he knew of her was strangely heady!

Dungarran cleared his throat and turned. 'Were you

with Hugo and Lady Sophia at Lady Sefton's soirée, Miss Perceval?'

'Last Wednesday? No. I was otherwise engaged.' Amusement threatened to bubble to the surface. It was hard not to laugh. What would the gentleman say if she told him where she had in fact been?

'Ah!'

With a touch of audacity she asked, 'Why? Were you, Lord Dungarran?'

'No. I too, had a previous engagement.' He turned as Lowell came back. 'Ah, Perceval!'

'Now, how can I serve you, sir?' Lowell cleared one of the chairs by the simple expedient of throwing a pile of journals to the floor. 'Do, pray, take a seat.'

Dungarran sat down. There was a pause. Then he began. 'I have to say I was surprised to find you in possession here, Perceval. I thought to meet a Mr Gaines—a Mr Woodford Gaines.'

The servant came in with some cool drinks. When he went out Lowell said casually, 'The house does belong to Gaines, yes, but he recently left London…'

'*Very* recently,' said Hester, giving Lowell a significant look.

Lowell nodded. 'Very recently. He lets me have rooms here, and for the moment I'm the sole tenant. Do you know Gaines?'

'Not…exactly. I thought I saw him with you the other night.'

'Saw me? Where?'

'At a lecture on mathematics.'

There was a small noise as Hester's glasses slith-

ered to the floor. Dungarran rose from his chair and
gathered them up.

'You're lucky, Miss Perceval. They don't appear
to be broken.'

'Oh…oh, thank you, but they're not mine, sir!' she
said nervously. 'I must have picked them off the seat.
Are they yours, Lowell?'

Lowell rose nobly to the occasion. 'They might belong to Gaines.' Then he turned to his visitor. 'I'm
sorry, no, I wasn't with Gaines on Wednesday evening. I was with my sister.' He laughed. 'A lecture
on mathematics would be the last place my friends
would expect to find me!' His sister looked at him
sharply. Lowell, too, was enjoying this game, but she
hoped he wouldn't overplay it. He went on, 'But why
do you ask?'

Dungarran smiled lazily. That smile, thought
Hester viewing it objectively, might well charm an
unwary bird out of a tree—but the bird might end up
feeling it had made a mistake. 'I'm sorry. You must
think me impertinent. At the risk of boring you, I
should like to explain. I have a…slight interest in
mathematics myself, and for some time now I've been
in correspondence with a gifted mathematician, someone whom I only know as Euclid…'

He went on to give them an account, which they
didn't need, of the events on the evening of the lecture. 'And now I am at a loss. The young gentleman
in question did not turn up at the end as I had hoped.
I rather thought I had tracked him down when I traced

him to this address. Tell me, how long is Mr Gaines likely to be out of London?'

'Till the autumn.'

'Ah.'

Greatly daring, Hester asked, 'May I ask why you are so anxious to meet this...Eugene?'

'Euclid, Miss Perceval. Euclid. He was an eminent mathematician in ancient times.'

Hester opened her eyes wide. 'Mr *Gaines* was? I don't understand.'

'Why should you?' Dungarran smiled indulgently. 'The journal for which both he and I write has the rather bizarre custom of giving its contributors pseudonyms from the past—'

'Do you mean to tell me that you actually *write*, Lord Dungarran? For a journal?'

'Pray do not disturb yourself, ma'am. I do not permit my work to interfere with my social commitments.'

'So I have observed. But what do you write?' she asked ingenuously. 'Poetry?'

'Not exactly.' He turned to Lowell. 'I should very much like to meet the fellow. Though he appears to be very young, he is extremely talented. There are aspects of his work which interest me greatly. Are you quite certain that you cannot help me?'

Lowell spread his hands regretfully. 'I'm afraid I can't,' he said. 'Gaines is in Devon on a walking tour with his godfather. I've no idea where is at the moment, only that he will be back in the autumn.'

'Ah. That's a pity. Then I apologise for wasting

your time. I'll finish up this very good ale and then go. May I escort you home, Miss Perceval?'

'Thank you, sir, but my footman is waiting outside,' said Hester, not without a certain satisfaction.

He nodded in approval, sat back and took another draft of his beer. Still looking into the glass, he said casually, 'So you're not a mathematician?' and followed this with a quick glance at Lowell from grey eyes which were unusually keen.

'Far from it!' exclaimed Lowell. 'I was never so glad in all my life when the time came to put my primers away for good.'

Dungarran nodded. 'A heartfelt reaction—and one most people share. That's why I keep rather quiet about my own fascination with the subject. Few wish to hear about the application of algebra, or the new research into calculus.'

'Calculus?' Hester asked sharply. Lowell and Dungarran looked at her in astonishment. She gave a little laugh and faltered, 'Oh, you must excuse me! My mind was wandering. Were you talking about another of your friends? Like Eugene? Was Calculus at the lecture, too?'

'Er…no. Just Euclid. But we must be boring you, Miss Perceval. Forgive me.'

Hester bit back the protest which rose to her lips, gave a bell-like laugh and said, 'It would be rude of me to confess to being bored! But I daresay many ladies would have better uses for a ballroom than holding a lecture on mathematics in it!'

Dungarran looked at her thoughtfully, then smiled

and got up to go. 'I'm sure you are right! And if you don't need my company to Bruton Street, I'll take my leave.' He bowed, then turned to Lowell. 'Should you hear anything from the mysterious Mr Gaines, Perceval, I'd be obliged if you ask him to get in touch with me.'

He went out. Lowell breathed a deep sigh of relief. Hester frowned and said thoughtfully, 'All the same, Lowell…'

'Well?'

'All the same, if I were you I would prepare a very good reason for being at that lecture. Dungarran, I can assure you, is far from stupid. I don't think he was completely convinced by your evasions.'

'What nonsense! Why on earth should he think I'd go to a lecture on mathematics, of all things?'

'That's what you must think out for yourself!'

'Unnecessary, my dear sister. You wait and see— it will be quite unnecessary!'

Lowell would not have been quite so sure of himself if he could have seen into their recent visitor's mind as he walked back to Curzon Street. Dungarran was quite certain that Lowell Perceval had been at the lecture. How else would Hester Perceval have known that it had been held in a former ballroom? Obviously because her brother had mentioned the ballroom in the St James's Street house when he had told her about the lecture. He had also let slip that he knew when it was held. Interesting. Young Mr Perceval had enjoyed playing with him! That would account for the air of suppressed amusement about both the Percevals which had so intrigued him. Still deep in thought, he entered his house, handed his hat and cane to the footman waiting at the door, and sent for his man.

'Ah, Wicklow. Good. Come through to the library and shut the door, will you?'

It would be difficult to describe Wicklow's exact role in the Dungarran household. He was his lordship's manservant, everyone knew that. Indeed, he was the very epitome of a gentleman's gentleman. Neat as a pin himself, with a thin, pale, somewhat melancholy face, quietly discreet in his movements, he looked after Dungarran's wardrobe with consummate skill. But he had other functions connected with his master's less well-known activities, and it was for this work he was now needed.

'Wicklow, you were prompt in finding Mr Woodford Gaines's address. Did you learn anything else about him?'

'Not much, my lord. He appeared to be a perfectly normal young man. A bit of a dandy, they said. Your lordship asked for speed and discretion in the matter, so I did not spend more time than necessary with his associates.'

'Quite right, quite right. You did well. But now I want you—still with discretion—to establish two things. Mr Gaines left London recently, possibly for Devon. I want you to find out first exactly when he left, and second exactly where he went—Devon, or anywhere else. And Wicklow!'

Wicklow, who had been about to leave the room, turned and waited.

'I would prefer you to avoid annoying Mr Lowell Perceval with your enquiries. You will obviously not approach Mr Perceval's sister, either. Thank you, that is all.'

After Wicklow had gone Dungarran sat in silence reviewing his conversation with the two Percevals. He had seen from the outset that they were very close, and he rather thought that Lowell would confide fairly freely in his sister. They had been quite good, those two. Only two slips—one by Lowell, one by his sister. He smiled grimly at the neat way in which Master Lowell had ostensibly denied having been at the lecture, without actually lying. 'A lecture on mathematics would be the last place my friends would expect to find me.' Very neat. But why avoid that lie when he had told one already? 'I was with my sister.' And why say it with such amusement? If he *had* been at the lecture he could not possibly have been with his sister. There was no doubt that Hester Perceval would support anything her brother said, but why had he felt the alibi necessary? It might be odd that Lowell Perceval should wish to attend a lecture on mathematics, but there was nothing *wrong* with it... Unless there was something suspicious about Gaines himself...?

Where the devil was Euclid? Why had he vanished from the Society's rooms last Wednesday, and why had he left London immediately afterwards? Robert Dungarran got up and walked about the room restlessly... Perhaps they were all wasting his time—it wasn't certain that Gaines and Euclid were one and the same person. The signature in the register was no real proof. Had Lowell Perceval signed it, using Gaines's name...? As a wager, perhaps? Lowell Perceval was known for his mad escapades. He gave a gesture of impatience. There were too many questions. He would have to wait till Wicklow found some answers. Meanwhile, there was work to be done... Dungarran went to the handsome desk in a corner of the room and took out some papers.

But after a moment he sat back with a sigh of exasperation. The situation was absurd. Buried in the papers, which had been removed with great difficulty from Napoleon's headquarters in Paris and brought to England at considerable risk, there could be vital background information about the food and weapons situation in France and the army's lines of supply. But they were all in cipher. If they were to be useful to the Allies then they would have to be transcribed before very long. The War Office would soon get impatient. He needed help, and Euclid, with his outstanding talent for ciphers and the speed with which he worked, was the very man. And now the wretch had become elusive! It was to be hoped that Wicklow would find him...

But the result of Wicklow's investigations only raised more questions. Mr Woodford Gaines had left London for Totnes in Devon on 15 April—two weeks before the lecture ever took place. He had not been seen in Half Moon Street since then, and was generally assumed to be walking in the Dart valley with a godfather of whom he had great expectations. There were no other inhabitants of the Half Moon Street house, and Mr Perceval's other close friends had all been at a reunion.

So who was the second young gentleman who had been in St James's Street with Lowell Perceval? Where was he?

Over the next few days Dungarran pondered this mystery. It had become important to him to solve it—and not just to satisfy his curiosity. He had had confidence in Euclid. The correspondence with the fellow had given him a great deal of pleasure. It was rare to find a mind so much in harmony with his own, and all his instincts had been to trust him. Whether Euclid realised it or not, he had been deciphering bits of foreign documents for some time now—aiding and confirming Dungarran's own work for the government. Any mystery about him was most unwelcome.

He decided to investigate from another starting point—the collection and delivery of Euclid's contributions—and went round to the Society's headquarters to question the staff himself. The day porter at the entrance was old and half blind, and only vaguely remembered receiving and handing out various sealed papers over the months. He provided a description of the agent which could fit Lowell Perceval—and a hundred others as well. The junior porter's description of the young man who had signed the register on the

evening of the lecture, however, could hardly be anyone else.

'Yes, I remember 'im, my lord. A very 'andsome
young gentleman. Young, tall, wiv fair 'air and blue
eyes. Looks as if 'e's laughin' all the time...'

When questioned about any other young gentleman, the porter was less certain. 'There was someone
else... But whether 'e was wiv the first young gentleman, I couldn't rightly swear to... Very shy, 'e
was—kept in the background. One thing I do remember—'e wore glasses. I didn't see nothink else. Oh!'
He pocketed the coin, Dungarran had handed him.
'Your lordship's very kind. I'm sorry I can't 'elp you
more.'

Things seemed to have reached an impasse. He decided to consult someone whose good sense and intelligence he considered as good, if not better than his
own. He betook himself to his aunt. Lady Martindale
was a childless widow and lived alone in a large
house in Grosvenor Street. She had been the late Lady
Dungarran's favourite sister, and was Robert
Dungarran's godmother. They were frequently seen
together. Society knew that Lady Martindale was very
attached to her nephew, but most would have been
astonished to learn how highly the nephew thought of
her intelligence and discretion, and how much he confided in her. She was one of the few people in London
who knew of his activities at the Foreign Office. Her
husband had been a diplomat, and it was through his
persuasion that Dungarran had taken up his work
there.

'I have a problem, Godmama—' he began.

'You seldom come unless you have, Robert. What is it this time? Could it possibly be a woman?'

Dungarran smiled. 'You never give up, do you? Why do you doubt my ability to manage my own love affairs?'

'Love affairs, indeed!' Lady Martindale gave an unladylike snort. 'You don't know what love means! You mean flirtations, or liaisons with ladies of more beauty than virtue—that doesn't mean love to me!'

'Whatever you say, dearest. I won't argue,' he said indifferently. But she was not to be put off.

'You've been spoilt, my boy! Ever since you came of age women—of every kind—have found you fascinating—'

Dungarran made a face. 'Please! We both know that any rich, reasonably personable man would interest the ladies, don't we?'

'That may be so. But it is a fact that when you exert yourself you usually find most women responsive. And that isn't good for you.'

This frank speaking was not to her godson's taste. 'You make me out to be a veritable coxcomb, Aunt,' he said somewhat coolly. 'As far as I know, I have never raised false hopes in any female breast. Except perhaps once...' he stopped. 'No matter.'

His godmother waited hopefully, but it became clear he was not going to amplify. She took up her theme again. 'When you do fall in love, Robert—and I hope I may live to see it—you might not have such an easy time. Things don't always go as we plan when the heart is involved. You might be glad of a shoulder to cry on then.'

'Let us not get into the realms of fantasy, Aunt Martindale,' he said impatiently. 'It is highly unlikely, if not impossible, that my heart would ever rule my head to such an irrational extent. I'm surprised at you. I thought you had more sense.'

Lady Martindale shook her head. 'Stronger men than you have fallen, Robert.'

'But not, I think, more logical ones. Now, may I consult you on a certain problem, or are we to carry on spinning fairy tales?'

'What is it?' she asked in a resigned tone.

He had no need to tell her of his correspondence with Euclid, or of his work on ciphers. She knew all this. So he briefly related the puzzling events of the night of the lecture, and the information he had since gathered. She requested him to repeat his account of the meeting with the Percevals in Half Moon Street, and asked one or two questions. At the end she said slowly, 'Why are you so sure that Euclid is a man?'

He looked at her in surprise. 'What else could he be? There are no women in this case.'

'Oh, come, Robert! You are not usually so stupid! There is one at least!'

'You mean Hester Perceval?' He began to smile. 'You've met her?'

'I've seen her. But I haven't spoken to her.'

'Well!' He looked at her as if he had said enough. When she continued to look at him in silence, he went on, 'Godmama, Euclid is a man of the quickest wits, and a penetrating mind. He has a very good feeling for mathematics and has an instinct for finding the key to difficult ciphers which almost amounts to genius.'

'So?'

'What is more, he has a sense of humour, an appreciation of the ridiculous, which is very like my own. You've seen Hester Perceval. How can you possibly think that she could be Euclid?'

'Why not?'

'She…she's dull! She's…she's… Well, that's it, really. She's dull. Boring.' Lady Martindale was still silent. 'Look,' he said in exasperation. 'Euclid has the flexibility of mind that all the great decipherers have. Hester Perceval is as rigid, as fixed in her ideas as a woman can be. Did you know her six years ago?'

'No, I didn't. Your uncle and I came late to London that year. And she left halfway through, after that business with Canford. I heard about her, of course.'

'You must have been told how she came to town with a mission, ignoring all advice and insisting on spreading her half-baked theories, learned by heart from her schoolteacher's preachings. She was supposed to have been a prize pupil, but, I assure you, there was little indication of cleverness in her dealings with the world! We all were heartily sick of her.'

'Robert, she cannot have been very old. What was she—seventeen? Eighteen? I feel sorry for the girl.'

'So was I. But I was even sorrier for her family, I assure you. And I think I may safely say that she hasn't changed much. Six years later she may be quieter, but in all our meetings she has not uttered a single original thought. Hester Perceval as Euclid? Impossible.' He got up and walked about the room. 'Impossible!'

'I don't think I can help, then. As far as I can see, there doesn't seem to be any other candidate for Euclid.' She looked at him, with a slight frown. 'You are usually very open-minded. But you seem to have a very strong prejudice against Miss Perceval. Are you quite sure she is as stupid as you say? Have you paid particular attention to her since she has come back?'

'I haven't dared,' he muttered.

'Aha! So she's the one...' He looked faintly exasperated as she smiled at him. 'Six years ago she thought she was in love with you, is that it? Don't be so conceited, Robert. Six years is a long time for a girl to hold on to an unrequited passion.'

'Hester Perceval cordially dislikes me, Godmama. So much is perfectly clear.'

'In that case, where is the danger? But you may observe her from a safe distance. She just might surprise you.'

'I doubt that very much. But since I still haven't yet finished with her brother, I may see something new. They might well be at tonight's reception at Carlton House.'

'Are you still free to take me?'

'Of course! What makes you think I might not?'

'I heard about the state they're in at the Horse Guards about those papers...'

'My dear godmother, they're always in a state at the Horse Guards! I'm about to go to work on their confounded papers, but there's this business of Euclid to settle first. We'll forget the Horse Guards this evening and enjoy ourselves—as long as we can keep our distance from Bathurst and his minions.'

'Let's hope the wine at Carlton House is better than it was the last time we dined there!'

After the concert Dungarran observed the Perceval family making its way into the Long Gallery. He decided to make use of the occasion. 'Aunt, you said you haven't been introduced to Miss Perceval...'

'I've met the senior Percevals, and I know Hugo, of course, very well. But not the two younger ones. Do you mean to introduce us?'

'I'd like to. As you know, I want to have a further word with Lowell Perceval, and this seems a good opportunity.'

'I'm disappointed. I hoped you wanted me to meet the young lady.'

Dungarran pulled a face. 'Hester Perceval is not my kind of young lady.'

'You must tell me some time what is, Robert,' sighed his godmother, as she followed him through the crowd. It was an ambition of hers to see her nephew settled, but as time went on she was growing less and less optimistic. It was not for want of opportunity. Over the years she had observed more than one accredited beauty fluttering her wings in his direction. But though he gave every sign of being charmed, he had never succumbed. Even now, as they greeted their acquaintances on the way through to the Perceval family, she was amused by the many languishing glances cast by ladies who should have known better. It was not only his handsome face and tall figure which women found attractive, she thought. He had an air of detachment which most women found an irresistible challenge. She smiled. If they only knew its origin! Robert had had his fair share of mistresses, but when it came down to it he was far more interested in the mysteries of mathematics than the mysteries of love! Too well bred to show complete indifference in society, he was nevertheless bored by most social exchanges. What sort of woman would it take, she wondered, to break through that barrier? Not one of your conventional society beauties, that was certain!

They had reached the Percevals. She greeted the parents with a friendly smile, and exchanged a few words with Hugo. Then Robert said, 'Aunt, I'd like to introduce Miss Hester Perceval…and Mr Lowell Perceval.' The lady curtsied, the young man—and what a personable young man he was!—bowed.

She studied them with interest, while Robert joined in general talk with the family. At first sight it seemed that all the good looks in the family had gone to the male line. Hester Perceval was almost as tall as her brother—too tall, perhaps, for a woman. She was rather thin, and fashionably but quietly dressed in a pale muslin evening dress with a somewhat limp fall of lace round the neckline. Her hair was fair like that of her brothers, but its natural curls were smoothed down at the front and drawn into neat bands behind. If the girl had set out to make herself as dull and inconspicuous as possible, she could not have done better! Her brother, on the other hand, was every bit as good-looking as Hugo, but with a more immediately charming manner. In contrast to Hugo's air of calm assurance, there was a reckless air about him, and laughter seemed to hover round his mobile mouth and deep blue eyes. He was still young—younger, perhaps, than his years—but when he once grew up… A real charmer, though essentially a lightweight young man. It was obvious that the two younger Percevals were devoted to each other, though she suspected that the sister had the stronger character.

When Hugo and Sir James and Lady Perceval started to move off Lady Martindale took a step back, but Robert gave a slight shake of his head and looked briefly in the direction of Miss Perceval. Lady Martindale was as quick as the next woman at taking a hint.

Chapter Six

'I hear you come from Northamptonshire,' Lady Martindale said, turning back to Hester. 'Tell me, do you know Lord Yardley and his delightful family? I don't believe I saw you at the ball the Yardleys gave for their daughter's come-out. That was a splendid affair…' For the next few minutes she chatted with the sister while Robert held the brother in conversation. Hester Perceval was polite, if rather colourless in her manner. But she was noticeably uneasy. She kept looking towards the two men as if anxious to know what they were saying, and her sigh of relief when they turned back to the ladies was almost audible.

Lowell Perceval was looking ruefully guilty, rather like a small boy caught out in some mischief.

'Hester, I'm afraid it's all up! Lord Dungarran has flushed me out. I've had to confess that I was at the lecture the other night.'

'I am surprised Lord Dungarran is so interested,' said Hester coolly.

'I hate mysteries, Miss Perceval,' said Dungarran with one of his charming smiles. His aunt's interest quickened. Robert was dangerous when he smiled like this.

'What is mysterious about my brother's attendance at a lecture?'

Lady Martindale decided to take a part. 'A mystery? A lecture? Robert, what is all this about?'

'I'm sorry, Aunt. I'm being very rude. Forgive me. Mr Perceval was at a lecture at the Society last Wednesday, and when I quite mistakenly thought he was denying it, I was puzzled—and, yes, a little put out, too. It was one of the best I've heard.'

'I see. But where is the mystery in that?'

'Mr Perceval claims he has no interest in mathematics. So what puzzles me is why he was there at all!'

For a moment Lowell looked at a loss, and the girl next to Lady Martindale stiffened. Then she said with a laugh, 'I can see you're going to have to tell them about your wagers, Lowell!' She turned to Lady Martindale, and with the first sign of vivacity she had shown she said, 'You must know, Lady Martindale, that my brother cannot resist a wager. Have you heard of his exploits in Piccadilly?' She went on to explain in some detail how Lowell had ridden his horse at full gallop down one of London's main thoroughfares. She omitted no detail, describing the horses he had startled, the wagons he had narrowly missed, the carriages, the personages... Lady Martindale listened while she watched her nephew from the corner of her eye. Miss Perceval was making a brave effort to distract attention from the subject of Lowell's attendance at the lecture, but Robert, she knew, would not be put off. For all his relaxed air of someone who is enjoying an amusing anecdote, he was only waiting for the end of the recital to repeat his original question.

When Hester finally ran out of breath, he said, 'And all without real injury to anyone! You must be quite an accomplished horseman, Perceval! But what sort of a wager could entice you into the lair of the New Scientific and Philosophical Society?'

Lowell once again hesitated, and his sister once again came to his rescue.

'It was probably because of something I said, Lord Dungarran. I…er… I could not believe that Lowell would survive a lecture on such an uninteresting subject for more than half an hour. Oh! Forgive me, I mean no offence. I merely meant that it seems a dull subject to those who do not understand it.' She paused. 'To those who do, I am sure it is fascinating.' Her words were innocent enough, and the tone was obviously meant to convey that Miss Perceval was not to be counted among them. But Lady Martindale sensed something more than this about it. Was it irony? Or mockery? There was certainly a thread of amusement. She looked at her nephew, but he appeared not to have noticed. His eyes were on Lowell Perceval.

He said with a smile, 'And was it such a penance? The young man who was with you seemed to be an enthusiast. I have seldom heard such impassioned words in defence of the subject! It can't have been Mr Gaines, surely?'

Mr Perceval was now on his guard. 'Why not?' he asked warily.

'You told me yourself. He's in Devon with his god-father. And someone told me—can that have been you, too?—that he left London well before that Wednesday evening.'

The two Percevals exchanged glances. Lady Martindale was now in complete agreement with her nephew. These two were playing some game of their own. She could see that Robert was intent on chal-lenging them. There was steel behind the amusement in his voice, and he did not take his eyes from Lowell's.

'Lowell! That's too bad of you!' Hester's exasper-ated exclamation cut into the pause. 'My wager was that you should go alone, without other distractions. If you had the company of another young man to keep you amused, then I consider that you have lost!'

'Lord Dungarran is mistaken, Hester, I swear. I wasn't with another man! It's true that someone next to me made a speech. He seemed to get a bit burned up, but I thought the whole thing very boring. You still owe me.'

Two pairs of eyes turned to Dungarran. Lady Martindale could see Hester's clearly for the first time. They were as deep a blue as those of her brother, and had the same limpidly innocent look in them. Her mouth twitched as she heard her nephew say, 'So you cannot help me, after all. How very annoying! I shall have to think again.'

And she wondered if the Percevals were as little deceived as she was by these words. They might well be congratulating themselves on winning the first round in this war of wits, but she would venture a considerable sum on her nephew to win the match—and, unlike the Percevals' so-called wager, the bet would be genuine!

Lady Martindale had derived considerable amusement from witnessing this exchange. She had no doubt that her nephew would be the victor in any battle of wits, but she suspected that he had at last met a worthy opponent—and not in the person of Lowell Perceval! She spent the next week or two watching the young Percevals closely and found nothing to cause her to change her mind. Hester Perceval was an enigma. When she said as much to her nephew he laughed at her.

'My dear aunt! In what way can Hester Perceval possibly interest you? What on earth is enigmatic about her?'

'You are very scornful of Miss Perceval, Robert. But in my view she must be unique! Young ladies enjoying a Season in London usually take endless pains with their appearance. Every skill known to their mamas, their dressmakers and their maids is employed to enhance their charms.'

'With varying success,' said Robert with a grin. 'And in Miss Perceval's case, very little.'

'But that's just it! She doesn't try for success, Robert! That is what makes her unique! I have never before met a girl who appears to make every effort not to *improve*, but to minimise her looks.'

'Oh, come! That cannot be so.'

'I mean it! Her aim seems to be to disappear into the background. Her manners are well-bred, but they lack any personality. Her clothing is so un-noteworthy that five minutes after leaving her one has difficulty in remembering what she was wearing—'

'But that's because she is a very dull girl!'

'You think so? I don't believe I can agree with you. It surely did not escape you that it was the sister, not the brother, who found the excuses for Lowell's behaviour at your famous lecture? And I suspect she put herself forward in a most uncharacteristic manner to do so.'

'So you didn't believe in Lowell's reasons any more than I did?'

'No. But did you not notice that it was Hester's quick-wittedness which saved him each time?'

'And frustrated me.' He thought for a moment. 'I must confess I was concentrating on the young man. I didn't notice his sister's efforts. Are you sure it was so?'

'Yes, Robert!' said Lady Martindale firmly. 'And if you have not seen Miss Perceval when she is unaware of being watched, then I have. She is a different creature altogether. Altogether livelier and much more attractive.'

Robert Dungarran's tone revealed his continuing

scepticism. 'I cannot claim to have watched her as assiduously as you apparently have, but in my experience Hester Perceval could be described as neither quick-witted nor lively, and, though I'm sorry for the girl, I simply cannot imagine she could ever be attractive!'

'You belong to the wrong group of people, my boy! With Lowell Perceval's friends, where she is perfectly at ease, she is a delightful creature—she laughs and teases, and is clearly popular with them all. It is only when she comes into Society with a capital "S" that she is suddenly subdued.'

'You're imagining things!'

'I assure you I am not! As soon as Hester Perceval comes into contact with anyone who could be described as "eligible" she freezes. I have seen her!'

'Then why else is she in London?'

'I have heard that she is here most unwillingly. Her parents more or less insisted on it.'

He was silent for a moment. Then he said, 'It would not be surprising if the poor girl was reluctant to venture into society again. Her first attempt ended in disaster... And if she finds amusement with Lowell Perceval and his friends then I am glad for her, though I am surprised. They seem very immature with their tricks and wagers. But my dear aunt, let us now talk of something else. I confess that I still find Miss Perceval a very boring topic of conversation!'

Lady Martindale gave up and talked of other matters. But she did not change her mind about Hester Perceval, and unobtrusively cultivated the girl's acquaintance. To this end she invited the Perceval family to one of her dinner parties.

She invited her nephew, too, and though he was still preoccupied with his translation of the French documents, he agreed to come. He was less than pleased, however, when he discovered that his partner for the evening was Hester Perceval. But since his manners were impeccable, apart from casting a speaking glance at his aunt, he saw Miss Perceval to her place and sat down beside her with every appearance of pleasure. There was a short silence while he considered what the devil he should say to the girl.

'Are you enjoying your stay in London, Miss Perceval?' he finally asked.

She looked at him thoughtfully as if debating what to reply. He wondered irritably what on earth the problem was. Surely a purely conventional 'Very much!' or 'Naturally' or even a noncommittal 'Sometimes' would do? Then they could safely go on to discuss the latest balls and concerts. That should last through several courses.

'I didn't at first, Lord Dungarran. But now I am enjoying myself very much.' He was so surprised at this that he threw her a quick glance. She looked down immediately, but not before he had caught a hint of mischief in the blue depths of her eyes.

'Oh? Why is that?'

'I… I have discovered that an old friend of mine is here,' she said demurely. 'Someone I have known for several years, but have not till now met in person.'

'Ah! Do I sense a romance?'

'Oh no! Nothing like that. Our friendship is based on a meeting of minds. But it is very...interesting, nonetheless, to meet him.'

Dungarran nodded but sighed inwardly. He was doubtless about to hear of some worthy lady or elderly gentleman from the north, a missionary, or a reformer or something of that sort. He braced himself for a dissertation on the virtues of some undoubtedly very boring person.

'I don't suppose I know him, do I?'

'He is not known to society in general,' she said somewhat evasively. 'His talents are not ones which are commonly valued by the Ton.'

It was as he had thought. A preacher, or possibly one of the new radical thinkers, earnest in manner and depressingly dull in appearance. He persevered. 'And are you happy with your new acquaintance? Are his appearance and conversation as you imagined them?'

'They are radically different! In fact, I even occasionally find myself disliking him. But then I remember my former admiration and then...' She shook her head. 'To tell the truth, I am not yet sure what I think of him. It is...most interesting.' She glanced at him, and he was once again surprised by a gleam of amusement, mockery almost, in her eyes. What the devil was Miss Perceval up to? Her eyes were lowered again as she asked, 'But may I ask if you have yet traced your elusive mathematician?'

There was no doubt this time. Miss Perceval's manner was conventionally polite, the question harmless enough, but Robert Dungarran was nobody's fool. All his instincts—instincts which had served him well in the past—confirmed his suspicion that Miss Perceval was somehow making fun of him. A most unaccustomed flick of temper gave his next words unusual sharpness.

'Not yet. But I will.' His eyes rested for a moment on Lowell, seated further down the table. 'And I am quite certain that your brother knows more about Euclid than he will admit, Miss Perceval.' Keen grey eyes locked on to hers. 'Moreover, I strongly suspect that you are in his confidence. Am I right?'

Her eyes did not waver as she stared calmly back at him. 'Are you suggesting that my brother is Euclid? I assure you that he is as ignorant as a swan on mathematical matters.'

'I accept your word for that. Besides, it agrees with what I have discovered. Your brother's talents did not lie in the sciences in Cambridge. I am sure, however, that he knows Euclid, and was with him at that lecture. The signatures in the register for the evening are both in his handwriting.'

There was a pause. Then she said with not the slightest trace of amusement in her voice, 'I do not quite understand why you are pursuing the question of Euclid's identity with such determination, Lord Dungarran. But if you think Lowell knows more about Euclid than he has admitted, then you must talk to him—at another time, perhaps. I do not think Lady Martindale's dinner table a suitable place for...for such an inquisition. Excuse me.' She turned to her neighbour on the other side, who happened to be free, and began a conversation with him.

She had at least stopped laughing at him, he thought, with a certain amount of satisfaction. Really, what his aunt had said was perfectly right. Hester Perceval was an enigma, and would repay further observation. But not tonight—the girl was right, of course. His aunt's dinner table was not the place for serious investigation. And, to anyone who did not know how important it was to decipher the French papers as quickly as possible, his pursuit of Euclid must seem illogical, against the conventions of good society. But he would tackle Lowell Perceval very soon on his own ground and, meanwhile, he would watch Miss Perceval more closely.

Dungarran could observe without being observed when he chose to. And for the next week he observed Hester Perceval. He saw with surprise how animated her conversation with Lowell Perceval's young friends could be, what a teasing, laughing relationship existed among them all. He saw her dancing, obviously enjoying every minute, and displaying a marked grace. But not with anyone who could be classed as 'an eligible young man'. Her partners were members of her own family, friends of her parents, friends of her younger brother. As soon as she was asked to dance with anyone who had been in London six years before, or anyone who could be regarded as husband material, she stiffened and went silent and unresponsive. The transformation was amazing.

* * *

A few days later he was with his godmother being driven along Piccadilly when they saw Miss Perceval entering Hatchard's bookshop. 'Robert, look! Here's our chance. Biggs! Stop here! I wish to get down. Come, Robert. Let's find out a little more about our young lady. Is she buying Sir Walter Scott's latest offering? Or is Byron her choice? Or what?'

'She doesn't like poetry,' said her godson grimly, as they entered the shop, 'but I can see one thing— Miss Perceval is once again walking out with neither groom nor maid to accompany her. And in Piccadilly, too!'

'Shocking. But never mind that. I want to see what she does. Come!' They saw Miss Perceval had walked past the tables displaying novels and poetry, and was standing in front of a shelf holding a variety of scientific works. Even as they entered she started talking earnestly to an assistant there.

Dungarran put his hand on his aunt's arm. 'Don't go any further!' he said quietly. Picking up a fine volume of *Ackermann's Views of London* from a table by the door, he added, 'We'll look at this for a moment or two.' After a while Hester Perceval turned and made her way back towards the entrance. She was carrying a small parcel. He intercepted her.

'Why, Miss Perceval!' he said. 'What a surprise to find you here!'

'Lord Dungarran! Lady Martindale! How…how pleasant to see you.' She didn't look as if she was pleased. In fact, she had turned a little paler. But she rallied and said, 'What a splendid shop this is! I could spend hours looking at it all.'

'You appear to have bought something.'

She looked at the parcel in her hand as if she had forgotten it. 'This? Oh, yes! P...poems.'

'I thought you didn't like poetry?'

She looked blank for a moment. 'Oh yes! No! I mean, since coming to London I have decided that I should find out more about it, Lord Dungarran.'

'A great deal of nonsense is talked about poetry, Miss Perceval,' said Lady Martindale, smiling. 'There are some excellent poets, of course—but some very bad ones, as well. I find Lord Byron's effusions quite ridiculously overvalued. Do you?'

'I... I haven't read any. Yet. Whom do you admire, Lady Martindale?'

They talked for some minutes, at the end of which Dungarran said, 'My aunt's carriage is outside. May we offer you a lift back to Bruton Street, Miss Perceval? Or would you prefer to walk?'

'Thank you, but I would prefer to walk. The...the exercise is good for me.'

He looked at her sardonically. 'Then I'll call your footman, shall I? Or is your maid with you?'

Lady Martindale took pity on Miss Perceval's dilemma. 'I have a better idea, Robert. I should like to take Miss Perceval back to Grosvenor Street with me. I should like to show her the picture of her grandmother painted by one of my aunts when they were both young. A watercolour. Hugo says he can still trace a likeness, even after all these years. I would dearly like you to see it, too, Miss Perceval. Can you spare the time?'

Hester hesitated. She was strongly tempted. Lady Martindale had a most attractive manner.

'Do come,' said Lady Martindale persuasively. 'Robert can walk back. We'll look at the picture and chat until he arrives, and then we shall all have tea together. Would that not be charming?'

Robert Dungarran saw with amusement that, like many another before her, Hester was slightly dazed, but unable to refuse Lady Martindale. His aunt had a way of making it impossible. He handed the ladies into the carriage and watched them drive off. Then he went back into the shop. The assistant, who knew him well, was very ready to oblige.

'The young lady has made several purchases in the last week or two, my lord. But I'm afraid I was unable to oblige her today in her chief request. She wished to purchase, on her brother's behalf, I understand, something on the recent researches into calculus. I suggested he might more likely find such a work in Cambridge. The subject is somewhat remote for our London clientele.'

'Were you able to help her with anything else, Behring?'

'Yes! We had a volume of Mr Lagrange's dissertations on number theory and algebraic equations, which she bought. In French, naturally. But she assures me that her brother is fluent in French.'

'An erudite young man.'

'Oh, very. If I remember correctly, you have such a volume yourself, my lord.'

'I believe I have. Thank you, Behring.'

Dungarran walked along Piccadilly and through Berkeley Square towards Grosvenor Street so deep in thought that he completely ignored the greetings of several passers-by. Such discourtesy was so unlike him that his friends were quite worried. They would have been even more concerned if they had seen his behaviour a few minutes later. On the far side of Berkeley Square he stopped abruptly, paused, then turned round and strode swiftly back to his own house in Curzon Street. He reappeared a few minutes later carrying a small parcel and resumed his progress to his aunt's house.

Here he found his aunt and Hester Perceval in animated conversation over the teacups. A watercolour of a young lady lay on the table.

'Where have you been, Robert? As you see, we found we couldn't wait any longer—we have started without you.'

Dungarran helped himself to tea, and settled himself comfortably in a chair opposite his aunt's visitor. He had already placed his parcel on a small table beside the chair.

'What do you have there, my dear?' asked Lady Martindale. 'It looks like a book. From Hatchard's? Did you return there? Is that what kept you?'

'Which question would you like me to answer first, Godmama? Yes, it is a book. Yes, I did go back into

Hatchard's. No, the book is not from there. It is one of my own, which I propose to lend to Miss Perceval. I understand she would be interested in it.'

Hester shifted uneasily under Dungarran's steady gaze. His last words had surprised her, and she made an effort to smile gratefully. 'Thank you, but if it is poetry, Lord Dungarran, I cannot promise to read it with great understanding—more as a willing beginner.'

'That may well fit the case exactly, Miss Perceval, though I'm afraid it isn't poetry.' With these words he got up and handed the parcel to Hester. She hesitated. He seemed to tower over her, and there was something in his manner which was not reassuring. She threw a look of appeal at Lady Martindale, who said, 'Pray open it, Miss Perceval! I am most intrigued. I cannot imagine what it is. Do tell me.'

Reluctantly Hester undid the string and unwrapped the book. She looked at it in silence for a moment while she felt a wave of scarlet colour her cheeks.

'It…it is a book on calculus,' she said in strangled tones.

'I understand from Behring that you were asking about such a work.' Then he added sardonically, 'For your brother, of course.'

Lady Martindale, looking concerned, came over and sat by Hester. 'Robert, I am not certain I approve—'

'Please, Aunt Martindale. I surely do not have to remind you, of all people, how urgent the matter is.'

Hester had not heard this exchange. After the initial

shock she concentrated on rallying her forces. This detestable man with his spying ways had nearly reached the end of his search for Euclid. But she was not about to give in without a fight.

She stood up and said coldly, 'Am I to understand, Lord Dungarran, that you questioned a tradesman about my activities? A shop assistant? You must allow me to tell you that even in Northamptonshire we would not consider that to be the action of a gentleman!'

'You are right, of course, and I apologise—I am only sorry that it was necessary.'

'Necessary! To whom? To you? To satisfy your own idle curiosity?' The scorn in Hester's voice was devastating.

Lady Martindale, who had been prepared to intervene on Miss Perceval's behalf, sat back and decided to wait. Life in London was often rather dull, but this tea party promised to be much more interesting than the usual insipid exchange of gossip. It looked as if the unmasking of Euclid was imminent—which in itself was exciting. Meanwhile, she would enjoy watching Hester Perceval attempting to hold her own, even against her masterful nephew—and, all things considered, she was doing rather well, too.

'But then I should have learned,' Hester continued with equal contempt. 'Necessity has a habit of causing you to forget you were born a gentleman! Prying into my affairs today is no worse than hitting me, defenceless as I was, six years ago. You claimed necessity then, if I remember.'

'Robert! You didn't!'

Dungarran smiled grimly at his aunt's startled protest. 'It is, sadly enough, perfectly true, Godmama. I ought to tell you in my own defence that Miss Perceval was in the grip of raging hysteria at the time. Nothing else would have got through to her.'

Lady Martindale looked quite fascinated. 'I never realised that your earlier acquaintance with Miss Perceval was so…eventful,' she said.

Dungarran ignored his aunt's curious gaze. He turned to Hester and smiled disarmingly. 'But I assure you, I have regretted that, and what I said afterwards, ever since. Can you forgive me?'

Hester was not to be placated. 'Fine words! But your 'regret' does not seem to have inhibited your ungentlemanly conduct today!'

With delight Lady Martindale noted that her nephew, unaccustomed as he was to having his charm ignored, was disconcerted. He said sharply, 'If we are talking of ungentlemanly conduct, ma'am, may I remind you of your own present behaviour?'

'What do you mean? I don't know what you mean! Explain yourself, sir!'

'I should have thought my meaning was obvious to the poorest intelligence—and we both now know that yours is far from that, my dear Miss Perceval. Since coming to London you and your scapegrace of a brother have done your best to deceive me. Evasions, half-truths, lies, even—'

'We did not lie!'

'Oh? I suppose you really do have one or two

books of poetry in your possession? The first one was ballads, was it not? Lent to you by brother Lowell?'

Hester turned away suddenly. 'The first one,' she said in a low voice. 'The first one… It…it wasn't mathematics, I promise you.'

'And the rest?'

When Hester remained silent he said, 'It would not have been necessary to question servants and shop assistants if you had been more forthcoming with the truth.'

Hester recovered her voice. 'But why on earth should we? What is it to you?'

'We shall come to that later. Meanwhile, Miss Perceval, will you finally admit that you were Lowell's companion at that lecture? I should tell you that there can be no other explanation.'

Hester glanced at Lady Martindale, then sighed. 'Yes. Yes, I was. Is it not shocking? Dressing up as a man, and braving a masculine preserve? Does that satisfy you? You can surely condemn my behaviour now, Lord Dungarran.'

'On the contrary—if it was the only way you could hear such an excellent lecture then I admire you for your enterprise. I expect your brother had a hand in it, too. But this is unimportant—'

'Unimportant? Do you realise what it would mean if society got to know of it? I should have to retire once again in disgrace. My parents would be devastated.'

'There is no reason at all why the world should hear anything at all of the matter. I have far more important things on my mind than tattling to society, and my aunt's discretion is world-famous. But tell me—does this mean that you are prepared to admit that you are indeed Euclid?'

Hester paused. Her mind was racing, but she was forced to discard one evasive explanation after another. Dungarran would never now believe that either Hugo or Lowell could cope with the work she had been doing. There was no one else. Finally, she said simply, 'Yes.'

Lady Martindale got up and kissed her. 'Brave girl! Wonderful girl!'

Dungarran was shaking his head. 'Incredible girl! What a dance you have led me! My aunt was the first to suggest it, but I refused to believe her.' He gazed at her bemused. Then, still shaking his head in amazement, he said, 'My dear Miss Perceval, let me tell you at once what a delight my correspondence with Euclid has been.'

'I... I cannot tell you how much I have gained from my association with Zeno,' Hester said shyly.

'Give me your hand.' Hester slowly raised her hand and Dungarran took it in his own and kissed it. Hester looked at his bent head. This man holding her in his own strong, warm hands, his lips on her fingers, was Zeno, her friend, her mentor, her inspiration... She had never imagined anything like this... A feeling of purest delight, unlike anything she had ever experienced before, ran through her veins like fire. It frightened her and she snatched her hand from him and turned away, trembling. After a moment she added, 'I shall miss our work together.'

Chapter Seven

'Miss it? What do you mean?'

'I shall have to give it up. You must see that I cannot continue, not now that we both know the truth.'

Disappointment made Dungarran's tone sharp. 'Why the devil not?'

'Isn't it obvious? Zeno was a friend—but you…? Oh no!'

'This is nonsense! I know you dislike me—you have made that very clear. But you can surely forget Robert Dungarran. I'm still Zeno!' He took her firmly by the shoulders and turned her back to face him. 'And I need you more than ever! You must not give up! I won't let you!'

Hester shook herself free. 'Who do you think you are—to tell me what I must do or not do! You cannot force me to work with you! Indeed, I would find it impossible! I am astonished, Lord Dungarran, that you still wish to do so, now that you know Euclid is such an ill-educated, ignorant, conceited fool of a girl!'

'Damn it, why do you have to throw in my face words uttered six years ago in the direst circumstances. I've told you I regret saying them—though they were true enough at the time—'

'Ha! And I suppose you haven't considered me stupid and dull since?'

'Well, yes— But that was before—'

Lady Martindale, who had been sitting forgotten, decided it was time to intervene.

'Children, children,' she said. 'This discussion is clearly going nowhere. Sit down, Miss Perceval. Robert has something to explain to you. It is important. Please, sit down.'

Hester, looking mulish, sat down again on the sofa. Dungarran, with a nod of thanks at his aunt, took a deep breath and began to explain the situation he faced in the matter of deciphering the French papers.

He spoke well and clearly, but Hester was hardly listening. Six years of regaining confidence, of learning to be tolerant, of developing a sense of humour, had vanished like the wind. She was filled with the old fury against the young men who had so humiliated her six years before, chief among them this man. Stupid and dull, indeed—that's what he thought her! It did not occur to her that, since returning to London, she had done her best to convince society in general, and Dungarran in particular, that she was both. She quite forgot that she had enjoyed deceiving him, persuading him that she was the ninny he thought her.

The logic and balance so superbly evident in Euclid's work were notably absent for the moment—swamped under Hester Perceval's purely feminine sense of insult. No! It was impossible to think of Zeno as separate from Robert Dungarran. She would not even try. When he had finished she shook her head and stood up.

'I am sorry. The trust and confidence I had in Zeno have gone—I only see Lord Dungarran. I do not think I would be *able* to work with you. Besides, what would society say about the amount of time we should have to spend in each other's company? How could I explain that? No, I am honoured, of course, Lord Dungarran, but there must be others—'

'Dammit, there is no one else! Why the devil do you think I've spent so much time and energy seeking you out? Oh, ye gods! Why did Euclid have to turn out to be a woman?'

Hester turned triumphantly to Lady Martindale. 'You see, ma'am? It is exactly as I have always said. Men are incapable, completely incapable, of doing justice to a woman's intelligence! Now that your nephew knows Euclid is female, look how his attitude has changed! If I were idiotic enough to agree to work with him my efforts would soon be dismissed as irrational and foolish, and he would, in no time at all, cease to have any confidence in what I did. And he expects—no! He *demands* that I should help him! Ha!'

Lady Martindale said gently, 'You are doing my nephew an injustice, Miss Perceval. But I think that neither of you is in a state at the moment to discuss this very important subject sensibly and without prejudice. May I suggest that he calls on you tomorrow morning, when you have both had time to reflect?' She turned to her nephew. 'Meanwhile, Robert, I should like you to escort Miss Perceval back to Bruton Street,' adding with a smile, 'but may I advise you not to mention Zeno, or Euclid, or ciphers on the way? Talk about the weather, or the latest fashions— or even poetry!' She took Hester's hand. 'My dear, I congratulate you. Whatever Robert may have said, no one's work in ciphers has impressed him more than yours. Remember that when you are considering what to do. I shall see you very soon, I hope.'

The walk back to Bruton Street was accomplished almost in silence. Hester's thoughts were in turmoil, and her companion seemed preoccupied. At her door he bowed and handed her the two books which had precipitated the scenes at Lady Martindale's.

'At what time may I call tomorrow?' he said calmly.

'I keep early hours—country hours, you might say. I am usually available from ten o'clock. But it will do you no good—'

'Please! We promised my aunt we would not discuss the matter today.' He pointed to the book on calculus. 'Start reading this one. You will be fascinated, I assure you.'

She looked at him suspiciously, but he was completely serious. 'Thank you,' she said. He took her hand, and kissed it. The gesture was a conventional one—not at all like the kiss he had pressed on her fingers at Lady Martindale's. But even so, she experienced a faint echo of the same tingling sensation. This would not do! She moved somewhat jerkily away, bowed her head briefly and, avoiding his eyes, went in.

'Hester! Hester! Was that Lord Dungarran with you?' Her mother's voice greeted her as she entered the salon. 'Where have you been, child? I've been expecting you this age.'

'Lady Martindale invited me to tea, Mama, and Lord Dungarran kindly escorted me home.' Hester was unable to suppress an ironic smile at this tame description of a somewhat fraught afternoon. Her mother, seeing the smile, drew her own conclusions.

'How kind! I have always admired Dungarran. He has such style—and such an eligible young man, too!'

'Mama, believe me, for I mean it very sincerely, I will not change my mind about men and marriage—least of all in favour of Lord Dungarran. Indeed, if anything, I have become more than ever convinced that I would prefer to remain a spinster. Can we not return to Northamptonshire quite soon? Surely I have satisfied your conditions?'

'But Hester! It is far too soon to leave London! Why, we are only in the second week of June.'

'But Robina has left London, and the Cleeves as well. Can't we go too?'

'Be patient, Hester. We shall stay a little longer. Your father and I are enjoying London life, and it is so delightful to see Hugo again.'

Hester gave up. She was not to escape further acquaintance with Dungarran, it seemed. What her mother would say when he called the very next morning she could not begin to think!

The Bruton Street house had a small room to the right of the entrance, where the occupant of the house could entertain casual visitors. The next morning Hester waited there for Dungarran. She had not changed her mind overnight, but she was by no means clear quite why. His plea for help was a reasonable one, though she could hardly believe that her expertise was so vital to the country. But in some indefinable way she felt that this man was a threat to her peace of mind, her settled way of life, and she wanted no more to do with him. The curious feeling his touch had roused in her had not been unpleasant—far from it—but it represented danger, she was sure. So she faced him with determination.

'I expect to return to Northamptonshire quite... quite soon,' she said. 'Communication would be too difficult.'

'I agree the distance would complicate matters, but we've managed well enough for several years—why is it suddenly impossible?'

'Lowell was my messenger, and he does not plan to come to Abbot Quincey so frequently in the future.'

'I can have packages sent—'

'No! That...that would not do.'

'For God's sake let us quit these prevarications.

Miss Perceval, I don't think you understand how important these documents are—'

'I don't care how important you may believe the documents to be! I am not going to help you! Do you understand?'

'Oh yes, I understand. I understand very well. You will let your dislike of me override everything else— your love of the work, your sense of duty, your patriotism…all must give way to Miss Perceval's grudge—which she has cherished for six long years— against this monster Dungarran, who, God knows, doesn't deserve it. Can you be surprised that I despise the pettiness of such a mind? That my opinion of Euclid is seriously affected by what I hear from you?'

The door suddenly opened and Lowell burst into the room. He did not observe Dungarran, who was standing behind the door.

'I say, Hester! Have you heard? No, you can't have done, it won't be in the papers till tomorrow. Sywell has been murdered! And it's just as you described Rapeall's end in your book—every detail! The razor, the blood all over the bedchamber, Sywell was even in his nightshirt… The resemblances are uncanny! By Jupiter, this ought to increase the sales of *The Wicked Marquis* no end!'

Hester had been trying in vain to stem Lowell's flow. But now he saw her gestures, turned and saw the figure by the door.

'Oh my Lord!' he said.

'Exactly,' said Dungarran grimly. He surveyed them. Finally he said, 'You are full of surprises, Miss

Perceval, some more pleasant than others. Do I gather from this that you are the author of *The Wicked Marquis*?'

Lowell would have said something but Hester silenced him with a gesture. 'Yes,' she said. 'Have you read it?'

'I have—as have all your other victims. You have a gift for satire. The pictures you drew of us all were cruel, but very funny. I take it they were based on your experiences in London six years ago?' Hester nodded, and he went on, 'But the rest—the cheap sensationalism, the salacious details... Were they perhaps based on experience, too?' He stopped and stared at her. For a moment there was in his gaze a boldness, a contemptuous familiarity which Hester had never in her life seen directed towards her by anyone.

'How dare you, sir!' she exclaimed. She lifted her chin and stared back angrily, but she could not sustain it. After the briefest of moments the full significance of what he had said overcame her and her eyes dropped. Her hands moved in a gesture of repudiation, as she turned away, her head bent in shame.

Lowell took a step forward. 'Sir, I—'

Dungarran turned to Lowell. He said softly, but so dangerously, 'Ah yes! I should have known! It was you! By heaven, it was you! Her brother! She could never have written those descriptions, not in a lifetime. You did!' When Lowell nodded miserably, Dungarran exploded. 'By God, you may have done some reckless things in your time, Lowell Perceval,

but you have never done a more wicked one! And
you claim to love your sister! What the hell do you
mean by exposing her to the sort of comment that
book aroused? Putting her in danger of the censure
of most of society, and the lewd curiosity of the rest!
If she were ever discovered she would most certainly
be an outcast for the rest of her days—even her parents might well disown her. You are despicable!' He
went over to Hester, who was standing with her back
to them, battling against the tears which threatened to
overcome her. His voice softened. 'Miss Perceval,
forgive me, please forgive my over-hasty words of a
moment ago. Believe me, I was so shocked I hardly
knew what I was saying. I swear I did not mean
them.'

Hester swallowed. 'I… It was understandable, I
suppose. As soon as I saw what Lowell had written I
knew I should not have allowed it.'

'By heaven, you should not! Were you mad? How
could you let your partiality for this half-witted
scoundrel blind you to the risks you were taking?'

Hester swallowed. 'I… I—'

'I stole the book,' said Lowell sulkily. 'I took it
from her cupboard. She never intended to have it published. I added the saucy bits. She didn't know anything about it before she came to London, and by that
time it had been on the town for weeks.'

Hester wiped her cheeks and said firmly, 'But the
original idea was mine. If I had not written the book
in the first place Lowell would never have been

tempted. So what…what do you propose to do, Lord Dungarran?'

'What do you think I should do? Your brother has put you in danger of complete ostracism from decent society. Do you not think that he deserves some sort of punishment?'

'I'll take whatever you can devise, sir, if you could spare my sister from public disgrace.'

'You should have thought of the public disgrace before you embarked on this latest lunatic escapade!' Dungarran said in biting tones. He paused in thought while the two Percevals regarded him in silence. Finally he said slowly, 'Your parents are the proper people to deal with this, but I am reluctant to give Sir James such a shock. Perceval, I would like to talk to your sister in private. Perhaps you could leave us alone for a few minutes?'

Lowell looked doubtfully at Hester, but she nodded. 'Don't worry, Lowell. Things will be all right, you'll see.' Uncertain and ashamed he went out, closing the door softly behind him.

'Have you always spoilt him, Miss Perceval? Saved him from his just deserts?'

'Not at all. Lowell has been a great help to me in the past, especially after I returned from London six years ago. It was he who introduced me to the New Scientific and Philosophical Society, which led to the…the work on ciphers. I think that saved my sanity. You and your friends had almost destroyed me. His efforts then did much to repair the damage. Oh no, I owe Lowell more than I could ever repay.'

'He has something to his credit, then. But all the same, he should not escape punishment for this piece of madness. Do you realise the potential seriousness of what he has done to you? My reaction was mild compared with what you might meet with from others.'

'I...do now. And I am sure he is aware of it, too.'

'Perhaps I should consult Hugo...'

'No! Not Hugo!' Hester cried. Dungarran looked at her in amazement. She went on, 'Please, you don't understand. I am sure that Hugo is a very good friend. And he is the best of brothers, too. But his standards are impossibly high for someone as...as volatile as Lowell. I cannot imagine that any good would come of involving Hugo.' She stopped. It went sorely against the grain to plead with this man, but she bit her lip and said stiffly, 'Could you not simply forget that you ever heard Lowell's words this morning? I would do anything to save him from the loss of Hugo's good opinion.'

Dungarran considered her in silence. Then he smiled, that dangerous, charming smile, the sort to charm an unwary bird out of a tree. Hester just had time to think, 'But I am not an unwary bird, and I will not be charmed!' before he spoke.

'I should not allow your brother to escape, I know. But I will do it on one condition, Miss Perceval.'

'Which is?'

'That you remain in London, of course, and work with me on the French ciphers.'

'I knew it would be that!' Hester said bitterly. 'You are blackmailing me, sir.'

'Of course I am!'

'You have no gentlemanly scruples about it?' He shook his head with a little smile and she added with scorn, 'Naturally not. No doubt you will claim necessity!'

'I do. You may think of me as you will, but I will do anything to have these transcriptions done as soon as possible. Perhaps you should remember that I am doing you—and your family—a considerable favour in remaining silent about that book.'

Hester looked at him with dislike. Then she shrugged and asked, 'Where are we to work? It won't be easy to arrange without stirring up unwelcome gossip. Or do considerations of that sort not affect you?'

'I had thought that my aunt might help. Surprisingly, she has developed a liking for you.' The corner of his mouth twitched. 'Especially since you proved her right on Euclid's identity... You should get on very well with each other. You resemble her in so many ways. Like yourself, she has strong views on the manner in which women are treated in the world.'

Hester looked at him in astonishment. 'I have never heard her expound them!'

He raised an eyebrow. 'Perhaps she is...wiser in the ways of society than an inexperienced seventeen-year-old once was? I think you would be surprised at how much influence she has in certain important circles. But this is by the way—to business! My aunt is

prepared to put a room in her house at our disposal.
We could meet in the mornings, before half of
London is awake. It means you would have to visit
Lady Martindale rather more often than you have
done. Would your parents object?'

'Oh, no! Especially as...' She smiled with some
irony. 'Especially as you are Lady Martindale's
nephew. You must know that you are regarded as
eminently eligible by most mamas, including my
mother.'

'I hardly—'

'But you need have no fears on that score, Lord
Dungarran,' Hester went on. 'I have no intention of
marrying anyone at all—least of all you.'

'Succinctly, if unkindly put. I am relieved, however, to hear it.'

Hester added loftily, 'My interest in mathematics
is far greater than my interest in a possible partner.'

'Strange! That is exactly what my aunt says of me.
We should make an ideal pair—that is to say, ideal
colleagues. How soon can you arrange to visit my
aunt? I can have the papers at Grosvenor Street tomorrow.'

'Then I shall come tomorrow. At ten?'

'Ten it is.' He came across and took her hand. To
her relief he made no attempt to kiss it. 'Miss
Perceval, I shall do my best not to irritate more than
I can help. And, in spite of our differences, may I say
how relieved I am to have Euclid as my co-worker?'

She looked at him coldly, not giving an inch. 'I
hope I deserve your confidence. In return, I shall try

not to let my dislike of being coerced into it interfere with my work for Zeno.'

He said softly, 'You have now given me your word that you will do this work with me. You cannot change your mind. The consequences, if not for yourself, then for Lowell, could be serious.'

The short, difficult silence was only broken when Lady Perceval erupted into the room.

'Hester! Why did you not tell me that Lord Dungarran was here? Please, sir, forgive my daughter's rag manners and allow me to offer you some refreshment. My husband is upstairs. I am sure he would be delighted to speak to you. And we expect Hugo any moment.'

Lord Dungarran allowed himself to be ushered out of the door and up the stairs to the salon. Hester followed demurely. It was plain that her earlier words to her mother were being ignored—Lady Perceval had not abandoned her hopes of a match. She was wasting her energies, but she only had herself to blame! As Hester went up the stairs she thought how strange it was that, however much she disliked Dungarran, she trusted him. She was quite confident that, having given his word, he would keep her secrets. Dislike him she might, but of his integrity she was certain.

In the salon Sir James was sitting by Lowell, looking very shocked. 'This is a shocking affair!'

'My dear, what are you talking about?' asked Lady Perceval. 'What has Lowell been telling you?'

'He says that that villain Sywell has been murdered!'

'Oh! Oh! Never say so!'

'Lowell seems to have it on good authority. Did you ever know him, Dungarran?'

'No, Sir James. His adventures were before my time, but if his recent reputation is anything to go by... He's from your part of the country, is he not? Doesn't he own Steepwood Abbey?'

'Yes, but it was never rightly his. Sywell won it from its true owner eighteen or nineteen years ago. That was a black day for all of us.'

'What happened?'

'It was back in '93. Edmund Cleeve was the Earl then. He was told that his only son had died and seemed to go mad. He came to London, came across his old friend Sywell and they started gambling. But Edmund Cleeve's luck was right out. In one night he lost everything—Abbey, lands, wealth...everything. They all went to Sywell.'

'Cleeve shot himself, didn't he?'

'Aye, that he did. And Sywell has lived in the Abbey ever since. It's been a sorry business for the neighbourhood. The land hasn't suffered too badly— he sold a good deal of the estate back to Thomas Cleeve. But it's not that. He's a man of no morals at all, and his scandalously villainous behaviour has brought misery and disgrace to many a poor girl in the neighbourhood.' Sir James looked at his wife. 'But no more of that before the ladies.'

'I've heard the stories,' said Lord Dungarran

gravely. Hester threw him a quick glance, but he ignored her. 'I don't suppose there'll be many to mourn him.'

'Least of all Thomas Cleeve. After he inherited the title he badly wanted to buy back the Abbey itself, but Sywell would never sell. For years Thomas has had to watch the ancestral home of the Earls of Yardley falling into ruin without being able to do a thing about it. I wonder if he knows about the murder?'

'I doubt it,' said Lowell. 'It's not yet generally known.'

'And the Cleeves have left London,' added Lady Perceval. 'My dear, these are unpleasant topics of conversation. I didn't invite Lord Dungarran up here for this!'

Sir James seemed not to have heard her. He frowned. 'It means there'll be some changes round the district.'

'For the better, I would think. But... I really came this morning with a request from Lady Martindale. She was most interested in the work Miss Perceval has been doing, and I've come with a request for a further opportunity to talk to her. Is that possible?'

Lady Perceval was clearly delighted. Apart from her relationship to Dungarran, Lady Martindale was one of society's most influential hostesses. 'Of course!' she cried. 'What work is this, Hester?'

'Er...something I was working on in my attic, Mama. You remember I was studying Grandpa Perceval's papers? It's something arising from that which interested Lady Martindale.' Hester smiled affectionately at her mother. 'So you see, Mama, that not everyone thinks books a waste of time for a woman! I could work with her in the mornings. I would still be free for...for visits and social occasions.'

'Well, if Lady Martindale wishes...'

'Thank you!' said Dungarran briskly. 'I'll call for you tomorrow morning, then, Miss Perceval. And now, alas, I'm afraid I must go. My aunt will be delighted that you have given your consent, Lady Perceval. Sir James, I hope this news of Sywell's death does not disturb your enjoyment of London. The world would seem to be well rid of such a scoundrel. Lowell—' He paused. 'Are you walking my way? I thought I would visit Tattersall's.'

Lowell looked a little apprehensive but agreed. The two men left together.

'My dear girl, what an opportunity! Lady Martindale moves in the very highest circles. Sir James, do you not think it wonderful?'

'Of course, of course.' Sir James seemed rather abstracted. The news of Sywell's death was clearly causing him some thought.

Hester sat without speaking. The morning's events had left her mind in turmoil. She was full of apprehension about working with Dungarran, though she knew she must. It would be foolhardy to arouse his displeasure. If she was reckless enough to go back on her word, not only would he take his revenge, but the delight and interest she had found for so long in the world of ciphers would be lost to her. The correspondence with the *Journal* would naturally cease.

But there were more positive arguments in favour of doing as Dungarran wished. She had found Lady Martindale an interesting and likeable woman, the first lady of fashion she had met who also cultivated the mind. The prospect of getting to know her better was an attractive one. And, she had to admit, now that she had been forced to cooperate with Dungarran she was growing interested in the work he had described—she knew she could do it.

True to his word, Dungarran called for her the next morning some minutes before ten o'clock. Hester was waiting, and they set off at a brisk pace. Apart from a few errand boys and tradesmen they saw no one on the way. London was still asleep. With any other companion Hester would have enjoyed the unaccustomed exercise. Walking was a favourite occupation at home in Abbot Quincey, and the rather tame promenades in the park, which was all she was offered in London, were no substitute.

'Lord Dungarran, it is kind of you to have fetched me this morning, but I would prefer to make my own way to Grosvenor Street in future,' she said as they drew close to their destination.

'I'm afraid that is simply not possible, Miss Perceval. This is not Northamptonshire. The streets of London are no place for an unaccompanied female.'

'I could use one of the footmen—'

'And how long would it be before you were dispensing with his services? No, I shall fetch you my-self. It is simpler and safer.'

'Oh, why do you always have to be so…so high-handed? Always to know better? You are as bad as Hugo!'

He turned and grinned at her—not the dangerously charming smile, but in genuine amusement. 'Such outrageous flattery is embarrassing. I have the highest possible regard for your elder brother! But you forget, Miss Perceval. I know you a good deal better than I did a month ago. You are, I have discovered, neither dull nor simple. Nor are you very biddable. Is the pot calling the kettle black?'

This made her laugh in spite of herself. When Lady Martindale received them she was pleased to observe that they were in a better humour with each other than she had seen before.

After leaving their coats with a servant they were shown into a light, airy room with two windows. Under each was a table with plenty of paper, ink, pens, a slate and chalk practically covering the sur-face. A comfortable chair was placed at each table in such a way that the sitters would have their backs to each other.

'I thought it safer,' said Lady Martindale with a smile. 'But you seem to have settled some of your differences? I am so glad, my dear, that Robert has managed to persuade you to work on the ciphers.'

'His arguments were…very convincing, Lady Martindale. I found myself unable to refuse.'

Robert Dungarran cast a glance at Hester. Her blue

eyes were innocent of guile, her voice conventionally polite. His aunt was unconscious of any double meaning. The delicate irony of her words was meant solely for him, he was sure. How could he have missed till now the wit and subtlety of this girl? How many times must he have overlooked the hidden humour, the barbs behind her façade of demure nonentity! How often had she made a fool of him without his even noticing? Well, those days were over. He had Miss Perceval's measure, and they were now battling on equal terms. He said easily, 'Don't count on the peace lasting, Godmama. I am still a monster in Miss Perceval's eyes. But we mustn't waste time. Where are the papers?'

'I locked them in the bureau here.' Lady Martindale went to a substantial but beautiful bureau in the corner of the room, and opened the front. She took out an untidy bundle of papers and handed them to her nephew, who spread them out on one of the tables.

'The ones I've already transcribed are on top,' he said to Hester. 'I thought they would be useful for comparison. Do you remember the St Cloud set?'

'St Cloud? I don't think I ever saw…'

'Ah yes! You did, but we didn't tell you what they actually were. Do you remember a rigmarole about Caesar and Gaul and crossing the Alps?'

'Ah, those! Yes. I thought they were nonsense, but they were a real challenge to solve.'

'There are more like them,' he said grimly. 'It's a slow business deciphering them.'

Hester hardly heard him. She was already sitting down at the table, eagerly perusing one of the papers. After a moment she took a pen and started jotting down a set of numbers. Lady Martindale smiled, took out a book, and made herself comfortable in an armchair by the bureau. Lord Dungarran looked at Hester, shook his head in a bemused fashion, then sat down at the other table with another of the documents. The silence was complete except for the occasional scratching of a pen.

Chapter Eight

When Hester got up to go at the end of that first morning, she was disconcerted to find both Lady Martindale and her nephew regarding her with amusement. Somewhat stiffly she asked if there was something wrong with her appearance.

'You look delightful, my dear!' said Lady Martindale. 'But unless you wish to have your activities questioned on this very first day, you had better remove a telltale spot of ink from the end of your nose!'

'Is there one? Oh, it's too bad! It always happens at home, but I tried so hard not to let it happen here!' Hester took out her handkerchief and scrubbed at her nose.

'Not that side—allow me,' said Dungarran, smiling broadly. He took her handkerchief, adjured her to lick it, then carefully wiped the offending stain. 'There!' he said. 'All gone. But I'm afraid there's some on your dress, too.'

Hester gave a cry of horror and looked down. A

spot of ink marred the bodice of her simple muslin gown. 'I don't know why it should be so,' she exclaimed. 'I take such pains, but there's always something!'

'I think that you forget to take such pains when you're working, Miss Perceval. I have seldom seen such complete concentration—especially not in a wo—'

'Be careful, sir!' Hester said in warning tones.

'In anyone,' he amended. 'But what will you do?'

'My maid will wash the muslin if I can just get to my room without seeing my mother. At home I use a large apron to cover me, but I didn't bring it to London.' She looked at him severely. 'I never suspected that I should need it!'

'I think I can help there, Miss Perceval,' said Lady Martindale hastily. 'I can find something for you. It will be here tomorrow. I should hate our little scheme to founder for want of an apron!'

The next morning she produced an ideal garment. It was very like the apron Hester used at home, of coarse material with a front bib, shoulder straps and a tie at the back. The chief difference was that it was in a bright, clear blue, not the dull grey that Hester was used to. Hester eyed it doubtfully.

'Put it on, Miss Perceval. It is not an elegant garment, but it will protect your dress. And the colour will suit you perfectly.'

The colour seemed to Hester to be far too vivid, but she shrugged and put it on. Then she thanked her hostess and sat down to work, losing herself almost immediately once more. Lady Martindale exchanged a smile with her nephew and sat down in her armchair by the bureau.

From then on Dungarran and Hester worked together in the room at Grosvenor Street. Lady Martindale read or sewed in her corner, occasionally looking up as one or other of them exclaimed or sighed, or took a paper over to the other table and consulted. There was nothing in the least romantic about their conversations, but Lady Martindale was beginning to think that Hester Perceval would be the ideal wife for her nephew. Though neither was aware of it, their rapport was very strong. In spite of Hester's initial antagonism, each had an almost instinctive understanding of the other's mind, and the sum total of their joint work was far greater than either would have achieved alone. There was as yet no sign of any physical attraction—but, Lady Martindale smiled to herself, that might come with time and propinquity!

Hester soon found that the mind of the unknown French ciphermaster was much in tune with her own. She had considerable success with a passage which had defeated the best minds at the War Office for months, and Dungarran's surprised, but perfectly genuine, admiration went a long way to make up for the humiliation of the past. She began to look eagerly for his approval, and in return was always ready to watch him use his own considerable, more intellectual, gifts to solve a problem which had defeated her. Though she was completely unaware of it, Hester's dislike of him was slowly but surely fading. Zeno, her friend and trusted guide, was imperceptibly becoming one with the figure of Robert Dungarran.

For his part he grew impatient with the tedious consultations at the War Office which kept him from her company. He wanted to be back with Hester Perceval in the room in Grosvenor Street, working with her to fathom the mysteries of the ciphermaster's mind. He rejoiced in the sight of the slender figure in blue, bending over her papers in such concentration. Even the spectacles which she had now taken to wearing for the work became an important part of the scene—and the usual spot of ink on her nose. Euclid, after all these years, had taken on a most surprising form!

The work went on apace, and the pile of papers was growing gratifyingly smaller when their plans received a sudden and unexpected threat.

The news of the Marquis of Sywell's demise had been dealt with in detail in the newspapers. 'It is with horror and dreadful dismay,' the *Morning Post* announced, the day after Lowell's revelations, 'that this paper has learned of the shocking death by stabbing of the most noble the Marquis of Sywell at his home, Steepwood Abbey, in the County of Northamptonshire earlier this week…' The paper, and others which took up the story, went on to describe in gory detail the scene which met the eyes of the Marquis's 'devoted retainer', Solomon Burneck, when he entered his master's bedroom on the fateful morning.

'"Devoted retainer", indeed!' muttered Sir James

rustling the paper impatiently. 'Partner in crime, more like! A more surly, unpleasant fellow I never met.'

'Did Burneck see the assailant? Or is he himself suspected?' asked Lady Perceval.

'The report gives no indication. As usual the press is short on facts and long on unnecessary and probably imaginary detail!' replied Sir James testily.

But if Sir James regarded the report as unsatisfactory, London did not. It was not long before the sparse details of the real-life death of the Marquis of Sywell were being compared with the fictional and far more sensational account of the murder of the 'Wicked Marquis'. The coincidences were very quickly remarked and in no time at all the details of the two murders were hopelessly confused. Rumour grew on rumour and soon the public imagination pictured the scene of the crime as a veritable blood bath, with indescribable atrocities inflicted on Sywell's corpse.

As a delicately bred female, Hester was spared the worst of the rumours. But in any case her preoccupation with the French documents left her little energy for the gossip and speculation which were flying round the capital.

Later in the week the newspapers, lacking any firm evidence or further facts, started to debate the consequences of the murder. This unsettled Sir James far more than any gruesome account of the crime.

'Lady Perceval! Listen to this!' he said, some days after the murder. He took up the newspaper and read out, '"The affairs of Lord Sywell are in some disar-

ray, and our correspondent tells us that inhabitants of
the surrounding villages, especially the tradesmen, are
already worried about unpaid bills and unsettled accounts. The future of the estate must be in doubt.
Following the mysterious disappearance of the
Marchioness last year, the Marquis lived alone, and
he appears to have no obvious heir. Moreover, surrounding landowners will also have their anxieties, as
long neglect has already led to disturbing occurrences
on the Steepwood estate.'" He got up and walked
restlessly round the room. His wife eyed him anxiously. After a while he said, 'It's a damnable affair!
As if the fellow had not caused enough trouble in his
lifetime! There's bound to be unrest in the district.
My dear, I must return to Northamptonshire as soon
as possible! Things will be in turmoil, and a good
many people will be looking to me to help them.'

'B… But Sir James! You must not leave London!'
exclaimed Lady Perceval. 'Just when Hester is at last
having some success! Lady Martindale has taken such
an interest in her this past week, and Lord Dungarran
has been really quite attentive. We cannot take her
away now!'

'What makes you think Robert attentive, Mama?'
asked Hugo, who was paying one of his frequent calls
on his parents. 'I have not seen any evidence of it—
and Hester seems to avoid him in public. Are you
sure you're not confusing the aunt with the nephew?
Lady Martindale certainly seems to have a strong liking for my sister, and I can see why—they are two
of a kind! But it would be unwise to resurrect Hester's

interest in Robert. Remember what happened last time!'

'I'm afraid I agree with Hugo, Lady Perceval! You set your hopes too high, my dear! I see no change whatever in Dungarran's attitude.'

'But given time…'

'You are always so optimistic! Why don't you listen to Hugo? He surely knows better.' Lady Perceval set her lips and remained obstinately silent. He sighed and added, 'Well, we shall no doubt eventually find out which of us is right…'

'But nothing will happen if Hester is removed from London just at this point, Sir James!'

'No. No, I quite see that.' He paused and thought for a minute. 'Would it suit if I went alone to Abbot Quincey and you and Hester stayed here?'

'Oh no! That would never do! I should be quite lost without you!'

He patted her hand. 'But what else can I do, my love?'

'Could I go, Father?'

Sir James regarded Hugo thoughtfully. 'It's certainly time for you to take a greater interest in the estate… But no. You couldn't do this alone. You've been in Abbot Quincey so seldom in the last few years that our people don't know you any more.'

Hugo said a little stiffly, 'I always promised to come back to Northamptonshire this year, Father. Before my thirtieth birthday.'

'Oh I don't blame you, my boy! I was very happy for you to enjoy town life before you settled down.

But you couldn't possibly deal with this situation. No, I must go myself.'

'Then I shall come, too! As you say, I ought to take up some of the responsibilities.'

Sir James beamed. 'Excellent! I shall be very pleased to have your support. It won't be an easy matter.'

'But what about Hester?' persisted Lady Perceval. 'If Hugo stayed in London she could remain with him!'

'My dear, you are talking nonsense! Hester couldn't possibly stay with Hugo in a bachelor's establishment! No, though I'm sorry for it, it looks as if you and Hester will have to come with us.' He took her hand and said persuasively, 'I should think she would be delighted to come back with us to Northamptonshire. Remember her reluctance to come here in the first place! Now, how soon can we be ready? Two days? One?'

Lady Perceval's pleas were in vain. Sir James remained adamant, and the family was informed that they would be returning to Northamptonshire very soon. But Sir James was wrong about Hester's reaction to the news. Such a short time ago, it was true, she would have given anything to leave London. But now the news dismayed her beyond measure. She was astonished at the depth of her disappointment.

When Dungarran heard of Sir James's plans he first of all swore comprehensively in private, then, in his usual calmly competent way, set about finding a way out of the dilemma. After some thought he went back to his aunt and asked for her help. She was equally unhappy at the prospect of losing Hester Perceval's company, but found what he proposed a little too unconventional.

'Invite Miss Perceval to be my house guest till the end of the Season? I cannot do it, Robert!' she protested. 'I like Hester Perceval very much—I am sure I would enjoy her company! But her parents will surely think it extremely odd if a woman they hardly know suddenly invites their only daughter to spend several weeks with her, while the rest of her family return to the country! And I trust you realise what conclusion society would most certainly draw!'

'That I am interested in Miss Perceval? Well, I am, though not in the way they might think!'

'That is all very well—but what of Miss Perceval?'

'Oh, you need have no scruples on that score, Godmama. Hester Perceval has already declared in the clearest terms that she has no interest in matrimony, least of all with me!'

'All the same, she will not enjoy the gossip which is bound to arise.'

Her nephew was silent for a few minutes. Finally he said, 'Well, perhaps we should encourage such gossip. The idea that Miss Perceval and I are romantically interested in each other would be an excellent alibi for the time we already spend in each other's company.'

'Really, Robert, I could get very angry with you! You are so single-minded when it comes to your work! What happens when the Season is over? Does Miss Perceval retire once again to Northamptonshire with a broken heart?'

'That is nonsense, you know it is! Yes, at seventeen she thought her heart was affected, but she soon grew up and recovered. She is now as clearsighted as I am about the sentimental rubbish talked of love.'

'But society will never believe it. And they will say that Miss Perceval has remained in London in the hope of capturing one of London's most eligible bachelors. You know how cruel people can be.'

'They won't say that, if we make it clear that I am the one in pursuit. Vain pursuit.'

'This is too complicated for me.'

Robert Dungarran took his aunt's hand. 'My dearest aunt, it will be very simple. I am positive that Miss Perceval is as eager as I am to complete this work. It only needs a week or two, but she must remain in London for that time. I shall pay Miss Perceval a great deal of attention in public, and she will carry on behaving towards me with her normal indifference verging on dislike. I think I could persuade her to act out our little comedy—especially if you were prepared to support us. There will be no danger to her reputation, I assure you!'

Lady Martindale smiled. 'If she is seen to reject the advances of London's eligible but elusive Lord Dungarran, her reputation can only be enhanced! You have been the target of every matchmaking mama for the past ten years!'

'Stop talking nonsense and tell me if you consent.'

'You must consult Hester first,' she said warningly.

'I will.'

'Then if the Percevals agree, I will help you. But I still think it is a madcap scheme!'

After Hester had most reluctantly agreed to Dungarran's plan, Lady Martindale approached the Percevals with her invitation. Persuasive though she was, it looked for a while as if their scheme would founder on Sir James's notions of what was proper, but she had an ally in Lady Perceval. Left alone with her husband, Hester's mother represented to him all the advantages of Lady Martindale's interest in their daughter.

'I am surprised, Sir James, that you even think of rejecting such a flattering invitation! I would not dream of arguing with your decision that we should return to Northamptonshire. I am sure your reasons are perfectly sound. But I hope I may claim some influence in a matter which so closely affects our daughter's prospects. You not only run the risk of offending one of society's great ladies, but you are also putting Hester's future at risk! I do hope you will reconsider.'

Hugo added his voice. 'Lady Martindale is just the sort of woman you would wish Hester to be, Father. She is undoubtedly as intelligent and as strong-minded as Hester, if not more so. I believe her to have quite an influence in government circles. But she has such tact, so much charm, that few people suspect this. Hester could learn a great deal from her.'

Sir James finally gave in to persuasion and Hester was allowed to accepted Lady Martindale's kind invitation. On the day the Percevals left London for Northamptonshire Hester was installed in a very pretty bedroom in the Grosvenor Street house. Lady Martindale made her most welcome, but spoke seriously to her before they came downstairs.

'Miss Perceval, I hope there are no unfortunate consequences to this scheme of Robert's. I wish you to promise that if you have any doubts about it—at any time—you will confide them to me. Though I am delighted to have your company, I am not at all sure that we are doing the right thing.'

'I hope you don't think the worse of me for agreeing?'

'Not at all. I consider you a brave woman.'

'Brave? In what way?'

'Robert can be very charming when he chooses—'

'Not to me, Lady Martindale. Pray have no anxiety on that score. I am in no danger from your nephew. I… I daresay you have heard what a fool I made of myself six years ago?'

'Something of it, yes. But it was a very long time ago. You were a mere child.'

'Perhaps. But the experience was enough to convince me that marriage was not for me.'

'I… I hope Robert was not the sole cause of such a harsh decision, Miss Perceval?'

'No. I don't even blame him—not now—for my disillusionment. I was a child and I misunderstood his intentions. I… I thought he was in love with me. But he was merely being a good friend to my brother.'

'My dear!'

'The shock caused me to…to behave very…very badly. It took six years to get over it.' Hester smiled wrily. 'I am most unlikely to make the same mistake again, I assure you.'

Lady Martindale looked at her closely and seemed satisfied with what she saw. She smiled brilliantly. 'Then let us enjoy ourselves with a clear conscience, Hester! Do say I may call you Hester!'

'I should like you to. But what do you mean ''enjoy ourselves''? I am here to work.'

'My dear Hester, do but consider for a moment! You and Robert will of course continue to work as before—probably even harder. But in the evening we shall all be on public show. I am willing to wager that you will be more of a success than ever. But Robert? Will he enjoy playing the part of a rejected suitor? Such a role has so far been outside his experience! I wonder how he will cope?'

Hester smiled slowly at the picture conjured up by Lady Martindale's words. Then she said, 'Do you know, Lady Martindale, I think I am about to enjoy the social life of London for the first time in my life.'

Her hostess burst into laughter. 'Cruel, cruel girl!'

For a day or two there was a lull in London's festivities. Hester had a chance to settle into her new circumstances, including Robert Dungarran's constant presence. They worked harder than ever on the transcriptions, but the last few documents seemed to be more difficult than all the rest put together. The work which had been going so well suddenly came to a halt.

Halfway through one morning Hester threw her pen down, for once not minding that she spattered ink liberally over her apron front. 'I give up! I've tried everything I can think of. I thought I knew that Frenchman's mind, but this time he's been simply too clever for me! What the devil can he have used as a base?' She put her elbows on the table, rested her head on her hands, and gazed down in frustration at her scribbled efforts.

Dungarran leaned back in his chair with a sigh and stretched his long legs out before him. 'I haven't had any success, either! Damn the man! I've wasted half the morning on a single page.'

Lady Martindale looked at the two despondent backs. 'My dear children, you are both stale! You have been cooped up for far too long in this tiny room with nothing but the scratching of pens to entertain you! Give yourselves a rest from the puzzle and it may all become clear. Take Hester for a drive, Robert. It's time you were seen together in public.'

'As usual, you are right, Godmama. Come along, Euclid! Let's give our poor brains some fresh air. We'll have a drive round the park.' Hester got up without taking her eyes from her papers.

'Hester, dear,' said Lady Martindale patiently. 'Remove your apron, take off those hideous glasses and wipe your face, before you go. Otherwise the world will never believe our myth.'

'Myth?' asked Hester vaguely.

'The myth that I'm in love with you,' said Robert Dungarran, gently removing Hester's glasses. 'But I don't know that I agree with you, Godmama. There's something highly appealing about a suitably placed ink spot.' His finger touched Hester's nose. 'It draws attention to the purity of line…'

Hester, still abstracted, spoke much as she would have addressed Lowell. 'And I suppose you will say that this apron adds to my beauty?'

'It suits you.'

She looked up, startled. Then seeing his teasing smile, she pulled herself together. 'Thank you,' she said ironically. 'Well at least I know my place—a kitchenmaid! No, don't say another word—I shall clean myself up, then put on my hat and gloves. Though I doubt it will make an atom of difference to London's view of our relationship.'

When Hester had disappeared, Lady Martindale said, 'Did you mean it?'

'Mean what?'

'About the apron.'

'Well, I half meant it. I was teasing her. But yes, it does suit her.'

'It's the colour, of course. She always wears such insipid garments. As I said once before, her dresses are completely unmemorable, part of her desire to be invisible. But…if we are to convince society that she has attracted you…' Lady Martindale fell silent for a moment. Then she said suddenly, 'Robert, I will try to persuade Hester that she needs a new evening dress for the ball at Harmond House! You must help me.'

'How the devil do you think I could help? I can't imagine that Miss Perceval would be swayed by any recommendation of mine!'

'You must! But no more—here she comes! Hester! That's better. My dear, we've just been talking about the Duchess of Harmond's ball. It will be a splendid affair, and Robert has agreed to escort us both. It is a perfect opportunity to demonstrate his interest in you. How would it be if you had a new dress for the occasion?'

Hester said reluctantly, 'Mama insisted I needed one, but I already have so many…'

'This ball is worthy of another one,' said Lady Martindale firmly. 'And I know just the dressmaker you need—we shall pay her a visit this afternoon. I saw a bolt of absolutely lovely silk when I was last there—a dark azure blue peau-de-soie, just a shade deeper than the colour of your apron. It would be ideal.'

'Oh no! Thank you, but no! I always wear pale colours. Such a blue would be far too striking.'

'We could tone it down with an underdress of white, perhaps. Don't disappoint me, Hester dear. That blue suits you so well,' said Lady Martindale.

'So you have said, but I think not…' Hester's tone demonstrated her reluctance to offend Lady Martindale, but it was quite firm.

'Robert, can't you add your persuasion?'

'I would…if I thought it necessary,' he drawled. 'Miss Perceval is right. She has somewhat insip…er…delicate colouring, and surely strong colours are better suited to…more dashing personalities?' Robert Dungarran noted with secret amusement that Hester's 'delicate colour' was rising in her cheeks. He went on, 'She is very wise to choose colours which suit her retiring nature. Besides which, unlike most of her sex, she is more interested in matters of the mind. Clothes which flatter, and the pursuit of beauty are beneath her. Fortunately.'

'Robert!'

'…Fortunately, I was about to say, for those of us who need her other skills.' He smiled charmingly at Hester, observing with pleasure that the colour was now high in her cheeks and that her fists were clenched inside her white gloves. He continued, 'But why are we wasting time on a topic which holds so little interest for Miss Perceval, Godmama? I'll wager that she believes clothes are meant to conceal our faults, not enhance our advantages.'

'I take it you mean the tailors' use of padding in the shoulders and stiffening in the jackets, sir?' Hester snapped, casting a glitteringly critical eye over Dungarran's excellent figure, his dark green coat immaculately smooth over broad shoulders and narrow hips. 'They certainly achieve marvels.'

Dungarran burst into laughter. 'Come, Miss Perceval! Enough sparring! We shall take some air. All this talk of dresses has wasted time which we can ill spare—especially if my aunt is taking you off to the dressmaker this afternoon. We still have to fathom the work of that ill-begotten son of a Frenchwoman.'

Nothing more was said, though Hester was noticeably silent on their drive. After their return Lady Martindale sought out her nephew in private and expressed strong disappointment in him.

'I cannot imagine what possessed you, Robert! You were unkind to Hester—and unfair! Her colouring is not at all insipid! And now she will insist on choosing yet another nondescript off-grey sort of colour, and the world will wonder what on earth you see in her! It's too bad of you!'

'Will you take a wager on the off-grey, dearest Godmama?'

Lady Martindale refused the wager, which was as well, for she would have lost it. On seeing the azure silk Hester said she had changed her mind, and declared it to be the very thing she was looking for. Madame Félice had received them graciously, for Lady Martindale had been one of her earliest patrons, but after a minute during which they discussed details of style, she apologised and asked if she might leave them in the competent hands of her assistant. She then withdrew. Hester was unmoved by this, but Lady Martindale was surprised, and said so.

'I expect she has large numbers of orders for the Harmond ball,' said Hester. 'And it's not as if I am likely to be a regular client. I really don't mind in the slightest. Compared with the seamstress at Abbot Quincey, any London dressmaker is a genius!'

It certainly seemed that Madame Félice's assistant was one. On the night of the ball Lady Martindale dressed early, and then sent Régine, her maid, along to Hester's room to add, she said, the final touches. Hester's own maid was young and inexperienced and very much in awe of Régine, who had come from France before the Revolution. She looked on while Régine dressed Hester's hair, and watched in admiration as the constricting bands of hair were undone, brushed vigorously, twisted and knotted by skilful fingers, and the whole finished off with a rope of pearls and crystal drops artfully arranged in the coils.

'But…but these are not mine. Where did they come from?' asked Hester.

'Her ladyship sent them, mademoiselle. And the earrings. Hold your head still, please, while I put them in… *Voilà*!'

Régine's tone was so businesslike that Hester felt she dared not argue. And when she looked at the result of the maid's ministrations she decided not to try. Her hair had been dressed by an expert, and for once it was evident that, along with her brothers, Hester too had inherited the famous golden gilt hair of the Percevals. Curling tendrils framed and softened the classical Perceval features, and behind them gleaming twists of hair dressed high emphasised the graceful line of head and neck. Pearls and crystals hung from delicate ears.

Régine allowed herself a small smile before she became businesslike again. 'Now for your dress.' Hester stood like a doll in her simple slip of white satin while the two maids twitched the heavy folds of deep blue silk into place. She was not used to such a low neckline, accustomed as she was to covering up her lack of curves with numerous frills of lace, and she twitched the bodice a little higher. Régine pursed her lips, pulled it back into place and said sternly, 'The neckline is perfectly modest, mademoiselle. You will spoil the line if you pull it so.'

'Of course,' said Hester meekly. 'It was just that I seem to have more…more figure than usual.'

'That is the art of cutting. I have not often seen such a beautiful piece of workmanship, no, not even in France. Would mademoiselle like to see herself?'

Hester stared at the figure in the looking-glass. Burnished hair glinting with stones, dark blue eyes wide with amazement, glittering drops at her ears, a slender throat, unmistakeable curves covered in satin overlaid with a simple layer of delicate white lace… All enhanced and enriched by the gleaming blue folds of silk.

Lady Martindale came in and clapped her hands. 'My dear girl!' she exclaimed. 'My dear Hester! Your hair! I never imagined… Régine, I congratulate you—that hair is divine!' Then she examined Hester from every side, and pronounced the dress a great success. 'The fit is excellent. Why have we never seen that very pretty figure before, Hester, my love?' Hester was still wondering what to reply when Lady Martindale smiled and said, 'But we must go down to the salon. Robert will be here shortly. I can't wait to see his face! Come, my dear.'

While they waited in the salon, Lady Martindale asked Hester if she had had a dress with a train before. 'They can be difficult to manage, but yours is a very small one. See? It has a tiny loop to hold it up when your are dancing. Yes, just like that! It really is a beautiful dress, Hester. A great success. Do you like it?'

'I... I'm not sure... I've never had anything as striking as this before.'

'You will be the belle of the ball, I swear. You must dance with Robert once, you know—he is our escort. But after that you can refuse him as often as you please.' Lady Martindale started laughing. 'London will be so sorry for him!'

'I can't wait to see it!' said Hester gleefully.

They were both still laughing when Dungarran was announced. If Hester had secretly hoped to see him struck dumb with admiration she was disappointed. He stopped, it was true, but merely to raise his eyeglass and examine her appearance with all his usual calm.

'Well, Robert? Admit you were wrong! That dark blue silk is perfect for Hester!'

'I knew it would be,' he said as he kissed his aunt.

'I beg your pardon?'

'I said I knew it would be.' He came over and smiled as he took Hester's hand to kiss. 'I also knew that Miss Perceval would be more likely to choose the blue if she believed I thought she should not. Am I right?'

'You...you...!' Hester controlled herself. She said

calmly, 'You are right, of course. How perceptive of you, sir. And how devious!'

'But in such a wonderful cause. May I say that you look magnificent, Miss Perceval? If I were a marrying man—'

'Which you are not.'

'I would find it impossible not to make reality of our myth tonight.'

'My dear sir,' said Hester, giving him a provocative look. 'If I were a marrying woman...'

'Yes?'

'I just might consider being more receptive. But as it is....' She smiled at him maliciously. 'Prepare to act the part of a rejected suitor, Lord Dungarran!'

Chapter Nine

Though a number of important families had already left London, enough were left behind to give lustre to the Duchess of Harmond's ball. As Dungarran entered the reception room accompanied by his two ladies, a perceptible stir ran round the room, and one or two eyeglasses were raised. Hester stiffened and her hand on Dungarran's arm tightened.

'Courage, my friend,' he said. 'Think of it as a play. I know you can act a part—I've seen you do it, and very cleverly, too! This can't be more difficult than acting the man!'

These words helped Hester through the following, nerve-racking minutes. So many of the ladies and gentlemen of the Ton, people who had in recent weeks practically ignored her, found some reason or other to talk to Lady Martindale and her protégée. While they made polite enquiries about her parents, they eyed her covertly, clearly wondering what had happened to dull, quiet Miss Perceval. In some cases their curiosity was so open that it verged on impertinence, and Hester could not prevent the colour from rising in her cheeks. But she remembered Dungarran's words and acted her part. After a few minutes it was no longer so difficult to be at ease with these people. The sense of failure, which had caused her to be stiff and awkward in society, had been replaced with the knowledge that in one sphere she was truly admired and valued for the work she had been doing. The man beside her, one of society's most influential members, was willing to let his unblemished reputation for success with the ladies suffer a severe setback rather than lose her. Hester lifted her head proudly and continued to astonish the Ton with her charm and self possession.

All the same, she was immensely relieved when Dungarran offered his arm and asked her to dance. And when he suggested taking a long way round via the conservatory she almost forgot to hide her approval of the idea.

They made their way through leafy pathways towards the huge ballroom at the back of the house.

'My congratulations. You're doing splendidly,' he said, looking down at her with a smile.

'I found it less difficult than I thought. And dancing is no longer the nightmare it once was.'

'You dance very gracefully, Miss Perceval.'

She felt the colour rising in her cheeks. 'We both know that I owe my skill to you in the first instance, sir,' she answered.

'But not much else,' he said abruptly. 'If you knew

how much I have regretted my cruelty to you all those years ago!'

She suddenly wanted to tell him how her attitude towards that disastrous début—and towards him—had changed. 'I can now see that I deserved something of what you said—perhaps not all. But I no longer brood on it, nor bear any grudges. During the past few years Zeno has done more than anyone to heal that injury. And only recently I've come to realise that in a curious way you and he have balanced it all out between you. So…shouldn't we forget the past? The present is so much more interesting! Don't you agree?'

'You look so enchanting that I would agree with anything at the moment, Miss Perceval! But this is not according to plan! You are supposed to be treating me coldly, not offering an armistice!'

'Well then, having said my piece, I will! Come sir! Enough of this tête-à-tête! I wish to dance!'

Hester had no shortage of dancing partners, though neither Lowell nor any of his friends was there to support her. Dungarran asked her to dance again and was refused, but he tried once more two-thirds of the way through the evening. Hester, who had found most of her partners tediously predictable in their remarks, was glad to accept, though she once again gave a show of reluctance. They took the floor for a set of country dances.

But halfway through a progression down the middle of the set Hester suddenly stopped. 'A pentacle!' she said. The couple behind cannoned into her, and a moment or two of confusion followed. Hester apologised gracefully, Dungarran shook his head with a deprecating smile at the rest of the set and they were soon under way again.

As soon as they were close enough he whispered, 'What happened?'

'It suddenly came to me. The base! It's not a rectangular grid—it's a pentacle! It could be, at least. It would account for the oddness in it.'

'You're talking of the cipher?'

She looked at him scornfully. 'Of course I am!'

'We'll try it tomorrow! That look of contempt was very convincing, by the way. I am suitably crushed.' They were separated again by the movement of the dance.

As soon as the set was finished Hester made her way swiftly to Lady Martindale without waiting to see whether her partner was following. Dungarran caught up with her just as she arrived.

'I think we've given society enough to think about for tonight,' he said. 'My self-esteem is feeling quite bruised.'

'My dear Lord Dungarran, I have hardly begun!'

'I only wish that you and my aunt were not deriving quite so much enjoyment out of it all, Miss Perceval!' He had been smiling, but he suddenly became serious. 'Ah!' he said. Hester followed his eyes. An exquisitely dressed gentleman, who had clearly just arrived, was standing in the doorway, surveying the scene. He was not above average height, but very handsome, with dark hair and eyes, and beautifully moulded mouth and chin.

Lady Martindale said softly, 'Our dear friend the Comte de Landres is here, Robert.'

'Thank you, I've seen him.' He turned to Hester and his voice had an urgent note in it as he said quietly, 'Be on your guard with the gentleman at the door. He poses as a French émigré, and is accepted everywhere in society, but his secret allegiance is to the present régime in France. He would give much to know where the French documents are, and even more to learn how much of them the War Office has managed to decipher.'

'He's coming over here, Robert.'

Dungarran said rapidly, 'Look as if you are bored beyond measure, Hester, but listen to me! The myth we have concocted will serve us very well. I know he suspects me, but he mustn't be given the slightest reason to connect you with any of it. Do you understand?'

As de Landres approached Hester turned away, saying somewhat petulantly, 'Of course I do, Lord Dungarran! Pray let us talk of something else!' She eyed the newcomer with interest as he bowed over Lady Martindale's hand.

'*Mais* Lady Martindale! How is it that you look more lovely every time I see you? The secret of eternal youth must be yours, I think…'

He would have continued in this vein but Lady Martindale smilingly interrupted. 'I see that your absence from London has not impaired your silver tongue, monsieur! Hester, my dear, you must beware of this gentleman. He can be charming in four different languages at once! May I present Monsieur de Landres? Miss Perceval is at present staying with me, monsieur, while her parents are in the north.'

'*Enchanté*, Mademoiselle Perceval.' Black eyes surveyed her with obvious pleasure. '*Mais vraiment enchanté!* Are you staying long in London? Please, I beg you to say that you are!'

Hester blushed. 'You are very kind, sir. I… I'm not yet sure…'

'Then you must give me a chance to persuade you! Or…' The black eyes went from Hester to Dungarran. 'Am I trespassing, perhaps?'

'Oh no!' cried Hester with emphasis.

Dungarran smiled coldly. 'Miss Perceval shows little inclination to listen to anything I say, de Landres. Perhaps you might be more successful.'

'What? Where the great Lord Dungarran has failed? Most unlikely—but of course I will try. Mademoiselle, may I begin by persuading you to dance with me?'

'Thank you, I'd like to, sir.'

'Robert, you may take me to the supper room,' said Lady Martindale. 'Hester, we shall see you there after your dance, I hope. Meanwhile, I am sure Monsieur de Landres will take very good care of you.'

The particular dance did not allow much opportunity for long conversations, but as they met and separated again the Comte asked any number of questions. They all demonstrated a flattering interest in

Hester and her family, and had she not been on her guard she would perhaps not have noticed how many of them involved her present association with Lady Martindale and her nephew. She took pride in the fact that her answers, apart from displaying a coolness towards Dungarran, were innocently free of any real information. The dance ended and they walked towards the supper room. The Comte returned her with a flourish to Lady Martindale and went off to find some refreshment. There seemed to be something of a crowd round the supper table. He would be some time.

'You seemed to enjoy your dance with that popinjay,' said Dungarran.

'Oh, I did!' Hester replied with a bright smile.

Dungarran frowned. 'You will remember that he's not all he seems?'

'I did. And I will.'

'What did you talk about?'

'Really, Lord Dungarran, you are as bad as he! He asked me a lot of questions, and I answered them.'

'Such as?'

'Well, some of them were flatteringly personal. But I expect you wish to know about the others. They amounted to one question really. He wanted to know what you were doing. He asked whether you spent a lot of time with the people in the War Office.'

'He must have thought you very simple, to ask outright like that.'

'You underestimate me. He did not ask outright, he was as devious as you. But that was the real question.

He also commented that you spent a great deal of time at your aunt's house.'

'What did you say to that, Hester?' asked Lady Martindale.

'I blushed and implied, without actually saying so, that Lord Dungarran's frequent visits to Grosvenor Street were on my behalf, and that his attentions were not very welcome.'

'Good!'

'But he also asked whether your nephew spent any time working on papers while he was there.'

Dungarran stared and frowned. 'The devil he did! Now I wonder how he got wind of that? What did you say?'

'I said that you were a nobleman. That you probably didn't know how to work.'

For a fraction of a moment Dungarran looked offended. Then he grinned. 'You are a minx, Hester! A cruel minx. But that was quite in the Lord Dunthinkin style!'

Hester said quickly, looking as innocent as she could, 'Lord Dunthinkin…? I've heard several people mention him. Who is he?'

Lady Martindale looked severe and shook her head at her nephew. 'Robert!'

'Oh, I'm sorry, Miss Perceval. I shouldn't have mentioned the name,' Dungarran said gravely, and only Hester could see the mocking gleam in his eye. 'He's a character in a most unsavoury book. I can't say more—it has amused my aunt, but she doesn't consider it fit for innocent girls.'

'Like most of society, Hester, I have read the book. Unlike most of the ladies of society, I even admit to having done so. But I really don't think that your parents would approve of your reading it. It is true that parts of it are extremely amusing, but much of the rest is disgusting.'

Hester was saved from further awkwardness by the return of the Comte.

At the end of the evening the conspirators all felt that their campaign had begun very well. Lady Martindale and Hester returned to Grosvenor Street in high spirits, recounting with glee the various remarks made to them by ladies whose daughters had been ignored by Dungarran in the past.

'Did you hear Lady Pembrook, Robert?' asked his fond aunt. 'She really feels for you! She complimented me on Hester's improved appearance, and added that you seemed to be quite taken with my young guest.' Lady Martindale started to laugh. 'Then, positively drooling with pleasure, she said, ''Not that I noticed any corresponding warmth in Miss Perceval's manner towards your nephew, Lady Martindale. *Au contraire!* She is distinctly cold. He has always been so successful, too… It cannot be pleasant for him.'' What do you say to that, my dear nephew?'

He looked at her in exasperation. 'That you know as well as I do that she has detested me for years. Ever since she failed in her efforts to push her unfortunate daughter into my arms, in fact. And I don't believe the poor girl even liked me!'

'Then what about Mrs Gartside?'

He sighed in resignation. 'I suppose you were listening, Godmama. You must enjoyed that!'

'What did she say?' asked Hester.

Dungarran turned towards her. 'She was very fulsome about you. Then she said she was impressed at the change in your manner—especially towards the *eligible* young men in the room.'

'Oh!' Hester exclaimed. 'How unkind of her!'

'She is famous for her spiteful remarks. You needn't worry about her,' he said reassuringly.

'But what about the rest, Robert? Hester would like to hear that, I'm sure! Go on!'

Dungarran gave his godmother a look. Then he turned to Hester. 'I ought to tell you first that Mrs Gartside has an exquisitely lovely daughter. God knows where she got her looks from, but there's no denying that Phoebe Gartside is very beautiful. For a short while I thought I was in love with her, and the Gartsides made it very clear that they would consider me a suitable son-in-law.'

'What happened?'

'The girl has the brains of a pea! Fortunately I found this out before it was too late and withdrew. She soon found someone else—a Viscount whose intellectual gifts are on a par with her own.'

'And what did Mrs Gartside say tonight?'

'She commiserated with me! How sad it was, she said, to see a reformed flirt learning what rejection was! Even though my fortune must be such a strong temptation.'

Hester grew slightly pale. 'I was right in the first place, Lady Martindale,' she said. 'I am happier with my symbols and ciphers—they may be difficult, but they are not malicious.'

Dungarran took her hands in his. 'Hester—may I call you so in private?' She nodded. 'Hester, you mustn't let the envious spite of one or two tabbies spoil this evening. You were magnificent! Your manner towards me was perfectly judged. It is as well that I know it to be part of our game, for otherwise I would be feeling all the chagrin that those two tabbies wish on me—and more!'

Hester tried to smile, but her lips trembled. She removed her hands from his. For some unaccountable reason she suddenly felt out of spirits.

Lady Martindale looked at her sympathetically. 'Hester is tired, Robert. And if I know you both, you will be at work on your ciphers before ten o'clock tomorrow morning. It's time you left.'

Dungarran nodded, and after bidding them both goodnight he went. Lady Martindale took Hester's hand and led her to her bedroom. 'Sleep well, my dear. Robert was right. You were indeed magnificent.'

'Was she really as lovely as he said?' Hester asked sadly.

'Who?'

'The…the girl he said he loved.'

'Phoebe Gartside? Yes. She was every bit as lovely—and just as silly, too.'

'But he was in love with her. He fell in love once.'

'He was just a boy. And it lasted about a month. It wasn't real love, of course, it was pure infatuation with her looks. And as soon as he started talking to her the dream was shattered. I am sorry to say, Hester, that he has never to my knowledge been seriously in love with anyone. He has had a number of mistresses, of course. I've been told that he is a very generous lover. But properly in love? No. I doubt he ever will be—he is too...too detached.' She stole a glance at Hester. 'You are very alike, you know. Neither of you lets your heart rule your head. Isn't that true?'

'Yes!' said Hester. 'Yes! And it is better so!'

By morning Hester had recovered from her curious lack of spirits the night before. She was eager to test her new theory on the French cipher, and was already downstairs in their study when Dungarran arrived.

'You're an early bird,' he said. 'I thought I would be here first. I suppose my aunt is still in her room?'

'Yes, it was very late when we finally got to bed last night. We talked for some time after you had left.' Hester spoke absently. She was carefully drawing a figure on a piece of paper. He came over and looked at it.

'Tell me,' he said, 'how did you come to think of a pentacle?'

'Well, we both noticed a curious symmetry in the cipher—but it wasn't a circle, or a rectangle or any of the usual geometric shapes. I tried all the figures I could think of, and you did, too, but nothing seemed to work. But the pentacle is not an ordinary mathematical symbol.'

'It belongs to magic. An unusual choice for our level-headed Frenchman, surely.'

'Ah, but think of the Greek names for it!'

'One is the pentagramma, or pentagram…'

'And the other is the pentalpha. Penta alpha, Robert! Five As.'

'Because it's formed from five As! Of course! And each A would govern a different set of letters. But that would make a very complicated grid. Hours of work.'

'Exactly! But we seem to have tried all the simple ones. Let's test it! I should imagine we should quite soon see if it was working.'

After half an hour of concentrated work a coherent sentence began to appear. They looked at each other in awe.

'It's worked! It's worked, Hester! You little marvel!' An unaccustomed flush of excitement was on Dungarran's cheeks. He jumped up and dragged Hester after him. Together they danced round the room in a wild jig. At last they came to a stop by Hester's table. She went to sit down, but Dungarran put his hands on her shoulders and pulled her up against him. Hester struggled to free herself.

'No!' she protested. 'No!'

'Don't you want me to kiss you?'

'No. I don't like…kisses.'

He smiled at her, but did not release her. 'Has anyone ever kissed you before, Hester? Apart from your family?'

'You know someone has! Lord…Lord C…Canford k…kissed me. It was horrible!'

'My poor girl! That wasn't a kiss! It was an insult.'

'All the same…'

'Let me show you what a kiss can be, Hester.' His voice was persuasive, but though his hands were still on her shoulders, he was making no effort to pull her closer. 'You mustn't go through life believing that all kisses are horrible.'

'But…but surely all kisses are the same. What makes you think I should enjoy your kiss better?'

He spoke gravely, but there was a distinct twinkle in his eye. 'If you believe that all kisses are the same then it's time I taught you otherwise. I promise that you would enjoy my kiss better—I'm nicer than Lord Canford. And I think you like me more.'

'What has that got to do with it? I like working with you, talking to you—but not…not… I've never thought of…of…'

'This?' He still made no effort to draw her closer, but instead leaned forward and gently kissed her on the lips. Then he drew back and asked, 'Was that so bad? Be honest, Hester.'

'I… I don't know.' She thought for a moment. 'No, I think it…it was rather agreeable.'

'Shall I try again?' His arms slid round her and he pulled her towards him, almost imperceptibly. This time his lips met hers with more force, though he was still perfectly controlled. After a moment of panic, she felt a strange warmth taking possession of her, and she relaxed in his arms.

'Not a bit like Lord Canford,' she murmured.

He laughed and looked down at her. She smiled dreamily back at him. His expression changed, the grey eyes grew dark and she felt his arms tightening round her. This time the kiss was demanding, passionate, requiring a response. She could feel the length of his body against hers, and a wave of glorious feeling overtook her. Without volition her arms went round his neck and she returned kiss for kiss until her own body was on fire... His arms tightened till she could hardly breathe, but she rejoiced in their closeness, this strange glorious sensation fizzing along her veins like champagne...

But after a moment sanity returned to her. She pulled herself free and held on to her chair, seeking to still the trembling in her limbs. She couldn't look at him, but she heard him walk swiftly away. He was angry, it seemed. He stood by his table for a moment, and she thought she heard him cursing under his breath. Then he turned and took a step towards her. She shook her head and stammered, 'N...no more! Please! I... I...'

'Hester, for God's sake forgive me! I'm sorry! I don't know what happened! I lost my head. I can't really believe it, but it's true. I lost my head... I don't know when that last happened. I...I...' He turned away again and when he spoke his voice sounded bewildered and ashamed. 'I suppose you think me no better than Canford.'

Hester lifted her head and protested, 'Oh no! Never! You...you were very k...kind. It was my fault. I... I still don't know how to behave.'

He swung round, looking astonished. 'You really don't know what happened there, do you?' he said harshly. 'You've lived such a nun's life in that attic of yours. I very nearly lost all control! And I was supposed to be reassuring you, trying to wipe out the memory of that kiss of Canford's. I don't know what came over me. Can you possibly forgive me, Hester? I'll find it hard to forgive myself.' He came nearer. 'You are in no way to blame for what happened, believe me.'

Hester shook her head. 'Don't say any more. Please! I'd... I'd rather forget it happened.' She swallowed, and wondered if her heart would ever stop pounding. 'Can't we dismiss it from our minds? Carry on as we were before?'

His expression softened and he came towards her again. When she stiffened involuntarily, he smiled and held up his hands. 'Don't look like that. I promise you, Robert Dungarran is himself again. You're in no danger. It won't happen again, I swear.' He watched her steadily until she nodded and gave an answering smile—a little tremulous perhaps but a smile nonetheless. He went on, 'You were shocked by that last kiss, Hester. And so was I. It was not what I intended, and I agree that we should forget it. Such a triumph of emotion over reason is not our style, is it?'

Hester said wrily, 'No, indeed!'

'Then are we friends?'

When she nodded he held out a hand, and after a slight hesitation she took it. Holding it firmly in his, he said gently, 'But, all the same, you should learn a little more about life. You've been shut away in your attic for the past six years, absorbed in your figures, cut off from contact with the outside world. That's something for which I feel I share the blame. You said last night that I—Zeno—had helped to restore your confidence. Can't you let the other half of me— Robert Dungarran—teach you how to enjoy contact with the world. Confess it. You took pleasure in your success last night, didn't you?'

'Ye…es.'

'It's time you learned how much more pleasant a little light dalliance, a few light-hearted kisses between friends can be.'

'I don't think I want to try any more kisses. They're too…too unsettling.'

Lord Dungarran looked regretful. 'No kisses? Never? Not of any kind? Not even between friends?'

She said nervously, 'Well, not another like the…the last. The first two were pleasant enough. But we must get on with the transcriptions.' She sat down and pulled one of the pages towards her with determination.

He regarded her bent head with a smile in his eyes. 'You're quite right, of course. That's what we're here for.' He returned to his table, and took up his pen. After a few minutes he said thoughtfully, 'These Pentacle papers look to be quite different from the rest. Wouldn't you agree, Hester?'

'I haven't got very far, but yes, they seem to be a report on an exchange of letters...' When Lady Martindale appeared they were each busy with a bundle of papers, and once again the only noise was the scratching of pens.

In the evening they went to a less formal affair at the house of one of Lady Martindale's friends. Lowell and his friends were also invited and Hester was looking forward to relaxing in their undemanding company. Dungarran invited her as usual to the first dance, and as usual she accepted with a show of reluctance. But this time the reluctance was not completely feigned. They had worked harmoniously enough during the day, lost in the importance of the work they were doing. But outside their room, as soon as they were physically close to each other Hester remembered the feel of the tall body dominating hers that morning, her astonishingly fiery response, and she was immediately self-conscious.

'Look at me, Miss Perceval,' said Dungarran as they made their way up the set. 'I am not an ogre.'

'No, of course not. It's just that...just that...'

'You are remembering this morning, no doubt. I thought you had decided to forget it? That we were friends again.'

'It's not so easy,' replied Hester with spirit. 'I am not as used to such occurrences as you obviously are.'

For a moment they were relatively isolated at one end of the set. 'If you are talking of the first two "occurrences",' said Robert Dungarran, 'then I would agree with you. Age and experience make it inevitable. But the third kiss…' He shook his head with a fleeting echo of the morning's bewilderment. 'Would you believe me if I told you that I resent its effect as much as you do? It is most unlikely to happen again.'

'That, sir,' said Hester as they rejoined the progression down the set, 'is just as well!'

When the dance was over she excused herself to Lady Martindale and joined Lowell at the other end of the room with a sigh of relief. Here was someone uncomplicated, familiar and dear to her. With Lowell she could be completely herself without having to act a part or pretend. Perhaps in his company she might forget the curious ache which was rapidly developing inside her. She shook herself mentally and set her mind on enjoyment. Within minutes she was part of a laughing crowd.

'Enchanting, is she not?'

Dungarran turned. The Comte de Landres was standing at his shoulder, his eye on a figure in red and white at the other end of the room. Hester was wearing one of her muslin dresses, but had put over it a short-sleeved, wine red velvet top. Her golden head and the striking contrast of her dress were easily discernible among the young people surrounding her.

Dungarran looked at them all with a jaundiced eye. Hester had danced with her brother, then they had spent long minutes talking animatedly. After that she had turned to a friend of Lowell's with a smile and danced with him. They had returned to the group and started chatting again. At that point Dungarran had decided to stop watching, and had invited an accredited beauty, one of the Season's successes, to join him in the quadrille. The girl had twittered her way through every movement of the dance, and he had returned her to her chaperone when it finished with an inward sigh of relief. But when he had looked for Hester she was dancing with yet another green, half-grown youth. What the devil did she see in them all? Lowell was her brother, it was natural she should wish to exchange a few words with him—but why spend such a time with his friends? He was surprised, really surprised, that Hester Perceval, who had as fine a mind as he had ever met, should wish to waste her time on such lightweights. He had half a mind to go down there and ask her to dance with him again. It would at least remove him from de Landres's presence. But after a moment's thought he decided not to. It would be too painful if she refused him in front of all those striplings. And she almost certainly would—because of their damned pretence, of course!

De Landres looked at him with knowing amusement. 'She seems remarkably happy with those young people.'

'One of them is her brother, de Landres.'

'Ah! That accounts for it. And I daresay she finds them something of a relief after the rarefied atmosphere of Grosvenor Street. How is your work on ciphers progressing?'

Dungarran turned and gave him a cool stare. 'Ciphers?'

'I hear you are an expert, milord. Everyone at the Horse Guards sings the praises of Zeno.'

'Come, you are trying to flatter me. I dabble in mathematics under the name of Zeno, you're quite right there. But ciphers?'

'I heard about the lecture at the New...what was it again? The New Scientific and Philosophical Society. Did you ever trace your Euclid?'

'Er...no. That young man seems to have disappeared completely.'

'A pity. Apparently he was an enthusiast. He could have been a great help to you,' said de Landres sympathetically. 'It's a slow business working alone.'

Dungarran examined the Frenchman with cool disapproval. 'Working? I don't know what you mean. You're obviously confusing me with someone else.'

'Come, milord! Why do you try to fob me off like this?' de Landres said gently. 'It's common knowledge at the War Office that Zeno, alias Dungarran, is deciphering some documents stolen from the French. Am I not right? There's nothing wrong in my knowing that, surely? I am as eager as anyone to see the tyrant Napoleon defeated. What are they? Reports on supplies?'

Dungarran eyed him grimly. It was obvious that some idiot at the War Office was being far too indiscreet with someone he thought was an ally. De Landres's true allegiance—to Napoleon—was still unknown to all but a few.

'Your friends at the War Office may well be prepared to broadcast their secrets to the world, sir. I am
not.'

'Such discretion! But I wonder why you find it necessary to work at Lady Martindale's house rather than
your own? Can it be that you are letting yourself
be…distracted by her young visitor? Is that why the
task is proceeding so slowly? Or is that because the
ciphers are too difficult?'

'Are these French ways, de Landres? I have to say
that, in an Englishman, I would find such curiosity,
such questions about my deeper feelings, damned impertinent! We will not discuss Miss Perceval, if you
please.'

'As you wish, Dungarran. But I warn you, I shall
carry on asking questions of my friend at the War
Office.'

'And who is that?'

'What? And have you order him to keep a watch
on his tongue? No, no! You will have to find that out
for yourself, *milord*!' He bowed and walked away
with a self-assurance which Dungarran found immensely irritating.

Chapter Ten

If Dungarran had only known, Hester was finding her brother's company less amusing than she had expected. Lowell had begun by introducing her to Mr Woodford Gaines.

'How nice to meet you, sir,' she said. 'But I thought you were in Devon with your godfather?'

'Indeed I am, Miss Perceval! That is to say, I'm not with him at the moment, but I was till yesterday. And I shall go back to him quite soon. I came up to town to try to persuade old Lowers to join me, don't y'know. Dashed boring in Devon with only a godfather for company! He wants to walk or play chess all the time!'

'Lowers? Oh, you mean my brother!' She gave Lowell a sisterly look. 'And has Mr Gaines persuaded you, Lowell?'

Lowell, looking rather uncomfortable, said, 'I was going to tell you, Hes. I'm off with Gaines the day after tomorrow. You'll be all right, though, won't you? I know it means that you're on your own in

London, now that Hugo has gone back with Pa and Ma. But they were happy to leave you with Lady Martindale. And Dungarran is there. He'll keep an eye on you.'

Hester kept her voice even. 'You know what I think of Lord Dungarran, Lowell.'

'I thought that had all changed? He seems to be pretty nutty on you now!'

'That doesn't mean to say that I am "nutty" on him!' she replied sharply. Then she relented and spoke as warmly as she could. 'Of course I shall be all right. Lady Martindale is very kind to me.' She gave him an ironic look. 'And I am sure you'll enjoy walking and playing chess in Totnes.'

The two young men burst into laughter. 'The old man has a nap in the afternoon and goes to bed at ten, Miss Perceval,' cried Mr Gaines. 'And the cider is strong and plentiful in Devon.'

'From what I hear, so are the barmaids, eh, Gaines?' The two gave another roar of laughter. Hester was not particularly amused. She had not seen a great deal of Lowell since she had joined Lady Martindale, but he had always been there in the background, a reassuring family presence. Now she would be the only Perceval left in the capital. Lowell saw her disquiet and tried to make amends.

'Come and dance, Sis.' As they walked on to the floor he said, 'If you're really upset I won't go. It's just that Gaines was so keen to have my company, and…and you seemed to be quite settled with Lady

Martindale...and Dungarran.' He gave her a sideways
look. 'I've hardly seen you for days.'

As they danced Hester wrestled with the temptation
to tell him the truth. But was she sure what the truth
was? She had been blackmailed into a reluctant working relationship with Dungarran, that was true. It was
also true that his present admiration for her was
feigned, put on purely for the benefit of society. Even
Lowell had no idea that it was merely a ruse, a device
to enable her to continue working with Dungarran
without rousing comment. But...how had this morning's events affected that 'working relationship'?
Those kisses had surely not been in the plan...

Lowell was worried by her silence. 'Shall I not go,
Hester? Shall I stay in London?'

'No, no!' Hester made up her mind. The secret of
her deciphering work was not hers to reveal. It was
tempting to confide in Lowell, especially as he obviously felt neglected, but she must not. She must
keep up the pretence.

'No, you must go with Mr Gaines,' she said firmly.
'I confess I have qualms about the strong cider, but
the barmaids, being equally strong, will keep you both
in order, no doubt. No, Lowell, you mustn't give up
your trip for my sake. I am very happy with Lady
Martindale, she is a delightful hostess. But I hope
you'll be here to escort me back to Abbot Quincey
when the time comes?'

'Oh, I will! I'll be back well before then! Er...that
is to say...when were you thinking of going, Hester?'

Hester experienced a strange reluctance to name a

day. The deciphering of the documents could not possibly take longer than another two weeks. But to state in so many words that she would leave Grosvenor Street so soon, say goodbye to Lady Martindale and her nephew... 'I... I'm not sure,' she said. 'We must both be back home by the middle of next month.'

'For the July fête—'

'And Hugo's birthday.'

'But that's a long time ahead.'

'It doesn't seem so long to me,' said Hester, perhaps more sadly than she realised.

They danced in silence for a while. Then Lowell said, 'Perhaps Dungarran would come to Abbot Quincey for the fête?'

'Robert Dungarran? The perfect London gentleman? Come to a country fête, complete with farmers, sideshows, Morris dancers and bucolic merriment all round? Don't be silly, Lowell!'

'Then perhaps for Hugo's birthday? That's only a day or two later.'

'Why on earth should he? I neither expect him nor want him!'

'I was only thinking he was Hugo's friend,' said Lowell meekly. 'Nothing to do with you, of course, Sis.'

Hester gave her brother a sharp glance. 'Well, he isn't! Don't start imagining things, Lowell.'

Her brother said no more, but since he was a kind person at heart he exerted himself to distract her, and when the dance ended and they returned to his friends he made sure that Hester never lacked a partner.

His efforts were appreciated when Hester observed Dungarran dancing with a ravishingly beautiful, dark-haired girl dressed in pale pink. He was looking down at her, his head bent in its familiar pose, an indulgent smile on his face. The mysterious pain inside Hester was suddenly so acute that she had difficulty in breathing.

'Hes! What is it? What's the matter?' Lowell's voice seemed to come from a long way off. She conquered her malaise with an effort and forced a smile.

'I... I...don't know. It suddenly felt stuffy in here. I'm all right now.'

'You went whiter than your dress. Are you sure you're all right?'

'Yes, yes, please don't make a fuss, Lowell. It was nothing. I... I think I should go back to Lady Martindale. She will be wondering where I am.'

'Don't worry! Her nephew will reassure her. He's hardly taken his eyes off you ever since you joined us.'

'Really?' asked Hester, with a glance at the couples now leaving the floor. 'I find that very difficult to believe!' Dungarran was totally absorbed in ushering his partner tenderly towards the chaperones' corner. He was bowing over her hand and the silly girl was looking completely enchanted... Hester pulled herself together. She would not look at them, she would not! She turned and smiled brilliantly at Mr Gaines. 'If you are depriving me of Lowell's company for the next week or so, Mr Gaines, you may console me with the next dance!'

Mr Gaines went scarlet with embarrassed pleasure. 'Miss Perceval! What an honour! No, I mean it!'

The return to Grosvenor Street was by no means as merry as that of the night before. Dungarran seemed preoccupied, and though Hester talked gaily to Lady Martindale about Lowell and his friends, it was evident that she was not as happy as she pretended. Lady Martindale looked from one to the other and grew thoughtful, but she waited until they were in the house again before she spoke.

'What did de Landres have to say, Robert? Whatever it was, you were both quite absorbed.'

'He worries me. He asked again about the ciphers, and made no attempt to disguise his curiosity—nor to hide the fact that he knew a great deal about them already.'

'Do you think he knows that you suspect him?' asked Hester.

'I am sure he doesn't. It's more that he is desperate to know how fast we are progressing, and especially whether I have any assistance. He mentioned Euclid, but I told him the young man had disappeared.'

'Which is no more than the truth,' said Lady Martindale with a smile. She grew serious and went on slowly, 'It must be important to him. He took quite a risk in showing how much he knew. I wonder who his informant is?'

'Some sprig of the nobility with more pedigree than brains. There are several such in the Horse Guards. It won't be difficult to find and deal with him. But de Landres is a different matter...'

'I wonder why he is in such a hurry?' asked Hester. 'It's almost as if a time is important to him.'

'I agree. Of course, timing is always important in military campaigns. But I would be surprised if his concern is about the French supply lines in Eastern Europe; if he knows as much as I think he does, he knows that keeping that information from the Allies is a lost cause—those documents have already been deciphered and sent off.'

'It must be something to do with the Pentacle papers! But what? We've only just started on them.'

'Then we'll have to work longer hours, Hester! We'll start earlier in the mornings.'

'You're a slave-driver, Robert!' protested Lady Martindale. 'The poor girl works hard enough! She is in London chiefly for the Season, don't forget! She's supposed to be enjoying herself.'

Hester thought of the party they had just attended. It would be no pleasure to her to watch while Robert Dungarran indulged in more of his light-hearted flirtations with lovely young girls. 'I think I enjoy my ciphers more, Lady Martindale. I know I am odd, but to me they are still far more fascinating than the...than the dances and courtesies of the polite world.'

'I'm not sure your parents would be pleased, however! And what about your brother?'

'Lowell is leaving London for a while. He is joining Mr Gaines in Devon.'

'Ah, Mr Gaines! The fellow with the useful wardrobe, and a godfather in Totnes! I had quite forgotten him,' said Dungarran.

'What are you talking about, Robert?'

'An earlier episode in my acquaintance with the Perceval family. But I digress. You were accusing me of being a slave-driver, I think.'

'Hester seems to be reconciled to it. However, I hope you will leave our evenings free. Or are you going to keep her prisoner here till the Pentacle papers are done?'

'I don't have to, Aunt. As Hester has said, the difficulty is to teach her to appreciate, even to enjoy, the pleasures of society. I have no intention of reducing her opportunities for light-hearted dalliance—quite the contrary. But I don't believe starting earlier on the ciphers will disturb her.'

'Then we must all go to bed right now!' Lady Martindale said briskly. 'It's very late, and you will both be at your tables long before I am up—as you were this morning. I hope your parents never learn what a poor sort of chaperone I am, Hester. But there! They don't know my nephew as I do. You are as safe with him as you would be with me. In spite of what he has just said, I know that the work you do together is far more important to him than any light-hearted dalliance.'

It was as well that she was already halfway out of the door, and so did not see the scarlet flooding Hester's cheeks and her nephew's slightly self-conscious look.

* * *

When Hester entered the study early the next morning she found Dungarran already hard at work.

'Have you been to bed at all?' she asked in astonishment.

'Good morning.' He got up and took her hand in his. 'For a short while. There's a possibility that I may have to go to Portsmouth later. A note was waiting for me when I got back last night.'

'Portsmouth! But you can't! We have work to do here!'

'I know we have work to do, and I've told the Admiralty so. But I may not have any choice. I'm still waiting to hear what they decide.' At her sigh of exasperation he went on, 'It's connected with the work we've been doing, Hester. Some fool of an Admiral wants me to explain parts of our transcription to his captains before they set sail for the Baltic.'

'But…but what about the Pentacle papers? Aren't they important, too?'

'Of course they are! So shall we get down to them?'

Hester sat down at the table without replying. At first she found it difficult to settle, but after a short while she was fascinated once again by the sentences gradually unfolding before her eyes. When the messenger came with word for Dungarran she was surprised to see that they had been working for two hours. It was half past ten.

'I'm sorry, Hester,' he said after reading the note.

'I have to go after all. But I ought to be back in three or four days.'

'Three or four days!'

'I assure you I'll finish there as quickly as I can.' He took her hand. 'You'll miss me?'

'Of course I will!' she said and snatched her hand away. 'I shall have to work twice as hard!'

'I have no doubt that you will!' He grew serious. 'Avoid conversation with de Landres. The time is coming when we shall have to do something about that gentleman, but meanwhile he mustn't have the slightest suspicion of your involvement. Promise?'

She cast a glance at the papers strewn on the table. 'I don't think I'll have time for conversations with anyone! Yes, I promise.'

'Then I shall leave you. But…before I go… Have we time for a little—a very little—light-hearted dalliance, would you say?' He took her hand again and pulled her closer. A kiss, light as a feather, touched her lips. 'A reminder,' he said softly. 'So that you don't forget our agreement.'

'A…agreement?'

'I promised to teach you the pleasure of kisses between friends, remember?' He observed the rosy colour in her cheeks with satisfaction and kissed her hand. 'It's time I went!'

But halfway to the door he stopped, came back and kissed her again, this time more comprehensively. Once more the blood ran through her veins like fire and she would have responded just as passionately as the day before, if she had not exerted every ounce of self-control. His arms tightened, and he kissed her again. Then he slowly let his arms fall and gave a short laugh.

'You must be a witch! Given time, I think you could prove my aunt wrong. Goodbye, Hester!' He was gone.

Hester was left staring at the door. What had he meant? Lady Martindale had said that his work was more important to him than light-hearted dalliance. Did that mean...? Hester put her hand to her throat. Then she shook her head as if to clear it. Given time, he had said... There was her answer. Robert Dungarran would never give himself time to fall in love, never!... Fall in love? Where had that idea come from? Hester Perceval was not interested whether Robert Dungarran fell in love or not! Falling in love was not in her own plan for the future! She turned with determination to the Pentacle papers.

Lady Martindale came in a little later looking worried. 'Hester, this trip of Robert's is very annoying! He's away for three, perhaps even four days! And I've promised to go out to Richmond to spend the day with an old friend on Monday. That's only the day after tomorrow. Shall I postpone my visit? Or would you like to come with me?'

'You're very kind, but I don't think I could do that, Lady Martindale. Now that your nephew has disappeared off to Portsmouth it's more than ever important that one of us is working!'

Lady Martindale smiled. 'Robert's work in

Portsmouth is just as important, my dear. For some reason or other the people there don't trust anyone else as much. They regard him as indispensable.'

'Oh. Well, in view of what we said last night about urgency I shall be fully occupied with these!' Hester made a gesture to the papers on the table. 'But please don't postpone your visit for my sake. I shan't have time to feel lonely!'

'I would prefer not to disappoint her...' said Lady Martindale, still a little undecided. 'She's an invalid and doesn't have many visitors... Are you sure you won't come with me?'

'Quite sure! In fact, if on Monday you could tell your servants to say there is no one at home, that would suit me even more. I'd like to work undisturbed.'

'Of course! Most of them have leave to be out in the afternoon, so you should have complete quiet.'

Apart from meals and a walk in the park insisted on by Lady Martindale, Hester worked quietly and steadily the next day. She was aware of feeling slightly lost, of missing the tall figure at the other table, and if she had allowed herself the indulgence, she would have been miserable. But the work became more and more absorbing. Unlike the previous documents which had all concerned supply lines to the army throughout Europe, the Pentacle papers summarised an exchange of letters between Paris and the French command in Spain. At first they dealt with the demands made by Napoleon on his generals in the

Peninsula, demands which the men on the ground clearly regarded as unrealistic. Later, however, the sentences grew more veiled. They seemed to be hinting at a plot of some kind... Lady Martindale had difficulty in prising her away for an early night.

When Lady Martindale came in to bid her goodbye the next morning Hester was already totally absorbed in her papers.

'I'm still not sure I should leave you like this. You'll work yourself into a brainstorm.'

Hester looked up blankly, then rose and took off her glasses. 'Dear Lady Martindale, I shall be perfectly happy working away here. In Northamptonshire I often spent hours alone in my attic and loved every minute of it. Enjoy your visit to your friend and forget me.'

'Very well. But promise me that if you feel tired you will take a short walk! Bertram would go with you. Make sure you take him! I shall see you tonight, my dear.'

The house was indeed quiet after Lady Martindale had gone, but Hester laboured on without noticing. It was becoming clear that the plot concerned an assassination attempt. But whose? Obviously someone important—the letters described him as one of Napoleon's greatest enemies. Hester sat back in thought. Who was this person? She suddenly sat up again and stared at the papers before her. Could it possibly be *Wellington*? He was in Spain at the moment and his recent campaign in the Peninsula had posed practically the only successful resistance in the whole of Europe to the Emperor's armies. But there had so far been no mention of a name. She bent over her work again.

But by mid-afternoon her back was stiff and her head was aching. After she had made several stupid mistakes she decided that the short walk required by Lady Martindale was called for. Apart from Bertram, an elderly footman at the door, the house seemed devoid of servants. They were clearly taking advantage of Lady Martindale's absence to have a day's freedom. Hester fetched her hat and went out, waving away Bertram's offer to accompany her. She murmured something about going to see her brother and this seemed to satisfy him. But once outside, her feet turned as if by instinct in the direction of Hatchard's, and soon she was on her way past the table of new books in the front of the shop to the shelves on mathematics. She would just snatch a quick look before returning... She froze when she heard a familiar voice, and drew back behind a tall bookcase.

'Well, Behring, what do you have for me today?' said the Comte de Landres. 'Have the new French classics arrived? No? A pity! I'll have a look through the shelves over there, however. I may have missed a treasure the last time I looked.' Hester leaned further back. She had no wish to meet the Comte. There was silence for a moment, then de Landres's voice could be heard just on the other side of the shelves. Someone else had joined him. They were speaking softly and in rapid French, but Hester, suspicious now, could hear every word.

'Did you find anything?'

'Nothing at all.'

'Then the papers can't be at Curzon Street. And they aren't anywhere at the Horse Guards, either. It is as I thought, they must be in the Martindale house. Probably in the small room on the right.'

'What do you want us to do?'

'The timing could not be better! With Dungarran in Portsmouth and the two women in Richmond for the day, the house is empty.'

'Servants?'

'All out, except for one footman. He's old, Armand could easily deal with him. No need to hurt him. Where did you leave Armand, by the way?'

'I took him back to the inn. He's safer there. He can't speak English, and he's doesn't exactly look the gentleman. So—what do you want us to do? Bring the papers to you?'

'No. It's very risky, but I think I'll join you in Grosvenor Street. I want to be sure we get the right papers. I can't read the things but I'll recognise them—and the sooner they're burnt the better. That's vital. If anything should go wrong, if we're caught, those papers must be destroyed—understood?'

'We won't get caught.'

'Get rid of the papers!'

'All right, all right! I understand. I'd best be on my way. I have to collect Armand.'

'When will you be at the house?'

'In an hour. Less, perhaps.'

'I'll call there in an hour. I can pretend to be visiting, if necessary.'

Hester waited until de Landres had followed his accomplice out of the shop, and then she scurried out. The Pentacle papers were in danger and she must rescue them! De Landres's desperation to get rid of them before they could be deciphered proved their importance. Hardly knowing what she would do, she half walked, half ran back to Grosvenor Street. The door was shut but not locked, and the footman was nowhere to be seen. He was old and lazy—he had probably decided to have a rest, leaving the door unlocked in case she came back sooner than expected. Inside the study she gathered up the papers and the notes she had been making and stuffed them all into Lady Martindale's sewing bag, which was on the floor by her chair. She looked round frantically. Her glasses! They were lying on the table. She snatched them up and hurried out again, not quite knowing where she was going, only desperate to put as great a distance as possible between herself and the house in Grosvenor Street. Lowell! She would find Lowell. Halfway to Half Moon Street she stopped dead. Lowell wouldn't be there! He had left for Devon with Woodford Gaines, and the house would be empty. Her heart sank. But after a moment's thought she rallied again. Mr Gaines's servant knew her. If he was still there he would let her in. She might find an hour's refuge there—enough time, at least, to decide what to do next. Oh, *why* was Dungarran so far away just when she needed him most? How could she keep the Pentacle papers out of the hands of de Landres for another two days? She hurried on...

But Dungarran in fact returned earlier than expected from Portsmouth. He had finished his business there without ceremony, finding that half the captains he had been required to speak to were already at sea. Cursing the inefficient dotards at the Admiralty, he had set off early, wasting no time on the road. He used the importance of deciphering the Pentacle papers to explain his urgent desire to be back in London, but as he drew nearer to the capital, he had to acknowledge to himself that he was equally impatient to see Hester Perceval again. Try as he might to dismiss the feeling as irrational and illogical, it simply would not go away. He was more than a little irritated by this lack of control over his emotions. It didn't help that he found himself making for Grosvenor Street instead of his own home. His aunt and Hester would be out at a soirée, but he could wait for them there, and meanwhile examine what Hester had been doing on the papers.

He reached Grosvenor Street just after eleven o'clock, but he arrived at a household in chaos.

'Robert! Oh, thank God you're here!' Lady Martindale's normal air of self-possession had vanished and she clutched her nephew's arm with desperate fingers. 'Hester has vanished!'

'What?'

'She's gone! And that's not all. So have the papers!'

'To hell with the papers. *What has happened to Hester?*'

'She sent this note.' Lady Martindale looked round distractedly and produced a crumpled piece of paper. Dungarran smoothed it out and took it to the window. He let out a long breath.

'It is her writing,' he said. 'I recognise it. And she says she is safe.'

'But where is she? Bertram saw her go out about three o'clock this afternoon and she hasn't been seen since. That's nearly eight hours ago!'

'Where did the note come from?'

'The servants tell me it was delivered just before I returned—by someone they didn't recognise.'

'Man or woman?'

'A man. But they were in such a state themselves that they didn't really notice anything more about him.'

'Why? What happened, Godmama? Why did Hester go?'

'That's what I was trying to tell you. The house has been ransacked, Robert! While I was out at Richmond two men broke in, bundled Bertram into a cupboard—he could have died of suffocation for all they cared!—and searched the place for your papers. They made such a mess... Come and see.'

Dungarran looked round grimly at the devastation in the study. His face twisted as he saw on the floor a bright blue apron, spotted with ink. He picked it up and stared at it for a moment. Then he said as if to reassure both his aunt and himself, 'The note said she was safe. Was she here when the men came?'

'I don't know! Bertram says not. He says she went out long before they appeared. But…'

'Well?'

'He's certain she wasn't carrying anything.'

'No papers. Did she have anyone with her—a footman? No, of course not! Did she say where she was going?'

'Bertram thinks she said she was going to see her brother.'

'And he didn't see her return?'

'He is a little evasive, Robert. I think he left the door unattended for a while—he sometimes does when left to himself, and she might have come in then. But he is quite sure he didn't hear her voice while the two men were here. Surely she would have made some protest?'

'She has spirit—she would have protested a great deal!' He looked at the apron. 'Unless she was hurt?'

Lady Martindale sat down suddenly. 'Robert! Oh no!'

He took a deep breath and said firmly, 'We must believe that she wasn't here. Let me think about that note…' After a pause he said slowly, 'Hester must have left before the intruders arrived—she says the papers are safe. That means she had time to gather them up and take them with her.'

'I suppose so… What I don't understand is why she took them at all! How could she have known in advance that the men were coming?' Lady Martindale put her hands to her head. 'But if she didn't know, why did she run away? I shall go mad, Robert! It goes round and round in my brain till I can't think at all! And in spite of the note and what you and Bertram say, I'm so worried about Hester. Where on earth can she be?'

'What have you done so far?' Dungarran's voice was still calm. Only his knuckles, white against the blue apron, betrayed his tension.

'I thought she might have gone home, so I sent every man I could find round all the inns with coaches for the north. No one has hired a coach for Northampton since last Friday, and no one answering Hester's description travelled on the Mail or any of the stage coaches. The fellow at the ticket office said there were no women at all on the Mail tonight. He noticed particularly.'

'What else?'

'There hasn't been time for much else, but one of the maids says that she saw Hester crossing Berkeley Square. I wondered if she had gone round to see Lowell, as Bertram had said. I was just about to send someone to ask.'

'I'll go,' Dungarran said brusquely. 'It won't take long.'

But when he roused the sleepy manservant in Half Moon Street he was informed that Mr Perceval had left London that afternoon for Devon.

'Accompanied?'

'Mr Gaines went the day before yesterday, my lord.'

'But was there no one else with Mr Perceval?'

The manservant looked puzzled. 'I cannot say. I was out at the time. He was here this morning when I left, but the house was empty when I got back at about eight o'clock. Mr Gaines allows me to visit my mother on the last Monday of the month, my lord,' he added, a touch defensively.

Dungarran rewarded the man and returned to Grosvenor Street. 'That must be where she's gone, Aunt! With Lowell to Totnes!' The apron was folded over again and tucked inside his pocket.

'Totnes? But why—oh, of course! Devon. Lowell was to join Mr Gaines there. That must be it... Robert! Where are you going?'

'To Curzon Street. I'll pick up my man and be off to Devon within the hour.'

'But you've only just come back from Portsmouth. You must have some kind of rest! It's almost two days' journey to Totnes!'

Lord Dungarran came back into the room and took his aunt's hands in his. 'I shan't rest until I know where Hester is. And if she has those papers the matter is all the more urgent.' He made to go again, but Lady Martindale held him back.

'What can I do to help?'

'Make sure that our friend the Comte de Landres doesn't follow me!'

'How can I do that?'

'Get some of your friends at the War Office to arrest him. He must be behind this.'

Chapter Eleven

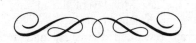

Robert was back in three days, but he had no good news. Mr Gaines's godfather was seriously ill and Lowell Perceval's plan to spend time with his friend in Devon had been abandoned the day after it was formed. So far as Woodford Gaines knew, Lowell had never left London.

'So we are none the wiser?' said Lady Martindale anxiously.

Her nephew shook his head. 'I haven't seen a trace of either of the Percevals. What about de Landres? Does he know anything?'

'He's been questioned. He admits he engaged the men to search for the papers, but claims that they didn't find them. He has even admitted that he was there himself. But there was no sign of Hester,' he said. 'Except for Bertram the house was deserted. And while I wouldn't believe a word the villain said, Bertram confirms it. He still thinks Hester went out to visit her brother. And now both Percevals are missing! What are we to make of it?' Lady Martindale

walked up and down in agitation, hardly able to suppress tears. 'Robert, I shall soon have to send a message to Sir James and Lady Perceval! What am I to
say?'

Dungarran's face was lined with worry and fatigue,
but he said firmly, 'Wait a little. We don't wish to
give them an unnecessary fright. Wherever they are,
I believe Hester and Lowell are together. We must
hope so, at least. If she *did* know that de Landres was
coming to steal the papers—'

'How *could* she?'

'I don't know, Godmama, but it's the only thing
that explains her behaviour.' Hearing the impatient
irritation in his voice, he endeavoured to speak more
calmly. 'She took the papers to a place where de
Landres couldn't find them, and she got her brother
to help her. She must be somewhere we haven't
thought of. I think we should have another talk with
the servant in the house in Half Moon Street. Come,
Godmama!'

Together they went to Half Moon Street. Here they
found the manservant very ready to talk. He reiterated
that he had seen neither Hester nor Lowell, but he
told them of two used brandy glasses he had found
since talking to Dungarran, and taking him to one side
he said softly, 'I don't like to mention it before her
ladyship, but there was women's clothing in Mr
Lowell's chamber, too. I've folded it up but it's still
there.'

'Fetch it, man!'

When he brought it down Lady Martindale exclaimed, 'Why, that's Hester's dress!' She looked fearfully at her nephew. 'W...What does it mean?'

For the first time since coming back from Portsmouth Robert Dungarran's features relaxed. 'Not what you fear, Godmama. In fact, I think I know now what the Percevals have done and where they are.' He thanked the manservant suitably, and took his aunt home.

'If you will write a note for Lady Perceval I shall deliver it in person. But I think... I hope it will not be needed.'

'You know where they are? But how?'

'They are almost certainly in Northamptonshire.'

'How could they have got there? We enquired...'

'After a young lady. Do you remember that Hester Perceval once attended a lecture in St James's Square?'

'Dressed as a young man! Of course! Those clothes of hers... She changed her clothes in Half Moon Street. Oh Robert! I think that must be the answer. And what a clever disguise!'

'I shall have to go straight away. I think they are safe in their own home, but I won't be at ease until I see them there.'

'Yes, yes! Shall I come with you?'

'I'm not sure you would enjoy the rate at which I propose to travel, Aunt.'

'Then you must send a message back as soon as you know! I shall be on the rack until I hear from you. Oh, Robert, I pray with all my heart you are right!'

Robert looked at his aunt's face. Lady Martindale had aged by ten years in the last week. Her cheeks were pale and dark circles lay under her eyes. Her hands were trembling. He took one in his and pressed it comfortingly.

'They are! I know they are!' he said gently, putting as much assurance into his voice as he could. 'And I shall send a message telling you so. Trust me.'

Dungarran travelled overnight in a hired chaise and four. His activities of the last week caught up with him and, in spite of his worries, he finally fell asleep. But his slumbers were fitful and broken by nightmares and nameless fears. He was not as certain that Hester was at Abbot Quincey as he had led his aunt to believe. But if not, where else would he look? The note said she was safe, but was she? The thought that she might be in the hands of strangers, with only Lowell to help her, was torture. He was incapable of rational thought, unable to persuade himself that, logically, he was very likely to find Hester comfortably installed in her own home, engaged in the further decipherment of the Pentacle papers. Strangely, none of his anxieties were for those same papers. All his thoughts were for Hester.

Daylight restored him to something of his former self. He started planning what he should do. It was too early to go to Perceval Hall, nor was he in a state to call on anyone. He must find somewhere to repair the damage of five days' almost continuous travel. At the first likely-looking inn he ordered the coachman to stop, and asked his man to step inside and order a room. The landlord was just stirring and was astonished at being asked to provide a room at what seemed to him to be the wrong end of the night.

'Do you have a room?' Wicklow asked coldly.

'Oh yes, sir. Several.'

'Then we shall take the best. His lordship would like breakfast in half an hour. But first we should like plenty of hot water and towels.' Then as the man stared he added, 'As soon as possible!'

Aided by Wicklow, Dungarran made himself more respectable. He washed and shaved, then put on a clean shirt and cravat. His coat was shaken and brushed, and his boots polished, though not altogether to his man's satisfaction. The breakfast was a hearty one, and Dungarran made himself eat a fair amount. However impatient he was, he must try to be sensible. The next hour or two might very well be a testing time. At last the hour was sufficiently advanced for Dungarran to be received at Perceval Hall. Outwardly his usual imperturbable, well-dressed self, he got in the coach once again and gave the order to drive off.

As he approached Hester's home the beauty of the house and grounds made no impression on him. It was taking all his considerable strength of character to retain an air of polite calm, and presenting himself and his mission to the Percevals in a reasonable manner would test every social skill he possessed. He did not know what he would do if Hester were not here…

The door opened as the coach came to a halt.

'Good morning. My name is Dungarran. Are Sir

James and Lady Perceval at home?' He went in and waited in the entrance hall while the servant disappeared to consult. Of course they were at home! It was a ridiculously early hour to call—any sensible person would still be at breakfast, or in bed... Perhaps it would have been better to ask for Hugo? Less conventional, but safer... What a time the wretched man was taking!... He strode restlessly up and down the hall, stopping before a portrait of a young lady dressed in the clothes of the previous century, where he tried to trace a similarity to Hester. What would he do if she were not here?

'Will you come this way, please?'

He followed the servant into a small parlour. Lady Perceval was sitting by the window. Sir James, looking rather puzzled, came forward to meet him.

'Good morning, Dungarran. Er...what can I do for you? Did you wish to see Hugo? He's just coming...'

'No, Sir James. It was you I wanted to see.'

'Of course! How stupid of me! You've brought a message from my daughter! How is she? And Lady Martindale? Both well, I hope?'

Lady Perceval came over to him. 'How very kind of you, Lord Dungarran! Though I was rather hoping to see Hester before too long. We miss her, you know.'

An icy hand was clutching Dungarran's throat, making it impossible for him to speak. Hester was not, after all, here. His worst fears, the fears he had refused to give way to, had been realised.

The silence was broken by Hugo, who came striding into the room, a broad smile on his face and his hand outstretched. 'Robert! What the devil are you doing here? It's damned good to see you! Can you stay?'

The moment could not be put off any longer. Dungarran took Lady Martindale's letter out of his pocket and handed it to Sir James. 'I…I'm sorry, sir,' he said.

Lady Perceval turned to her husband. 'What is it? What is it, James? Something's wrong! It's Hester!' He was busy with the letter and didn't hear her. She turned again to Dungarran. 'Is she ill?'

Sir James led her gently back to her seat. After a quick look Hugo came over to sit next to her. 'I'm afraid it's bad news, my dear. Lady Martindale tells us that Hester is missing. She has not been seen for…' He took out his glasses and looked at the letter again. 'Nearly five days?' His voice expressed shock and growing anger. Lady Perceval gave a little scream.

'You don't mean it! You can't mean that Hester…my darling— No, no! It can't be!' Hugo put his arms round her, but she shook him off. 'Your aunt promised to look after her!' she cried to Dungarran. 'I trusted her! What happened? What can possibly have happened?'

Dungarran was white but he remained calm. 'I was in Portsmouth, and Lady Martindale was visiting a friend in Richmond. My aunt had urged Miss Perceval to go with her, but she refused. I am aware that it was very wrong of us to leave her alone, but she was insistent that she wanted to carry on with…with some work she had been doing. As far as we can tell she left the house of her own accord, taking the…the work with her.' He turned to Sir James. 'We thought we knew where she was, Sir James. As soon as I returned to London and heard what had happened I went straight down to Devon in search of her. But we were wrong. I've since wasted no time in coming here. She…she left this note with one of Lady Martindale's servants.' He handed over the scrap of paper—the only source of hope. His hand trembling, Sir James took it and read it out.

'"I am quite safe and so are the papers.—Hester."' He looked up. 'But this was four nights ago? And not another word from her since? Good God, man, what can have happened to her?'

Dungarran's lips tightened. 'I…I don't know,' he said.

Hugo cried angrily, 'Don't stand there saying you don't know! Why aren't you out there looking for her? Father, if you don't mind I'll collect my things and set off straight away for London. Hester must be there somewhere.'

'We think Lowell is almost certainly with her,' said Dungarran. 'There is some evidence for it.'

There was a shocked silence, then Hugo said, 'He can't be. Lowell can't be with her. He's here. I've just been out for a ride with him.'

'Heavens above, Lord Dungarran! Where is my daughter?' cried Lady Perceval in great distress.

'Yes, Dungarran,' said Sir James grimly. 'Where is Hester now?'

'Here, Papa,' said a new voice. Everyone turned. Hester Perceval stood in the doorway, one hand clutching the doorframe, the other holding a sheaf of papers.

After a moment's stunned silence the family converged on the door. Mother and father, Hugo, even Lowell, who had followed his sister into the room, hugged Hester in turn, exclaiming, laughing, admonishing, expressing their delight that she was safe.

Dungarran took one long look at the figure in the doorway, then went over to the window, leaving the Percevals to rejoice among themselves. Ordinary courtesy would demand that he left them to their jubilations unwatched by an outsider. But it was not anything so conventional as courtesy that had moved him to stand with his back to the room, staring at the landscape outside. He had a battle to fight unseen. Never before had he been subject to such a riot of feelings as was now threatening to overwhelm him. His famous detachment had in the past carried him through many a dramatic situation with no loss of dignity or control. Now it had deserted him. Nothing in his life had disturbed him so much as the sight of Hester Perceval in that doorway.

He put his hands against the window-pane in an effort to absorb its coolness into his blood. He was struggling against a primitive urge to snatch the girl into his arms, to hold her so passionately close that she could hardly breathe, to carry her off to some remote island where they could live for ever and lose all sight of the world... At the same time he felt an absurd tenderness, a desire to cherish her, protect from all harm, to throw away the hideous clothes she was wearing and replace them with lace and satin and jewels, to demonstrate to the wide world his pride and joy in her...

But at war with both of these was a growing anger. How *dare* she subject him to such anxiety! If she had thought half as much of him as he of her, she would have sent a message before now to reassure him! The thought of his fruitless journeys, the long road to Devon and back, the nightmares of the night before, enraged him beyond measure. How *dare* she have so little consideration for his feelings! How *dare* she have taken such a hold on his heart that he had lost all sense! The coolly logical mind, in which he had taken such pride, was now, thanks to this woman, at the mercy of a maelstrom of completely irrational emotions!

'Lord Dungarran!'

He turned. Hester was inside the room, still clutching the folder of papers, the family in a protective circle behind her. She looked red-eyed and thin, as if she had neither eaten nor slept for a week, and the drab, ink-stained garment she wore hung about her like a tent. The dress was short for her tall figure—it revealed ankles in wrinkled stockings and feet encased in clumsy boots, servants' boots. Her hair was dragged away from her face. With a sharp pang, he saw that the face itself had the inevitable smear of ink down one side.

And yet, on seeing her in the doorway his first thought had been that he had never seen anything so beautiful. Now, under the eyes of her family, it was a struggle to restrain himself from wiping the smear from her face and kissing her as he had kissed her, a century ago it seemed, in the little study in Grosvenor Street. Or would he first shake her till she cried for mercy, begged him for forgiveness for her heartless behaviour?

'Lord Dungarran?' Her manner was hesitant, as if she was unsure of what he would say.

Robert Dungarran hesitated. What *was* he to say? He was so fluent in society, so polished in address. What could he say to this girl? The feelings at war within were making it impossible for him to say anything. He looked at the papers still clutched in her hand. Their familiar look, the memory of the work Hester and he had toiled over for so long, loosened his tongue. Calmly—he must speak calmly—he said, 'Miss Perceval. You have the Pentacle papers there, I see.'

Her lips tightened. Surprise, then resentment showed in that tired face. 'Where else would they be?' she asked sharply.

Why hadn't she run to him, why hadn't she shown delight to see him, or regret that she had caused him such trouble! Anger won the battle for supremacy in Robert Dungarran's emotions. 'How the devil would I know where they would be, ma'am? With you, perhaps—but where was that? Vanished into thin air! Do you realise how much valuable time has been lost while you have been playing hide and seek, and I have been combing England for a trace of you?'

'Lord Dungarran—'

'Have you any idea of the confusion and distress you have caused with your silence?' he continued, sweeping aside her interruption. 'Look at your family! A few moments ago your mother was close to collapse. Her worry was short-lived, thank God, and is now at an end, but have you thought at all of Lady Martindale's feelings? I have never seen my aunt so distracted in her life—not even when my uncle died!'

'I am sorry for your aunt's distress, Lord Dungarran. Truly sorry. You will be able to reassure her when you return.' Hester's face was stony as she added, 'But instead of wasting valuable time berating me, you should be on your way to London. I have transcribed enough of the papers to know their secret. Lord Wellington's life is in danger. Some of the Spanish high command are in a plot to assassinate him.'

The news brought him up short. 'When? Where?'

'On the twentieth of next month—' She passed a hand over her forehead. 'Or is it this month? I have lost count of the days.'

Hugo said gently, 'Today is the third, Hester. The third of July.'

'Is it? The twentieth of this month, then—or very soon after. The Spaniards are due to meet Wellington for a conference on the road between Ciudad Rodrigo and Salamanca. The letters are not more precise than that.'

'They can't be—not with the uncertainty of the campaign. But they'll find him somewhere on that road. Our men must simply find him first. We have time—just! Hester, this is not the moment I know, but please forgive—'

'You should leave immediately, Lord Dungarran.' She put the folder down on the table with deliberation. 'There are the papers. Take them and finish them at your leisure. You needn't trouble to come back when you have delivered the message—I don't expect to see or hear from you again.'

'I must explain—'

'Don't try! I meant what I said. Goodbye. And— for Wellington's sake—God speed!'

Dungarran held out his hand, but she ignored it and with a quick look of apology at her family went out of the room. He was still staring at the door when Sir James spoke.

'Dungarran, I don't pretend to understand what has been going on,' he said with a troubled frown. 'But do you take what my daughter has said seriously?'

'Oh yes! It's perfectly serious—extremely serious, Sir James.'

'Then shouldn't you be going? I would invite you to eat something with us, but speed would seem to be essential. I'll get one of our people to put something up for your journey. Hugo, you might think of accompanying Lord Dungarran. If what Hester has told us is indeed true then we must make sure the message reaches the War Office safely and as soon as possible.'

'I shall leave immediately. Will you come, Hugo?'

'Of course! I'll get some things.' He went out. Dungarran turned to Sir James.

'There isn't time to explain why I behaved as I did a few moments ago. I…I was not myself. Could you perhaps talk to your daughter—persuade her to give me a chance to say how much I regret it?'

'I'll do my best, Dungarran.' The expression on Sir James's face was not reassuring. With a gesture of despair Dungarran picked up the folder of documents, turned on his heel and followed Hugo out.

After the two men had gone Hester wanted nothing more than to retreat from the world again. But her parents were hurt and angry at her deception of them. They could not understand why she and Lowell had kept her presence in Abbot Quincey such a secret. She owed them an account and an explanation. Lowell in fact did most of the telling, while she sat, her hand in that of her mother, listening and reliving the events of the past five days…

When Lowell had opened the door of the house in Half Moon Street Hester had such a shock that she burst into tears. 'Lowell! Oh, thank God you're still here!' she cried. 'I thought you had gone. Let me in— quickly!'

To his credit Lowell didn't ask questions there and then, but ushered her straight into the little salon. Here she sank into an armchair and tried to get her breath back. But she leapt up again when she heard noises outside in the street.

'The door! The door, Lowell! Is it shut fast? Tell your man not to open it to anyone! Go, Lowell, go!'

'There's no one else here, Hes. And the door is shut.'

'Bolt it, Lowell! Please!'

When Lowell returned he looked in concern at his sister's pale, tear-stained cheeks and trembling limbs. He pushed her back into the chair, then went in search of brandy and glasses. When he came back he demanded, 'What on earth has happened, Hester? Is it Dungarran? What has he done?'

'No, no, no! It's the Comte de Landres. He mustn't find me!'

'De Landres? What the devil has de Landres to do with you?' Hester tried to stammer out a few words, but between fright and lack of breath she was incoherent.

In deep concern Lowell said gently, 'Hester, take a sip of that drink, then calm down and tell me why you're in such a state. Slowly now!'

Hester sipped the brandy, took a deep breath and started an account of the morning's events. Before she knew it, she was telling Lowell the whole story, beginning with the means Dungarran had used to blackmail her into working with him...

'I should be shot, Hester! To give him such a hold over you! But I would never have believed it of Dungarran! I would have thought him incapable of such ungentlemanly behaviour.'

'He…he would never have carried out his threat, Lowell. I realise that now. He is, truly, a gentleman. But let me tell you why he thought it so important for me to help him.' She went on to describe the days of patient decipherment, the feelings of triumph when they had found the key to the Pentacle papers… In the end Hester told him almost all of it, leaving out only Dungarran's kisses, and their astonishing effect on her. Such things were not relevant to her tale. But the rest of her story took a considerable time, for if Lowell was to help her he must know everything, including the newly discovered importance of the Pentacle papers. It was a relief to unburden herself to him. Lowell had been her confidant and accomplice for so many years, but the secret work she had been doing with Dungarran had recently put a wall between brother and sister. Now all was open again—except Dungarran's efforts to educate her in the tenderer arts. That was still private ground.

When she had finished, Lowell, who had been standing at the window, turned and asked, 'When did you say Dungarran will be back?'

'Not for forty-eight hours.'

'Hm.' Lowell finished his brandy. 'Well, I don't wish to worry you further, Hes, but there's a gent on the other side of the street who has been watching this house ever since he arrived five minutes ago. No! Don't come closer to the window! He's seen me, but he mustn't see you. Wait! He's coming over! Upstairs with you, and take your baggage with you!'

Hester waited round the bend at the top of the

stairs, heart beating so loudly that she thought their visitor must hear it.

'Mr Perceval? Mr Lowell Perceval?' The man's English accent was good, but not perfect.

'Sir?'

'Oh, excuse me, let me introduce myself! My name is Razan, Charles Razan. I am a friend of the Comte de Landres. May I come in?'

Hester heard footsteps entering the hall and going into the salon. Then Lowell's voice. 'May I know your business, sir?'

'Monsieur de Landres has charged me with a message for Miss Perceval. May I see her?'

Lowell's voice again, expressing polite bewilderment. 'My sister, sir? What makes you think she lives here?'

'Oh, I don't! But the servant at Lady Martindale's said he thought she might have come here to visit you.'

'Lady Martindale's servant was mistaken. Miss Perceval wouldn't even expect to find me here, I assure you. She thinks I'm out of London. And, except for a change in my plans, I would be. As it is, I shall be leaving very shortly, so I can't even offer to deliver a message if I see her. I'm sorry, but I can't help you.'

'Then I apologise for having disturbed you.' There was a pause. 'You are quite sure she isn't here?'

This time Lowell's voice was cold. 'Quite sure. I'll see you out. Good day, sir.' The door opened and was then shut and bolted. Lowell came up the stairs.

'You heard?'

Hester nodded. 'He wasn't convinced.'

'I'm not surprised. He saw the two brandy glasses. He'll be back—possibly with friends. I'm not sure what we should do.'

'Let's go to Abbot Quincey! The papers would be safe there. Lowell, let's go home! I can't think of anywhere in London where I could hide, and it's two days at least before Dungarran's return. I daren't go back to the house.'

'The Holyhead Mail leaves Wood Street at half past seven. We could catch that easily,' said Lowell thoughtfully. 'But what about Lady Martindale?'

'Heavens, yes! I hadn't thought! She'll be so worried when she comes back from Richmond! If I write a note for her can you get it delivered to Grosvenor Street?'

'I'll see to it. Say you're safe, but don't say where you are or what you're doing.'

'Why not?'

'Just in case the note falls into the wrong hands. I'll take you to the Cross Keys, leave you there to wait for the coach, then cut back to Grosvenor Street. If Lady Martindale is there I'll talk to her. If not, I'll leave the note with one of the servants. We'd better prepare to leave. Hester, I hope you'll be safe—de Landres and Razan won't be looking for you at the inn, will they?'

'They won't be looking for a young man. Are those clothes of Mr Gaines still here? Then fetch them and

I'll change. And I'd like a more suitable bag for these papers. But hurry!'

Lady Martindale had not yet returned when Lowell called, but she was expected at any moment. Though the house was in confusion, he was able to leave his note with one of the servants with strict instructions to deliver it the minute she arrived. He wasted no time for, as he later told her, he was not easy in his mind until he saw Hester safely waiting for him at the Cross Keys. No one would have recognised Miss Perceval in the young dandy sitting, one leg crossed over the other, quietly reading a newspaper in the corner. And Lowell was much reassured when she told him that, as far as she was aware, no one had shown any undue curiosity about the passengers for the Mail. They left on time, and the two Percevals, whose experience of such a mode of transport had till now been slight, spent an uncomfortable night as the coach rattled along until they reached Northampton in the early morning. Here they climbed out stiff and hungry, Hester still clutching her precious bag. They didn't stop for any refreshment. Lowell hired a couple of horses, and they set off for Abbot Quincey.

'I've been thinking, Lowell,' said Hester as they rode along the country lanes. 'It would be better if no one knew that I've come back.'

'Why not?'

'Mama would never let me work the way I need to if I am to decipher these papers in time, you know she wouldn't. And if de Landres or any of his henchmen should come to Perceval Hall, how long do you think it would be before they found out from Mama that I was here?'

Lowell nodded. 'But where could you hide? And where would you sleep?'

'In my attic. There's bound to be some sort of bed we could fetch in from one of the other attics. Food might be more of a problem…'

'I suppose I could bring you some, but if I came too often someone would be bound to ask what I was doing. And wouldn't you need clothes and someone to look after you?'

Hester thought for a moment. 'Could we ask Maggie to help? She wanders all over the place and no one ever takes any notice of her. She'd manage the clothes, and I should think she could manage the food, too.' Hester was tired and suffering from reaction, but she managed an affectionate smile. 'Think of the way she managed us when we were children! I'm sure she'd do it—especially if *you* asked her, Lowell! You were always her baby, her favourite. Maggie would never say no to you!'

So they decided that Lowell would help Hester up to the attics by an unused staircase at the back of the house, and then go to find Maggie. They would have to improvise from then on. Whatever happened, Hester was determined to work without interruption until she had finally found out the secret of the Pentacle papers. When Lowell asked her she told him why.

'Those papers have become a…a sort of challenge.

To me personally. I'm not particularly proud of deceiving Mama and Papa, or of playing a part with Dungarran in front of society. I took the papers in order to save them, and if I can find out their message then I shall feel the things I've done have been justified.'

'I thought you might have been doing this for Dungarran…?'

'Of course not!' Lowell raised an eyebrow at her, and Hester pulled a face and went on, 'Well, in a way I am. I want to show him. I want to prove to him that I'm a force to be reckoned with, not just a…' She glanced at Lowell. 'Well you know as well as I do that Dungarran is a…a…' She tried again. 'He enjoys what he calls 'light dalliance', and I want him to take me seriously.'

'You're in love with him!'

'That's nonsense! Absolute rubbish! You're an idiot, Lowell! I didn't mean as a woman—I meant take me seriously in my work!' Lowell looked at her speculatively as they rode on. It seemed to him that his sister was protesting just a little too much, but he decided not to pursue the subject. Hester had enough to worry about.

They reached the stables behind Perceval Hall before the household was stirring. By this time Hester was near to collapse, but Lowell was always at his best when facing a challenge. In no time, Hester found herself in her attic, sitting in her favourite armchair while Lowell set about rearranging the furniture.

'Bear up, Hes! Don't give in now! We'll soon have

you settled.' He cast a satisfied glance round the
room. 'There! There's space for a bed in here, and
Maggie will know where I can find one. I'll go now
to fetch her—I won't be long.' He came back and
hugged her. 'Don't look like that, Hes! A few hours
sleep and you'll be as good as new.'

Lowell soon returned with their old nurse. Maggie
might grumble, but she was too soft-hearted to refuse
her favourite. Sworn to secrecy, she fetched sheets
and pillows from the linen cupboard, while Lowell
dragged a truckle bed from a neighbouring attic.
Hester hardly heard her scolding, barely felt Maggie's
work-roughened hands gently exchanging Woodford
Gaines's clothes for a cotton wrap. Before she realised it she found herself tucked up in bed between
cool, lavender-scented sheets in her own, dear, familiar refuge. The last thing she saw before falling
asleep was the bag of papers on the floor beside
the bed.

Chapter Twelve

She slept for several hours, then woke with a start. Maggie was putting a cup of chocolate and some rolls beside the bed. Then she disappeared again. Hester was so hungry that, by the time Maggie returned carrying a basin and ewer, the food was all gone. 'I'll fetch some clothes for you as soon as I can,' she said, looking disapprovingly at Woodford Gaines's clothing, now somewhat the worse for wear. 'You canna wear those garments, Miss Hester. It isn't fit.'

'It isn't important what I wear, Maggie. No one will see me but you and Master Lowell. But I must start on those papers straight away.'

Maggie sniffed. 'I'll fetch the things your mother left for the village. There'll be something there that'll fit you.' A few minutes later she was back with some undergarments and a rough, brown cotton dress. Hester, still in her wrapper, was already laying the Pentacle papers out on her desk and arranging her pens. Within minutes she was hard at work, her hair screwed back out of the way, and the drab dress already christened with ink.

About halfway through the morning Lowell appeared to see how she was. He laughed at her absorption, but seemed comforted by it.

'No need to worry about you, that's obvious.'

'What did the family say when you came back so unexpectedly?'

'They exclaimed, of course, and asked what I was doing here. I told them I'd been planning a trip to Devon, but it had been called off at the last minute—which is perfectly true! I forgot to tell you yesterday—Gaines's godfather has been taken ill. That's why I was still in London. To say the truth, the family are all so busy with the Steepwood business that they hardly noticed I was there! What a mess it is, Hester! However, Pa and the others seem to be managing, though the neighbourhood won't really settle down until we all know who the new owner is. What about you? Do you need anything else?'

'I shall need more pens. These wear out so fast, and I haven't time to mend them.'

'Give them to me. I'm a dab hand at mending pens.'

Over the next few days, with Lowell to give her the necessary support and Maggie to look after her physical needs, Hester devoted all her attention and energy to the business of deciphering the Pentacle papers. Buried in the long, elaborate phrases of Spanish diplomatic language, accompanied with terse French comments, a picture was emerging of a tiny group of dissident Spaniards. They had no cause to love the French—Napoleon had invaded their country, taken over Madrid, their capital, and installed his brother Joseph there as their upstart king. Yet these

Spanish grandees were in secret correspondence with French agents. Their letters expressed their burning resentment of the British command in the Spanish Peninsula—in particular, the high-handed manner in which all strategic decisions were taken without reference to some of the noblest, the greatest, the most talented generals in Spain. The flames of their anger had been fanned by skilful handling on the part of the French, and matters had reached a point where one or two of the Spaniards were ready to take action. Assassination was mentioned. But whose? The Spaniards were still too cautious to mention names. Hester toiled on, barely taking time for sleep or food. She had saved the Pentacle papers from destruction. But in bringing them to Abbot Quincey she had also taken on a heavy responsibility. Someone's life—probably that of Lord Wellington—was in danger. She must not rest until she knew it all.

And eventually, after working till she was in danger of dropping, she had it. She had just finished writing the summary of everything she had learned when Lowell came bursting into the attic with the news that Dungarran was in the hall asking to see her father.

Lost in her own reliving of the story, Hester had barely been aware of Lowell's voice, her parents' questions and his replies. Now she roused herself. Lowell had brought them up to the moment when she had appeared in the doorway. She turned to her mother.

'Mama... I'm sorry! Indeed I am! I didn't think of anything but the papers. It wasn't until I saw your

face…and…and Dungarran spoke… Forgive me…'
Her voice choked.

Lady Perceval put her arms round her daughter. 'Of
course you're forgiven!' she said. 'Your Papa and I
are proud of you, Hester. But now you must go to
bed. You need rest. We'll talk of all this later, when
you aren't quite so exhausted. Come!'

Sir James kissed his daughter on her way out. 'I
suppose I must forgive you, too, though I still think
you could have told us. But Dungarran was very
harsh. It's all up to him and Hugo now. I wonder how
they're faring?'

After telling her story Hester found it impossible
to stay awake. She fell into an exhausted slumber
which lasted almost forty-eight hours, broken only for
a sip of water or some of the soup brought by her
mother or one of the maids. Waking or sleeping, she
had no thought for anything outside her bedchamber
walls—London, Lady Martindale, the Pentacle papers, Wellington himself, might never have existed.
Even Robert Dungarran. But this respite did not last.
After two days she was restored to full activity and
consciousness, and…misery.

The day had still been young when Hugo and
Dungarran had set out, and they travelled as speedily
as the post horses would take them. They were in
London by early evening. Dungarran took a few
minutes to inform his aunt that Hester had been
found, then hurried on to the Horse Guards. Here he
was lucky enough to catch one of Lord Bathurst's
most able lieutenants. The situation was quickly explained and as quickly understood. In no time two of

the army's best men had been despatched to Lisbon with the message, and four others had been called in and given instructions. Two of them would take a different sea route to Corunna, and make their separate ways through Northern Spain with the aid of the Spanish guerrillas. The last two would be smuggled in at Calais, and travel the more dangerous land route, using ways known only to themselves through the hostile territory of France. The message was sure to reach Wellington by one means or another.

Robert Dungarran took Hugo back to his aunt's house. Over dinner Lady Martindale and Hugo talked. Robert was markedly silent.

'I am not at all surprised you're tired and out of sorts, Robert,' said Lady Martindale. 'You've been chasing about the country without stopping for days! You've earned a long rest.'

'Thank you. I suppose I shall take one,' her nephew answered shortly.

Hugo exchanged a look with Lady Martindale. 'Why don't you come back with me?' he asked. 'I'd enjoy your company, now that things seem to have settled down on the estate.' He grinned. 'You could come to our fête on the eighteenth. Now, you would enjoy that!'

His friend looked at him sourly. 'I don't know why you always think of me as a town-lover, Hugo, indeed I don't! Have you forgotten the Dungarran lands in Hertfordshire? And the house in the Cotswolds—not to mention the Irish estates, and the hunting lodge in Leicestershire? I am well used to country pursuits and duties, believe me.'

'Then you won't mind coming to our fête!' Hugo turned to his hostess. 'What about you, Lady Martindale? Would you like a sojourn in the country? London society must be getting rather flat now. You were very kind to Hester. My parents would welcome you.'

'I hardly think so, Hugo! What? Welcome the woman who lost their only daughter for more than four days?'

'The circumstances were…a little unusual. Part of the blame lies with Hester, surely? And she is now quite safely restored to them. No, I'm sure they have forgotten. I think you should both come.'

'I am certain your sister would like to see Aunt Martindale. But she would refuse to see me.' Dungarran got up from the table and went over to the fireplace. 'I was unforgivably rude to her this morning.'

'You, Robert? Rude? Unforgivably rude? I don't believe it!'

'I was in a rage. Hugo was there. He'll tell you.'

Lady Martindale looked astonished. 'Can this be true, Hugo?'

'Yes. In fact, Robert was deuced unfair to Hester. I asked him about it on the journey down, but he wouldn't explain. I've never seen him like it before. In fact—' Hugo hesitated. 'In fact, if it wasn't Robert we were talking about, I'd think he was…'

Lady Martindale leaned forward. 'Yes?'

'I'd think he was…in…'

'In love?'

'Ridiculous, isn't it?'

'Of course it is!' Robert Dungarran said bitterly.

'Go on, laugh, both of you. Thirty-one years old and I've fallen in love for the first time. Ridiculously in love. I've lost my head, my reason, my self-respect, and this morning I lost my temper. Your sister, Hugo, has never shown a liking for marriage, and not much for me, but now she will never be persuaded to consider either. Very amusing!'

'Robert! Dearest! I never thought to see this day! Oh, I'm so happy for you.'

'Happy for me? My dear aunt, are you mad? Did you not hear? Hester Perceval will refuse even to meet me. She will never let herself love me.'

'Unless I am very much mistaken, she already does.'

'Lady Martindale, Robert is right.' Hugo's face was troubled. 'Hester has always sworn she would never marry. You may be right about her sentiments, but she can be remarkably pig-headed when she chooses.'

'As we all know,' said Robert Dungarran.

'I am ashamed of you! If a personable gentleman, with everything to recommend him, cannot persuade a young lady, who is more than half in love with him already, to marry him, then I shall... I shall eat my best hat! Mind you, I am not saying it will be easy, but that is not at all a bad thing. You've always found too much favour with the ladies.'

'So you have told me, Godmama. I am pleased that one of us can be happy.'

Lady Martindale smiled at Hugo. 'Hugo, I don't think it wise in the circumstances to accept your parents' hospitality. But I think cousins of my late husband live somewhere in the neighbourhood, and we shall wheedle an invitation out of them. I look for-

ward to seeing Hester and your parents again, and
would love to come to your fête! Robert must please
himself.'

Lady Martindale wasted no time. She managed to
catch her relatives just before they left London for the
country, and received an enthusiastic invitation.
Within a day or two she and her nephew joined them
at Courtney Hall, just five miles from Abbot Quincey.

Hugo had preceded them to Northamptonshire,
anxious to assure his sister that Wellington's life was
secure. It was the only part of his news which pleased
her. The rest—that Lady Martindale and Robert
Dungarran were only five miles away, that Dungarran
intended to call again very soon—was enough to send
her back up to her attic, like a wounded animal seeking a hiding place. But the attic, which had been such
a refuge in the past, held little consolation. She sat
huddled in her armchair for hours, using all her pow-
ers of reason, all the intelligence she had so prided
herself on, to cure the ache in her heart. She had been
perfectly right to dismiss Dungarran as she had. Why
on earth should she waste another moment's thought
on him? He was an ingrate, a cold-hearted opportun-
ist, who used people for his own ends, ignoring the
fact that they were living, feeling human beings. She
had overcome her panic to rescue his papers for him,
gone through so much anxiety until she had found
Lowell, she had undertaken a hideously uncomfortable overnight journey to Abbot Quincey, deceived
her family, starved and gone without sleep to finish
the transcription... And what were his first words?
Not that he was glad to see her, not that he was

amazed at what she had done for him. She hadn't existed. His concern was for the papers. *'Miss Perceval. You have the Pentacle papers there, I see!'* He was a man without a heart and she would have no more to do with him. A feeling of desolation overcame her. Zeno would have to go, too. What was she to do now that her friendship with him was over? How would she fill her days?

'Hester! Hester!' Lowell's voice. She pulled herself together and got up. Lowell came bursting into the room. 'Dungarran's here and Mama wants you!'

'Please tell Mama that I'll come down in a little while. When Lord Dungarran has gone.'

'I can't do that,' said Lowell, shocked. 'She was very insistent. I think Dungarran has come to see Papa. You'd better come down, Hes.'

Hester followed Lowell down the stairs and into the main body of the house. As soon as she was visible her mother caught her by the arm and dragged her along into her bedchamber. 'My dear, clever girl, what a conquest! You must change, Hester! Your maid has laid out a dress for you, and she's waiting to do your hair.' She was bustled into her room, where the maid started her ministrations.

'Mama, why the fuss? I don't intend to meet…anyone.'

'Yes, you will, Hester! I insist! And so does your Papa!'

Hester grew pale. 'I assume you mean me to see Lord Dungarran. Mama, you can't be so unkind!'

'Unkind? Unkind?' Lady Perceval was outraged. 'Allow me to tell you, Hester Perceval, that not many young ladies are given the chance to marry into one of the richest families in England!'

'Marry! Do you mean to say that that...that man has the effrontery to come here with a proposal of marriage?'

'What are you saying? Effrontery? Really, Hester, I sometimes wonder whether your studies have turned your brain! Robert Dungarran comes from an old and respected family, he is rich, charming and altogether extremely eligible. A matrimonial prize of the first degree, and a very elusive one! It is a most flattering offer! Now let me hear no more nonsense! You will receive Dungarran, and you will listen to what he has to say!'

Lady Perceval was not to be swayed and Hester resigned herself to facing the man she had sworn to avoid, and, if her mother was right, to listen to a proposal of marriage she was determined to refuse. She received him in the small parlour.

'Lord Dungarran,' she said coldly, as she curtseyed.

'Miss Perceval, I...I have your father's permission to...' He stopped, then said abruptly, 'Would you take a walk in the grounds with me? It's a fine day, and this room brings to mind a scene I would rather forget.'

Hester made no move. 'Why should that be? It was surely the scene of one of your greatest successes— the secret of the Pentacle papers delivered to you in time to be effective. And, by someone who, being a woman, would hardly expect any acknowledgement, any respect or admiration for work involving the mind competently done. It was quite astounding that I was trusted with it in the first place.'

'That is rubbish, and you know it! Give me ten minutes in the privacy and peace of the grounds and I can show you how highly I regard you, how much I acknowledge the superiority of your gifts. And how very much I love you and hope you will marry me.'

'Very flatteringly put. But too late. I do not need ten minutes anywhere to remind you, Lord Dungarran, that I have never had the slightest intention of marrying anyone. And after our closer acquaintance I can now assure you that, if I ever did change my mind, it would not be in favour of you!' Hester could hear her voice rising angrily on these last words and stopped. This was not the behaviour recommended by books on deportment for young ladies receiving a proposal of marriage. She took a breath and said sweetly and falsely, 'I am sorry if this causes you pain, but—'

But Robert Dungarran, fortified by a short, informative chat with Lowell on the way in, said with a wry grin, 'I doubt that! I doubt that very much indeed. And if it gives you any satisfaction, yes, you are causing me pain. But I refuse to depart as I no doubt should, with a manly smile and protestations of undying, if hopeless, regard! I am convinced that we could find happiness together in spite of your obstinate insistence—'

'The arrogance of men! I've heard enough! It's time you went, sir!'

'I'll go for now—it's obvious you won't listen to me today. But I'm not giving up, Hester. It's too important to me.' He came up to her and, taking a firm hold of her hands, looked deep into her eyes. 'Have you any idea how rare this is—this harmony of mind and body that flows between us? No, don't argue! Harmony, Hester! Think of the hours we spent working together—can you deny the instinctive understanding between us? And as for the body... I can remind you of the sweetest harmony of all...' He bent his head and though Hester pulled frantically away from him he refused to let her go. He trapped her in his arms and gave her a gentle kiss. But gentle or passionate—it made little difference. Her treacherous body melted as soon as their lips met...

'No!' she cried, and tore herself out of his arms. 'No! I won't be seduced into marriage by—what did you call them?—"the pleasures of light dalliance". I won't be your wife! I refuse to be any man's chattel or slave! And you may come here as often as you choose, Lord Dungarran—I shall not see you! Whatever my parents might say!'

His face was stern as he said, 'Chattel? Slave? You demean yourself, and me, by such talk! This is no light dalliance, Hester! I want you for my companion, my partner, and I offer you a home, and children...and a lifetime's devotion. I won't let you cast them aside. Not without a fight. Be warned.' He turned on his heel and went out.

Hester ran to the window and watched him striding away from the house towards the stables. He had always seemed tall, but here in the country he looked broader, more powerful. It was easier to believe that he was as gifted an athlete as Hugo. She turned away. This morning she had caught a glimpse of a new Robert Dungarran. The elegant man of the London drawing-rooms, with his air of detachment, his drawl and his lazy manner had been replaced with something more disturbing. His last words had revealed an aspect of his character which was, she was sure, known to very few. He had spoken seriously, almost severely, with a sense of deep sincerity. Was this the real Robert Dungarran? In speaking slightingly of herself as his wife she had offended him. Why? Was it because he really did have a view of marriage which demanded equal respect and support between man and wife? If so, it was an ideal which was radically different from her own jaundiced view. Which of them was nearer the reality?

Hester sought the isolation of her attic while she debated these questions. She considered her parents' marriage. Her mother did not pretend to be clever, but her father treated her with respect and love, and recent events proved what a support they were to each other. Among her own generation Beatrice Roade's marriage was full of love and humour, and what an asset Harry had been to her in dealing with her somewhat difficult father! Others came to mind, perhaps not so obviously ideal, but the couples involved seemed to be satisfied. Had she been over-influenced by her education at Mrs Guarding's? Had her first experience of London prejudiced her for life? And was she cutting herself off from something which could be…wonderful?

She resolutely refused to come down when Dungarran called. He had weapons to persuade her, which she was sure he would not scruple to use, and she wanted to think things out for herself. Each time he came he left a note for her with Lowell. They were all in cipher, which was as well, for some of them were not the sort she would have wished her mother to see. They all contained the wit and humour which she had associated with Zeno, and, though perhaps she did not realise it, they were, in their way, as disarming as his physical presence. But then one came which sent her raging out into the grounds like an avenging fury.

She found the note, as usual, on her desk, and, as usual, set about transcribing it. But before she was halfway through her cheeks were scarlet. It was one of the more lurid passages from *The Wicked Marquis*. Attached to it was a message. It ran: 'Only three people in the world know the author's name, though many more would like to. Shall we tell them? Or would you like to discuss the matter first? Two o'clock this afternoon by the big cedar.' No signature—but none was necessary.

She stormed out of the house and over the lawns at ten past two that afternoon ready for battle.

'You're early! That's good.' He gave her one of his smiles, the dangerous sort, the sort to charm an unwary bird out of a tree.

Hester stopped in her tracks. The smile was doing things to her, she had never felt more like an unwary bird. She pulled herself together. 'You said two o'clock!'

'I expected you to keep me waiting at least half an hour. Shall we walk on?' When Hester hesitated he added, 'It's perfectly proper. Your mother knows you're in the grounds with me. She trusts me.'

'She doesn't know any better,' said Hester bitterly. 'She thinks you're a gentleman, not a blackmailer.'

She fell into step with him and they walked towards the bridge by the lake.

'I had to do something, my love. You were never going to give me a chance to explain otherwise.'

'I'm not your love!'

'Oh, you are! Whatever you might say or do, you will be my love. For ever. Don't ask me to explain that, Hester, because I can't. And that reminds me…' He took a parcel out of the pocket of his coat. 'I must give you this.'

She unwrapped it and looked up at him in surprise. 'My apron! My blue apron.'

'I found it on the floor of the study after you had disappeared. From that moment on I was hardly rational.' He gave her a whimsical smile. 'Absurd, isn't it? Robert Dungarran, the advocate of logic, Zeno, the mathematician and believer in the supreme power of reason, both turned upside down by a girl in a blue apron with ink on her face! That's what happened, Hester. I fell in love with you in this blue apron, though I didn't realise it till much later. And when the truth did hit me I had no idea how to deal with it! You stood in that doorway, surrounded by your family, and I didn't know whether I wanted to kiss you, beat you or ravish you on the spot. A fine, mixed-up state for Robert Dungarran to be in—especially as not one of them was possible! So I went back to what I did know, what we had chiefly shared—the Pentacle papers. I knew it was the wrong thing to say. But I couldn't for the life of me think of anything else! I was paralysed.'

'I was so hurt! When Lowell told me you had ar-

rived I could hardly stand on my feet, but I wanted
to see you… And then…and then…'

'You believed my only thought was for the papers.
Hester, I swear to you that when I saw you my head,
my heart—everything I am—was full of you.
Mentioning the papers was merely a…a line of communication when everything else was so confused
that I didn't know where to begin.'

'You were angry.'

'I was furious! Try to understand what it was like,
Hester. I can't remember a time when I was not in
control of my feelings—my aunt would tell you that
I was always too detached, never cared enough.
Mathematics was my passion, and formulae and equations are not likely to arouse violent emotion. I had
always shunned irrational attachments, even despised
them. But you had taken possession of my heart before I knew it!'

Hester was in a state of agitation, her restless hands
twisting the apron into an unrecognisable rag. Robert
Dungarran gently removed it. 'I'll hold this for you,
Hester. I don't want it lost.'

'You say your world has been turned upside down,'
she cried. 'But so has mine! Ever since I was seventeen I have known what I would do with my future.
Marriage played no part in it. And now…and now…
You have come along again with your smiles, and
your wit, and your looks…and…the rest—'

'My kisses?'

'Yes, damn you, your kisses! And I no longer know
what I wish for…' Tears started to trickle down
Hester's face. 'How do I know what marriage to you

would be like? How do I know whether we should be happy?'

He took her chin and lifted her eyes to his. 'You can't,' he said gravely. 'Some things have to be taken on trust. But would you be any happier without me?' She was silenced. He took out his handkerchief and wiped her face. 'At least it isn't ink,' he said with a faint smile.

Hester turned away, still silent.

'Hester, you've now heard what I had to say. I cannot imagine life without you. But you are clearly not yet convinced. May I make a suggestion?' He saw that she was listening. 'May we meet tomorrow—and every day after that—until you are certain of what you want? Let me try to persuade you that we have the best possible chance of happiness together. And if you are still not convinced...' Hester looked at him. His smile was twisted. 'I shall not bother you after that.'

For the next few days Hester met Robert Dungarran in the grounds every day. Every day she learned more about him—his quirky sense of humour, his consideration, his deep love of the countryside—aspects of his character which had never appeared during their acquaintance in London. Together they helped with preparations for the fête which was imminent, and she saw how easy he was with a wide variety of people— her family, visitors, tradesmen, servants, farmers.

Every morning he sent her a love letter—love letters which must be unique, for they were all in complicated ciphers which she had to work hard to solve. Some sentences made her laugh, some moved her beyond measure, and parts of them brought a vivid blush to her cheeks. At the end of a week Robert Dungarran had succeeded. Hester Perceval, one-time dedicated spinster, had so changed that she was seriously contemplating marriage. But how was she to tell the man of her choice?

The day of the fête dawned bright and sunny. The whole family was thrown into a welter of last-minute preparation, followed by appearances during the fête itself. This was a huge success, the only mishap being the collapse of an awning over Hugo's head, just when he was about to present the prize pig. No damage was done except perhaps to Hugo's dignity, and much innocent fun was had in the attempts to retrieve the pig. But eventually the crowds had gone, the servants were beginning the work of clearing up and Hester could wait no longer. She sought out Robert Dungarran.

'We...we haven't had our walk today,' she said nervously.

'Would you like one now?' he said instantly. 'I think we have both done enough for Abbot Quincey and its fête, don't you? Come! Let's walk through the woods.'

The sun was still hot enough to make the shade of the trees very welcome. By now they were usually at ease in each other's company, but today the mood was different. The bright flashes of sunshine, glinting and dancing through the leaves, enhanced the atmosphere of bright expectation. They stopped.

'Well, Hester?'

'I...er...I...' She took a deep breath and began

again. 'Your note this morning... The cipher was harder than usual. I...I didn't manage all of it.'

'Dear me—didn't you?'

'Er...no. This bit...' She took out a piece of paper and showed it to him. 'Wh...what does it mean?'

He looked at her with a gleam in his eye. 'Shall I show you?'

'Er...yes. Please.'

Robert Dungarran took her in his arms and kissed her, sweetly and gently. 'Was that it?'

'N...not all of it. There's more.' And she pointed to the following paragraph.

'That? I wouldn't have thought that difficult. Let me see... How do I begin?' His hold grew tighter and this time his kiss lasted until Hester was trembling in his grasp. Her arms crept round his neck and she returned the kiss with fervour. The passion between them slowly mounted, their bodies melting into each other in the dancing leaping light surrounding them...

'Hester!' Robert Dungarran raised his head and held her away until the white hot feeling running between them gradually cooled. He considered her for a moment.

'Unless you are an unprincipled wanton, my sweet love, you've just made a declaration.'

Hester held shaking hands to her cheeks. 'I...I didn't know how to bring the subject up,' she said. 'And you have recently been so discreet...'

'Discreet! If you knew the restraint I've had to put on myself... So you knew what was in my note all the time?'

'Most of it, yes. There's a piece at the end...'

'Ah, yes! The last paragraph. That was quite deliberately hard. And it defeated you!' His smile was complacent.

'I could have done it if I'd had more time!' cried Hester, jealous of her reputation. 'But with the fête…'

'How sad! Time is not what you're going to get.'

'Oh! Then will you tell me? Or…' she smiled invitingly. 'Show me?'

'I'll tell you, if you do something first. Showing will come afterwards.'

'After what?'

'First,' he said, taking her in his arms again, 'you have to kiss me and promise to marry me.'

Hester put her arms up and brought his head down to hers. This kiss was different again from all the rest. It was long, sweet, and serious, a solemn dedication. 'I'll marry you, Robert, and do my best to be what you want me to be.'

'My dear love!' He lifted her into the air, laughing with triumphant joy, and then brought her slowly down again to his lips.

'And now will you show me?'

'No, my darling Hester. Not now. That comes later. After we are married.'

'Tell me then!'

He bent his head and spoke softly in her ear. Hester's eyes grew round and her cheeks grew rosy. 'Robert!' she said. 'Is that really so? Then…how soon can we be married?'

An Unconventional Duenna

by
Paula Marshall

PROLOGUE

Spring 1812

Athene Filmer, twenty years old, poor and illegitimate, had only one aim in life and that was to make a good marriage. She fully intended to marry a man who was not only rich but also had a title. By doing so she would settle her mother for life as well as herself. Today, out of the blue, an opportunity had come for her to achieve her ambition and all her mother could do was try to make her reject it!

'For goodness sake, Athene,' she was saying, 'if you must accept this offer of a London Season from Mrs Tenison, I must beg you to be careful. It may be my own sad experience which is affecting my judgement, but I should not wish you to end up as I have done—a lonely woman in a country village. I would much rather that you stayed with me than risk that.'

The country village to which Mrs Charlotte Filmer

referred was Steep Ride, where she and her daughter
lived in what was little more than a cottage, ambi-
tiously called Datchet House. Steep Ride was pleasantly situated in the wooded neighbourhood of
Steepwood Abbey, not far from the River Steep and
its tributary which ran through the Abbey grounds.

Mrs Filmer was, not without reason, looking anxiously at her daughter. Alas, Athene was not only
clever, but she was also determined and wilful—one
might almost call her headstrong! In that she was the
opposite of her mother, who was gentle and retiring,
and whose one lapse from the straight and narrow
path of virtue had been cruelly punished. In her first
and only Season the young man whom she had loved
had betrayed her, and though she called herself Mrs
she had never been married. Her one consolation lay
in her pride in her beautiful child.

'Dear Mama,' said Athene, leaning forward affectionately and kissing her anxious parent, 'I shall only
be going as a mixture of a companion and a friend
for my dear old schoolfellow, Emma. You may be
sure that Mrs Tenison will keep a firm eye on both
of us. Depend upon it, she will not allow me to outshine Emma, since her intention is to secure a good
match for her.'

'She will have no trouble doing that,' fretted Mrs
Filmer. 'What I do not understand is why she isn't
engaging some decent, middle-aged woman to look
after her rather than trying to persuade you to be her
companion. After all, you are not very much older

than Emma and might be considered to need a guardian or a chaperon yourself.'

'Now, Mama, you know as well as I do what a timid little thing Emma is. The sort of dragon you are describing would extinguish her, whereas I am her good friend and guardian from her school-days who protected her when she needed protection. I am also old enough for her to look up to me, but not so ancient and stern that I frighten her. I shall stand between her and the Tenisons' sponsor, Lady Dunlop, who is somewhat of a dragon. Besides, would you deprive me of the delights of a London Season because you were unfortunate? You were young and inexperienced in the ways of the world, whereas I have had the benefit for the last few years of being made aware by you of the traps which await the innocent in the often cruel world of the ton.'

'There is that,' sighed her mother. 'Nevertheless…'

'Nevertheless nothing,' said Athene firmly. She had the advantage of always having won her arguments with her mother in the past. Her own internal reaction when Mrs Tenison had called earlier that afternoon with her exciting proposal had been: At last! Here is the chance I have always wished for—and so soon, before I have reached my last prayers.

'You might not wish to take up this offer, my dear, once you have thought it over. You will, in effect, be one of the Tenisons' servants, little better than a governess. You will be kept in the background. I know that Mrs Tenison said that she would provide you with a suitable wardrobe, but you may be sure that it will not be either becoming or fashionable. I am sure that she will not want you to rival Emma…'

'Now, how could I do that,' wondered Athene, 'when Emma is all that is fashionable and I am not. She is blonde, blue-eyed and tiny, whereas I am dark, grey-eyed and tall—an unlikely sort of creature to attract the young bucks of the ton.'

Her mother forbore to say that Athene always caused heads to turn at the dances at the Assembly Rooms in Abbot Quincey and was already noted for her wit and address, even if her hair and her grey eyes were the wrong colour and her turn-outs far from being in the latest fashion. It would not do to over-praise her: she thought quite enough of herself as it was.

Instead she offered in as neutral a voice as she could, 'I still think that you should give this whole notion more thought than you are doing. For one thing, if anyone should learn—or suspect—that you are illegitimate you will be ruined.'

Athene tossed her head. 'I'll think about it again tonight, Mama, and tell you in the morning what my decision is.'

She had no intention of doing any such thing. Her mind was already made up. Here was her chance. Somehow, however much Mrs Tenison tried to extinguish her, she would make her mark in London society and hook her rich and titled fish. She remembered one of the older girls saying that immediately before she left Mrs Guarding's school to go to

London for the Season. She had certainly managed to hook *her* fish: a baronet—admittedly not of the first stare—but a fish with a title nonetheless.

An irreverent Athene had once wondered how much like a fish he *had* looked. Was he a shark—or a simple-seeming goggle-eyed cod? She hoped that her fish would be handsome, good and kind as well as rich and titled—which might be asking rather a lot, but one ought always to aim for the highest...

Naturally she would not allow either her mother or Mrs Tenison to guess at her true reason for accepting this somewhat surprising offer: she would be as good and demure and grateful as a poor young lady could be. Consequently, when they were both invited to the Tenisons' to be informed of the details of her employment, Mrs Tenison thought that Miss Athene Filmer had gained a quite undeserved reputation for being outspoken and downright in her manner.

Emma, of course, was delighted. Her face shone with pleasure when Athene and her mother were shown into the Tenisons' drawing-room, and for once she acted impulsively.

'Oh, Athene!' she exclaimed, running forward to take her friend's hand. 'You cannot know how pleased I am that you have agreed to come with us! I shall not feel frightened of anything if you are standing by my side!'

'Come, come, Miss Tenison,' said her mother coldly, 'that is no way to behave. Thank your friend quietly and in a proper fashion. Remember also that she is to be your companion, almost a chaperon, not your bosom bow, so you will address her as Miss Filmer. You, and only you, are to be presented to the Prince Regent. I trust that you understand what your proper place will be, Miss Filmer?'

Athene bowed submissively. 'Oh, indeed, Mrs Tenison. I am to accompany Miss Emma as her support, not her equal in any way.'

'But I shall allow you to call me Emma in private,' exclaimed her daughter eagerly. 'After all, we were friends at school, were we not?'

'True,' said Mrs Tenison, still cold, 'but you will not refer to that fact in public. I have called this meeting today in order to inform Miss Filmer of her duties, and to make arrangements for her wardrobe to be made in the village before we leave. You, Emma, will have a small number of dresses run up in Northampton, but your best toilettes will be ordered from a London *modiste* when we reach there.'

It was quite plain, thought Athene, that Mrs Tenison intended her to have no illusions about the humble nature of her post in London. This judgement was immediately reinforced when Mrs Tenison added, 'If you have any reservations about accepting my offer, Miss Filmer, pray raise them now. We must not start out on a false note.'

'No, indeed, Mrs Tenison,' agreed Athene, dodging her mother's rueful glances in her direction, while Mrs Tenison continued to reinforce her subordinate position. 'I quite understand the terms of my employment.'

'I hope you also understand,' said Mrs Tenison, 'that other than providing you with suitable clothing and bed and board, I am not offering you any money for your services. Your reward is to visit London in the height of the Season as the companion of a young lady of good family.'

She did not, thought Athene cynically, refer to her daughter as an heiress. An heiress who was looking for a husband with a fortune and a title. While the Tenisons were not enormously rich, Emma would be inheriting £15,000, enough to attract at least a baronet—or a Viscount if she were lucky. She also had the possibility of inheriting further wealth from a maiden aunt.

Without waiting for an answer Mrs Tenison turned to Mrs Filmer. 'I trust that you, too, madam, are happy with the splendid opportunity which I am offering your daughter.'

That gentle lady cast another agonised glance at Athene. She was as charmingly pretty and withdrawn as Mrs Tenison was handsome and forthright. A stranger to the room would have thought that Emma was her daughter and Athene Mrs Tenison's.

Of course, she was not happy—but how could she tell Mrs Tenison that? For was not Athene's patron the leader of local society in the village of Steep Ride, whose word was law, who had the ear of the parson at Abbot Quincey and the assorted nobility and gentry of the district around Steepwood?

'If that is what Athene wishes...' she began hesitantly.

'Then that's settled,' said Mrs Tenison loudly and sweepingly taking poor Mrs Filmer's reply for granted.

She rang the bell with great vigour and demanded the tea board of the servant who answered. She had heard that some members of the fashionable world had been drinking tea in the afternoon instead of after dinner and had decided to lead the fashion as well.

No need to allow her two humble dependants to know how much it pleased her to have gained a companion on the cheap while appearing to be conferring a favour on them!

'Truly remarkable, m'lord!' enthused Hemmings, the valet of Adrian Drummond, Lord Kinloch. 'Between us we have achieved a *nonpareil!*'

He was referring to his employer's cravat which, after several perilous minutes, he had managed to tie in one of the latest modes. Adrian, not sure that he was totally satisfied with Hemmings's masterpiece, swung round to show it off to his cousin, Nick Cameron, who was seated in an armchair, watching the pantomime which Adrian made of preparing himself for the day.

'What do you think, Nick?' he asked anxiously. 'Will it do?'

If Adrian was tricked out almost beyond current fashion in his desire to be recognised as one of London society's greatest pinks, Nick showed his contempt for such frivolities by dressing as casually as though he were back at home in the Highlands of Scotland—a country which Adrian had not visited for many years.

'Who,' Adrian always declaimed theatrically when asked why he had never returned to his family's place of origin since he had left it when little more than a boy, 'would wish to be stranded in such a wilderness?'

Now Nick put his head on one side and said in a voice as considered as though he were being asked a serious question about the current state of the war in Europe, 'Do you really want my honest opinion, Adrian?'

'Indeed, Nick. I would value it.'

'Then I wonder why you spend so much of your time worrying about the exact way in which a large piece of cloth is arranged around your neck. Would not a simple bow suffice? And also save you a great deal of heartache.'

Adrian said stiffly, for once reminding Nick of the difference in their social standing, 'It is all very well for you to ignore the dictates of society, but I have a position to keep up. It would not do for *me* to go around dressed like a gamekeeper.'

'I scarcely look like one,' murmured Nick, examining his perfectly respectable, if somewhat dull, navy-blue breeches, coat, simple cravat and shining boots from Lobbs. 'But I do take your point. The Earl of Kinloch must present himself as the very maypole of fashion.'

There had been a time when the two young men had been boys together when such a set-down from Nick would have had them rolling on the ground in an impromptu battle: Adrian struggling to make Nick take back the implied insult and Nick striving to justify it. Afterwards they would rise, shake hands and remain friends. Nick had a bottom of good sense which Adrian always, if dimly, respected and on many occasions had saved the pair of them from the wrath of their seniors.

Hemmings said helpfully, 'I think, m'lord, that a little tweak to the left would improve what might already be seen as satisfactory, but which would make it superb. Allow me.'

Adrian turned round; Hemmings duly tweaked. Adrian, admiring the result in the mirror, said to Nick, 'There, that is exactly the sort of adjustment which I was asking you to supply. A fellow cannot really see it for himself—he takes his own appearance for granted.'

'True,' said Nick lazily. 'May I ask why you are so bent on displaying yourself to your best advantage today?'

'I'm driving us to Hyde Park, of course. There, one must be seen to be caring of one's appearance, as you would allow, I am sure.'

'We have been to the park before, but seldom after such a brouhaha. May one know why?'

Adrian signalled to Hemmings that, his work over, he might leave, and came and sat opposite his cousin. This was a somewhat difficult feat since he chose to wear his breeches so tightly cut that sitting down became almost perilous. On the other hand the breeches showed off a pair of splendid legs—the whole point of the exercise.

'The truth is,' he said, 'that my mother has been besieging me again about marriage. She is becoming so wearisome on the subject that I fear that I must give way and oblige her. She does have a point in that I am the last of the Kinlochs and when I pop off there will be no one left to assume the title if I don't oblige. I intend to look over all the available heiresses who possess some sort of beauty. I couldn't marry an ugly woman, however rich, because if I did I shouldn't be able to oblige Mama over the business of offspring. My wife must be as attractive as my dear Kitty. A pity that I can't marry *her*—no difficulty about offspring, then.'

'My dear Kitty' was Adrian's ladybird, whom he had set up in rooms in the fashionable end of Chelsea and to whom he was as loyal as though she were his wife. A great deal more loyal, in fact, than many members of the aristocracy were to their legitimate wives.

'Mmm,' said Nick gravely, suppressing a desire to laugh at this artless confession. 'I do see your point.

Very well, I will come with you and help you to make a list of all those young ladies whom you might consider eligible.'

'Excellent!' exclaimed Adrian. 'I knew that you would be able to assist me if you put your mind to it.'

He rose. 'Tallyho and taratantara! Let's make a start, then. The sooner I find a wife the sooner Mama will cease to badger me.'

'I would point out,' offered Nick, slipping an arm through his cousin's, 'that the Season has barely started and all the new beauties who will be on offer have not yet arrived. I shouldn't be too hasty, if I were you.'

'There is that,' agreed Adrian happily. 'Besides, what about you, Nick? Shall you join me in this exercise? I know that your parents never badger you about providing Strathdene Castle with an heir, but you really should, you know. After all, it's years since that wretched business with Flora Campbell—time to forget it. Perhaps I could badger you. It's time I badgered you about something. You have had your own way with me for far too long.'

'Badger away,' said Nick easily, refusing to rise to Adrian's comment about Flora. 'I am quite happy to remain single. I've never yet met the woman I would care to live with—or whom I could trust—but who knows, this Season might be different.'

He didn't really believe what he was saying. 'That wretched business with Flora Campbell' had inevitably, and permanently, coloured all his feelings about women of every class, but it would not do to tell Adrian that. What he would do was look after Adrian now that the inevitable fortune-hunters were circling round to secure him as a husband for their daughters.

All in all they were as unalike as two men could be. Nick was dark, dour, clever and cynical; Adrian was bright, fair, trusting and relatively simple-minded. Their only resemblance lay in their height: they were both tall. Adrian had once said in a rare fit of understanding, 'If I were King, I'd appoint you Prime Minister, Nick. We'd make a rare team.'

So they would, Nick had thought. They were closer than brothers and nothing had yet come between them. Now, he slipped an arm through Adrian's and they walked to the stables where Adrian's new and splendid two-horse curricle was waiting.

CHAPTER ONE

'For goodness sake, Emma, do stand up straight,' hissed Mrs Tenison at her daughter. 'Do not hang your head. Take Athene as your model. She at least is aware of the proper carriage of a gentlewoman.'

'I'll try, Mama,' faltered Emma, 'but you know how much I dislike crowds.'

'Enough of such whim-whams,' commanded Mrs Tenison severely. 'Be ready to curtsey to your hostess when you reach the top of the stairs. And you, Athene, remember to stand a little to our rear and refrain from drawing attention to yourself.'

'Of course, Mrs Tenison,' said Athene submissively.

They were at Lady Leominster's ball which, although it was always held in mid-April, was the first truly grand event of the Season when everyone who was anyone had finally arrived in London, and everyone who was anyone would be present at it. The Tenisons had previously attended, under the wing of

Lady Dunlop, who accompanied them everywhere, several minor functions where they had met no one of any consequence and all of the young gentlemen present appeared to be already married.

Emma was looking modestly charming, but provincial, in her pale pink gauze dress, made in Northampton. She was wearing on her blonde curls a wreath of red silk rosebuds nestling amid their pale green leaves. Her jewellery was modest: a pearl necklace and two small pendant pearl earrings. Mrs Tenison possessed enough good sense to realise that the famous Tenison parure made up of large emeralds surrounded by diamonds would have appeared garish if worn by her delicate-looking daughter. The misery of it was that they would merely have served to enhance Athene's looks had she been entitled to wear them.

She had also made sure that Athene would not diminish Emma by having her attired in a dark grey, high-necked silk dress of even more antique cut than Emma's. Finally to extinguish her, as though she were an over-bright candle which needed snuffing, Athene had been made to wear a large linen and lace duenna's cap which covered her beautiful dark hair and hid half of her face. As a final gesture to remind Athene of her subordinate position, her hair had been scraped so tightly back from her face, and bound so severely, that its deep waves had disappeared and would not have been seen even without the ugly cap.

Athene had borne all this with patience, since it

was the only way in which she would ever be able to attend anything half so grand as the Leominsters' ball. Her party was surrounded by all the greatest names in the land on their long and slow walk up the grand staircase. Mr and Mrs Tenison had already spoken to several cousins, including their most grand relative of all, the Marquis of Exford.

Athene liked Mr Tenison. Unlike his wife he always spoke to her kindly, and when he had found her reading in the library of his London house shortly after they had arrived in town he had been pleased to discover that, unlike Emma and Mrs Tenison, she had a genuine interest in its contents.

He had taken to advising her on what to read, and had provided her with a book-list of recommended texts. On those afternoons when Emma and her mother visited friends and relatives, leaving Athene behind, since her guardianship and support was not needed on these minor social occasions, he enjoyed listening to her opinion of her latest excursion into the world of learning. He had already discovered that she had a good grasp of Latin and had lamented to him that ladies were not supposed to learn Greek.

Today, when they had been alone together in the drawing-room before the Tenisons had set off for Leominster House in Piccadilly he had said, 'Good gracious, my dear Miss Filmer. Is there really any need for you to wear anything quite so disfiguring as your present get-up?'

Athene had lowered her eyes. She had no wish to

provoke the unnecessary battle which would follow any attempt at intervention on her behalf by Mr Tenison. More than that, she was already aware that he always lost such encounters. Worldly wisdom also told her that Mrs Tenison might become suspicious of her husband's intentions towards her if he chose to become too openly friendly with the unconsidered Miss Filmer.

'It is important,' she said quietly, 'that I do not attempt to outshine my dear little Emma in any way, nor lead any gentleman to imagine that I am present in London in order to look for a husband, since I have no dowry. My duty is to look after her and give her the courage to enjoy herself in a crowded room. You must know how distressed she becomes whenever she is in a crowd.'

He had nodded mournfully at her. 'Yes, I am well aware of why my wife has asked you to accompany us, but I cannot say that I quite approve of you being made to look twice your age.'

'That is part of the bargain to which I agreed,' said Athene, astonished at her own duplicity and at her ability to play the humble servant so successfully. 'I beg of you not to trouble yourself on my account.'

'So be it, if that is what you wish,' he had said, and his wife's entrance, towing along a reluctant Emma who was suffering from a severe case of stage-fright at the prospect of being among so many famous people, had put an end to the conversation.

Now, looking around the huge ballroom, aglow

with light from a myriad of chandeliers beneath which splendidly dressed men and women talked, walked and danced, Athene felt like the man in the old story who said that the most amazing thing about the room in which he found himself was that he was in it.

Stationed as she was, standing behind the Tenisons, who were of course, all seated, she wondered distractedly how she was to begin her own campaign. It was going to be much more difficult than she had imagined. No doubt in his early days Napoleon Bonaparte himself must have had such thoughts, but look where he had ended up—as Emperor of France!

Well, her ambition was not so grand as his, and she would be but a poor thing if she made no efforts to attain it. Perhaps in the end it would all be a matter of luck, and occasionally giving luck a helping hand. Yes, that was it.

One thing, though, was plain. Tonight there was no lack of young and handsome men, many of whom were giving young girls like Emma bold and assessing looks—doubtless wondering how large their dowry was and whether they were worth pursuing. Thinking about dowries made her more than ever conscious that not only did she not possess one, but she also had the disadvantage of ignoble birth to overcome—if anyone ever found that out that she was illegitimate, that was.

To drive away these dreary thoughts she peered around the room from beneath her disfiguring cap, trying to discover if there was anyone present whom she might find worth pursuing.

There were a large number of men of all ages in uniform—was that where she ought to look for a possible husband, or should she try for one of the many beaux present? Perhaps an old beau might be more of an opportunity for her than a young one? The very thought made her shudder.

Emma looked over her shoulder at her and said plaintively, 'I wish that you were sitting beside me, Athene. I should not feel quite so sick.'

'Nonsense,' said Mrs Tenison robustly. 'You ought to be on your highest ropes at being here at all. Besides, I think that you may already have been found a partner. Cousin Exford expressly told me that he would introduce us to some suitable young men and here he comes with two splendid-looking fellows.'

Emma gave a small moan at this news. Athene, however, turned her grey eyes on the approaching Marquis of Exford and his companions to discover whether Mrs Tenison's description of them was at all apt.

Well, one of them, at least, was splendid. He was quite the most beautiful and well-dressed specimen of manhood she had ever seen, being blond, tall and of excellent address. The young man with him, however, could scarcely be described as splendid-looking in any way: formidable was a better word. He was tall, but he was built like a bruiser—as Athene had already learned boxers were called. He was as dark as his friend was fair, his face was strong and harsh, rather than Adonis-like, and his hair and eyes were as black as night.

Indeed, Athene found herself murmuring, 'Night and day.'

Mr Tenison overheard her and, turning his head a little in her direction, remarked in a voice equally low, 'Acute as ever, my dear—but which is which?'

This cryptic remark would have set Athene thinking if the Marquis had not already begun his introductions when the Tenison party stood up. Athene, already standing, wondered what piece of etiquette was demanded from her which would acknowledge the superior social standing of the Marquis and his guests. A small bob of the head might suffice, so she duly, and immediately, bobbed.

The slow dance of formalities began. It appeared that the fair young man was Adrian Drummond, Lord Kinloch, from Argyll, and that his companion was Mr Nicholas Cameron of Strathdene Castle in Sutherland. Emma blushed and stammered at them. The lowly companion was introduced as an afterthought. Nick and Adrian had spent the early part of the evening discreetly inspecting those young women present whom they had not seen before. As usual they had found little to please them. Nick indeed had gone so far as to mutter to Adrian, 'I don't think much of the current crop of beauties if this is the cream of it.'

Adrian had replied dolefully, 'Lord, yes. Mother is

going to be disappointed again. Not one of them is a patch on Kitty.'

His cousin could not but agree with him, and when their mutual relative, the Marquis of Exford, had come up to them saying enthusiastically, 'There's a pretty little filly here tonight that I think you two rogues ought to meet. That is, if you're both determined to marry, which Kinloch here says that you are,' Nick had groaned, 'Let him speak for himself—I'm in no great hurry to acquire a leg-shackle.'

Exford smiled mockingly. 'They're taking bets in the clubs that both of you will be hooked by the Season's end. If you really meant what you said, Cameron, I'll lay a few pounds on you *not* being reeled in. Let me know if you change your mind.'

Nick was not sure that he cared for being the subject of gossip and bets made by bored and light-minded men. Adrian, however, had smirked a little, much as he was now doing at Emma.

'Charmed to make your acquaintance,' he was saying, and he was not being completely untruthful. She was after all one of the best of the poor crop which he had so far encountered, being blonde and pretty if a touch pale. He thought that if he married her, providing himself with an heir was not going to be too difficult a task. Exford had also told him on the way over that she had a useful, if not a grand, portion.

Not of course, that that mattered overmuch. Owning half of Scotland—only the Duke of Sutherland was richer than Adrian—meant that he was able to indulge his fancy where a bride was concerned.

Athene realised from Emma's flutterings that she was finding this gorgeous specimen overwhelming: he was so different from the callow young men whom she had met at Assembly dances at home. When he bent down from his great height and said softly, 'I am already claimed for the first few dances, Miss Tenison, but I should be enchanted if you would stand up with me in the quadrille,' she went an unlovely scarlet, looked frantically first at Athene and then at her beaming mama, before saying, 'You do me too great an honour, Lord Kinloch.'

'Not at all,' he swiftly, and gallantly, replied. 'It is you who are doing me the honour, Miss Tenison.'

At this, Emma blushed again and agreed to stand up with him. Satisfied, Adrian said, still gallant, 'You will forgive me, I trust, if I leave you now. I must find my partner for the next dance. I shall be sure to visit you in good time for ours.'

Nick said to him when they strolled away to find their partners, 'I thought that she was going to faint when you asked her to dance. Are you sure that you wish to pursue such a shy creep-mouse? I will allow that she is pretty enough for you, but she would not be my choice for a wife.'

'Oh, I like 'em shy,' said his cousin, 'while you, you dog, like them talkative and striking—or in need of assistance in some way. I half-thought that you might have offered the companion a turn on the floor—it must be a great bore to stand up all night watching out for her charge.'

'You mean grey-eyed Pallas,' said Nick. 'One can only just detect the colour of Miss Filmer's eyes under that horrendous cap. She has a good figure, though, and by the cut of it she is not much older than her charge. Odd, that.'

'Pallas?' queried Adrian, puzzled. 'I thought that Emma's father said that her name was Athene.'

Nick laughed. It was patent that if Adrian had learned anything about the mythology of the ancient Greeks while he was at Oxford he had promptly forgotten it. 'Athene was the goddess of wisdom in the ancient world,' he said, 'and one of her names was grey-eyed Pallas. She had an owl as an attendant, too. I wonder if Miss Filmer sports one.'

'Should think not,' complained Adrian, 'not much use at a ball, owls. Nor at the theatre, either,' he added as an afterthought. 'You do come out with some weird things, Nick.'

Behind them Mrs Tenison was busily reproaching Emma for being so backward in welcoming Lord Kinloch's advances.

'I wonder at you, child, I really do. A handsome young man of great fortune makes a fuss of you and all that you can do is blush and stutter. Here is your great chance. Be sure to talk to him if he chooses to talk to you, and if he wishes to meet you again then by all means accept any invitation he cares to make.'

'But I really do feel sick, Mama,' faltered Emma. 'It is very hot in here—and he is so…so…'

She wanted to say that Adrian frightened her because he was like a prince in a fairy tale and surely he could not be interested in a country girl like herself.

Athene, listening to this, wondered why Mr Tenison did not defend his daughter a little. She thought wryly that if Lord Kinloch had asked her to dance with him she would have accepted his offer with alacrity—charming alacrity of course. While she felt sorry for Emma, she could not help feeling impatient with her. Now had the dark man, Nicholas Cameron, offered to stand up with her she could have understood her charge's reluctance.

She had not liked the assessing way in which he had looked at them. He had even examined her carefully—not that he could tell what she really looked like beneath her appalling turn-out. Was it possible that this whole business was a great mistake? How in the world was she ever going to be able to charm anyone while standing like an ill-dressed scarecrow, mute behind her unkind patroness?

Emma said again, 'I really do not feel very well, Mama,' to which her mother replied angrily, 'Stuff, Miss Tenison, stuff!'

Mr Tenison put in a gentle oar. 'Do you not think that you ought to take note of what our daughter is telling you, my dear?'

His wife turned on him angrily. 'No, indeed, Mr

Tenison. You ought to be aware of her whim-whams by now. It is time that she grew up. I do not hear Athene whining and wailing about her situation. If we give way to Emma every time she whimpers we might as well not have visited London at all.'

Mr Tenison subsided, and no wonder, thought Athene. He said not another word until Lord Kinloch returned with Nick in tow. He had cajoled him into offering the companion a turn on the floor. 'I need to get to know the family better,' being the bait he had offered his cousin. 'It would be as well to have the young dragon on my side.'

Nick had refrained from pointing out that judging by the dominant mother's behaviour the whole family would be on his side if he began to court Emma so that there was no need to humour the companion. But for all his good looks and self-assurance Adrian was basically modest.

In any case the poet Burns had once written that 'the best laid plans of mice and men gang aft agley'. Those of Adrian and Mrs Tenison certainly did. Adrian had scarcely had time to bow a welcome to Emma before she sprang to her feet, and face grey, fled from the ballroom, her hands over her mouth, wailing gently.

Mrs Tenison sprang to her feet also and charged after her. Athene was about to follow, but Mr Tenison now also standing exclaimed, 'No!' with unusual firmness and held her back. 'Her mother must care for her since it was she who has ignored her pleas for help.'

Adrian was completely nonplussed by this sudden turn of events which left him stranded on the edge of the ballroom floor, the centre of curious eyes. Nick had not yet had the opportunity to ask Miss Filmer to join him in the dance, nor was he to be allowed to do so.

With great address Mr Tenison sought to smooth over the unhappy situation created by Lord Kinloch's sudden loss of his partner, by saying, 'I am sure, Lord Kinloch, that you would wish to make up your set in the dance by taking Miss Filmer for your partner instead of Miss Emma. I sure that my wife—and Emma—would prefer you not to be discommoded.'

To his great credit Adrian said, 'But, sir, what of your daughter? I should not like to entertain myself while she is ailing.'

'She rarely suffers these turns, but when she does they soon pass,' he said dryly. 'Athene, you would consent to partner Lord Kinloch, would you not?'

Would she not! Much though she regretted Emma's sudden collapse, Athene could not help but be delighted by this opportunity to get to know a rich and handsome young peer, a true Lord of All. Adrian hesitated a moment before offering her his hand, and saying, 'I would be grateful if you would oblige me, Miss Filmer.'

Her answer was to curtsey to him, bowing her head

a little when she did so—at which juncture her over-
large cap fell forward on to the floor at Adrian's feet.

Deeply embarrassed, she had retrieved it and was
about to resume it when Mr Tenison took it gently
from her hand.

'Come, come, my dear, you do not need to take
that disfiguring object with you into the dance for it
to trouble Lord Kinloch with its misbehaviour. Is not
that so, sir?'

Adrian did not hear him. He was too busy staring
at the vision of beauty which was Athene Filmer now
that she had lost her cap. She had, after entering the
ballroom, visited one of the cloakrooms on a pretext
and had loosened her hair from its painful and disfiguring bonds—which was why the cap had fitted so
badly that it had come adrift. Even the horrid grey
dress could not dim her loveliness. She reminded
Adrian of the beautiful female statues he had seen on
the Grand Tour which he had taken with Nick.

Nick was also staring at her. Grey-eyed Pallas, indeed, the very goddess herself. No owl, of course, but
a pair of stern and dominant eyes which she was turning on the moonstruck Adrian above a subtle smile.

Now, what did that smile mean? Nick was a con-
noisseur of the human face. When he was in Italy he
had come across an old folio containing drawings
which purported to show that facial expressions almost invariably revealed the true thoughts and motives of those who assumed them. Experience had
taught him that these very often slight indicators usu-

ally told him something important about those who displayed them.

He didn't gamble very often—he considered it a fool's pastime—but his ability to read the faces of those against whom he played gave him a marked advantage over them whenever he chose to. In the case of the one beautiful young woman whom he had hoped to make his wife he had ignored some revealing signs, only to discover later that they had told him correctly of her lack of virtue—thus adding to his suspicion of women's motives.

So, what was the true meaning of Miss Athene Filmer's smile? It was not at all the smile of a woman dumb-struck by Adrian's physical beauty. Miss Emma Tenison—and many other women—had worn that smile, but not this particular woman. Unless he were mistaken, it resembled nothing less than that of someone who has achieved something important: it was the smile of a man who was winning a game of tennis, or that of an angler who was about to land a large fish.

Oh, she was a dangerous creature, was she not? A true beauty with her dark hair, her grey eyes and her glorious figure… And what the devil was he doing, standing there, drooling over such a fair deceiver, even if she were named after the goddess of wisdom herself?

He shook himself to restore his usual cold self-possession and began to pay attention to Mr Tenison, who was asking him to sit by him for a while since

both of them were now abandoned while Adrian ca-
vorted with Pallas Athene on the dance floor. Nick
was only too ready to oblige him. He wanted to know
more about this unlikely beauty. At first he and Mr
Tenison spoke of general matters: the Season, the
news from Spain, the wretched business of Luddism
in the Midland counties.

It seemed that his family, and their companion,
lived not far from Steepwood Abbey, where, if Nick
were not mistaken, there had recently been yet another major scandal concerning its owner, the debauched Marquis of Sywell. He had taken some nobody for a wife—presumably no one else would have
him—and the nobody had suddenly, and mysteri-
ously, disappeared. It had even been suggested that
Sywell had done away with her, which, considering
his reputation, was a not unreasonable assumption.

Since nothing further had occurred, either in the
lady's reappearing, or Sywell or someone else being
accused of disposing of her, the scandal had finally
died down, and would only be revived if there were
any further, exciting revelations.

'Are you acquainted with Sywell, sir?' Nick asked.
'Is he such a monster as rumour says he is?'

'Worse,' said Mr Tenison briefly. 'No, I am not
acquainted with him—who is? I am at present, however, disputing some boundary lines with him. He has
seen fit to enclose a large portion of my lands, not
that he intends to do anything useful with it, of

course, just to be a thorough nuisance to yet another of his neighbours.'

Nick nodded; so Sywell was the miserable scoundrel which the *on dit* said he was, and a bad neighbour into the bargain. He thought that now was the time for him to find out a little about Pallas Athene. So, while he was apparently idly watching her busily charming his cousin whenever they were joined in the dance, he said, 'Your daughter's companion seems strangely young for her post. They are usually middle-aged, or elderly, dragons. This one seems scarcely older than her charge.'

'Oh, yes,' said Mr Tenison, responding to this apparently reasonable statement. 'As you have seen, my dear little Emma is of a nervous disposition. My wife thought that the usual stern creature we might hire would overwhelm her. Fortunately she was able to find someone sensible who would guard her and whom Emma would not be afraid of but would obey. Miss Filmer was a few years ahead of Emma at her school and protected her from those who sought to bully her because of her timidity. It also meant that she was doing Miss Filmer a kindness by giving her the opportunity to come to London for the Season, something her widowed mother could not otherwise afford.'

If Mr Tenison was crediting his wife with a benevolence which she did not possess, Nick was not to know that. He had, however, learned something useful. The poor girl from the provinces had been handed an unlooked-for opportunity to make the acquaintance of one of the United Kingdom's richest young men. Hence, of course, the smile.

He might be doing her a wrong but he thought not. His instincts, finely honed over the years, told him that he was correct, particularly when Mr Tenison added innocently, 'Miss Filmer is a most unusual girl, since she is not only beautiful, but remarkably clever, something which my dear Emma is not. We have had some interesting conversations in which she has shown an intellectual maturity far beyond her years. I consider that we are fortunate to have her as Emma's companion—something of that must surely rub off on her.'

Nick, from the little he had seen of Miss Emma Tenison, sincerely doubted that! Mr Tenison's revelations told him that Athene was well-named, but only time would reveal whether or not he was judging her too harshly in believing her to be husband-hunting for herself.

On the dance floor Athene was busy doing exactly what he thought that she was about.

At first she was pleasantly demure, but when Adrian said in his cheerful way, 'I do hope that you are allowed to enjoy yourself a little, Miss Filmer. Standing around keeping an eye on that timid little thing must be dull work.'

'Oh, Mr Tenison has been extremely kind to me,' she ventured prettily. 'Did he not ensure that I have not lacked for a partner tonight by recommending me to you? I trust that by doing so when Emma had her *crise de nerfs* just now he has not discommoded you.'

Adrian, who was not at all sure that he knew what a *crise de nerfs* was, and hoped that it was not catching, said artlessly, 'Dear Miss Filmer, I was absolutely charmed by my first sight of you when you lost your ugly cap, and was delighted to have you for a partner instead of the mouse.'

Suddenly aware that in being so gallant to Athene he had impolitely slighted her charge, he added hastily, 'Not that I meant anything wrong about Miss Emma, not at all…' He rapidly ran down, aware that anything he said might make matters worse.

'Oh, quite,' said Athene. 'Poor little thing, it is quite an affliction with her. Crowds always seem to depress her.'

'But not you, I'll be bound,' offered Adrian. The dance temporarily parting them, he spent the next few moments thinking up compliments which would not offend and congratulating himself on having found a real beauty. No chance of not being able to provide Clan Drummond with the wanted heir if he married, and bedded, her!

By the time the dance ended Athene had managed to convey that if Lord Kinloch was charmed by her, she was charmed by him. She had given him the address of the Tenisons' town house after he had informed her that he wished to further their acquaintance. He was not so stupid as to be unaware that the

only way in which he could see more of Athene was
by showing an interest in the mouse.

Or perhaps he could persuade Nick to appear to
pursue the mouse whilst he cultivated Athene. On
second thoughts that was not a good idea. Nick would
never agree to deceive a woman by pretending to admire her. He was too stupidly honest for that.

Nick, meanwhile, was further cultivating Mr
Tenison by discussing with him Plato and his notions
about morality, until Mrs Tenison returned, a somewhat recovered Emma in tow.

'A drink of water with a little brandy in it has restored the dear child,' she announced, before looking
around her to discover that Athene and Lord Kinloch
were both missing.

'Where in the world has Filmer disappeared to, Mr
Tenison? I trust that she is not ailing, too. That would
be the outside of enough. Emma needs her protection.'

Mr Tenison allowed apologetically that he had suggested that Lord Kinloch having lost his partner, he
might still enjoy his dance if Miss Filmer acted as a
substitute for Emma.

'Indeed,' said Mrs Tenison frostily. She looked at
Nick and decided that he would not do as a partner
for Emma. He was not a lord, and she had never heard
of him. He was not on the list of eligible young men
which she and her sponsor, Lady Dunlop, had drawn
up between them.

Nick was saved by the return of Adrian and Pallas

Athene from asking Emma, to whom he had offered
his chair, to be his partner in the next dance. Athene,
delighted that Lord Kinloch was so obviously taken
by her, adopted a suitably demure manner when he
gallantly insisted on handing her to a chair instead of
restoring her to her usual humble station behind the
Tenisons. She had no wish to offend Mrs Tenison
more than was necessary. If she were to do so she
might find herself sent back to Northampton.

That lady took one look at her radiant face—so
different from Emma's pale one—and barked at her,
'Where is your cap, Filmer? What have you done with
it?'

To Athene's amusement, Adrian, wounded a little
on his beauty's behalf, said tactlessly, 'It fell off,
madam, because it did not fit Miss Filmer properly,
and she is not a dull old thing who needs to wear
something to hide her lack of looks!'

If this reproach both pleased and amused Athene,
it stung Mrs Tenison, who now had the task of pla-
cating the young man whom she had mentally marked
down as a prospect for Emma.

'Oh, quite,' she said, while looking to her husband
for guidance, something which she rarely did. 'Most
proper of you, Lord Kinloch. You may leave it off in
future, Miss Filmer.'

Oh, so she was Miss Filmer now, was she? And
Lord Kinloch had just saved her from the humiliation
of wearing her dreadful cap. She had barely time to
take in these two momentous concessions when she

registered that Mr Cameron was looking at her with the oddest expression on his face. If Nick was experienced in the art of reading other people's expressions well, Athene, who was a novice just acquiring this necessary skill, was already acute enough to grasp that, for some reason, Mr Nicholas Cameron did not approve of her.

Well, pooh, to that, he was not the man in whom she was interested, although judging by the manner in which the cousins spoke to one another it would be as well not to antagonise him.

She had scarcely had time to think this before she was astonished to find Nick bowing to her, and saying in his deep, gravel voice, quite unlike Lord Kinloch's charming, light tenor, 'I trust that you will do me the honour of standing up with me in the next dance, Miss Filmer.'

Here was another splendid opportunity to cement her new-found friendship with Lord Kinloch and all his hangers-on.

'I should be delighted, sir,' she replied, casting her eyes innocently down.

If she was not fooling herself in her pursuit of Adrian, neither was she fooling Nick. He could scarcely suppress a grin when he put out his hand to take her on to the floor.

'Athene,' he said to her charming profile. 'Grey-eyed Pallas. May one ask if you own an owl as well?'

He wondered if she were educated enough to catch the allusion. Athene turned towards him, and if grey eyes could ever glitter, hers glittered. Conversation with Mr Cameron was obviously going to be of quite a different order from that with his cousin. She wondered what Mr Tenison had been saying to him.

She decided to be honest and not pretend charming innocence. 'I only possess the name of the Greek goddess of wisdom, Mr Cameron, not her attributes. Owls are in short supply in our part of Northampton.'

'But not wisdom, I suppose. Tell me, does your young charge frequently suffer from these fits?'

There was something slightly cutting in his tone. They had reached their set, so she turned to face him before the dance began.

'They are not fits, Mr Cameron,' she told him coolly, 'and I am sure that when you and Mr Tenison conversed he spoke to you of them. I am merely her companion, not her physician, but they are, I am sure, nervous only and when she becomes more confident will pass in time.'

'And do *you* intend to help her to be more confident, Miss Filmer? I would have thought that the presence of another young woman as much in command of herself as you seem to be might have the effect of distressing, rather than helping, her.'

'Then you thought wrongly again,' she told him, sure now by his tone of voice and his expression that he was her enemy, although why she could not imagine. 'I happen to be able to comfort Miss Tenison. I have done so since we were at school together. It is others who have the opposite effect on her.'

She did not say, most of all her dominant mother, for that would have been neither proper nor polite. She was surprised that Mr Nicholas Cameron, who seemed a perceptive young man, had not noticed how much Emma's mama extinguished her.

'We are,' she went on, 'likely to make a spectacle of ourselves if we do not end our conversation immediately and ready ourselves for the dance as everyone else in our set has done.'

Oh, bravo, Miss Filmer, was Nick's internal reaction to this. *You are all and more what I thought you were: a resourceful adventuress on the make. One thing is also certain: cousin Adrian will be no match for such a determined creature as you are proving to be.*

Later he was to ask himself why he felt such hostility to the mere idea that Athene Filmer would trap his cousin into marriage, but at the time he was not yet able to consider her, or her apparent wiles, dispassionately.

The dance passed without further conversation, leaving Nick to discover that Miss Filmer's body, beneath her disfiguring grey gown, was as he had already supposed, as classically lovely as her face. He could not be surprised when, on the way home, his cousin Adrian spent the whole journey talking enthusiastically of Miss Filmer's beauty and charm.

'A stunner,' he kept exclaiming. 'A very stunner—don't you agree, Nick?'

Yes, Nick did agree, but although he also distrusted

Athene's motives in pursuing his cousin, he didn't think that it was yet politic to be critical of her. Like many not over-bright young men, Adrian could be extraordinarily obstinate, and Nick knew from experience that to oppose him at this point would make him even more determined to admire this new beauty to grace the London scene.

All he said was, mildly, 'I wonder who her people are? Listening to Mrs Tenison I gained the impression that she would not have approved of a total nobody being her daughter's friend and companion.'

Adrian snorted. 'She's a poor little creep-mouse, the daughter, isn't she? Not a bit like my Athene.'

My Athene! Goodness, thought Nick, amused, one dance and an hour of her company and he's really taken the bait to the degree that he thinks of her as his.

'I can't remember you having been so besotted with a female before on such a short acquaintance,' he ventured. 'We really know nothing of her.'

'Only that she's in good society, is beautiful and says jolly things,' riposted Adrian. 'I noticed that you were chattering away with her before the dance started. What in the world did you find to talk about if you weren't impressed by her looks and address?'

'Owls,' said Nick gravely. 'Owls. Apparently they are rather scarce in the wilds of Northampton.'

'Owls!' exclaimed Adrian. 'That's not what pretty girls like to talk about. If that's all you could think of to interest her, it's no wonder she didn't impress, or charm you.'

Nick refrained from telling him that he didn't think that Miss Athene Filmer was trying very hard to charm him, and that he, far from charming Miss Filmer himself, had been rather short with her.

Yes, the less said the better. Perhaps Adrian would grow bored with having to keep up mentally with the clever creature which he judged Miss Filmer to be. He would be far better off with the creep-mouse who would make no intellectual demands on him and who had spent the rest of the evening staring adoringly at him, but was unhappily aware that Lord Kinloch only had eyes and ears for her beautiful companion.

In the meantime he would keep careful watch over them both, for he felt certain that the besotted Adrian would be chasing as hard as he could the beauty who he hoped would rescue him from his mother's reproaches by consenting to marry him and thus give Kinloch lands an heir.

CHAPTER TWO

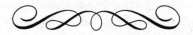

'If you are to accompany us to Madame Félice's, Filmer, then you must wear your cap, but you may leave it off when you go into society since it seems to distress Lord Kinloch.'

Of all things Mrs Tenison wished to please Lord Kinloch. He was quite the grandest young man who had been presented to Emma since she had arrived in London, and Mrs Tenison took his wish to be allowed to call on them as soon as possible to mean that he was showing an interest in her daughter.

Lady Dunlop had told Mrs Tenison that if she wished Emma to cut a dash in London society then she must be dressed by the fashionable *modiste*, Madame Félice. Mrs Tenison had seen at once that Emma's clothes, whilst considered charming in the provinces, were by no means fit for a young woman who wished to be admired when she was presented to the Prince Regent.

Madame Félice's shop was in Bond Street, that

Mecca of the rich and the pretentious. The lady herself was famous not only for her taste, but for her beauty. She had arrived from nowhere: the *on dit* was that she must have a rich protector, because only that could explain how she had managed to find the money, not only to buy such prestigious premises, but also to furnish them in the best possible taste.

Athene was walking sedately behind Emma, her mama, and Lady Dunlop, who was again acting as their patron in this matter, for Madame Félice, it appeared, did not make clothes for everyone, but chose her customers carefully. She could only look around her and marvel since, except for a few long mirrors, strategically placed, they might have been in one of the drawing-rooms of the ton. A pretty young woman showed them to a long sofa before which was an occasional table graced by a bowl of spring flowers. There was no sign of either Madame Félice or the clothes which she designed and sold. Their escort offered them lemonade from a silver pitcher before departing to notify her of their arrival.

'The workrooms are at the back,' said Lady Dunlop reverently. She was another large woman, like Mrs Tenison and possessed, if possible, even more address. She was the widow of a one-time Lord Mayor of London and was consequently immensely rich. 'You will understand that French is Madame's first language but she speaks tolerable English. Ah, here she comes.'

Madame was as elegant as one might have expected. Her day gown was pale blue in colour, high-waisted and classically cut. Its small ruffled linen collar was tied with a simple bow. Emma, who had been a little worried that she might be expected to wear something *outré,* was relieved to see that Madame's toilette was of the plainest. Indeed, she would have worn it with pleasure herself. For her part, Athene could only wish that Madame was going to design clothes for her.

It was only when she drew near, greeting them all with a bow when they rose to meet her, that Athene had the oddest sensation that she had met Madame before. This was of course, a nonsense, since Lady Dunlop had told them that Madame had come from Paris via the Low Countries some time during the last two years, but had only recently set up in Bond Street.

'Pray be seated,' she told them in prettily accented English, before seating herself in a high-backed chair after Lady Dunlop had carried out the necessary introductions. 'I understand that it is Miss Tenison I am to dress. It will be both a challenge and a pleasure, since I must retain her charming innocence and yet create something which will be sure to attract attention. A difficult feat, that, but I am sure that it can be managed.'

Her eyes roved over Athene when she added, 'I am not required to dress Miss Filmer also?'

Mrs Tenison, having beamed at Madame's description of Emma, now bridled a little at the mention of Athene.

'By no means. I fear that Miss Filmer cannot afford the fees you will be charging.'

'A pity,' said Madame sweetly. 'No matter, we will concentrate on Miss Tenison's requirements.'

She proceeded to do so. A bevy of young women were summoned and came in carrying pattern books, bolts of silk, satin and gauze, lengths of ribbon and made-up silk posies of a kind which she said that she would create for Emma. A small sketchbook and pencil was handed to Madame, who began to draw very rapidly a series of elegant garments for Emma. She showed the sketches to Emma and asked her opinion of the style and the colours which she had chosen.

Mrs Tenison, always dominant, objected to this as firmly as politeness would allow, saying, 'I would prefer, if you please, to select my daughter's coming-out gowns myself. I am not sure that she is necessarily the best judge of what will suit her.'

Emma, who had been enjoying herself immensely, and had once or twice called on Athene to help her, hung her head a little at this and looked frantically first at Madame and then at Athene, who was the amused spectator of Madame's manipulations and who had also just remembered where she had seen the *modiste* before.

From the moment that Madame had begun to draw, Athene had recognised her. She knew at once where it was that she had last seen that intent and highly concentrated expression and who had worn it.

Yet, could it be possible? Could it be that Madame

Félice, so fine, so polished, who had recently arrived in London from Paris via the Low Countries, was in reality harum-scarum, flyaway, country-bred, ill-dressed Louise Hanslope with whom she had played as a child? Louise, the daughter of a mysterious never-seen French émigré, who had been adopted by the Hanslopes in place of the child it seemed that they could never have.

Later she had been sent away to Northampton to be apprenticed to a dressmaker, and she and Athene had corresponded with one another even though Louise was some years older than she was.

Now she knew that the lonely child which Louise had been had taken delight in befriending another lonely and unhappy little girl. Later when she had returned to become the Marchioness of Sywell their friendship had been renewed and the two of them had roamed the Abbey grounds enjoying its neglected, but wildly beautiful, scenery.

The last time she had seen Louise before she disappeared had been at the old Rune Stone, set in a stand of trees which was always known as the Sacred Grove. They had been painting it from different angles and she had looked up to see that Louise was lost in the world which she was creating on paper. Athene's own efforts, although creditable, showed nothing of the great talent for colour and design which Louise's possessed and which she was now turning to good account in her profitable business.

Perhaps she was mistaken. Athene thought not. She

was sure that she, and she alone, had discovered that the missing Marchioness was not dead, not starving in a garret, but was a rich and successful *modiste* serving the wives of the great ones of the world of society!

And now little Louise Hanslope was saying smoothly to Mrs Tenison, 'You may offer me your opinion, madame, but I must remind you that it is Miss Emma who will wear my clothes and she will not be happy in them if they are not to her taste.'

'But they are so extremely simple,' protested Mrs Tenison.

'It is charming innocence that I am dressing, remember?' countered Madame Félice. 'If you are not happy with what I am proposing then I suggest that you go elsewhere,' and she began to close her drawing-book.

Lady Dunlop shook her elegantly coiffed head at Mrs Tenison, who said hastily, 'Oh, no, madame, I am in your hands. Do as you think fit.'

Athene could scarce repress a laugh at this abject surrender by the tyrant. She gave a little cough, while Emma, released for the first time from the bondage of her dominant mama, said eagerly, 'Oh, Madame Félice, I have the most splendid notion. Would it be possible for all my gowns, however they are cut and in whatever material, to be white in colour? I think that it would suit me, particularly if you make me some sprays of lily-of-the-valley, white crocuses and small freesias to wear with them. I have always wanted to wear white.'

It was the first occasion on which Emma had ever asserted herself, and Athene could not fault her taste, so far removed from the dull and often garish toilettes which had been her mother's choice.

'But...' began Mrs Tenison, only to meet Madame's stern eye, and mutter, 'Oh, very well.'

After that, all went swimmingly. Madame and Emma, between them, finished with a splendidly simple wardrobe. Athene, still amused, managed to catch Madame's eye when she was inspecting a length of white silk which one of her minions was holding against Emma. Since she was out of Mrs Tenison and Lady Dunlop's line of sight she indulged herself in a daring wink, which had been one of her and Louise's jokes in the old days. Madame did not wink, but gave her a slow and meaningful smile.

Oh, yes, she had not been wrong! She had found her old friend, strangely changed. Now all that was left was to renew their friendship, although how she was to do so in front of the two harpies, as Athene naughtily thought of them, might be difficult.

She had not allowed for Madame Félice's resourcefulness. Before their session was over, that lady, on some pretext, retired to the workrooms at the back of the shop, returning a little later with some small sprays of white silk flowers, already made up as specimens of what she could do, and a pile of paper. After a short interval she handed Athene the paper to hold, having first made sure that none of her minions was near her.

'You will oblige me, I am sure,' she said to the poor companion who had stood, unheeded, through-out the lengthy morning. 'They are some sketches I have made which might it amuse you to look through while we conclude our business.'

Her French accent was stronger than ever when she came out with this. Athene duly obliged her by taking the papers and looking through them.

The first one was, as Madame had said, a drawing of a walking dress which would have suited Athene down to the ground, as the saying had it. Beneath it Madame had written, 'You would look well in this.'

The second paper had no sketch drawn on it. Instead a short note in Madame's fine hand said, 'I see that my old friend is not deceived. Is it possible that our friendship could be renewed? Surely the slave has some time of her own and could visit one who is a slave no longer?'

The note was unsigned, but its message was plain. Madame Félice, or rather, Louise, the Marchioness of Sywell, wished to meet her, away from her charge and the harpies.

Unobserved, Athene spent the remainder of the visit looking through the rest of the papers, which were all drawings of the most elegant gowns, coats, bonnets, gloves, and even parasols. Occasionally, she showed one to Lady Dunlop to admire. Mrs Tenison was too busy agonisedly watching Emma being fitted out in what she privately considered to be the most unsuitable clothing to be able to take note of anything else.

Eventually everyone but Mrs Tenison was satisfied and prepared to leave. Athene handed the papers back to Madame Félice, saying, 'My thanks, Madame. They were most instructive and I shall be sure to follow your advice.'

Madame smiled sweetly and said, 'I am delighted that I was able to offer you assistance. It has been a pleasure to dress Miss Emma—I think that she is someone who will improve when her confidence grows. I trust, Miss Filmer, that you will be of equal assistance to her.'

Athene nodded, guiltily realising that in her efforts to attract Lord Kinloch, far from helping Emma, she was taking his attention away from her! On the other hand, there would be many young men who would be only too happy to court Emma—or 'make a leg at her,' as the current fashionable slang had it, so she was not really depriving her of anything serious.

Nevertheless, what her old friend had said had made her feel uncomfortable, and she tried to console herself with the thought that if she did not look after herself, no one else would.

She took that thought with her into the drawing-room that afternoon when Lord Kinloch—with his attendant cousin—paid his promised visit to them. She had already decided that during her one afternoon off she would visit Bond Street and renew her friendship with Louise—or rather Madame Félice as she must now think of her.

She wondered crossly whether Lord Kinloch ever went anywhere without his interfering shadow: she was unhappily aware of Nick's sardonic eye on her, even though she sat, all prim and proper, a little away from the main company. She was not wearing her cap, for after some strong—and private—words between Mrs Tenison and her husband, she had been informed after nuncheon that she was to leave it off in future.

Adrian was on his high ropes at the prospect of seeing Athene again, although for form's sake he had to address most of his conversation to the Tenisons.

'I have the most interesting news for you,' he announced jovially. 'I have decided that now that I have acquired a curricle I shall waste no time in racing it to Brighton. I intend to make it known that I am ready to accept any wager from anyone.'

'A reasonable wager, I trust,' said Nick sardonically.

'Of course,' said Adrian grandly—although no such proviso had entered his head. 'I am not so green as to waste my fortune on it.'

Nick refrained from pointing out that his cousin had had little or no practice in driving his new toy, and to race it before he was fully ready to do so might be unwise, if not to say dangerous.

It was left to Mr Tenison to say reflectively, 'I believe that curricle racing is not without danger, Lord

Kinloch. Only the other week two reckless young men were racing at full speed towards Brighton and found themselves side by side on the road in the way of a large cart being driven by a farm labourer. All three vehicles ended up in the ditch. One of the young men broke his arm and the other his leg.'

Athene could not resist asking, 'What happened to the poor labourer?'

'History does not relate,' said Nick. 'It dealt only with two feckless idiots, and had little to say on the matter of the one poor soul trying to earn a living and who had been deprived of the ability to do so.'

'I think,' said Adrian, 'that you may safely rely on me not to do anything foolish.'

Nick, knowing Adrian's cheerful, if not to say feckless, optimism, doubted that very much. But he did not wish to give his cousin a put-down before the Tenisons.

Emma, however, remarked anxiously, 'It sounds very dangerous to me. I beg of you to take care, Lord Kinloch, if you engage in anything so adventurous.'

'It's little more so than riding a horse,' declaimed Adrian, who had already had this argument with Nick and was determined not to be put off something which was so dear to his heart. 'Lots of fellows have raced to Brighton without coming to grief.'

Athene privately thought that Adrian was hardly the man to succeed in a venture which needed both skill and judgement beyond the common run, but she decided to say nothing, until Nick came out somewhat provocatively with, 'And you, Miss Filmer, what do you think of Lord Kinloch's engaging in this tricky pastime?'

'That it is not for me to question his judgement in the matter, since I have not yet seen him driving his curricle. If and when he feels that he is ready to take on all comers, then we must respect his decision.'

Nick could not help thinking, his expression growing more sardonic than ever, that Miss Filmer ought to be a man and then her talent for tactful and double-dealing answers could be put to practical use. His respect for her intellect grew as rapidly as his dislike for her apparent duplicity!

'Bravo, Miss Filmer,' said Adrian, who was quite unaware of the nuances in Athene's answer. 'So happy to see that not all of my friends are killjoys. You will be sure to cheer me on when I do decide to race.'

'Indeed, Lord Kinloch.'

'Come, come,' he said, beaming around on them all, 'since you are now my friends I must be Adrian to the ladies and Kinloch to you, sir,' he ended, addressing Mr Tenison.

Such gracious condescension was meat and drink to Emma's mother. Unaware that Athene was M'lord's real target and not Emma, she drowned him in effusive thanks, already thinking of the happy day when she would be able to speak of Emma to her friends as 'My daughter, Lady Kinloch'. She had,

however, already added Nick to her lengthy list of
people whom she disliked.

Mr Tenison remarked dryly, 'Nevertheless,
Kinloch, I am bound to support Mr Cameron's reservations about the wisdom of your trying to race
after such a short period of practice.'

His wife said sharply, 'It is just like you, Mr
Tenison, to throw cold water over young people's
pleasures. I am sure that Lord Kinloch knows what
he is doing. We shall certainly cheer you on whenever
you do race you may be sure of that, m'lord!'

Conversation, which had been general, now became particular. Adrian addressed himself to the three
women, while Mr Tenison quietly continued his conversation of the previous evening with Nick, which
had been interrupted by Emma's return.

'If the others would not consider it impolite, I
would like to invite you to take a short turn in my
library. I have a rare edition there of Burton's
Anatomy of Melancholy, of which we spoke last
night and which you might like to inspect.'

Adrian, overhearing this, said benevolently, 'By all
means, sir. Take Nick to the library. Grubbing among
the books will restore his high spirits.'

Nick said slowly, 'If our hostess agrees...'

Mrs Tenison rapidly interrupted him. 'By all
means, Mr Tenison. We must keep our guests happy.'

She was delighted to learn that she and Emma—
and Filmer, of course, but she didn't count—were to
be left alone with Adrian. She was even more de-

lighted when Nick, the spirit of mischief moving in him, added, 'On one condition, sir: that Miss Filmer accompanies us. I gather from something you said last night that she is something of a bookworm, too.'

Now, what's *his* little game, thought Athene inelegantly, and furiously. Oh yes, I have it, he's moving me from Adrian's orbit so that he is compelled to concentrate on Emma, and not me.

There was no way, however, in which she could refuse such an offer, which was enthusiastically seconded by Mr Tenison who thought—wrongly—that it would be a great opportunity for Athene not to have to join in the vapid conversation which would surely follow when the only persons of sense were removed from the room.

Nick, a subtle smile on his face, held out his arm to what he knew was the reluctant Athene, who was compelled to present a smiling face to the world at being singled out for such an honour. He knew that on the way home Adrian would roast him mightily for removing Athene from a place where he could see and worship her from afar. After all, had she not virtually approved of his decision to race to Brighton when everyone else had been so dashed dispiriting over the matter?

Adrian would like to bet that if ladies were encouraged to race curricles Athene would be a splendid performer. The image of her urging her team on entranced him so much that he barely heard what the two Tenison women were saying to him. Or rather,

Mrs Tenison, for Emma merely sat there, silently worshipping his handsome presence much as he had been worshipping Athene's.

Athene, meanwhile, was listening to Nick and Mr Tenison talk about Burton, whose book she had not yet read although Mr Tenison had recommended it to her. He had fetched it from its shelf and laid it on the big map table which stood in front of the window for Nick to inspect it.

After a short—and enthusiastic—examination of it, while Athene stood by, Nick said, 'I fear that we may be boring Miss Filmer.'

Athene returned, a trifle sharply, 'Not at all. I find it most interesting to listen to Mr Tenison—he offers me an education which I would not otherwise have achieved.'

Mr Tenison smiled at this and murmured, 'You see, sir, she is truly named Athene, and like the great Pallas herself no one could call her a bluestocking.'

'No, indeed,' agreed Nick. 'Miss Filmer is neither plain nor noisy—a very model of rectitude.'

Athene could have hit him. She now knew him well enough to know that he was roasting her. Mr Tenison was taking Nick's words at face value, and nodding vigorous agreement.

He removed the copy of Burton, reached down to a low shelf on which stood a run of giant folios, and lifted out one which he laid reverently on the table before opening it and saying to the pair of them, 'I'm sure that you would find this splendid volume of great interest. It contains the most wonderful engravings of all the Greek gods, including Athene who is pictured here with her owl.'

That owl again! For the first time Nick and Athene exchanged a smile at its reappearance. The smile's effect on them both was electric. Nick's harsh face, which Athene had always thought of as sour, was strangely softened when the light of humour danced in his eyes. Its sternness disappeared, and his attraction grew as his smile widened. Athene's face, too, changed. The touch of hauteur, which was the consequence of her feeling that she needed to defend herself in the face of a cruel and critical world, disappeared from it.

Each recognised in the other a similar understanding of the true nature of that world, and each of them was disconcerted to discover that the other possessed it, too. To cover their confusion both of them put forward a hand at the same time to point out something which interested them in the portrayal of the goddess—and their hands met.

The effect of this simple touch, coming as it did on the heels of the smile, surprised them both, since neither of them had experienced anything similar when they had danced together at the Leominsters' ball. It was as though a fire ran through them. For a moment they were locked together in a universe where only the other existed.

Mr Tenison, unaware of their strange epiphany, or moment of understanding, continued to speak, taking his hearers' silence for an appreciation of what he was showing them. Athene was the first to recover from the odd bodily sensations which touching Nick had induced. She wrenched her hand away and began to rub it, wondering why in the world she had responded in this strange manner to someone whom she disliked and who plainly disliked her.

Nick was in no doubt as to what had happened. Good God! Of all wretched things! He had fallen in lust with the siren who was chasing after his cousin! He was self-knowing enough to ask whether that was why he resented her so much—that he was jealous because he was not the object of her pursuit. No matter. He sternly told his unruly body to behave itself, for once he had had this dreadful thought arousal had not been long to follow.

For a brief moment they had been together, but now they were apart again. Athene, as strongly aroused as Nick, but in her innocence unaware of what had happened to her, made what she thought of as distracted conversation although Mr Tenison appeared to notice nothing odd.

'Was Pallas Athene what we would call a witch?' she asked, unaware that Nick, now recovered, was sardonically thinking: the goddess might not have been a witch but you plainly are, to have such an effect on me.

Mr Tenison considered her question seriously. 'In our terms yes, but I do not think that the Greeks thought of her as one.'

He turned the pages and, silent, his hearers allowed him to continue his impromptu lecture until he pulled his watch from its pocket and exclaimed, 'Goodness. It is time that we returned. I have no wish to fail in politeness to your cousin, but I am of the opinion that the library would not interest him.'

'Not at all,' said Nick, and, lying in his teeth, he added, 'Besides, I am sure that Kinloch is only too delighted not to have to share your daughter's conversation with me.'

'She does not care for the library overmuch,' said Emma's father mournfully. 'On the other hand, Miss Filmer does, and as you have already heard she asks the most interesting questions.'

Nick had discovered more than that about Athene, but he could not tell Mr Tenison of it.

They returned to find Adrian holding forth about the coming race again. Before he and Nick left to show themselves in Hyde Park, to which he had promised to drive the Tenisons in the near future, his last words were, 'I am sure you will not regret coming to watch the start at Westminster Bridge when I do race. It will be the most tremendous fun.'

On her first afternoon off Athene made her way to Bond Street and Madame Félice's shop. She was burning to know how Louise Hanslope, who had become the Marchioness of Sywell, had managed to disappear and transform herself into society's most sought-after *modiste* when half Northamptonshire had been looking for her dead body.

She remembered Emma saying to her with a shiver, 'Oh, Athene, do you think that the Steepwood curse has struck again and is responsible for her disappearance, or, hateful thought, her death? After all, everyone in the district knows that those who live on what was once sacred ground do so under the threat of reaching a terrible end—and the Abbey is sacred ground.'

Athene had said as gently as she could, 'Oh, that's superstitious nonsense, my love, of the kind one reads about in Mrs Radcliffe's novels, all of which happen in foreign parts. The English countryside is not the place where murder and kidnappings occur.'

'But she *is* missing,' Emma had said mournfully.

There was no answer to that, and now, improbably, Athene was about to find out the truth. Fortunately neither Emma nor Mrs Tenison had known Louise when she had been the Marchioness, so they had not recognised her in her guise of Madame Félice.

Athene's old friend greeted her with pleasure and a loving kiss before leading her upstairs into her living quarters above the shop. There, in a pretty room overlooking the street, she rang for tea and biscuits to be brought for herself and her guest.

'Now,' she said, when the little maid had returned with the tea board, 'we may have a jolly coze together. You must be wondering how I arrived in Bond Street and I am all agog to know how you came to be poor little Emma's companion. Poor, you understand, because I can see that she is under the thumb of her dreadful mother. She is an object of pity despite her splendid dowry.'

Athene again began to suffer pangs of conscience when she thought of how hard she was scheming to make Adrian Kinloch propose to her and not to Emma.

She tried to dismiss them by saying, 'Oh, my story is simple. Mrs Tenison had enough common-sense to grasp that if she gave Emma another taskmistress as hard as she is herself, the poor child would have been extinguished. In the guise of being kind to Mama and myself, she offered me bed and board for the Season in return for acting as Emma's companion.'

'You mean that the old baggage is not paying you?' gasped Louise incredulously. 'She is treating you worse than she would a servant!'

'Indeed, but since I am by way of being a gentlewoman the pretence is that it would not be proper to offer me a fee. Do not worry overmuch on my behalf, though. Mr Tenison is kind and gives me free run of the library and his conversation.'

'I trust that he is not too kind,' said Louise suspiciously. 'Gentlemen of a certain age, particularly when they have wives like Mrs T., are not to be trusted near pretty young ladies of any age. And despite your appalling clothing you are a very pretty young lady indeed.'

'Well, so far he has said and done nothing wrong,

and somehow, I don't think he will. But if he did, I would think up some excuse to return home immediately, you may be sure of that.'

'I'm happy to hear it. I always thought that you had a fund of downright common-sense. And now I suppose that I ought to tell you my story, which is a deal more like a novel by Mrs Radcliffe than is comfortable. There was a time when I thought such adventures as mine were simply the stuff of idle tales for idle ladies. No such luck for me, though. In an evil hour, mistaking the man completely, for remember, I was still young and green, I married the Marquis of Sywell. It was the worst day's work I ever embarked on. Before marriage he sought to charm me, after marriage, no such thing. I was his prisoner and his slave....'

She broke off and turned away from Athene, who reached out to put a gentle hand on her arm, saying, 'Do not continue, my dear, if it distresses you.'

'No,' said Louise, pulling herself together and regaining her normal composure. 'It is not only that to speak of it distresses me, but I cannot tell you, an innocent, unmarried female, of what that terrible man made me suffer... Suffice that suffer I did, and in ways of which I could not speak to anyone.

'One day at my wits' end, and terrified that he might kill me in one of his fits of cruel rage, I decided to run away and try to begin a new life. After all, I had a trade, and I knew of a friend in London, the great *modiste* Marie de Coulanges, an émigré like my mother, who would give me shelter. With the help of another friend, who shall for the moment be nameless, for if my husband knew of how he helped me, his life, too, might be at risk, I took with me as much of my husband's store of gold and cash as my friend could find to give me.

'So I ran away in the night, knowing full well that my disappearance would certainly cause my husband to be suspected of having murdered his wife. It may be wrong of me, but I gloried in the knowledge that I could make him suffer as I had suffered. Let everyone think that the Steepwood curse had struck again. This time, unlike my marriage to that monster—for that is what he is—I had made the right decision. You may imagine my surprise when, with my store of money and the help of my friend in London, my success as a *modiste* finally brought me to Bond Street. For the first time in my life I have felt both happy and safe.'

Athene nodded. She was well aware of the hardships which Louise had suffered as a dressmaker's apprentice, and was sorry to learn that they had been succeeded by the misery of her life as the Marchioness.

'You never told me,' she said at last. 'You should have come to me for help.'

Louise shook her head. 'Your own life was hard enough—as witness your present position. Your friendship and your letters in the long and difficult years of my apprenticeship kept me going, prevented

me from falling into despair. Now I can repay you
for that. I cannot deck you out as your figure and your
beauty deserve, for the old baggage would be sure to
wonder where such glory came from. What I can do
is dress you with a modest elegance which will appeal
to all those who possess real taste and can recognise
it in others. The old cat will not appreciate the beauty
of such a restrained toilette. Her own preference is for
the garish, but fortunately, I have prevented her from
overwhelming poor Emma with it.

'When we have finished our tea we shall go downstairs and I will begin the pleasant task of dressing
you almost as you ought to be dressed. I see no reason
why you should not end the Season with a husband
of your own—if you can find a man who is both good
and kind. I am hoping that Mrs T. will not sell poor
little Emma to some monster with a title.'

Well, Adrian Kinloch was not a monster, but
Athene had already secretly appropriated him for herself. She said hesitantly, 'You must know that I
cannot pay you. Perhaps I could give you a little on
account…'

'Nonsense!' exclaimed Louise robustly. 'You did
not grasp what I was saying. Consider your trous-
seau—for that is what it is—as some small repayment
for your many kindnesses.'

Appalled, Athene said, 'I don't deserve it.' She was
thinking of her scheming over Adrian.

'Nonsense again, my love. Come, let us make a

beginning. I will brook no argument over this. I am your *modiste* now, and my word is law.'

Athene gave way as gracefully as she could. 'I will only agree if we can renew our old friendship as and when we can.'

'Granted,' said Louise, rising. Everything she did was done elegantly and matched the delicacy of her face and figure with its crown of fine golden hair. 'To celebrate it after we have decided on your new toilette, let us take a turn along Bond Street. One of the few things I miss about Steepwood Abbey is its fresh air and its glorious views. Not that there is much fresh air in Bond Street, but at least we shall be in the open, even if for only a short time.'

'Yes,' said Athene rising and following Louise— whom she must remember to call Madame Félice— 'There is very little for you to paint in London's dirty streets.'

The two young women spent a happy hour deciding on Athene's new clothes before putting on their bonnets and shawls and walking arm in arm down a street crowded with passers-by of all ages and sexes. Athene thought afterwards that it was the first happy day she had spent since alighting from the Tenisons' carriage which had brought her to London. She and Louise laughed and talked together as easily as though they had never been parted. When, at last, they did separate, Athene to return to the Tenisons and Louise to her shop, they both congratulated themselves on an afternoon well spent.

Athene would not have felt so happy if she had known that she had had a critical observer. Nick Cameron, who had just spent an afternoon at Jackson's boxing saloon, had been one of the passers-by. He had recognised not only her, but also her companion. A friend of his had recently pointed Madame Félice out to him in Hyde Park one day when she had been driven there in her open carriage.

'No one,' the friend had said coarsely, 'could convince me that that particular high-stepper isn't there for a man's taking.'

Nick had nodded back. He didn't care for loose talk about women in public—or in private for that matter—but he had secretly agreed.

So what was Miss Athene Filmer, the Tenisons' supposedly virtuous young companion, doing walking along a public thoroughfare engaging in animated conversation with someone who was the butt of all the fashionable young bucks and pinks who frequented London society? What price her virtue now?

He made an immediate resolution to test it.

CHAPTER THREE

'A masked ball,' exclaimed Mrs Tenison doubt-fully. 'Are you sure that it would be quite the thing for us to attend?'

'Not everyone who attends a *bal masqué* necessar-ily wears a mask—or more properly a domino, which is the half-mask which used to be worn with a large black cloak, but the cloak is not now obligatory,' ex-plained Mr Tenison a trifle wearily. 'Besides, since the Mortimers who are giving this ball are of the first stare socially, we need have no fear that we shall be compromising ourselves in any way by attending it. Everyone who is anyone will be there.'

'Most of the cousinry in fact,' said Athene quietly. She had rapidly learned that this word described the majority of the leading aristocracy and gentry, all of whom were more or less related to everyone else of consequence in their world.

'Exactly,' said Mr Tenison.

Mrs Tenison said sharply, 'I do not see the point

of wearing a large cloak which covers one's toilette. I am glad to hear that its use is not necessary now.'

Emma offered, a trifle timidly, 'I suppose, Mama, that the notion was that the cloak makes it more difficult to identify who is wearing it.'

The fact that she was ready to challenge her mother a little when previously she had always been her abject slave in speech and behaviour amused Athene and pleased her papa. Separately they both saw it as a sign that going into society was beginning to have a liberating effect on her. Madame Félice's determination to design a dress to suit Emma's taste, rather than her mother's, had also had its influence on her.

Athene had already made up her mind to wear the gown which Madame had privately created for her. It was a dream of a thing in aquamarine silk so plainly, but so perfectly, cut that when Mrs Tenison first saw it she had no notion that it shrieked high-class in every line. Its only ornament was a tiny spray of silk forget-me-nots.

'You are not to wear any jewellery with it,' Louise had told Athene when she had tried it on.

'I haven't any,' said Athene, a trifle mournfully.

'All the better,' Louise had replied in her Madame Félice voice. 'Most women wear too much.'

'You don't regret leaving yours behind then?' asked Athene curiously.

'A little—but then I only had a little, and even so, I should never have worn everything at once like some women do!'

She handed Athene a tiny fan of the same colour as the forget-me-nots. 'That's a present from me to you, and when you make a grand marriage, which I am sure that you will, you must order all your clothes from me.'

Despite Mrs Tenison's failure to recognise Madame's handiwork, Athene knew that she looked her best when she walked a little behind Emma, whose own looks were enhanced by the pretty white gown which Madame had created for her.

Like Athene's it was too plain for her Mama's taste, but for the first time Emma was feeling happy to be going to a ball, since she had always considered herself to be monstrously over-dressed before.

'There they are, there's my beauty,' hissed Adrian to Nick.

They were watching the crowd making their way upstairs. The Tenisons' party, which included Lady Dunlop, who had given Athene's dress a long look, had not yet put on their masks, which were of the simplest kind. Adrian and Nick were wearing dominoes which had come from Venice and which possessed beaks like birds that covered their noses and made them harder to identify. They were not the only guests who were wearing more than the minimum required. Many, however, like Lady Dunlop, wore no mask at all.

Nick, after giving Athene a close examination—poor Emma was inspected by neither of them—thought, but did not tell Adrian, that the elegant gown which the lowly companion was wearing must also have been made for her by Madame Félice.

He was more intrigued by her than ever, dammit! If he had had to be attracted to a woman at all, why could he not have been dazzled by some perfectly respectable young miss of good family? Even if he had wanted to marry, which he didn't, he did not need to marry an heiress, for although he was by no means as rich as Adrian he was more comfortable—or warmer, as the money men had it—than most.

Instead he was lusting after a houri whom he was more than ever sure had set her sights on his cousin solely because of his rank and money. He reproached himself a little for being so angry about this. After all, were not the Tenisons doing exactly the same for their daughter by bringing her to London and to the marriage mart of high society? It was quite obvious that Miss Filmer had no parents wealthy enough to launch her into the *beau monde*.

So where had the money come from for the dress?—and why was Miss Filmer so friendly with a ladybird of dubious reputation, for his informant had also added that she must be financed by some man with money, since she had come from nowhere and had immediately opened her luxurious salon in the most expensive part of town. The current *on dit* was that only a rich protector could possibly explain *that*—the puzzle was: whoever could it be, since she was never seen in the company of a man?

Adrian chattered away all the time that Nick was

trying to solve his own puzzle. He was asking himself why, in the name of all that was holy, were the affairs of Miss Athene Filmer taking up so much of his time? Was it only because he did not want Adrian to be caught in a loveless marriage by a woman who was unsuitable? He shuddered reminiscently at the very thought.

Once he had thought to marry a girl whom he had believed to be kind and innocent: a girl with whom he had grown up and whom he had hoped to make his wife when his time at university was over. Instead...

At this point he gave up and concentrated instead on listening to his cousin. There was no point in raking over the unhappy past in a crowded ballroom— or anywhere else, for that matter. So instead, he gave Adrian the attention he deserved.

'I particularly wish to ask Athene to dance with me,' he was saying, 'but unfortunately, the Tenisons will expect me to ask Emma as soon as we meet, and not her companion. You could ask Athene first, while I take on Emma. After that it would not be odd for me to do the pretty and take pity on the companion for whom no one else will offer besides yourself. Provided, of course, that you have invited Emma on to the floor before I could ask her again. That way I would be able to have at least one dance with Athene without anyone thinking it odd.'

Nick was on the point of saying, 'Certainly not, I will not be party to such a deception,' when, to his astonishment, he heard himself saying, 'If that is what you wish, then I will oblige you. But just this once— and no more.'

What in the world was he thinking of? Had he not already made up his mind that he would never oblige Adrian in his pursuit of Athene, and here he was, doing that very thing!

On the other hand it would give him a splendid opportunity to try to provoke Athene into saying something which would give her little game away. Yes, that was it, that was why he was agreeing to help Adrian, and not because it would give him the opportunity to be alone with Athene.

Having comforted himself with this, he made a point of going over to the Tenisons in Adrian's wake and dutifully asking the scheming companion to join the dance with him. Not that he intended to take her on to the floor—by no means. He had a better plan than that, and one which might enable him to trump all of Pallas Athene's aces.

Athene, standing mute behind her charge, aware that more than one man had looked approvingly at Louise's creation, watched the cousins cross the ball-room towards their party. She recognised them immediately despite their masks, and watched Adrian bow and offer for Emma in the most gallant manner possible.

Emma blushed and allowed him to take her hand and lead her away. To Athene's great surprise Nicholas Cameron bowed in her direction and asked in as pleasant a voice as he could muster, 'Do I collect that you do not have a partner for this dance, Miss Filmer? If so I would be honoured to take you on to the floor.'

Athene offered him a small bow. 'It would be my pleasure, too, sir.'

This statement was not entirely untruthful. Something about Nick Cameron frightened her, but she could not, in decency, refuse him, and if she were honest she was beginning to find him strangely attractive. Besides, it was, after all a kind offer, for no one would have expected him to squire an insignificant companion.

He was holding his hand out to her.

She took it.

Immediately the strong sensation which had surprised them before surprised them again. Nick, stifling his own rapid response, led Athene towards the opposite side of the room, where a number of couples were assembling for the dance and, more importantly, where they were out of sight of the watching Tenisons.

Instead of joining the dancers, however, he murmured softly, 'I know that this is meant to be an evening for pleasure, but you may not know that Lord Mortimer has one of the finest libraries in England. It even rivals that of Lord Holland. I wonder if you would care to forgo the dance and join me in inspecting it. It is, I assure you, an opportunity not to be missed.'

Athene hesitated before answering him. 'Etiquette would say, Mr Cameron, that I should not leave the dance floor to allow a young, unmarried man to take me, unescorted by an older woman, to visit a library—however innocent such an excursion might seem to be.'

Nick's eyes glittered behind his mask. That, and its eagle-like beak, gave him, for the briefest moment, the appearance of a bird of prey about to strike. The effect was so momentary that Athene wondered whether she had imagined it.

Her original reaction was, however, reinforced when he merely said, almost idly, 'The proprieties do trouble you then, Miss Filmer? I had begun to wonder if they did. May I assure you that you are perfectly safe with me, although whether I am safe from you is quite another matter! Our absence is unlikely to be noticed and I was doing you the honour of supposing you would relish the prospect of improving your education. I have no intention of destroying your reputation.'

Athene shivered and looked around her. His effect on her was so strong that she would have liked to run from him in order to save herself from the powerful feelings which overwhelmed her whenever she was with him. They were, however, in the open, as it were, and she could not create a scene which would ruin her—but not him. He was now gently urging her through the press around them until they arrived before a pair of double doors.

Desperately, she said, 'If I could be sure that I could trust you…'

'You may trust me absolutely,' he told her, opening one of the doors into the corridor and leading her, unresisting, through it. 'I shall be as honest as you always are, Miss Filmer. I respect, and fully understand, your reservations about joining me in the Mortimers' library and will behave like a perfect gentleman at all times.'

Reason informed her that if Mr Nicholas Cameron truly respected her he would not try to persuade her to break the conventions which ruled the lives of women of their class. Reason also said, in an even more convincing voice, might it not be useful to find out exactly why he dislikes you so much? For she was sure that he did dislike her, from the manner in which he always examined her with hooded eyes. A private conversation with him might enable her to discover why he did.

More than that, was he also sharing the peculiar sensations which coursed through her whenever he touched her? Or were they simply something odd which she was experiencing? It could not be, surely, that she found him attractive, since he was the exact opposite in appearance and behaviour of the imaginary heroes who had filled her daydreams since she was a small girl.

He did not look like Apollo, or any of the pictures of the Greek gods which she had often admired in the drawings in the great folios in Mr Tenison's library.

Nor was he soft-spoken, charming or worshipful to her when he talked to her: Adrian Kinloch's admiration of her was as patent as Nick Cameron's lack of it was. Adrian's appearance, too, resembled that of an Apollo come to earth.

Nick, by contrast, was similar to the swarthy, physically powerful and dominating Mars, the god of war, and in Shakespeare's words, 'like Mars he possessed an eye to threaten or command'. He was of the earth, earthy, and when he spoke to her his voice always sounded as though he were mocking her and all her doings. That he was clever was beyond a doubt, and in that, too, he did not resemble his handsome, feckless cousin.

All this swirled through Athene's mind while her Nemesis, for so she had begun to think of him, led her silently down a corridor lined with the busts of Roman emperors, and through another set of doors into the magnificent room which was Lord Mortimer's library.

He closed the doors behind them, and saying, 'At last,' turned to face her.

'Now, Miss Filmer,' he began, 'we may start to know one another. Tell me, I do beg of you, by what means you have come to possess an evening gown made for you by London's leading *modiste,* when I understand that you're a penniless young lady brought into society in order to chaperon the Tenisons' timid young miss. Penniless young ladies cannot afford Madame Félice's prices.'

Her face paling, Athene swung away from him to wrench at the handles of the double doors. Over her shoulder she said to him in as fierce a voice as she could summon up, 'No! I shall not answer you. I was mistaken to agree to accompany you here. You persuaded me to do so under false pretences, and I demand that you return me at once to the ballroom. I want no more of you, or your lying insinuations.'

Nick leaned back against one of the pillars which supported a ceiling on which the god Jupiter was carrying off Europa.

'By no means,' he drawled. 'I merely asked you a question which many will be asking. My own curiosity was piqued by seeing you in Bond Street in the company of a mysterious woman who is as notorious for her lack of morals as for the superb gowns which she designs and sells. How came you to know her, my provincial butterfly? What price your innocence if you are her friend and confidante?'

Athene stared back at him, and said, still fierce, 'That is my business, sir, and none of yours. You may ask your questions, but I shall not answer them.'

She had the doors open now and was about to leave when Nick caught her by the shoulders and swung her round to face him before he released her. In that brief moment she felt the full power of his rough strength.

'By God, madam, you *will* answer me, for my cousin's business is mine, and you have made him yours. He thinks and talks of nothing else but you, and deludes that poor child and her parents into believing that she is the one he is interested in. What's your little game, madam? Or is it a big one? Pray do not tell me that you have fallen desperately in love with him. You are a clever woman but you cannot bam me.'

Athene's answer was as fierce as his question. 'I have no wish to bam you, sir, nor anyone else. It is *you* who have bammed *me* by luring me hither on pretence of inspecting Lord Mortimer's library in order to treat me as though you were a hanging judge and I were a convicted criminal in your court.'

Nick was full of a reluctant admiration for her fierce spirit, which had transformed her face so that she looked lovelier than ever. It was taking him all his strength of will not to fall upon her, to take her into his arms. Instead he continued to admonish her, reminding himself that, on the evidence, he was right to do so.

'Oh, madam, I think you would do well in a worthier cause than that on which you are embarked. The goddess after whom you were named could then be proud of you. Alas, I cannot believe that you are being honest with me—or with your employers—over your pursuit of my cousin or the origin of the clothes which you are wearing.'

'I repeat, sir. It is no business of yours who makes my clothes, any more than I have the right to choose your tailor and boot-maker. If I were to assume that right I should make sure that you would look less like an unmade bed and more like the cousin of one of society's finest beaux—for whom I happen to have formed a *tendre!*'

'Oh, brave,' was his answer to that. 'Nevertheless, I know full well that you are not telling me the truth so far as your feelings for my cousin are concerned— and I intend to prove that I am right.'

Athene, who had been ready to leave, and to return to the ballroom alone—and damn the consequences— made the mistake of saying, 'Indeed, and how *do* you intend to prove that?'

'Like this,' he said, and before she could stop him he had his arms around her and his mouth on hers. His desire for her, increased by her fiery resistance, had completely overcome his discretion, and worse than that—his honour.

Athene had never been kissed before, other than by her mother, and certainly never by a man. Her first impulse was to pull away from him, but the sensations which had previously run through her when they had simply touched hands now overwhelmed her so much that her power to resist the attraction which lay between them was as lost as his.

It was Nick who ended their first passionate embrace—and solely because reason told him that they must return to the ballroom before the dance ended and their absence was noticed.

'Now, madam,' he said, drawing back and sardonically registering her dazed expression, so different from the picture of dislike which she had been showing him only a moment before. 'Now, tell me after *that* that it is my cousin who engages your loving admiration—unless, of course, you respond to all men so enthusiastically when they kiss you!'

Athene's dream of desire was broken immediately. 'Oh, you are detestable,' she exclaimed. 'Take me back to the ballroom, at once, and never speak to me again. You promised that you would behave like a perfect gentleman and yet you immediately broke your word. How can I ever trust you again?'

What in the world could he say to that? For it was the truth, was it not? He could scarcely tell her that alone with him she had proved by her mere presence—and not because she had encouraged him—to be temptation itself.

'No,' he said, his voice sober. 'I cannot deny that I have behaved badly, and I must ask you to forgive me for my ungentlemanly conduct, but consider…'

'No, sir, I will consider nothing, nor will I forgive you. I shall immediately return to the ballroom and you must do as you please, since nothing you can do would please me. Had you done as you had promised I might have enjoyed inspecting Lord Mortimer's library with you, but, as it is…'

As it was, Athene was as good as her word. She was through the door and along the corridor before Nick started after her. He was the victim of a strange mixture of conflicting emotions. On the one hand he suspected her honesty more than ever since she had, in effect, denied nothing. On the other hand he could not but admire her fighting spirit. The phrase she had thrown at him reverberated in his head—you would look less like an unmade bed—and had him smiling at it ruefully.

Oh, yes, she had a way with words, had Miss Athene Filmer. It was like arguing with a leading lawyer in the courts at the Old Bailey, so quick was she to quibble at *his* every word. Nevertheless his own honour demanded that she did not return alone to the ballroom to be quizzed by every idle gossip in society.

He need not have worried. He rejoined her at its entrance to discover that the crowd was all agog over the latest public indiscretion of Lord Byron and Lady Caroline Lamb. Consequently the adventures—or misadventures—of a country miss were hardly likely to attract their attention away from that salacious piece of gossip.

All eyes were upon the Lady and her flushed face. She had apparently started a blazing argument with M'lord on the edge of the dance floor—to which he had replied by limping out of the ballroom, leaving the spectators and the dancers all agog. By morning the *on dits* would be flying around London!

Only Mrs Tenison said crossly to Athene when she reached her station behind her, 'Wherever have you been? I missed seeing you in the dance, and then the commotion which Lady Caroline caused was such that I could not even watch Emma and Lord Kinloch! If Lady Caroline were my daughter I would make it my business to see that she did not disgrace herself in public. They say that her husband was gaming in one of the salons and could not be troubled to come and control her. It was left to her mother to pick up the pieces and not, I understand, for the first time.'

Naturally Athene could not express her relief that Lady Caroline's behaviour had managed to prevent her own misadventure from becoming public knowledge. Emma and Adrian's return to the family party meant that she had no need to reply to Mrs Tenison's petulance, since Emma's mother immediately began to tell Adrian that she had brought her daughter up properly so that she would never disgrace her husband and family in public.

'Quite so, and I compliment you,' replied Adrian tactfully. He spoilt this piece of flattery by adding, 'Miss Emma is a very unicorn of virtue, is she not?'

All three Tenisons and Athene stared at him when he came out with this unlikely statement. Nick, who had also joined the party, muttered in an undertone to his cousin, 'I think that you meant paragon there, Adrian.'

'Oh, did I?' exclaimed Adrian innocently. 'Forgive me, Miss Emma. I fear I neglected my books when I was a lad, but Nick is quite the scholar and always rescues me.'

Athene said as sweetly as she could, giving Nick a sideways basilisk stare, 'Oh, I think I like unicorn better than paragon, Lord Kinloch, seeing that the unicorn is the symbol of virtue.'

This earned *her* two sideways looks: one from Mr Tenison and the other from Nick, but Adrian, brightening up after his *faux pas,* said in his cheerful inconsequential way, 'Is that so, Miss Filmer? I must remember that in future, it could be useful in conversation. I am most grateful to you.'

He ended by giving her another sideways look in which adoration and admiration were equally mixed.

Mr Tenison made a muffled sound which could have been understood as a strangled cough rather than the strangled laugh it actually was. Nick said dourly, 'Miss Filmer's grasp of language is unequalled. She would make an excellent writer—all she needs to begin is a first-rate plot—but perhaps she has thought of one already.'

Athene was saved from having to answer this two-edged compliment by Mr Tenison who said jovially—which was in itself remarkable, for he was by no means a jovial man—'May I suggest that we repair to the supper-room? Both dancing and watching others dance are dry work, and a refreshing drink would do us all the world of good.'

It was Athene's turn to stifle a strangled laugh. She had long been aware that Mr Tenison was more *au fait* with the realities of what was going on around him than either his wife, his daughter, or his friends. He was one of life's observers and the undertones of the recent bout of conversation were apparently as plain to him as they were to her.

Emma, looking worshipfully up at Adrian, who had

eyes only for Athene, said gently, 'I like being called a unicorn. I think that they are splendid creatures, but I always think of myself as more of a mouse,' she ended, a trifle mournfully.

For the first time Adrian took a good look at her. 'Certainly not, Miss Emma. There is nothing of the mouse about you. I would rather say that you resembled a...' He had begun his sentence carelessly and could not think how to end it.

Inspiration struck. 'A robin, perhaps. I think that they are jolly little birds, bright-eyed and hopping merrily about. Is not that so, Nick?'

'Oh, indeed,' said his cousin. 'They also have the advantage of not being showy birds, like some, but they do have a rare integrity,' and he bowed in Emma's direction.

Discomposed, she coloured, but retained enough *savoir-faire* to say simply, 'I think that you both over-compliment me—but, yes, I think that I like being called a robin.'

Mrs Tenison was not sure that she approved of Emma being called a robin, but her husband was pleased. At least Lord Kinloch had had the goodness to look properly at his daughter for once instead of mooning after her companion. It was not that he disliked the thought of Athene attracting the noble lord, but he did not approve of M'lord using Emma as a diversion.

It was as plain to him as it was to Nick that Athene and Adrian were not suited to one another. M'lord would bore her to tears in a week if they married, and he would not know what to say to her when the week was up. In the long run he would probably prefer someone who would worship him, rather than that it would be he who would have to do the worshipping. Now someone like young Cameron would be a far better bet for Athene—*they* would never run out of conversation, that was for sure.

The pity was that young people never quite knew who it was that they ought to be running after. Usually they hankered after the moon when a shy star would be much better for them. He took his wife's arm to prevent her from saying something unwise, and watched with some amusement Nick Cameron hastily annex Athene so that Kinloch was left to escort Emma.

He also knew that, in the usual way of things, the cousins were not likely to ask poor Athene Filmer to marry them since she possessed neither family nor money, but at least she would have had a few evenings' admiration from the pair of them, even if it came to nothing.

Neither he, nor any of his party, noticed that, as in Bond Street with Nick Cameron, Athene had attracted a man's attention.

A middle-aged nobleman with a handsome face full of character stood at a little distance from them. Another gentleman who was somewhat younger was beside him. As Athene's party passed him the nobleman said abruptly to his companion, 'Have you any notion who the beauty on the arm of young Cameron might be?'

'None, Duke, but I can find out for you. I would have thought, though, that she is a trifle young for your taste.'

'As to that, Tupman,' said the Duke of Inglesham coldly, 'since my wife died I have had no taste at all for women, either young or old. But this particular child interests me because she greatly resembles someone whom I knew years ago when I was a green boy. I merely wondered whether she was related to her.'

Now, this was intriguing. The Duke's reputation so far as women were concerned was spotless, despite the fact that he had married a shrew who had led him an unholy dance before she had expired suddenly from a syncope brought on by a fit of raging temper.

'Leave it to me,' Tupman said. 'I promise to be discreet. They are walking to the supper room. I know Cameron and I can have a quiet word with him there about his companion.'

The Duke sighed. 'As you please,' he said with apparent indifference. The likeness which he thought that he had seen had moved him greatly, but he did not wish Tupman to know that.

Nick, Adrian and Mr Tenison were standing at the supper table, having found a quiet corner for the ladies to seat themselves. Nick was moving away from his companions when he saw that wretched gossip, Tupman, coming towards him holding a plate of food and a glass of wine.

'Hello, Cameron, thought it was you I saw in the distance. Who was the beauty you had on your arm? You always seem to be able to corner them, you dog, I wonder how you do it.'

Nick returned stiffly, 'That was Miss Athene Filmer. She is by way of being the companion of Miss Emma Tenison.'

'Oho, the Northamptonshire heiress? A little backward in coming forward is she not, despite all the money? Is Miss Filmer an heiress, too?'

'Not that I know of, but we haven't discussed that yet. She and the Tenisons are very recent acquaintances.'

'And does she hail from the wilds, too? You must introduce me later.'

'Indeed,' said Nick, desperate to get away before Adrian joined them and began to enlarge on Athene's merits, thus giving the vacuous beau who was quizzing him fuel for more gossip to spread around society. 'You will forgive me if I leave you. I must do my duty by my friends.'

He left Tupman behind as quickly as he could. That gentleman stared after him in surprise. Nick Cameron had a reputation for being abrupt, but he was seldom as curt as that. Now what fly was buzzing round his head to make him so exceedingly testy? It might be a good idea to find out.

In the meantime he would take Miss Filmer's name

back to Inglesham and watch his reaction when he told it to him.

He was to be disappointed. Inglesham was as calm and collected as ever, and quite indifferent when he was told of the beauty's name and origins.

'From Northamptonshire, you say. Hmm, perhaps I was deceived over the likeness. Nevertheless, accept my thanks for your kindness.'

One person not deceived was Nick Cameron. Some instinct—an instinct which had served him well before—had him watching Tupman return to the Duke and engage him in urgent conversation the moment he reached him.

Now why, in the name of wonder, should Inglesham be interested in Athene Filmer? For the same instinct told him that Tupman was reporting back about her to the man he was toadying to. The toadying was not a surprise—Tupman toadied to everyone great—but that Inglesham should encourage it was.

Another surprise, although when Nick thought about it later it was not a surprise at all, was that Inglesham was not the only person to be interested in Athene. Every male eye in the room seemed to have noticed that the Tenisons had brought an unknown beauty with them. Athene, without doing anything but be her own lovely self, had made the impression on society which she had intended when she had left Northamptonshire.

Louise's dress had helped her, of course.

The result of this turn-about was that Adrian's cunning ploy to ensure that, after supper, he had a dance with Athene without offending the Tenisons, came to nothing!

Nick and he arrived to discover that Athene and Emma were now promised to other interested men for the rest of the evening. Fortunately for Emma, those who arrived to claim Athene's hand and were disappointed turned their attention to her charge, who found that, reflected in Athene's glory, she was as much in demand as any other débutante in the room.

Mrs Tenison wailed to her husband when Nick and Adrian discovered that both girls were being led on to the floor by other young hopefuls, 'Whatever has come over everyone, Mr Tenison? Why should Athene become such a centre of interest? She is a nobody, and her dress is modest, to say the least.'

'But very charming, and her deportment is incomparable. On the other hand, Emma is in looks tonight, and is having her share of admiration.'

Mrs Tenison made a face. Her husband interpreted it correctly. He said gently, 'Do not envy Athene her evening of glory, my dear. Young men will cheerfully dance with her, but once they know of her lack of fortune, they will never offer for her. Emma, on the other hand, is a double prize—looks *and* money. Given time she will blossom in these surroundings, Mrs Tenison, be sure of that. No, grudge poor Athene nothing.'

'So long as Filmer does not get above herself,' his wife sniffed.

Filmer, as Mrs Tenison preferred to call her, was enjoying herself. She was not only basking in male admiration, but she was also showing Nick Cameron that she was attractive to other men besides his cousin.

If these other men did not particularly attract her as much as Nick Cameron did, then he was not to know that. Indeed, he must never know it. Adrian Kinloch was still her goal. With his wealth and power in society he could, in marrying her, give her everything which her mother deserved, and if she had to sacrifice something to marry him, then so be it.

She saw, moving through the arabesques of the dance, that he was watching her with sad eyes. The expression on Nick Cameron's face was unreadable.

Oh, the evening had been a triumph, no doubt of it. Adrian, seeing her admired by others, would admire her the more.

So, why did she feel so empty?

CHAPTER FOUR

'This arrived for you by a special messenger a few moments ago, Miss Filmer. He did not wait for an answer.'

The Tenisons' butler handed Athene a letter when she walked into the entrance hall on the way to enjoying a very late breakfast the morning after the Mortimers' ball.

The servants never knew quite what to make of her. She always behaved with the utmost propriety, knew her place—which was somewhere between them and the Tenisons—but they also knew that it was whispered that there was some mystery attached to her widowed mother.

That no one appeared to know what exactly what the mystery consisted of simply made it more mysterious than ever! Mrs Filmer had certainly arrived out of nowhere and she appeared to possess no relations, for none had ever been seen visiting her.

Athene duly thanked the butler before retiring to

the drawing-room to read her letter. She had no wish to be cross-questioned by Mrs Tenison about its origin and its contents. The only person she knew in London who might send her one was Madame Félice, and the less her domineering employer knew about her friendship with Louise, the better.

The note was short. It simply said: 'Some remarkable news has reached me. It may also have reached you by now. I need to discuss the meaning of it, and its possible consequences for me, with someone whom I can trust, and you are the only person in London I can safely call friend. I beg of you to visit me as soon as you can find the time to do so. MF.'

Athene crumpled the letter in her hand. Whatever could have happened to have resulted in such a *cri de coeur*? She would find her way to Bond Street that very afternoon, for if she was the only person Louise could trust, then the reverse was true. Louise was her only trustworthy friend and they must present a united front to an unkind world.

She walked into breakfast shortly before Mr Tenison, who arrived in a state of agitation: a state which was unusual for him. He was carrying a letter both larger and longer than her own.

'My dears,' he said, and his voice was as agitated as his manner. 'I have had some disturbing news from home. I thought that it would be better for me to inform you of it in private before you read about it in the public prints. It is sure to be in the *Morning Post* either today or tomorrow. Lawyer Simpkin tells me as a matter of urgency, seeing that I was having some contentious legal discussions with him, that the Marquis of Sywell was found dead in his bedroom at the Abbey several days ago. He had been brutally murdered by some person, or persons, unknown.'

Mrs Tenison gave a great moan. 'Another assassination,' she exclaimed. 'It is not long since the poor Prime Minister, Mr Spencer Perceval, was shot by that madman, Bellingham. We are none of us safe,' and she dabbed her handkerchief to her eyes to express her grief.

'Not that I ever liked the man,' she added, recovering as suddenly as she had been overcome. 'The Marquis, I mean, not Mr Perceval. We are surely not expected to go into mourning for him. He was only a neighbour, not a relative.'

'To be truthful,' said Mr Tenison, 'I can't imagine anyone who will mourn him. He was the most disagreeable of men. On the other hand that does not mean that I wished him dead.'

'The curse,' said Emma faintly. 'The Steepwood curse has worked again. First the Marchioness disappears and now the Marquis is murdered. Perhaps the same person killed them both.'

Athene, handing Emma her handkerchief, since Emma appeared to have lost hers and was paying the curse, rather than the Marquis, the respect of tears, murmured, 'That would be a great leap in logic. Does your letter say, sir, whom the authorities might suspect?'

Mr Tenison, surveying his tearful womenfolk and grateful for Athene's sturdy common-sense, answered her immediately, 'No. It appears to be as great a mystery as his wife's disappearance. The trouble is, I suppose, that there are many who had words with him—as I did—but one cannot assume that that necessarily means that one of us rid the world of him.'

Athene nodded. She thought that she now knew of what Louise was writing in her letter and why she needed to speak to someone straight away. She also thought that she ought to burn the letter immediately. One other thing was certain: the Marquis's murder would form the subject of gossip and conversation for at least a week before some other remarkable news superseded it. After all, who spoke of the late Prime Minister now?

'Sywell, murdered. I can't say that I'm surprised. Especially after having read the saucy squib about him that's been circulating recently.'

Nick Cameron and Adrian had just encountered George Tupman in Bond Street on the way to Jackson's boxing saloon. He had stopped them in order to pass on the news which had just arrived in a letter from his brother who lived near Steepwood Abbey.

'What saucy squib are you referring to, Tupman?' asked Nick.

'Oh, haven't you come across it? I suppose since you arrived in London some little time after it first surfaced, you missed all the original excitement it caused. It's a satire about Sywell, entitled *The Wicked Marquis*—he's called Rapeall in the book and half society is pilloried in it. It was published by one of those low fellows who make money out of such things, and it's been passed from hand to hand. If half of what was in it is true, most of the ton had cause to finish him off. The news of his death is sure to be in the *Morning Post* tomorrow,' he finished importantly. 'I thought that you'd like to be the first in the know.'

'Of all the many people who disliked or feared him,' offered Nick, 'which one would you put money on as the murderer, Tupman, if asked to place a bet?'

Tupman shrugged. 'Possibly a servant—or a Luddite, or some other malcontent. I can't imagine one of us doing such a thing. A bit extreme, that!'

Adrian said, 'I never met him. Was he as bad as the squib says? By the by, I should like to read it some time, particularly if I'm in it.'

'Worse, one might suppose,' said Nick briefly. 'I only had the bad luck to encounter him once. He was beating some wretched footman nearly senseless for some imaginary breach of etiquette. It took me all my self-command not to wrench the whip from him and use it on his sides. I was only a lad, then, and beating Marquises was a bit above my touch. It would be different now.'

'They say it's the Steepwood Abbey curse working again,' said Tupman, his eyes as round as Emma's.

'It's mentioned in the squib. You may borrow my copy of it, Kinloch, but only if you'll promise to return it. And no, you're not in it, and you should be pleased. Those who are have been given unkind names and made fun of.'

Adrian was not sure that he was happy about being left out, even if he would have been made fun of if he had been mentioned.

'So, it's true that there's a curse on Steepwood,' he finally said.

'They always come out with some sort of nonsense about curses when there's a mysterious death,' said Nick robustly. 'Who believes in them these days?'

'I do,' said Adrian. 'There are lots of them in our family history. Scotland is full of curses, Nick, you should know that.'

Nick shrugged his shoulders. He thanked Tupman for his news and the cousins walked on—in time to see Athene entering Madame Félice's shop.

'I say,' exclaimed Adrian. 'Wasn't that Athene? What splendid luck! We can make an excuse to go in. It will give me a chance to talk to her.'

'Depending on which famous gossip is also patronising Madame, it might be a splendid chance to have someone start to chatter about you and her after a fashion you might not like,' said Nick sensibly. 'Besides, what is she doing there? She can't afford Madame's prices—which is why it's a small mystery how she came to be wearing one of Madame's creations last night.'

'Are you sure she was?' said Adrian doubtfully. 'It didn't seem very up to snuff to me, rather ordinary, in fact. Can't see where the mystery comes in.'

Nick couldn't help thinking that his cousin's lack of judgement over Athene's turn-out was yet one more reason why the pair of them would never suit. Adrian's taste ran to the gaudy—he couldn't see Athene standing for that.

'I still say that you wouldn't be best advised to enter such a female paradise without any real reason for doing so.'

'Oh, very well,' scowled Adrian, 'you're always a wet blanket, Nick, but...'

'But I'm usually right,' said Nick, taking his cousin's arm and steering him away from temptation.

Inside the shop Louise rapidly found an excuse to send Athene to the workroom at the back, and having disposed of her current customer she took her upstairs again, leaving word that she was not to be disturbed for at least the next half-hour.

Instead of serving tea, she walked to a sideboard where a decanter of Madeira and some elegant cut-glass goblets stood. She half-filled two of them before handing one to Athene saying, 'Drink this. I fear that you will need it before I have finished.'

Her lovely composure, which Athene had always admired, appeared to have deserted her. She took a small swallow, shuddered and put her glass down.

'To business. I must not waste your time. I had a

letter from a confidential friend in Steepwood: the friend who helped me to escape. It contained some shocking news. I never had reason to care for my husband after I discovered how much he had deceived me into marrying him by pretending that he was madly in love with me, but I would not have wished on him what has actually occurred.'

She was, unknowingly, echoing everyone's epitaph for the dead man when the news was broken to them.

'He has been found in his bedroom, foully and brutally murdered. By whom is a mystery. It seems that he had sent all the servants away including Solomon Burneck, his butler-cum-valet, so he was alone in that great barracks of a place. If it were not for that, poor Solomon might have been a logical suspect, for there appears to be little doubt that he was Sywell's illegitimate son, and was very badly treated by him—giving him a good motive for murder.'

She paused before going on. 'He had been slashed to death with his own razor after what seems to have been a prolonged struggle. There was blood everywhere. Naturally, the question of my own disappearance has been raised again, although I gather from my informant that the nature of his death meant that no woman could have killed him. Some suspicion appears to have fallen on Lord Yardley—he had had yet another public and violent quarrel with Sywell, not long before. One problem for those trying to discover who might have killed him is that he quarrelled so violently with so many people—most of whom might have wished him dead.'

'Yes,' agreed Athene. 'I know that he and Mr Tenison were at odds, but he seems to me to be a most unlikely murderer—besides he has not left London since we arrived here in mid-April.'

'There is something else which you ought to know,' continued Louise. 'My informant told me that the authorities are beginning another urgent search for the missing Marchioness. It is thought that there is a possibility that she might have paid someone to murder Sywell because she would not be able to kill him herself. You understand now why I have sent for you.'

'They surely could not possibly suspect you,' said Athene numbly. 'No one who knew you could think you capable of ordering him to be murdered.'

'Ah, but who did know me—apart from you?' said Louise wearily. 'Very few people ever met me. Once I married Sywell I was kept almost a prisoner, leaving the Abbey only to roam its grounds. Before that I was a humble seamstress with few friends and none of them—apart from yourself—from Steepwood. Besides, I do not wish to be found—not even to prove that I could not have murdered him. That part of my life is over and done with. I made a mistake when I married the wretch and I have already paid dearly enough for it. Sadly, I might not have done so, except that my guardian, John Hanslope, thought that it might be a good thing for me.'

'But why should they think that the Earl of Yardley might have murdered him?' asked Athene, a little bewildered. 'That seems to me as preposterous as supposing that you might have connived at it. I only met him once, but he seemed to be a quiet man, most respectable in his ways—quite unlike the Marquis.'

'That is how he is now,' explained Louise, 'but he was not always so. Sywell used to laugh about him to me when he was drunk. It seems—if my late husband can be believed—that in his youth, before he inherited the title, he was as wild as Sywell was. They were part of a set, which included the then Earl of Yardley, which gambled, drank and ran after disreputable women. Sywell boasted that he had won Steepwood Abbey and all the Yardley estates from the Earl in a long gambling session which lasted for days. It had been the family home of the Yardleys for generations.

'The worst thing was that Sywell also boasted to me that he had cheated the Earl, and that when the Earl had lost everything he blew his brains out on the spot. He always laughed when he got to that part of his horrible story—he told it to me many times because he was proud of his trickery, not ashamed of it.'

Athene said faintly, 'I had heard something of this. My mother never spoke of it. She hated gossip, so it came to me in bits and pieces from giggling girls at Mrs Guarding's. But it all happened long ago and the present Earl has made a great fortune for himself in

India, and has bought his own estate, so why should he want to kill the Marquis—who has impoverished himself by his own wicked folly—even to get Yardley land back again?'

'Agreed,' said Louise, 'and this is why I wished to speak to you. You are so common-sensical and ask all the right questions. On the other hand, it seems to me that most men do not behave very common-sensically when their money or their honour is at stake, particularly when they are drunk. We can only guess why Lord Yardley should quarrel with the Marquis after all these years, and must guess again as to whether that quarrel led to Sywell's death.'

Athene was thoughtful. 'It's like one of those wooden puzzles where you are given the individual counties of England as separate pieces and have to put them together to make the complete map,' she said, at last. 'It's hard enough to do that when you have all the pieces—if you don't, it's almost impossible.'

'True enough, and really all that concerns me is that neither of us should say or do anything which might reveal that *I* am Sywell's runaway wife. If any-one asks how we came to be friends we must be able to say something convincing which will mislead them completely—but which, alas, will not be truthful.'

The two girls—for they were little more—looked at one another ruefully until Athene said, with a sad laugh, 'If I were writing Minerva Press novels I might be able to come up with a thundering lie to which no one could find an objection, but as it is…'

'As it is, I am as stumped as you are,' confessed Louise. 'I have told so many lies to account for how I happen to be here in Bond Street, under a false name, that I have quite run out of invention.'

'How about this,' said Athene, furrowing her brow, and thinking hard before speaking. 'I had a French governess for a short time, as you doubtless know. We could say that she had a little sister—you—who visited us for a short holiday once, and that when I came to your salon with the Tenisons I recognised you immediately as that child grown up, but said nothing because it is no business of theirs.'

Her own ability to concoct a fairy-tale appalled her—particularly since she could hear Nick Cameron's sardonic voice saying, 'What a practised liar and schemer you are, Athene, nearly as devious as the goddess whose name you bear.'

She silenced the voice by listening to Louise's praise of her explanation. 'That should suffice,' she said, 'not that I think that anyone will track me down, you understand, but there is always a remote possibility. One thing I have learned is that after the preliminary lie one must keep the rest of the story simple. Too many involved explanations can lead to trouble.'

Athene kissed Louise's sad face impulsively. 'Oh, what a horrid world it is when poor girls like us are driven to such extremes in order to survive.'

She was thinking not only of Louise, but of herself,

compelled to make her own way in the marriage market because her mother was unable to scheme for her. Even so, she now knew that she was in a better situation than Louise had ever been. Louise had had no one to introduce her into society, and the man who she had thought was her saviour had turned out to be a monster.

Louise, watching Athene's face change, wondered for the first time whether she ought to tell her friend the whole truth about her disputed origins. Alas, she knew only too well that Athene needed to be single-minded to survive herself, and to burden her with her own sad tale would help neither of them.

Perhaps that story could better be told on another day, when the news of the Marquis's horrible death had had time to sink in.

In the meantime all that was left to the pair of them was to finish off their glasses of Madeira and talk reminiscently of days gone by in order to forget the trying present.

'Dead! Goodness gracious—which one of his many enemies finally gave *him* the *coup de grâce?*' This comment, by a lady, was one of the kindest—and most repeatable—which the Marquis of Sywell's brutal death provoked in society. Worse, wherever one went, if the Earl of Yardley's heir was present, hushed whispers about his father's possible involvement in the murder followed him around.

Marcus, Viscount Angmering, was always easy to

identify. He was a well-built man with, like Nick Cameron, a strong, rather than a handsome face. He had a crown of unruly and bright red-gold hair which flamed like a beacon. On top of that he was of a practical turn and could never be troubled, despite his wealth, to play the society fop.

'The worst of it is,' he was confiding to Nick and Adrian one afternoon in Hyde Park, 'is that it is rather as though I have a strange disease which everyone knows about, but will not speak of. Those in society whom I most dislike behave towards me as though I am about to pass it on to them and the ones whom I do like speak to me with ill-disguised and heavy sympathy! The last person I would ever suspect of murder is my father—but that's hardly evidence is it? Just proof that I'm a dutiful son after all!'

'True, and there aren't many of them about these days,' agreed Nick, while Adrian, taking poor Marcus Angmering literally, asked anxiously, 'You haven't really got a strange disease, Angmering, have you?'

He was quite unable to understand why Nick and Marcus both began to laugh uncontrollably.

Marcus said, wiping his eyes, 'You're a good fellow, Kinloch, and I wouldn't risk your health by bamming you. No, I'm in fine fettle: it's just that my temper has grown rather short since the news of Sywell's murder arrived in town and started everyone gibbering nonsense at me.'

'Oh, splendid,' said Adrian, relieved, and then, 'I don't mean by that that I approve of Sywell's being killed—even though he did rather ask for it by the way he went on. I've just read that jolly tale about him, *The Wicked Marquis*. Nick says that lots of the fellows are in it. No, I'm relieved to learn that you're in good health. Sywell gave us all a bad name you know, helped those awful Radical fellows to tell lies about the House of Lords. Perhaps they'll shut up now he's gone.'

'Doubt it,' said Nick and Marcus together. Marcus added in a more sober tone, 'The oddest thing is that it seems that Sywell's manner of death was exactly like that in the book.'

'All covered in blood from being finished off with a razor,' exclaimed the entranced Adrian.

'Exactly,' replied Marcus. 'Either it's the most extraordinary coincidence, particularly since the book was written when Sywell was in good health—or relatively good health,' he rapidly amended, '—or the book suggested to the murderer the way to dispose of him.'

All three men reflected in their different fashion on Sywell's horrid end, before Nick decided to change the subject by taking advantage of Marcus's coming over to them by asking him if he knew the Tenisons of Steep Ride in Northamptonshire.

'Seeing that your family comes from Steepwood, Angmering, I thought that you might have met them. They are in London at present: their daughter is to be presented at Court.'

'Um, Tenison?' said Marcus thoughtfully. 'Yes, I

was introduced to him at the Assembly Rooms in Abbot Quincey when I was last there. Solid sort of fellow—a bit of a scholar. Had a chat with him about the history of the Abbey before my family owned it. M'father thought him a sound man, too. I can just about remember the daughter. A little thing, very silent—had one of those dominant mamas.'

'Had she a companion with her then?' asked Nick as though the question were an afterthought.

'Not that I remember. Who does remember companions, though?'

Adrian, who had been listening with half an ear, exclaimed rather testily, 'You'd remember this one if you'd ever met her, Angmering. She's a rare beauty, puts the little Tenison into the shade without even trying. Comes from the same part of the world.'

Neither Nick nor Marcus had ever seen Adrian so interested in anyone or anything before. Indignation at a possible slight to Athene poured out of him.

'What's the name of this paragon, Kinloch?—for paragon she must be to have engaged your interest— thought your taste ran to ladybirds.'

'Look here, Angmering, Miss Athene Filmer is no ladybird, she's a good girl, does her duty by the little Tenison, helps to bring her on, doesn't she, Nick?'

'One might think so,' said Nick noncommittally.

'Filmer,' mused Marcus. 'Can't say I remember a Filmer, and if she made such an impression on you, Kinloch, I'm sure I should have taken more than a passing interest in her if I'd met her.'

'Well,' said Adrian, still belligerent, 'you've a splendid opportunity to get to know her. I was hoping that the Tenisons would visit the park this afternoon, seeing that the weather is so splendid, and here they are. I shall persuade Miss Emma's mama and papa that it might be an excellent notion for her and her companion to leave their carriage and take a stroll with us so that you can judge her for yourself. After that I'm sure that you will agree with me that all companions are not elderly hags.'

He strode towards the Tenisons' open landau, leaving Marcus staring after him.

'I say, Cameron, what in the world has come over Kinloch? Surely he's not fallen head over heels in love with a lowly companion of all people? I would have thought he'd be the last man to do anything so odd. Not that he carries much weight in the attic, but I wouldn't have thought him as light as that!'

Nick, to his eternal astonishment, found himself defending Athene.

'You haven't seen the companion, Marcus. She is rather remarkable—and clever, too.'

'Clever! Then what in Hades do she and Kinloch find to talk about?'

Nick began to laugh. He'd forgotten what a downright fellow Angmering was, as downright as himself, in fact. And he had just put a blunt finger on Nick's own reservations about a marriage between Adrian and Athene.

He had no time to make a comment on these lines

to Marcus, since that nobleman was giving a whistle at the sight of Adrian—a young woman on each arm—striding proudly towards them.

'Good Gad, I see what he means. The little one has come on a bit since I last saw her, though. She's more than passable now, in fact, a pretty little thing. But the companion—she's a stunner and no mistake!'

Nick looked sourly at his old friend. What! This was the outside of enough! Was Pallas Athene on the way to getting yet another admirer! What, would the line stretch out to the crack of doom, as Shakespeare had it in *Macbeth*?

Marcus bowed deeply to both young women when Adrian introduced them.

'Delighted to meet you, ladies. What a lucky fellow you are, Kinloch! A belle on each arm. You told me before you went over to collect them that you were bringing me a pair of beauties, and you had the right of it.'

Emma blushed—charmingly—the days when she was overwhelmed by such praise were over. Athene said, 'You flatter us, m'lord.'

'No m'lords, Miss Filmer. I am Angmering to you—and also to Miss Emma, whom I remember meeting last Christmas in the Assembly Rooms at Abbot Quincey.'

'You honour me by remembering me, Angmering,' said Emma shyly.

'No honour—how could I forget you? I believe that

I did not then meet your companion—for I would have remembered her, too.'

Athene, noting that Nick was glowering at her—as usual—found herself liking this blunt young man. 'No, Angmering,' she offered, 'I was not present because my mama was ill, and so we were unable to attend.'

'You reside in Abbot Quincey, Miss Filmer?'

Athene shook her head. 'No, I live with my mother, who is a widow, in a hamlet called Steep Ride at the other end of Steepwood. It is very pretty—perhaps because it is so small.'

Steep Ride, said Nick to himself. I must remember that. I now have the opportunity to find out more about Miss Athene Filmer and her origins. He was on his own. Adrian had Emma on his arm, and Marcus was escorting Athene. He could hear what they were saying and it did not please him.

After a short time during which they engaged in the small change of conversation, Marcus said to her, 'You are the first person, Miss Filmer, to whom I have spoken since I arrived in London who did not look at me as though I were about to do something strange and remarkable. I congratulate you.'

'Oh,' said Athene, smiling, 'I am sure that if you wanted to do something strange and remarkable, you would, but at the moment I do not expect it of you. I suppose that it is the Marquis's murder and your family's association with Steepwood which is causing everyone to behave as though we are all in the middle of a Drury Lane melodrama.'

Marcus smiled at her. 'Well put, Miss Filmer. You have succeeded in making me laugh at what was previously annoying me. Nick Cameron told me that you were a clever young woman, and so you are.'

'Did he, indeed?' said Athene dryly. 'I suppose, seeing that he has a reputation for being clever, that I should be flattered.'

'No flattery—as I am sure that he would agree.'

Athene doubted that very much. She was not sure how much she liked, or trusted, Mr Nicholas Cameron. What she did know was something which annoyed her: that she was, in some mysterious fashion, greatly drawn to him. Whenever she entered a room or, as on this occasion, was driven into Hyde Park, she found herself looking around for him. Worse than that, simply meeting him was strangely exciting: the sensation which he always aroused in her very similar to the one occasion when she had, by accident, taken too much strong drink.

How stupid to say that the mere sight of a man could make her light-headed! It made her wonder what effect she had on *him*. She usually gained the impression that she annoyed him: his mouth always thinned at the sight of her, and the eyes which surveyed her were so coldly assessing.

Nick, just behind them, was in nearly as great an emotional turmoil as Athene. He was having the same thoughts about her as she was about him. He could not help overhearing her conversation with Angmering and, as a consequence, was more determined than ever to find as much out about her as he could.

His determination was reinforced when the Duke of Inglesham, whose carriage was parked beneath some trees, came walking over to them, accompanied by a large borzoi which he was leading on a silver chain.

On reaching Athene the borzoi was immediately as enraptured by her as most male animals appeared to be, and had to be restrained by his master from embracing her.

Inglesham said in his usual cool fashion, 'Angmering, my friend, you must introduce me to your charming companion so that I may apologise to her for the conduct of my animal, whom I have rightly named Ivan the Terrible, although he is not usually quite so mischievous.'

He bowed low to Athene when he had finished.

Another damned admirer, was Nick's furious thought. She ought to be named Aphrodite, goddess of love, not Athene, since every man appears to be ready to fall at her feet. She would not lack for customers if she set herself up as a courtesan, that's for sure!

Marcus was busy introducing Athene to the Duke—and to Ivan, who was barking his approval at her. She bent down to stroke his proud and haughty head, which simply resulted in her being rewarded with enthusiastic lickings of her hand.

The Duke, pulling Ivan away, overwhelmed her with apologies, ending with, 'My dear Miss Filmer, I can only say that I have never known him to behave in such an extreme fashion before. He has previously been distinguished by his dislike of human beings—and that includes myself. You should count yourself flattered.'

Flattery again! Athene smiled and Nick ground his teeth—which was something of a feat, since he was trying to look pleased at the Duke's advent and his conversation with them. Inglesham's reputation was that of a hermit, and he usually had little to do with his fellow men and women. It was rumoured that he had been disappointed in love in his youth, that his marriage had been desperately unhappy, and that since his wife's death he had become more of a recluse than ever.

And now here he was, making eyes at Miss Athene Filmer, and his damned dog had nothing better to do than imitate his master. It was at this point in his internal rantings that Nick Cameron realised that something appalling had happened: he was in love with Miss Athene Filmer himself, and every male animal, human or beast, was his rival!

No, it was not to be borne, it was lust he must be experiencing. Yes, that was it, lust; but he knew that it was a lie. He might deceive others, including Athene; but he could not deceive himself.

There was no doubt that the Duke was struck by her.

'Athene,' he was saying. 'A noble name: may I enquire whether it is a family one?'

'I don't think so,' said Athene, whose only family was her mother, but she could not tell the Duke so. 'My mother called me that because her father had been a great classicist and she thought the name a pretty one.'

'No prettier than its possessor,' said the Duke gallantly, again trying to restrain Ivan, who had for some minutes been gazing adoringly at her, but was now ready to lick her again. 'I understand from what Angmering has just said that you are in London as the friend of a daughter of the Tenison family who hail from Steepwood in Northants. I believe I met Tenison recently over some wretched business with the late Marquis of Sywell.'

'Possibly,' said Athene, trying to give away as little of her unhappy origins as possible. 'I know that he was engaged in some trouble over disputed boundaries.'

'Were you here on your own account I would have made you a present of Ivan, who, I fear, will be distraught when he is compelled to leave you. You, I take it, come from Steepwood, as well. You have relatives there? Your mama's, perhaps.'

Now what the devil is he at? thought both Marcus and Nick. They were each privately of the opinion that he was attracted to Miss Athene Filmer, which was a monstrously odd supposition, knowing the Duke's reputation for rectitude in all aspects of his life.

'None that I am aware of,' said Athene, who was beginning to feel a great deal of embarrassment as the Duke pursued the question of her family. Although she showed little outward sign of this, Nick's sensitivity to her every mood told him that the Duke was treading on thorny ground. What was even more interesting was that the Duke was doing it at all.

What the devil did he want with Athene?

Athene was asking herself the same question. She was absently patting Ivan's head, for that animal was now content to enjoy her mere company without being over-enthusiastic about it. She was thinking that if she had been anyone but the Tenisons' poor friend she would have gladly accepted the present of the dog. She had never possessed one. Mrs Filmer had always lived on the edge of poverty: her annuity was enough to keep her in only modest comfort, so the Filmer women had always kept a cat which was less expensive than a dog.

'Like the old witches of legend,' Athene's mother had once said with a sigh.

The Duke, sensing that he was going a little too far and too fast, rapidly and tactfully abandoned Athene and her family to speak generally of the recent Luddite murder of a merchant in Yorkshire and the sad state of the lower classes in England.

'It is the war,' he said, with Nick and Marcus nodding agreement. 'Things might have been bad enough without that and the French blockade, which has only made matters worse. Young Byron was right to raise the matter in the Lords, but while he expressed his indignation, he failed to suggest any practical measures which might alleviate suffering.'

Well, at least he's no longer badgering me about my non-existent relatives, thought Athene, but this is nearly as melancholy a subject. It came almost as a relief when Adrian, Emma on his arm, returned to greet them with, 'What the deuce happened to you and Angmering, Nick, that you fell behind...'

He was interrupted by Ivan, who had taken an instant dislike to him and had begun to bark furiously at him.

The Duke said, 'Bad dog. I must return you to the carriage. I'm sorry to leave so cavalierly, Kinloch, but I really must not allow Ivan to dominate the conversation. We may speak again another time. Delighted to meet you all, and to be introduced to you, Miss Filmer: honoured I am sure.' He bowed himself away, dragging after him an angry Ivan.

'Now, what was all that about?' exclaimed Adrian, staring after him. 'Was he the reason that you fell behind? Thought the man was supposed to be a hermit. Didn't care for the way he looked at you, Athene, nor his dog, either.'

The rest of the party refrained from laughing at his artless comment. There were times when Adrian in spite of, or perhaps because of, his simple-mindedness, came out with the very truths which the more subtle-minded suppressed, and this was one of them.

Athene remarked in as cool a voice as she could summon up, 'I think, Adrian, that he only paid attention to me because of the extraordinary behaviour of his dog.'

She was not being strictly truthful. There had been something insistent in the Duke's questioning of her, and whether this was because she had attracted him, or whether he had genuinely wished to learn of her family, she was not sure. Again, all unknowingly, her thoughts were an echo of Nick's.

Marcus, too, had been intrigued by the Duke's behaviour to Athene but before he could say anything, which he thought later was just as well, their party was accosted by an extremely well-dressed and handsome woman who appeared to be in her early thirties and was on the arm of an elderly man.

'Cameron! Nick Cameron, it *is* you. I thought it was, but Laxford wasn't sure. His sight's not what it was these days. How extremely delightful to meet you again, after so many years. You must know,' she announced addressing all her hearers as though she were running a public meeting, 'that Nick and I were playmates when we were children. Ah, happy days,' she sighed, and then, briskly, 'Pray introduce me to your new friends, Nick. Lord Kinloch and I are old ones.'

And all the time the elderly man, her husband, Lord Laxford, stood mumchance beside her.

Athene noticed that Nick, far from looking delighted by Lady Laxford's effusive greeting, had assumed the expression which he always wore when he was busily engaged in chiding her.

His bow to the lady was perfunctory, and he did not address her by her title, saying only, 'Very well, Flora, it shall be as you wish.'

More than that his manner was icy as, one by one, he made the demanded introductions to a lady whose beautiful face was marred by a pair of shrewd, assessing eyes. What interested Athene was that the person the eyes were assessing was none other than herself. So Nick's playmate was clever enough—or knew him well enough—to be aware that it was she who was the object of his interest and not Emma!

Now what did that tell her about the lady—and her relationship with Nick?

Small talk followed in which Nick played no part, even when Lady Laxford dragged him into the conversation with, 'Silent, Nick, most unlike you.'

He preferred instead to stand to one side and try to engage the interest of the Lady's Lord, whose baffled gaze indicated that old age had somewhat addled his wits. Despite this obvious fact his much younger wife frequently appealed to him most prettily, but never waited for the answer which she knew that she was never going to get.

Finally, to everyone's relief, Flora Laxford's husband tugged at her arm and muttered something in a hoarse, incomprehensible voice to which she responded with a little shriek, and, 'Oh, very well, my dear. We'll return to the carriage where you may make yourself comfortable. I'll bid *au revoir* to my new and old friends.'

With a nod of the head and a wave of the hand she moved away, dragging along her better-half, who might, thought Nick morosely, be more accurately described as her worst-half.

Everyone looked at everyone else, not knowing quite what to say. Marcus, indeed, in his usual bluff fashion, was the only one to come out with the socially unsayable. 'Goodness me, what an exhausting creature. Were you really bosom bows with her in your distant childhood, Cameron?'

'For a time,' he replied in a voice which was designed to deter further confidences.

To see Flora Campbell again, and so suddenly, had been a shock to him. Oh, she was still pretty, but had she always been so shallow? He tried to push the unhappy memories which her reappearance had revived to what he thought of as the dustbin of his mind, but found it difficult.

Fortunately for him, a distant cousin of Marcus's arrived who wished him to join his party on the other side of the park in order to assure the cousin's mama that neither Marcus nor his father were in danger of immediate arrest over Sywell's murder.

This meant that Adrian was now able to escort Athene and Nick took over Emma. He found her pleasant, but undemanding, and as unlike Athene as a girl could be.

She told him, quite artlessly, 'I was so relieved when Mama asked Athene to accompany us to London. She looked after me at school, you know, when I first went there. Some of the girls began to bully me because I was young and small, but she soon made short work of them. I owe her a great deal which I can never really repay.'

These acts of kindness described an Athene whom Nick did not know. On the other hand, he thought cynically, it was quite possible that she had cultivated Emma in order to secure her parents' patronage.

The more he learned of her the more determined he became to learn even more. Not only that, meeting Flora Campbell again had revived all his suspicion of women and their motives. He could never forget that they had once been friends, and later more than friends. They had laughed, walked and played together and he had thought himself secure in his love for her. Before he had left for his last term at university, he had proposed to her and arrangements had begun so that they might be married as soon as he returned home.

The marriage had not taken place. While he was away she had met Lord Laxford, already an old man who was looking for a young wife. Laxford was immensely rich, with a fortune nearly as great as Adrian's, so instead of marrying the girl he loved, and whom he thought had loved him, Nick had been condemned to hear of her grand wedding to another.

Worse was yet to come. On the first occasion on which they met again, some six months later, he had sought to reproach her for her faithlessness, and she had laughed at him.

The woman he had thought so pure and true had said, 'Oh, Nick, my darling, don't be stupid. Nothing has changed, we can have one another whenever we wish and when Laxford goes to his last rest, which cannot be long, I shall be left with a dowry which will make us rich and comfortable when we marry, instead of merely being content to trudge along on just enough.'

He had turned away from her in disgust, all his youthful ideals destroyed in an instant. She had made him hard and cynical, not only towards women, but towards humanity in general. He did not, could not, regret having lost her, for she was not worth having, but what she had done had changed him completely. Later, when Laxford took a long time in dying, she had tried to approach him again, but he had always refused her.

Only when she had cornered him in the company of friends, as she had just done, was he unable to hold her off as he might have liked, but the inevitable result of her having done so was that he hardened himself further against Athene.

Tomorrow he would contact his cousin Hugh Cameron, who worked in the Home Office, and ask him to recommend an ex-Bow Street Runner whom he could send to Steepwood to find out exactly who and what Miss Athene Filmer actually was.

And in the doing he might discover something that would set his mind at rest where this charming mermaid was concerned.

Or not—as the case might be!

CHAPTER FIVE

Cousin Hugh Cameron duly obliged. He had a soft spot for Nick, particularly since his other cousin, Jack, a Captain in the 73rd Highland Regiment, was a black sheep with whom he felt no affinity. 'Jackson's your man,' he said. 'He's damnably discreet and, to let you into a secret, he left the Runners because we like to use him unofficially. At the moment he's free. I won't ask you why you need him. As he's fond of saying, mum's the word in these matters.'

'You're a good fellow. Tell me where to find him.'

'Oh, and by the way,' Hugh said when he had duly done so, 'you'll be pleased to learn that Cousin Jack has been sent to the Antipodes to guard convicts in Botany Bay, so he won't be writing you any more begging letters for some time yet!'

Jackson turned out to look exactly as Nick had expected. He was a dour, stocky, but powerful man, who never questioned Nick as to why he wanted to discover everything there was to be known about Miss Athene Filmer and her family.

He simply nodded his head, before saying in his rough voice, 'You will be aware, sir, that what I may find out might not be to your liking. I always warn folk of that, since sometimes they reproach me bitterly over any bad news which I might bring them. After all, I am only its messenger, not the creator of it.'

'Good, or bad, I wish to know everything which you might unearth,' Nick told him. 'And I certainly shan't blame you if it proves to be bad.'

Jackson nodded. 'Fair enough. I like to know where I stand.'

He did not ask, 'Pretty young lady, is she?' because he didn't think that Mr Nicholas Cameron would be troubling his clever head over an ugly one. What was more, he didn't tell Mr Cameron that other parties were interested in the goings-on at Steepwood in Northants: it was none of his business.

It was his, Jackson's, though, and besides foraging around about the Marquis of Sywell's untimely end, he had yet a third, if minor, errand to carry out. The devil of it was that this meant that he would have to be more discreet than usual—the good thing was that he would make more money than his usual commissions guaranteed him because he would have only one lot of travelling expenses.

Emma was duly presented to the Prince Regent, who turned out to be a dreadful disappointment.

'He was a fat old man,' she told Athene despondently. 'And very ugly. Papa said that he had been handsome in youth but that he has gone to seed badly. A very fat old woman was pointed out to me as his lady friend. It seems that he likes them ugly.'

Yes, decidedly Emma was growing up. That same night the Tenisons gave a little reception to which only their intimate friends were invited. Poor Athene was made to resume her homely grey dress again, since Mrs Tenison had begun to realise that she was outshining Emma—nor was she allowed to sit down to dinner with the most favoured guests before the reception began.

Not that it made any difference to her admirers. Adrian, indeed, would have complained loudly about her absence, but Nick persuaded him that it would not be tactful.

'Worse than that,' he said, 'it might provoke the old dragon into dismissing her, which would mean that you would lose the opportunity to meet her again.'

'There is that,' Adrian agreed, and the moment that Athene appeared in the main drawing-room after dinner was over he immediately made a bee-line for her, his honest face glowing with indignation.

'So old mother Tenison banned you from the dinner party,' he said. 'I wanted to give her a piece of my mind, but Nick stopped me.'

'Quite right, too,' she told him, a little surprised that Nick should protect her from what would inevitably have been Emma's mother's wrath. 'I think that she is beginning to regret that she brought me to London, and I fear that your intervention might give her the opportunity to get rid of me.'

She spoke more truly than she knew. Mrs Tenison had already told her husband that she was of a mind to send Filmer back to Northamptonshire.

'That would be a great mistake, my dear,' he said gently. 'Emma is beginning to blossom, and a great deal of her improvement is due to Miss Filmer, who seems to know how to persuade her to overcome her lack of confidence.'

'But Filmer has set her sights on young Kinloch,' said his wife angrily, 'and I was hoping that he would show an interest in Emma. He will not do that while he is besotted with her companion. Not that Filmer behaves like one.'

'I agree,' he said, 'most companions suppress their charges. Miss Filmer, on the other hand, brings Emma out. As for Kinloch, you must leave him to make up his own mind. He is not, for all his simplicity, easily influenced. Besides, I have a feeling that matters at the moment are in a state of flux. Kinloch undoubtedly admires Miss Filmer, but remember, there are two parties to consider here.'

'If by that,' said Mrs Tenison inelegantly, 'you mean that when she gets the chance Filmer will not hook him and lead him to the altar, then I believe that you are gravely mistaken.'

'It is no mistake of mine,' he said gently, 'that Miss

Filmer is a clever young woman and Lord Kinloch, whatever his other virtues, is exceedingly backward in that line. Well, we shall see, but I think that you worry unnecessarily.'

Mr Tenison did not believe it would be wise to explain to his wife exactly why he was uncertain that Athene and Lord Kinloch would arrive at the altar because he did not think that her mind was subtle enough to understand what he saw as the undercurrents of their relationship. She was blind to all the hints and clues which her quiet husband was picking up, and saw Nick Cameron as only a none too wealthy hanger-on of his cousin.

On top of that, Nick's cleverness was beyond her. She did not value it, nor recognise it when she saw it in Athene and in her own husband. Her judgement of men and women was essentially superficial, and Mr Tenison feared that if she were not careful her obvious manoeuvrings in search of a husband for her daughter would ultimately be to Emma's detriment.

In the meantime Adrian danced attendance on Athene and included Emma in their orbit because that was the only way in which he could pursue the real object of his desire. Emma, indeed, was so innocent that the possibilities which troubled her mother never entered her head.

She liked Adrian, and when he started a jolly game of whist in an anteroom after he had persuaded Marcus Angmering to partner Emma while he partnered Athene, she was over the moon with delight.

The game was jolly because the players were not very serious, and Nick Cameron, a sardonic onlooker, was amused to discover how each of them betrayed their character in the manner in which they played their cards.

Marcus was all bluff aggression: he invariably overplayed his hand. Emma by contrast was prudent, but the nuances of the game were beyond her. Adrian played like the happy artless boy he was, while Athene showed an appreciation of the game's possibilities which was beyond that of the other contestants.

The sad joke of it was that, saddled with Adrian, she was invariably on the losing side. Nick suspected that were she his partner they could have taken on any pair whom the guests at the reception could have provided. The game ran out with a delighted Emma and her partner as easy winners. Emma's pleasure was all the greater because she had always previously been on the losing side.

'Now, Kinloch,' said Marcus, 'you must, as a penance for losing, pay for us all to go to Astley's amphitheatre as soon as you can book seats. The ladies have informed me that they have never gone there, and it is time that they did.'

'Pleased to oblige,' grinned Adrian, telling himself that it would be a splendid opportunity for him to hold Athene's hand in the dark of the box—why, he might even snatch a kiss. 'Nick should come, too, though.'

'If I must,' Nick said. He was trying not to sound

ungracious, but for some reason the thought of Athene and Adrian being together was beginning to disturb him mightily.

'Who taught you to play as well as that?' he asked her when, the game over, she walked away, telling herself that with Mrs Tenison's stern eye on her she must not monopolise Adrian too much.

'Mr Tenison,' she said, 'and the local vicar when they needed another lady, and since Emma has no real talent for the game, and her father found that I had, I was included in their foursome. Mrs Tenison was the vicar's partner.'

The small beer of country life, thought Nick, and Pallas Athene is a quick learner, no doubt of that.

'I should not like to play against you for money,' he told her, half seriously.

'No?' she raised her eyebrows at him. 'I think that you do not like to have much to do with me, sir, whether money is involved or not.'

She had inadvertently offered him a chance to throw a dart at her.

'Oh, Pallas Athene, I think that money has a great deal to do with why Adrian and I meet you so often, and I do not think that it is my money in which you are interested.'

Athene was surprised at how much this judgement, carelessly thrown in her direction, hurt her. That there was some measure of truth in it made the hurt greater.

'You are not kind, sir,' she told him, her beautiful mouth quivering a little. 'You will allow me to leave you, after informing you that I have never once thought of money either when with you, or away from you.'

Was that a tear gathering in her eye? He had not meant to touch her to the quick, but he had. He had thought her harder than she was: always before she had turned his poisoned arrows aside easily. Why had this time been different?

Nick found himself beginning to apologise.

'Athene,' he said, 'forgive me. That statement was unwarrantable. I had no right to make it. But...'

'Oh, there is always a but attached to whatever you are about to say,' she told him hardily, quite recovered from her moment of fleeting distress. 'Pray spare me the rest of the sentence. I am sure you were merely about to reproach me after a different fashion.'

If only she were as virtuous as she was witty and clever, what a nonpareil she would be: all the same, she had made him feel like a cur.

Nick opened his mouth. He was too late. Not only was there nothing which he could usefully say, but she was now so far away that to pursue her, mouthing apologies, would undoubtedly cause unkind comment.

All that he had done was to throw her into his cousin's arms, for Adrian had come looking for her. He was saying tenderly, 'My pretty dear, you look tired. Shall we find somewhere quiet to sit, away from the hurly burly?' and she was agreeing with him and they were out of Nick's line of sight.

Nick stopped cursing himself and began to hope that Jackson might bring him some news which would show the woman with whom he had inconveniently fallen in love in a better light.

Jackson was already installed in Abbot Quincey's cheapest inn. He had arrived in Northampton the previous day, and had hired a horse to take him deep into Steepwood. The landlord was a gossip and his talk was all about the dead Marquis and his runaway wife. There had been no need for him to raise the subject.

'Only mystery about that devil's end,' the landlord told him cheerfully, 'was why nobody ever did for him before. The one thing that can be said in his favour was that the gossip about him kept us all entertained for years.'

'Plenty of gossip still,' Jackson had said idly, hiding his face in a foaming pint of indifferent ale.

'Aye, mind you, I don't think that Lord Yardley did for him. The Earl's a real gent. Sywell's wife, now, that's another matter. He was a cruel beast there, and no mistake. Gave her a black eye more'n once. No way to treat a lady.'

'Or someone who wasn't a lady, either,' was Jackson's dry contribution. 'Who d'you think *did* do for him, then?'

'Hard to say. But the way he was done for wasn't a lady's way—though she might have paid for someone to do him for her, if she's still alive, that is. There are those who believe that he did for her—only her body has never turned up, so if he did kill her, he couldn't have been tried without a body. Too late, now, if one does turn up.'

'Wouldn't prove he'd done it,' offered Jackson.

'Aye, there is that. Another pint?'

'Wouldn't mind,' said Jackson, hoping that finding information about Miss Athene Filmer wasn't going to be as difficult as discovering something substantial about Sywell's murder and his wife's disappearance. Hugh Cameron had hinted that the Regent himself wished the murderer to be found as soon as possible. It seemed that he thought that yet another unsolved scandal in high life would be one too many.

Jackson didn't care how many scandals there were so long as he was paid for investigating them. One thing was odd about his present commissions: that the subjects of both of the major ones were, or had been, inhabitants of this wild and, up to the present, little-known corner of Northamptonshire. Since he didn't believe in coincidences, he wondered what the connection was between the Marquis of Sywell, his wife and Miss Athene Filmer and whether he could uncover it. The minor commission also involved the Steepwood district, but he didn't think that there were any hidden connections there with the other two.

He stopped showing any further interest in Sywell lest the landlord began to wonder why he, a stranger, was so interested in him, but his lack of interest lost him nothing, since everyone who visited the inn had only one subject of conversation and that was the late Marquis. Jackson only had to sit there, apparently half-asleep and listen to the buzzing going on around him, to gather even more information than if he had been busy questioning everyone.

One piece of gossip which he overheard while apparently half-dozing intrigued him. The name of Tenison was bandied about the bar as proof that the Marquis could rile even the mildest of men.

'Arguing about boundary lines between Abbey land and Tenison's, weren't they, and Tenison swore that he'd set the law on him if he didn't give way. Story was that the mad Marquis kept on shouting that it was a pity they weren't living in the old days, when he would have had Tenison hanged for his insolence to such a magnate as he was. Parson said as how he'd never seen Tenison so angry before.'

'Angry enough to do for him?'

'Perhaps, who knows?'

So Miss Filmer's employer was another who had fallen foul of the madman, and that would give him a fine excuse to visit Tenison and while questioning him weigh up Athene Filmer.

Dawn the next day saw the sun rising in a blue sky. A good time to saddle up and visit all the oddly named villages which were distributed around the old Abbey. While he was doing that he could think up some convincing reason for visiting the Abbey itself when he had finished investigating Miss Filmer.

Abbot Giles was his first destination. He rode down

the main street looking about him as though he were trying to find something. An old lady carrying a basket and with an equally elderly dog on a long lead seemed to be the kind of person who might know all the local gossip. He was well aware that the Filmers and the Tenisons lived at Steep Ride, but he was prepared to believe that in this odd corner of the world everyone knew everyone else. Besides, he'd always found that an indirect approach paid off.

He dismounted, hitched his horse to a nearby gatepost and walked towards the old girl, pulling off his battered hat.

'Excuse me, madam, but I wonder whether you could assist me? I seem to have been given an incorrect address. I was told to visit Datchet House in the main street here where the party I seek lives, but there seems to be no such place.'

A pair of sharp eyes scrutinised him with interest.

'Indeed there is not. You must have been misinformed. What, may I ask, is the name of your party?'

'A Miss Athene Filmer. I have a letter to deliver to her.'

'Oh, Miss Filmer! Yes, she did live at Datchet House, but that is situated in Steep Ride—I can give you some useful directions. You will not find Miss Filmer there, though, only her mother. Miss Filmer is in London. She has gone as a companion for the Tenisons' young daughter.'

The sharp eyes on him were curious and avid for information.

'You seem a knowledgeable lady, madam. I wonder whether you can help me further. I also have a patron who is anxious to discover the whereabouts of the Marchioness of Sywell—that is, if she is still alive. Have you any notion where she might have gone to?'

'How curious you should ask me *that*. I have none at all, but the young woman whom you seek might. I happen to know that she and Louise Sywell were very friendly. I found that out by the purest accident. My walks take me into the Abbey grounds and on several occasions I saw them walking and talking together. Quite by chance I saw the Marchioness there on the day before she disappeared. She was not with Miss Filmer, but was in the Sacred Grove, by the Rune Stone. I gained the impression that she had been weeping.'

So the Marchioness and Nick Cameron's lady had been bosom bows. Here was a right royal turn-up!

He was about to ask another question when the old lady said to him eagerly, only too delighted to have a new ear to pour her gossip into, 'I was not at all surprised that Miss Filmer and the Marchioness were friends. They were both of quite mysterious origin. Miss Filmer's mother calls herself a widow but I have my doubts about that. She came here when Athene was a baby and never a relative has visited her. Oh, she seems respectable enough, but one must admit that her situation is extremely odd. Is there or was there a Mr Filmer? One begs leave to doubt it. Not that Miss Filmer is other than a well-behaved young woman, you understand. Quite clever, they say, but one cannot hold that against her. Is there anything further I can help you with?'

'It would be useful if you could let me have the London address of Miss Filmer's employer so that I can arrange for a letter to be delivered there. I am exceedingly grateful to you for your assistance, madam,' Jackson said. He was being completely truthful. 'May I know your name so that I may write you a formal letter of thanks?'

'Indeed, you may. I am Miss Amy Rushmere and I live at the end house in the street in that direction. If you will come with me, I shall write down the Tenisons' address, and perhaps you would welcome a dish of tea while I do so.'

Jackson heartily agreed to drink tea with her, for the old gossip had saved him a deal of work. Had she told the authorities of the Marchioness's friendship with Miss Filmer? He would seek that young lady out when he returned to London and question her about it. The Marchioness might have said something to her which meant little at the time, but which his gentle prodding of her memory might bring to her mind. It was also quite possible that the Marchioness had confided in her before she disappeared.

Miss Rushmere had little further to tell him, but questioned him eagerly about London, after she had given him the Tenisons' address, which he already knew.

'I only visited London once,' she told him, 'when I was a girl. I understand it is greatly changed.'

He told her it was, before setting out on his travels again. He thought that a visit to Steep Ride might be useful. He found, however, little there to engage him. Datchet House was small and it was plain that its owner did not possess a great deal of tin, but neither was she poverty-stricken. Since Mrs Filmer appeared to have no occupation it must be assumed that she had some sort of income: an annuity perhaps? He had no intention of rousing further unnecessary speculation by visiting her. He thought that the old gossip had told him everything he needed to know about her and her daughter, and since Mrs Filmer had kept the secret of the identity of her unknown lover for over twenty years she was scarcely likely to blab it to him at first sight.

He had already discovered that the only bank hereabouts was a country one in Abbot Quincey, which contained the few shops and the small Assembly Rooms, which were actually a ballroom over the Angel inn, which made up the social life and the provender of gossip in the Steepwood district. He would go there, find out if there was a clerk whom he could bribe for information—and bribe him.

In the meantime he would continue his investigations into the matter of Sywell's death and his lady's disappearance.

* * *

Bribing the clerk was easier than Jackson had thought it might be. He visited Jordan's Bank, looked about him, and identified one scrawny-looking, threadbare underling occupying the bank's only public counter. He wore a permanently dissatisfied face.

Jackson presented a Treasury note for five pounds and asked to be given five sovereigns.

'Don't see many of these,' sighed the clerk, holding up the note before sliding the sovereigns across.

'Nor many sovereigns, either,' said Jackson who had rapidly summed up his man.

'You can say that again, sir. Pays badly, does Banker Jordan.'

'You might like to earn a little extra tin, perhaps,' offered Jackson, playing the Devil to the clerk's Doctor Faustus.

'Why, are you giving sovereigns away?'

'Come to the alehouse tonight, answer a few questions and I'll give you a half-sovereign for each of them—provided that you say nothing of this to anyone.'

'Take me for a fool, do you? I'll be there on the stroke of seven, and you'd better be there, too.'

Oh, yes, Jackson would be there, no doubt of it. Beneath the battered clock on the greasy wall, seated beside the fire, a pot of ale before him. He had no doubt that the clerk would be there, too—and so he was.

'Fire away, old fellow,' the clerk said eagerly, already spending the half-sovereigns.

'Over here,' said Jackson, moving into a pew set

away from the rest of the room, ensuring privacy for its occupants, after ordering a pot of ale for the clerk.

'I am assuming that the bank has a Mrs Charlotte Filmer for a customer.'

'Indeed, sir, indeed. Is that your first question?'

'Yes.' Jackson laid a sovereign on the table. 'Now earn the rest of it. Do I also assume that she has an income, probably paid into the bank quarterly?'

'Yes, she does,' grinned the clerk. This was easy. He was supposed to keep all customers' business confidential, but damn that for a tale if sovereigns were on offer.

'Now earn another sovereign by answering two questions. Is it in the form of a banker's draft, and if so on what bank?'

Oh, this was easy money indeed, for he knew the answers to his new friend's questions.

'A draft for a hundred pounds paid quarterly. It is drawn on Coutts.'

'Excellent, now let us drink our ale in the knowledge of work well done.'

Jackson slid the two sovereigns across the table, and the two of them drank to each other before Jackson leaned forward and said with quiet savagery, 'And if you tell anyone of this, I'll have your guts for garters, make no mistake.'

'Oh, mum's the word, sir, mum's the word,' chattered the clerk. 'By my life, sir. You may depend on me.'

'Good, I'd hate for you to have a nasty accident.

Enjoy your windfall and forget that you ever met me. And, one last thing, don't visit this alehouse until after I leave the district at the week's end.'

Jackson leaned back and enjoyed his ale. So, Miss Athene Filmer was someone's love child, and her mother was being paid off by a draft drawn on Coutts. By whom, he would never discover through Coutts, for the bank's confidentiality was rarely, if ever, breached. One thing was sure, though, anyone who banked with Coutts had both position and money— which told him something about the donor.

As a bonus Miss Filmer was Louise Sywell's friend—and there was another lead for him to follow, and another fact for Mr Nicholas Cameron.

It also meant that before he reported back to all his employers he would need to interview the interesting and clever Miss Filmer, whose name seemed to pop up at every turn.

Some feeling, some intuition which he never ignored when he was in the middle of an investigation such as this, told him that Miss Filmer might be the one person who could lead him to the missing Marchioness. He had no concrete evidence to support this belief, but no matter. When he visited the Tenisons in London he would take the opportunity to question her about her friendship with the missing Marchioness, citing his commission from the Home Office as giving him the right to do so. Naturally, he would say nothing to her which would give away his commission from Nick Cameron regarding her origins and reputation!

His final task was to gain entry to the Abbey itself, which he duly did by the simple expedient of breaking into it one night. He found nothing there of the slightest use to him. The bedroom where Sywell had been murdered had been cleaned up after a fashion, and his own easy illegal entry, made while Burneck was out drinking, told him that the murderer's entry had probably been equally as easy. Burneck he met, by apparent accident, in the Angel's taproom, but he gained nothing by talking to him. 'I was absent that night,' he offered, 'fortunately for me. I was over at Jaffrey House, as a dozen could tell you,' and nothing could shake him.

Jackson thought that confined to a cell in Newgate, where he could be manhandled at leisure, he might sing a different song, but there was no scrap of evidence which could justify detaining him, so that was that. Best to return to London and seek out the interesting Miss Filmer under the guise of questioning the Tenisons.

Dammit, thought Nick Cameron, more in resignation than in anger, what the devil is the man up to? He was watching the Duke of Inglesham make his way to their party, who were chatting together after having enjoyed the performance of a Haydn quartet at one of Lady Dunlop's musical soirées.

The reclusive Duke, who for years had never been

seen anywhere, was now being seen everywhere. And in that everywhere he always chose—apparently absent-mindedly—to pay his respects to the Tenisons before he had been in the room with them for five minutes!

Like Mr Tenison the Duke was bookish, and after he had done the pretty with all the Tenison party, he invariably began to converse with him at length upon all the erudite subjects which engaged both their interests. This was perhaps reasonable enough and could be considered as perfectly normal behaviour for two middle-aged men, except that the Duke always took the trouble to include Athene in their discussions, which today had centred around an appreciation of what they had just heard.

Oh, she never disgraced herself when he did: she was, being very well-read, perfectly able to join them in their wordplay whilst Adrian, not understanding anything which was being said, was happy to stand back—open-mouthed—admiring his beloved's wit and charm.

Nick, more worldly-wise, was asking himself whether it was Mr Tenison's scholarship which attracted the Duke—or was he merely a blind behind which the Duke was able to admire Athene and constantly encourage her to speak her mind?

Not that she needed much encouragement to do *that,* he thought a trifle glumly, having felt the edge of her tongue more than once.

Their conversation, which now included a somewhat baffled Mrs Tenison and Emma, who had just returned from the supper room, had moved on to a learned discussion on the origin of the place names around Steepwood Abbey.

'Steep Ride,' mused the Duke after Mr Tenison had told him that his family came from that village. 'I suppose it must either refer to the River Steep or to a small wooded hill there with a track, suitable for horsemen to ride up or down.'

'A very small one,' admitted Mr Tenison.

'And you, Miss Athene,' asked the Duke turning his penetrating eyes on her, 'do you come from Steep Ride? I can imagine that on long winter nights your father and Mr Tenison must have had some interesting chats about its name.'

'Alas, Duke,' said Athene, who was as puzzled as Nick by the Duke's interest in her, 'my father is long dead. I live with my mother, who has never remarried.'

A shadow passed across the Duke's face. He expressed his condolences before droning away—Adrian's words—about place names again and how those in the Midlands differed from those in the north and the south.

Ordinarily Nick would have enjoyed taking part in such a discussion, but his reservations and doubts about the Duke's behaviour prevented him from doing so. The thought that Inglesham might be using his erudition as a blind behind which to pursue Athene was quite spoiling his evening.

It was bad enough to have to endure Adrian, his friend and cousin, sniffing around her, but to watch a middle-aged Duke doing the same was even worse. Even the Duke's departure shortly afterwards did not sweeten his temper.

He took advantage of another pause in the programme, designed to allow the guests a further visit to the supper room, to take Athene by the arm and say, between gritted teeth, 'All that learned piff-paff must have exhausted you, my dear Pallas. Allow me to refresh your spirits by leading you to where I understand from Mrs Tenison there is an excellent display of food and drink. Unless of course, like your namesake, you prefer to partake of the food of the gods—whatever that might be.'

This was too bad of him, was it not? For was not his behaviour a form of blackmail, so that there was nothing for it but to allow him to walk her to where footmen paraded with wine and meat and salmon patties on trays, and where a buffet of unparalleled splendour and dimensions was laid out?

Unfortunately Athene had never felt less like food.

Why did it distress her so much that he disliked her? Why *did* he dislike her? She had done nothing to hurt him. That his cousin—and now the Duke—chose to admire her was not her fault. She had not missed the sour glances which he had thrown her way during the Duke's time with Mr Tenison, but she could not tell him that she was puzzled by the Duke's obvious interest in her, and wished most heartily that he would not single her out so often.

Instead she said, 'What I don't understand, Mr Cameron, is why *you* should so constantly demand to speak to me when you dislike me so much. If being with me makes you so cross, why do you persist in following me about when I obviously find your attentions unwelcome? Unless it is to keep me away from Adrian.'

. There was enough truth in her last statement to have him, unwillingly, admire the acuteness of her mind all over again.

'Come now,' he told her, 'can you not believe that I am yet another of your admirers? What is remarkable about that? You have so many that not to admire you has become unfashionable.'

Now *he* was surely telling the truth only in his last statement, for Athene could not believe that he was genuine in saying that he admired her. Oh, if only it were possible that he did. Whenever he was not at odds with her he was a charming companion: he could speak well on matters which interested her, but which were a closed book to his cousin. She had played chess with him at the Tenisons and again when they had all visited Adrian's splendid family home off the Strand, and had given him a good game. Chess was beyond Adrian's understanding.

Nick had found her one day in Adrian's neglected library, admiring the prints which adorned a wall above a set of low bookcases. She had recently asked

Adrian where they had come from and what they sig-
nified, but he had stared blankly at her and had said
dismissively, 'I believe that my grandfather brought
them home from the Grand Tour.'

His lack of interest had been palpable and it had
been left to Nick to enlighten her. 'They are prints by
an Italian master called Piranesi, and they are famous
because they hint at terrible things, but do not show
them happening.'

'Oh, Nick's the clever devil in our family,' Adrian
had once said to her. 'He even paints and draws a
bit.'

Privately she was beginning to wish that she and
Adrian were of a like mind, and that he roused in her
the same sense of excitement which being with Nick
Cameron brought her. Even his dislike of her excited
her and she had made valiant efforts to overcome it:
so far with no success.

'Quiet, tonight, aren't we?' said Nick, seizing a
glass of white wine from a passing tray and offering
it to her.

'I thought that you objected to me being noisy,'
was her riposte to that.

'Only when Inglesham is toadying to you,' Nick
could not prevent himself from saying. 'You know
that he's a great deal richer than Adrian even. Why
don't you pursue *him*? Becoming a Duchess would
crown your Season completely. What's a mere Earl
compared to that?'

Athene lifted her glass defiantly and said, 'I offer

you a toast, Mr Cameron. To your cousin Adrian, who, whatever else he is, is kind. You are not kind. Your cleverness does not attract me as much as his goodness of heart. Does that satisfy you, sir?'

She was shaking so much that the glass in her hand trembled before she lifted it to her mouth; that, and her description of Adrian as kind, shamed him. Also, she had never looked more beautiful, nor sounded more desirable.

Nick had to confess to himself all over again that not only was he madly in love with her despite his suspicion of her motives in encouraging Adrian, but he was equally madly jealous of every man who looked at her, who spoke to her, or on whom she smiled. She would not smile on him. He had been too unkind too often for her to want him. A bitter regret consumed him.

'Athene,' he began, 'I'm sorry…' and was secretly relieved when she stopped him, for he had not known what he might say next.

'No,' she told him, putting her glass down on the table before which they stood. 'I don't want an apology—if that's what you were embarking on. It has come too late. Now, pray excuse me. I do not wish to eat, and I crave for more congenial company.'

Nick made no effort to stop her. She walked away from him straight-backed and only she knew that her heart wept within her, for she was well aware that it was Nick Cameron who could have made her happy, and that Adrian, for her, would always be second-best—despite his kindness.

The Tenisons and Athene were enjoying a late breakfast when the butler announced that a Mr Jackson needed to speak to Mr Tenison and members of his family, on business which was urgent and which pertained to the murder of the Marquis of Sywell. He had the authority of the Home Office to ask questions of parties who might have some useful information to give him.

Jackson had said nothing about the business of the missing Marchioness, since he did not wish Miss Filmer to have time to make up a plausible story if she did have something to hide.

He would spring that on her when he had spoken to Mr Tenison.

'Sywell's death!' exclaimed Mr Tenison, throwing down the *Morning Post* which he had been reading over his coffee and rolls. 'What in the name of wonder does that have to do with me? I was in London when he was murdered. What information could I possibly have which would be of use either to the law or to the Home Secretary?'

'Perhaps our trouble over the boundaries might have come up,' suggested Mrs Tenison, who was not lacking in good sense where such matters were concerned.

'That must be it. Well, I suppose I shall have to

see him. Show him to my study and tell him I will
be with him shortly.'

Emma said in a worried voice when her father had
left them, 'Surely they cannot imagine that Papa had
anything to do with the Marquis's murder?'

Athene put a comforting hand on her arm. 'Dear
Emma, the Marquis was killed on the night when we
all went to Lady Cowper's ball. Two hundred people
must have seen your father there. The man is probably
clearing up odds and ends.'

Emma's face cleared, too, and Mrs Tenison grudg-
ingly admitted to herself that Filmer had a deal of
common-sense whatever other virtues she lacked. In
any case the man did not detain her husband long, for
he returned very shortly afterwards to say that he
wished to question briefly his wife, Emma and Athene
about various matters which he had discovered during
a recent visit to Steepwood.

Jackson had no real wish to interview either Mrs
Tenison or Emma, but he did not wish to single
Athene out. Mr Tenison suggested that he might like
to speak to Miss Filmer before he spoke to Emma.

'My daughter is less likely to be over-set if she
finds that Miss Filmer returns untroubled from her
interview with you. Miss Filmer is a very sensible
young woman.'

'Doesn't matter which I see first,' Jackson told him.
'Miss Filmer will do as well as any. Your missis and
daughter can come in afterwards.'

Privately he was beginning to be intrigued by Miss

Athene Filmer, who seemed to have made such a great impression on everyone who knew her and whom he had interviewed. She consequently sounded as though she would pay for questioning.

'Question me first?' said Athene doubtfully, and then, echoing Mr Tenison, 'Whatever for?'

'Goodness knows, my dear. He wants to see Mrs Tenison and Emma after you.'

'Oh, very well. But I still find it hard to believe that he really needs to question any of us.'

Athene did not betray it, but her mind was in a turmoil. She was remembering that Louise had warned her that she must not betray her identity as Madame Félice to anyone, and that would even include this emissary from the Government. Mr Tenison had already informed them that Jackson had revealed that he was acting on behalf of the Home Office and—indirectly—of the Regent himself.

Surely, though, the man could not be aware that she knew where the missing Marchioness was and the pseudonym she was currently using? She would have to keep her wits about her and be prepared to lie to him if necessary in order to protect her friend to whom she had promised secrecy.

She found Jackson staring out of the window in Mr Tenison's study, his full attention apparently given to the street below, before the butler's announcing her name had him swinging round to examine her with a pair of yellow eyes which reminded her of the drawing of a lion in one of Mr Tenison's big folios.

'Miss Athene Filmer is it? Pray sit down, my dear. I have a few simple questions to ask you which I am sure that you will be easily able to answer.'

'I hope so, sir,' she told him and gave him her most winning smile.

His answering smile revealed a set of predatory teeth which now had her remembering the Wolf in the fairy story who had bared his to Red Riding Hood, and when she had exclaimed, 'What big teeth you have,' he had replied, 'All the better to eat you with, my dear.'

She knew instinctively that despite his slightly oafish and workmanlike exterior and his blunt speech he was a very clever and dangerous man indeed—something which, unknown to her, Mr Tenison had not quite grasped.

His first questions, though, were innocuous ones which set her wondering why he had needed to interview her at all. They concerned her position in the Tenison household and her address back in Northamptonshire.

'Did you ever meet the Marquis?' Jackson finally asked, after he thought that he had set her completely at ease so that when he introduced the Marchioness into his questioning she would not be afraid of him.

'Not really. I saw him at a distance once. He was thrashing some poor ostler who had done something to distress him, I never knew what. All the girls at Mrs Guarding's school were told to keep well away from him.'

'Um…' He nodded and looked out of the window again as though what he was hearing bored him, and Athene thought hopefully that this interview might rapidly end without any difficult ground having been traversed.

She soon discovered that she was wrong.

In a bored voice he asked, 'And his wife, the Marchioness? She is—or was—a little older than you are. Did you know her?'

Well, at least she could answer that reasonably truthfully.

'A little. When we were small girls she lived at the Abbey and we played together. Then one day, she didn't come to our meeting place, and I never saw her again until the Marquis brought her home after they were married. I didn't recognise her when she was driven by in his carriage, but later on when I was walking in the Abbey grounds, she came up to me and told me that she was my old friend, and after that we met on a few occasions.'

'Um…' said Jackson again. He recognised the ring of truth when he heard it. Yet why was it that he thought that the beautiful young woman opposite to him still had something to tell him? It was not her manner. She was perfectly composed, her elegant hands folded in the lap of her ugly dress.

'Had you seen her recently? Before she disappeared, I mean. Did she give you any notion of where she was going? If she were going anywhere, that is, and has not been done away with.'

Athene could safely tell him the truth about her last meeting with Louise and did. 'I last saw her a few days before her disappearance. She was a good water-colourist and we often met to work and talk together as young women do. We were painting the Rune Stone in the Sacred Grove and she said nothing to indicate that she might be leaving. I did know that she was very unhappy.'

Still the truth. He made as though to speak and she looked levelly at him. Oh, she was a pearl of price was Miss Athene Filmer, for all her illegitimacy. He wondered who the unknown father might be.

He kept silent, apparently thinking, in an effort—a wasted one—to destroy her composure.

'Miss Filmer, I must ask you to be truthful, for it is the government's business I am on, and much hangs on this. Do you have any idea where the Marchioness might be living, or who might be pro-tecting her? A dreadful murder has been committed and she might be implicated. At the least she would repay questioning, and—who knows—it might even exonerate her.'

Now for the lie, and perhaps God would forgive her for not betraying her friend who had been dealt with so harshly by life.

'No, sir, I have no idea. None.'

Athene thought that the less she said the better. Louise had advised her of that, and it was plain that the advice was good.

'None?'

'No, sir.'

'When you had those long walks together did she never speak of any friends elsewhere with whom she might have found shelter?'

Someone at Steepwood had been talking. Who? No matter, she could answer that question truthfully, too. Louise had told her nothing at Steepwood—and so she informed her questioner.

Jackson's admiration for her was unbounded. Beautiful, clever, and the best liar he had ever met. He was sure that she had told him the truth right until he had asked the final question as to whether she knew where Louise Sywell was. How he knew that she was a liar was a mystery to him.

He also knew that he would gain nothing further from her. She was not to be bullied or tricked. The very care with which she had answered him told him that. Her brief answers when he came to the meat of his questioning were masterly.

He decided to try another tack. 'You must, I suppose, Miss Filmer, wish as much as I do that the man who did this dreadful murder is caught before he can commit further atrocities. You must also wish to see your old friend again—if she is still alive that is. I am going to give you an address where you can reach me. If you can think of anything at all which comes to mind and which might help me, then I would be greatly obliged if you would inform me immediately. You would be doing the state some service.'

His last statement baffled Athene. She could not

see what Sywell's murder had to do with the state—
nor poor Louise's whereabouts either.

She had half a mind to question him about that, but
wisely decided that to say as little as possible would
be the best thing. Instead she rose, and said, as coolly
as she could, 'May I go, now?'

'Certainly, Miss Filmer.'

She had her back to him and her hand on the door-
knob when he spoke again. 'You are quite sure that
you have nothing further to tell me, Miss Filmer?'

Athene turned and gave him her most dazzling
smile.

'Quite sure, Mr Jackson.'

CHAPTER SIX

'Questioned you all about Sywell's murder and his wife's disappearance? Whatever for?'

Nick Cameron had just walked over in time to hear Emma telling Adrian about Jackson's visit the previous day and to be amused by hearing Adrian's incredulous response.

The Tenisons, Athene, Nick, Adrian and Marcus Angmering had all gone to Richmond to picnic on the banks of the Thames. Adrian had wanted to drive Emma and Athene there in his curricle, but Mr Tenison had gently insisted that it would be better for them to accompany him and Mrs Tenison in their landau. Nick had also refused Adrian's offer of a seat and had chosen to ride instead, stabling his horse at a nearby inn before walking to the riverside, where he found the party already underway.

Servants were unpacking wicker baskets and laying out food and drink on lace-edged linen cloths. Adrian and Marcus were entertaining the women, Adrian having prevailed on Marcus to accept Nick's rejected seat. Adrian's driving had been so unsteady that Marcus had deeply regretted having accepted his invitation and had spent the journey trying to persuade Adrian not to set out yet on his proposed race to Brighton to break the record for the run.

Marcus was afraid that the only thing Adrian might break would be his neck and not the record! He was tactful enough not to say so, merely suggesting that Adrian needed a little more practice in driving a curricle and two.

Now he was listening to Emma saying in her low pretty voice, 'We thought that he had just come to question Papa about the murder, but he also wanted to interview Mama, Athene and me. Papa thought that it would be better to agree to him doing so rather than refuse him.'

Mr Tenison said quietly, 'I thought that to refuse might make it look as though we had something to hide.'

Nick, knowing that Jackson had recently been on an errand for him in the Steepwood district, but had not yet reported back, wondered what on earth the man was doing, and whether it had any connection with his own commission, and said, as calmly as he could, 'I can understand someone questioning you, sir, but why should he trouble the ladies? And who gave this man the authority to do so?'

'His name is Jackson,' said Mr Tenison. 'I understood from him that he wished to know whether anyone in my household had been friendly with the missing Marchioness and consequently might have some notion of where she could have gone—if she is still alive that is. The *on dit* is that her husband might have murdered her. As to the man's authority, he provided proof that he was working for the Home Office, and also for a very grand personage indeed. More I cannot say.'

Nick was fascinated by this answer. How many birds was the devious Jackson seeking to kill with one stone? And how soon would it be before he reported back to him anything which he might have discovered about Athene's origins?

'And could any of you help him?' he asked, directing his question to Emma and not to Athene, who was standing there quiet and demure.

'I couldn't,' she said, 'but Athene knew the Marchioness a little, I believe—but we understand that she couldn't help Mr Jackson.'

Athene had later learned that Jackson had told Mrs Tenison of her having been a friend of Louise's, and she had consequently been compelled to endure a stiff bout of questioning from her about the missing Marchioness.

Adrian snorted. 'If it isn't the outside of enough to have some great brute of a fellow questioning gentlewomen about their past friendships. I wonder you didn't have the vapours, Athene.'

He was so concerned and so vehement that Marcus Angmering gave him an odd look, thinking, so that's the way the wind blows, is it? It really is the incandescent companion he's after and not the demure young lady!

Athene thought to quieten matters down a little by saying, 'He wasn't a great brute, Adrian, and he was perfectly polite to me when questioning me. More polite, I might say, than some gentlemen I have known.'

If she gave a rapid glance in Nick's direction when she came out with this, Adrian failed to notice it, and exclaimed indignantly, 'If any gentleman is ever unkind to you in the future, Athene, you must inform me immediately and I shall soon mend his manners for him, you may be sure of that!'

'He was very polite to me, too,' said Emma. 'I was quite upset before I went in to see him, but he soon put me at ease, and Mama, too.'

'So you knew the Marchioness, Miss Filmer,' Marcus said. 'I have often wondered what the woman who chose to marry Sywell was like.'

There was no help for it, Athene thought ruefully. The last thing which she wished to do was discuss her friendship with Louise, but she could not refuse Marcus's unspoken question. It was quite natural that he should want to know something of the man—and his wife—whom it was suspected that his father might have killed. It would be unnatural for her not to say something.

'She was very young and very pretty,' she said slowly. 'We had been friends when I was a little girl, and then she was sent away—I never knew why, or to where. When the Marquis brought her to Steepwood I met her in the grounds one day and we renewed our friendship. She was lonely and seemed unhappy. She disappeared as suddenly as she had reappeared, and so I told Mr Jackson. I had no notion of where she went. That's all. I was sorry to lose a friend. We painted and sketched together, I'm afraid that I can't tell you any more.'

'Thank you, Miss Filmer. I trust that I have not distressed you. We none of us like to lose a friend.'

Athene nodded: Nick, like Jackson, cynically wondered whether she had told the whole story of her relationship with the Marchioness. He also wondered how long it would be before Jackson informed him of the results of his enquiry into Athene's origins. He would have dearly liked to have known what Jackson was really questioning Athene about.

'What is extraordinary,' he said slowly, 'is that so many of us, sitting here by the Thames and ready to enjoy the food and drink which the servants have set out for us, should have some involvement with Sywell and his missing wife.'

Adrian said, 'Well, I'm certainly glad that *I* never had anything to do with him. He sounds a most disagreeable person.'

'I think that we can all safely say Amen to that,' was Mr Tenison's final comment before he changed the subject and began talking about the other staple topic of conversation these days—the latest war news from Spain.

On the following afternoon Nick was reading in the drawing-room of his lodgings in Albany—which were not far from those which Lord Byron occupied—when his man ushered Jackson in.

The ex-Runner was looking uncommonly cheerful, which Nick hoped might be the consequence of an exceedingly fruitful foray into Northamptonshire. He thought to score a useful point or two before Jackson began his report by remarking dryly, 'I have been expecting you ever since I discovered that my little errand was not the only reason why you visited Steepwood recently.'

Oh, he was a fly boy, Mr Nick Cameron, was he not? Jackson rewarded him with a conspiratorial grin, and, 'So the Tenisons have been talking, have they?'

Nick nodded. 'And others, too. So, what did you unearth about Miss Filmer? Besides any possible clues to the fates of the murdered Marquis and the missing Marchioness, that is?'

'Something,' said Jackson, who thought that it usually paid to be honest. 'But not, perhaps, as much as you had hoped. There seems to be little doubt that she is illegitimate. She has a supposedly widowed mother who has behaved with impeccable virtue ever since she settled in Northamptonshire. The late Mr Filmer was unknown to the district, and none of his, or her, relatives have ever visited her during the twenty years since she settled there.

'I met a local gossip who implied with a nod and a wink that Miss F. is almost certainly illegitimate. After that I pursued other avenues, by which it came to my notice that her mother has been, and still is, in receipt of an annuity, paid quarterly, on a draft drawn on Coutts Bank—the name of the origin of the money being unknown. Regretfully, since with Coutts confidentiality for their customers is absolute, that is as far as I can take you. The annuity is not large, but has enabled the two women to live moderately well. As to who her father might be—that, I fear, is beyond discovery, since no one knows where Mrs Filmer lived before arriving in Steep Ride.

'Despite the rumours about Miss Filmer's birth, her mother is accepted by local society, teaches at the Sunday school and is known for being as charitable as her income will allow. There is one other thing of interest. Miss Filmer was a friend and confidante of the missing Marchioness of Sywell, and it is my belief that she is well aware of where that lady may be found—although she resolutely denies all knowledge of her whereabouts. Rumour has it that she is a clever young lady, and so I found her to be.'

So, Athene was illegitimate, some person of reasonable wealth's deserted bastard. Jackson's information explained much of her behaviour, and Nick suddenly felt a tremendous pity for her. What she was chasing was not only wealth, but respectability and acceptance. She must be aware of her mother's—and her own—precarious position in society. To marry Adrian would at once advance her to a position where she could out-stare the world.

'You are telling me, then,' said Nick carefully, 'that in some, perhaps distant way, Miss Filmer is involved in the Steepwood mystery.'

'Only to the extent that she may know where the Marchioness is. May I add that I believe that there is little more to be found about her, or her mother. The mother has been most remarkably discreet and I believe the young woman to be of a similar nature.'

He did not say that having met Athene he could not but admire her, but the suggestion was there.

'Do I understand that you regard your commission for me as at an end?'

'Indeed—unless you have any further information to offer me.'

Nick shook his head. 'None: so all that remains is for me to pay you, and thank you. I trust that your other investigations proved to be more successful than the one for me has been.'

It was Jackson's turn to shake his head.

'Alas, no. The business of the Marquis's murder is as mysterious as ever. Even if the Marchioness were to be found, it is doubtful whether she has any useful information.'

'You do not think that she *is* dead?'

'My instincts—which are seldom wrong—tell me

that she is not, particularly since I believe that Miss Filmer knows more than she is telling.'

'Miss Filmer always knows more than she is telling,' said Nick savagely, handing Jackson his guineas, and telling him to go to the kitchen where his man would give him a farewell tankard of porter.

He threw himself into his armchair—his book lay forgotten on the floor. One thing and one thing only was true—regardless of what Jackson had told him—whether Athene was legitimate or illegitimate, whether she was helping Louise Sywell or not, nothing had been solved for him.

He was like a man lost on the ocean in a row-boat without oars. Only one thing was certain, in honour he must not let Athene know that he had set Jackson to spy on her. Doubtless she thought the man had pursued her because of her relationship with Louise: that he had also pursued her on his behalf must remain, for the time being at least, his guilty secret.

'Will you accept Adrian if he offers for you?' Emma asked Athene one golden afternoon not long after Jackson had caused such a brouhaha in the Tenison household.

'What makes you think he will?' replied Athene. They were seated in the drawing-room, supposed to be engaged in canvas-work. Emma, however, had abandoned hers, and had been mooning over a novel before she had questioned Athene.

Now she said, 'It's the way he looks at you—full

of worship. I wondered, though, how you really felt about him. I don't think *you* worship *him.*'

This was perceptive for Emma, but then, she had grown very much more mature lately, and was no longer so ready to be stifled by her mother.

Athene thought for a moment before saying, 'Not exactly.'

'I thought not,' said Emma her voice wistful.

'But I like him,' said Athene hastily. After all, if she were to accept his offer, for despite what she had just said to Emma she thought that an offer was on the way, she must show some enthusiasm for marrying him.

The trouble was that lately, every time that she thought about what marriage really entailed, not just the going to bed bit, but also that one would have to spend one's days talking and engaging in the business of living with one's husband, the prospect of doing any of it with Adrian had become less and less attractive the more she knew him—and face it, Athene, the more she had come to know and appreciate Nick.

She could certainly spend her life talking to Nick— possibly disagreeing with him sometimes—sure that her days with him would always be lively. She preferred not to admit to herself that her nights might be livelier, too!

When once she had visualised marrying a man for his money and his title without thinking of everything else which that would entail, she was now thinking of the entail bit more and more and had begun to doubt whether she was cold-blooded enough to go through with it.

The worst of it was that she had, at first, done everything she could to attract Adrian to her, and now that she was no longer so welcoming Adrian had become so sure of her that he wasn't aware of how much her manner to him had cooled.

She wondered if Nick had noticed the change. Oh, bother everything—must she always be thinking of him? He had not been so unkind to her lately, but that was perhaps was because he was resigned to her marrying his cousin and did not wish to distress him.

Emma said suddenly. 'I wouldn't have thought Adrian to be best suited to you at all. I think he's dazzled by you rather than in love with you.'

Athene was surprised by her charge all over again. Emma's shrewd remark—which showed that she had inherited some of her father's sharp intelligence—added to the questions she was asking herself about her own behaviour towards Adrian.

Where once, if Adrian had asked her to marry him, she would have said yes to him on the instant, without further thought, she was now experiencing an increasing hesitancy. Which only went to show, she thought ruefully, how much practice differs from theory! Before she came to London she had felt no compunction at all about the prospect of marrying a man for his money and title, instead of for himself, but everything which had happened to her since she had set foot in the place had shown her what an innocent she must have been.

'He's a good man,' she said, as much to encourage herself as to explain her motives to Emma.

'And a good man deserves the best,' said Emma quietly, picking up her needlework again, before changing the subject by asking Athene to advise her on the best colour for the flower which she was working.

Athene looked across at her charge. Why all this worry from her about whether she and Adrian were suited to one another? Quick as a flash the obvious answer came. Emma was in love with him herself. He was exactly the sort of decent, slightly simple man with whom she would be happy, because she would ask little of him which he would be unable to give.

This insight had Athene feeling more disturbed than ever. She had not sufficiently prepared herself for the notion that her own activities, pursued to achieve her happiness, might cause unhappiness in others.

For the first time she began to understand why Nick Cameron was so critical of her, and to ask herself whether he might not have some right on his side.

The Duke of Inglesham was entertaining a visitor. Or, more correctly, he was receiving one whom he had summoned.

The ex-Bow Street Runner, Jackson, who had been recommended to him by no less a person than Lord

Liverpool, was standing deferentially before him, awaiting his instructions. In Jackson's experience such grand personages usually dealt with lesser lights like himself through their secretary or their flunkies. He wondered what it was that was so confidential that he was being received in person.

He was soon to find out, and what he was being asked came as some surprise to him—and brought a certain, hidden, amusement.

'I was told that you are discreet, and that I can rely upon you absolutely,' the Duke began, a trifle hesitantly. 'I would not care for my interest in this matter to be gossiped about. I would wish you to discover everything about the origins of a young lady and her mother who live in the Northamptonshire village of Steep Ride. When I say everything, I wish you to understand that, for me, the word means exactly what it says.'

Jackson nodded. 'Understood, Your Grace. Do not trouble yourself: the grave is no quieter than I am.'

Inwardly he was asking himself, what next? Did all roads lead to Steepwood these days, and was it, could it be, Miss Athene Filmer in whom the Duke was interested?

Indeed, it was. Out it all came, the Duke hemming and hawing as though the matter were some trifle— which Jackson was sure that it was not.

'I understand that Miss Filmer and her widowed mother have lived there since shortly after Miss Filmer was born. There are reasons, business reasons, which mean that I must have full knowledge of everything to do with them.'

Well, the ex-Runner was behaving like the Sphinx which Liverpool had said he was. He was listening, his head on one side, his craggy face gravely concentrating on every word that Inglesham was saying. The Duke was not to know that Jackson was debating with himself how truthful, how honest, he ought to be with his new master.

After all, he already knew everything that was to be known—other than the reason for the Duke's surprising interest—about the young lady and her mother. If he said nothing he could make another—cursory—visit to Steep Ride, and then return as though he had been urgently engaged on the Duke's business. Or he could inform the Duke of what he already knew, after telling him that his recent investigations about the Marquis of Sywell's murder, and his wife's disappearance, had led him indirectly to the Filmers. As a result he had seen fit to find out as much about them as he could. To do so, however, would probably mean that the Duke's fee would be less.

He said, slowly, after he had reluctantly decided on the latter, truthful, course, 'As it happens, Your Grace, quite by chance, I can inform you immediately of everything concerning the young lady and her mama.'

The Duke said sharply, 'How is that? They are not in trouble, I hope? Or under any suspicion?'

'Oh, no,' Jackson said, reassuringly, and went on

to explain to His Grace his commission from the Home Office and his discovery of the friendship of Miss Athene Filmer and the missing Marchioness. 'Just dotting all the i's and crossing all the t's as is my way—but to no purpose this time. The young lady denied all knowledge of the Marchioness's whereabouts.'

'Go on,' urged the Duke. So Jackson informed him of everything which he had told Nick Cameron, without mentioning Nick's name and his interest in Athene.

'Coutts,' said the Duke hollowly when the man had finished. 'The banker's draft came from Coutts.'

'Which, as you doubtless know, Your Grace, means that we have reached *point non plus*.'

'Yes,' said the Duke wearily. 'It would be as well if I knew further details of it, but what you have told me is sufficient to my purpose: I am sure I know who arranged it. You say the young lady is both beautiful and clever and that her mother has been chaste despite the rumours about her daughter's birth.'

'Indeed, Your Grace. I would be wasting your money if I returned there, since I believe that nothing further of use remains to be found in Northamptonshire.'

'Yes, and I see also that you are an honest man.'

The Duke went to a splendid ormolu desk, opened a drawer and took from it a full purse which he handed to Jackson. 'I am giving you what I intended to reward you with had it been necessary for you to visit Steepwood. Should I need to do so, I would not hesitate to employ you again.'

After Jackson had gone, the Duke, his face a picture of grief mixed with hope, walked over to the desk and fetched from a locked drawer a small miniature of a beautiful young woman dressed in the fashion of some twenty years before.

'I never thought to see you again,' he said, after kissing it, 'nor do I deserve to, but God may be kind and give me a second chance.'

Adrian had made up his mind. The Season was wearing on. He knew that Nick was dubious about the notion of his marrying Athene, and probably his mother might be, too. On the other hand she had never yet refused him anything, and when she saw how lovely and clever Athene was, she would be sure to approve of his choice.

The beauty of it was that by marrying her he could please himself and also give the Kinloch estates the heir which all his relatives were blithering about whenever they saw him.

Since she had no mother or father with her, he would do the proper thing and approach Mr Tenison first. He was never quite sure what the Tenisons thought of him. Mrs Tenison was always polite, but that might be because she wanted to catch him for Emma, who was a pretty little thing, but not Athene's equal.

Now had he not met Athene then Emma would

certainly have been his target. Partly because of that, he was not sure of Mr Tenison's approval of his choice of Athene. He was such a clever devil and had a way of looking at a fellow as though he were an insect on a pin. Well, it wasn't him he intended to marry, so what of that!

He came to these interesting conclusions on the night that they all visited Astley's. Marcus Angmering should have gone with them but he had cried off. 'I have to go into the country to see some relatives on my father's business,' he had said. 'A great bore, but there it is.'

Rumour said that Angmering also thought his father a great bore, but not so much of one that he suspected him of murder!

The following afternoon saw Adrian outside the Tenisons' home. He was dressed even more *à point* than usual, and his hair was a miracle of the hair-dresser's art. It took him some minutes to summon up enough courage to order his driver to knock on the front door. He had not come in his curricle lest the journey spoil the perfection of his appearance.

Fortunately for Adrian's resolution Mr Tenison was neither out, nor engaged, and was prepared to see M'lord at once.

If Mr Tenison knew why Adrian, dressed to kill, wished to see him, he gave nothing away. He looked at the poor fellow in his usual searching manner, so that Adrian dismally concluded that whether or not he impressed Athene he had certainly not impressed her employer.

'I am at your service, m'lord,' was all Mr Tenison said.

'Yes, yes, indeed,' gabbled Adrian. 'I have approached you, sir, because Miss Filmer has no other relative or protector in London, and I felt that it would not be proper for me to propose marriage to her without asking the one person who might be thought to be her protector if I might approach her.'

'Very laudable of you,' said Mr Tenison dryly, somewhat astonished at the spectacle of Adrian coming out with a sentence which had so many words in it, and some of them long! Doubtless love was responsible for this achievement.

Adrian bowed, before saying eagerly, 'I may speak to her alone, then?'

'Only after I have informed her of the reason for your errand. I shall ask you to retire to the drawing-room, where I shall send her when I have told her why you are here.'

Everything was going swimmingly, Adrian thought, sitting in the pretty little room, waiting for his intended to arrive. He was sure that she *would* be his intended before he left the house. They had dealt so well together since they had first met that he could not believe that she would refuse him.

Upstairs Athene was listening to Mr Tenison informing her of Adrian's intention to propose to her. If ever she had thought that such a day might come, she had always imagined that she would immediately be over the moon with joy. Instead she did not know how she felt. Fright warred with delight. Now that the moment had come, could she really go through with it?

She tried to show as little emotion as possible while Mr Tenison was speaking, and he could not have guessed at the conflicting passions which consumed her.

Perhaps he did, though, a little, since before he dismissed her he said in his calm, kind way, 'You must have been aware, my dear, that His Lordship was about to propose, and I trust that you have given a great deal of thought to the answer you ought to give to him.'

Unaccountably Athene's eyes filled with tears. 'Oh, yes, I have,' she said simply. 'A great deal. Only…' and she fell silent until he prompted her by saying, 'Only, my dear…?'

'Only that when these things happen they often take on a very different complexion from when one merely thinks about them.'

He nodded his head. 'I know what you mean. I can only say to you, trust in your God and be true to yourself, Athene, and you cannot go wrong.'

She was holding these words in her mind when she faced a smiling Adrian downstairs. She knew at once that he was sure that she would accept him, and the panic which she felt at the idea of tying herself irrevocably to him surfaced again. More than that, she was frightened of hurting him, for had she not given him the impression that he meant more to her than he actually did, so that he was taking her acceptance for granted?

His first words told her that she was right on that count.

'Oh, Athene, you must know why I have come—even if old Tenison hadn't told you why I am here, you surely would have known. I cannot live without you, and my dearest wish is that you should become my wife as soon as we can arrange the marriage.'

He was so full of innocent delight that he fell on one knee before her and took her cold hands in his to kiss them.

Be true to yourself, Mr Tenison had said, and in order to do that she must not let Adrian go any further until she had told him the whole truth *about* herself.

His smile slowly disappeared when she did not immediately answer him, but loosed her hands gently from his and said, 'Oh, Adrian, before you say anything more there is something which I have to tell you.'

'No need for that,' he said, smiling again. 'All that you need to say is yes.'

Athene shook her head and said, stiff-lipped, 'I must tell you, Adrian, that I am not legitimate. Worse than that, I have no notion of who my father might be. Can it be possible that your family would agree to your marrying someone who has no right to the name which she bears? Someone who has no fortune and no known relatives?'

To do him justice, he showed no signs that he was shocked. He simply said, 'My darling Athene, it is you whom I wish to marry, not your father, nor your mother. What you have just told me makes no difference to my feelings for you. I repeat again, will you marry me?'

If she accepted him now it would be for two reasons, neither of them satisfactory. The first reason would be because of his unthinking generosity in not allowing her dubious social position to weigh with him, the second would be that she would say yes out of pity, not wishing to hurt him when he had been so good and kind.

Reason told her, yes, he can say he would marry you, despite all, now, at this minute, but later—how will he feel later when the vile gossip begins, as it surely will. I can only accept him if I truly love him, but if I am honest I cannot say that. I like him, yes, but, given everything, liking is not enough.

The longer she hesitated the more his honest face began to cloud over. 'I had not thought that you would refuse me,' he muttered sadly. 'I thought that you felt for me what I feel for you.'

She would try to let him down lightly, find some form of words which might delay things, give him time to think over the enormity of what she had told him. To have told him the truth might cost her ev-

erything, but at least it was one less lie on her conscience.

'Adrian,' she said simply, 'I am not sure exactly
what my feelings for you are, and I'm also not certain
what yours are for me. If I suggested to you that you
give us both a little time before you require an answer
from me, then we can consider most carefully whether
we really wish to marry one another.'

He shook his head. 'I already know that I wish to
marry you.'

'Ah, but does not my hesitation tell you that we
might be reading one another wrongly?'

By his puzzled face it was clear that this was beyond him. Athene thought ruefully that Nick would
have known immediately what she had meant, and
that pinpointed the difference between the two men,
and the reason why she was now hesitating about accepting Adrian's offer.

'Think,' she told him gently. 'We lose nothing by
waiting a little, say a week. It will give us an opportunity to get to know one another even more than we
do.'

'I know you well enough already,' he said stubbornly, 'to know that I want you for my wife.'

'I haven't refused you,' Athene said, now a little
desperate. 'Only asked you to wait a little for an answer.'

'You promise to give me one soon? I do not need
a week, but I will accept that.'

'Indeed, I would not keep you forever on the end of a piece of string.'

This provoked the ghost of a chuckle from him. 'No, indeed. I cannot think that in the end you will refuse me.'

'And we shall not speak of this to anyone?'

'If that is what you wish.'

'I do wish it. For the moment it must remain our secret.'

It was over. He kissed her hand and bowed to her, his face melancholy, leaving Athene standing there, alone, among the ruins of all that she had schemed for, ever since she had first known she was going to London with the Tenisons.

Mr Tenison had told her to be true to herself, and so she had: but what might it cost her?

CHAPTER SEVEN

'I've done it, Nick. Popped the question—it was easier than I thought. She wants a week to think my
proposal over, and she did ask me to keep it a secret,
but I can't think that it would trouble her if I told
you—and no one else of course.'

'Of course,' echoed Nick mechanically. 'I take it
that you are speaking of Athene Filmer.'

'Who else? Mind you, I was in the boughs until
she asked for a week to consider it, but I can't believe
that she will refuse me. Women like to keep you on
a string, you know.'

'So they do,' said Nick, his mind reeling from the
knowledge that Athene, after what he considered her
careful campaign, had not immediately accepted
Adrian. She must have some ulterior motive for refusing to accept him at once—but whatever could it
be? To keep him dangling would reinforce her power
over him, but she was risking a possible change of
mind from his cousin. He could scarcely believe that

she would do other than accept him joyfully at the end of the week.

'You are sure that you are prepared for your mama's shock that you have not proposed to one of the golden dollies who are on offer this Season?'

He did not tell Adrian of his discovery of Athene's low birth, because to do so would have betrayed the fact that he had set spies on the trail of the woman his cousin loved. And what would that do to their long-standing friendship?

'No, thank you, I wouldn't have a golden dolly as a gift. They are so taken up with all their riches that they think that they are doing you a favour by marrying you.'

'There is that,' agreed Nick.

He could not explain why he felt so numb at the prospect of Pallas Athene's marriage to Adrian. He had a sudden burning wish to confront her with his knowledge of her origins and of how she was tricking Adrian, and at the same time, yet another contrary wish—never to see her again: it would be too painful.

'You seem a little glum, old fellow. I thought that you'd be happy for me. Congratulations are in order, you know.'

'Not until she has actually said yes,' returned Nick, who had just made a sudden decision to leave London and visit his sister in Hampshire who was constantly complaining that she saw him so seldom.

But not before he had had a last interview with Athene.

* * *

'Oh, Louise, I have so much to tell you. My life has become so complicated that I often think sadly back to the peace of Steep Ride: a peace which I wished to escape, but now that I have, oh dear...' and Athene did something her friend had never seen before.

She burst into tears.

'Come, come. This is not like you, my dear,' said Louise tenderly, putting an arm about her weeping friend.

'I know. I'm usually brave. I can never remember crying before, but whatever choice I make, and I need to make one, seems to me to be a wrong one.'

She had found time somehow to visit Louise in order to warn her of Jackson's busy-bodying around Steepwood, which could constitute a threat to her anonymity if he discovered where she was, and also to ask for her advice over Adrian's proposal.

Where to start? In fairness to Louise she ought to begin by telling her of Jackson, so, sniffling occasionally, she did.

'I hope that I gave nothing away, but I could tell that he did not believe me.'

'If you denied everything then all he has is guess-work.'

'True,' Athene said, 'but I nearly didn't visit you, because I am terrified that I might be followed. I brought a big bag with me—as you see—with another shawl and bonnet in it, and when I was well away from Chelsea I changed into them, stuffing what I had been wearing into the bag so that I should be difficult to identify from a distance.'

Louise said admiringly, 'You would make a good conspirator, Athene.'

Athene sniffed again. 'Nick Cameron would say that I am well named. The goddess was cunning, too.'

Nick's was a new name for Louise to remember. She had heard of Adrian Kinloch before, but little of anyone else.

She said, 'If you are telling me the truth, and I know you are, he cannot trace me through you. I shouldn't worry about Jackson unduly. Is that all which is troubling you? It scarcely seems worth so many tears!'

This small sally set Athene smiling tremulously.

'No, it's not that. It's just…just…that Lord Kinloch has proposed to me and I don't know what answer to give him. I told him yesterday that I'd give him one in a week, and I haven't the faintest notion what my answer will be.'

'Is that the Kinloch who owns a third of Scotland?' Louise asked.

'Yes. He's exactly the sort of person who, before I came to London, I hoped might offer for me: he's handsome, immensely rich and has a title—what more could a poor girl wish for? I have to confess that I encouraged him from the moment we met—he seemed interested in me straight away.'

'I don't understand why you can't make up your

mind to accept him. He certainly sounds like someone any girl would want, let alone a poor one.'

'Oh, Louise, it's not as simple as that—it's just that he's such a simple creature. He's like a friendly puppy, I like him very much as a sort of kind friend, but the idea of marrying him frightens me because, if I am honest, we have nothing in common. I'm not even sure that he really loves me. My charge, Emma Tenison, has suggested that I dazzle him. What happens when that wears off? When he discovers that we have nothing in common? That everything which interests me, bores him? If I marry him it will be because he's rich Lord Kinloch—and anything more mercenary than that, I cannot imagine. How can I be true to myself *and* marry him?'

Louise said slowly, 'You don't love him at all? Not at all? It would then be a kind of arranged marriage— an odd one, which you have arranged for yourself?'

'Yes. I mean, no, no, I don't love him. You have put it perfectly.'

Louise leaned forward, grasped Athene's hand and looked her in the eye. 'My dear, all that I can say to you is this. It is not for me to decide for you, but I made the mistake of marrying Sywell mostly because I needed to feel safe, to gain a place in the world. Oh, he showed me his best side—which he discarded once we were married—but I must face the fact that to some extent we deceived one another. You understand me. Lord Kinloch doesn't sound like Sywell, but there are many ways of being unhappy.'

Athene kissed Louise on the cheek. 'You are a good creature and I will bear what you have said in mind.'

'Excellent, and now, because you have been honest with me, I will be honest with you. I, too, might be illegitimate, as you have told me that you are, but I cannot prove whether I am or not. More than that, if I am legitimate, then I have a claim to be considered a member of one of the great families of England: a member who has been cheated of all her rights of birth.'

She paused, and Athene said, her brave spirits rapidly returning, 'Oh, we are a sorry pair, are we not? I am almost beginning to believe that all of us who live in and around Steepwood Abbey are indeed cursed.'

'Indeed we are, and like you, I am beginning to believe in the curse—however much I wish not to,' said Louise. 'My story is very similar to yours, except that there is this strong possibility that my father did marry my mother. He was the Yardley family's black sheep, Rupert Cleeve, Viscount Angmering, the seventh Earl's heir. He went to France in the middle of their Revolution, convinced that the reformers there were about to transform the world. When it began to turn violent, he and the young Frenchwoman with whom he had fallen in love travelled back to England. Either before they left, or afterwards, he married her.

'What my father had not reckoned with was my grandfather's behaviour when he learned that my mother, Marie de Ferrers, was a Catholic. For some reason my grandfather detested them, why, my father never knew. The Earl's first action on learning of my mother's religion was to disinherit his son, which he could do because the estate was not entailed, and banish him from the family home.

'I was told that my father left England for France vowing never to return until his wife was accepted. As it happened neither of them had long to live: my mother died of a wasting disease and my father was killed in one of the Parisian bread riots in 1793. After their deaths all their letters and papers disappeared. My guardian, John Hanslope, who was the Yardleys' bailiff, believed that my grandfather destroyed them so that his son's daughter—myself—would have no claim to be recognised as a legitimate member of the family, preferring everything go to a distant cousin, leaving me without so much as a halfpenny for my dowry.

'My guardian was convinced that my parents were married, but could find no proof that such a ceremony had ever taken place. So, there you have it. Not only was I Sywell's unconsidered wife, but I am also the Yardleys' abandoned Lady Louise, reduced to earning a living as a country seamstress and then as a London *modiste*.'

The two young women stared at one another, and then, improbably, they began to laugh.

'If I read such a farrago as I have just told you in a Minerva Press novel,' said Louise at last, after wiping her eyes, 'I would say that it was the most immense nonsense, but my guardian, a most down-to-earth man, swears that it is all true.'

'My employer, Mr Tenison, once told me that real life is much more improbable than anything which one might find in a romantic story, so I have no difficulty in believing every word you say.'

'As I believe in yours.'

'I,' said Athene, 'have no claim to legitimacy, but if your parents did marry some evidence must exist somewhere. A proper search ought to be made. A man like Jackson would surely be able to track it down.'

'I can't afford him yet,' Louise told her. 'Everything I earn at present goes into my living expenses and into the business; little is left over. One day soon things will improve, but until then...' and she gave an elegant shrug of the shoulders which did much to convince Athene of her French origin.

Athene was still thinking things over when she reached Chelsea. It was her day off, and Mrs Tenison and Emma were out with Lady Dunlop paying duty calls, so she repaired to the library and amused herself by pulling down one of Mr Tenison's legal folios and looking through it for anything which might help Louise.

She was deep in a learned discussion relating to the laws of entail when the butler came in, looking somewhat disapproving.

'Mr Nicholas Cameron has just arrived, Miss Filmer, and is asking to speak to you. I told him that you were alone this afternoon, but he insisted that I should ask you if you will receive him for a few moments.'

Athene hesitated. She was well aware that it was quite against the rules for a single young woman to entertain a man alone, and she could not help wondering why Nick wished to see her. Could Adrian have informed him of his proposal? Yes, that seemed the most likely explanation. He had probably come to bully her again, to insist that she should not accept him.

Even so she suddenly made her mind up.

'You may tell Mr Cameron that I will receive him here, in the library, but for a few moments only.' The butler's face grew even more disapproving on receiving this order, but he left to do as he was bid.

His expression, however, was less forbidding than the one Nick was wearing when he entered.

Goodness! She was right. He *had* come to hector her. Athene put her hands behind her back, stood straight and tall before the map of the world which covered part of one wall, and stared bravely back at him. She did not offer him a seat.

'Yes, Mr Cameron, what is it you want?'

He was as stiff as she was and bowed to her as though she were a stranger.

'It is perhaps no business of mine but I understand that my cousin has proposed to you...'

Athene could not prevent herself: she interrupted him, her voice icy. 'You are right, it is no concern of yours. But, pray continue, I am all agog to hear what you have to say on the matter.'

'This: I understand that you are keeping him dangling, whether for a genuine reason or to demonstrate your power over him, or perhaps because you prefer to wait for a better offer of some sort from Inglesham.' He paused.

She had no notion of how the mere sight of her, standing there beautiful, proud and tall, affected him. Frustration drove him on. 'What I do know is that you have, so far, successfully deceived the world as to your origins. What would he have to say to you if he knew that you are...'

Nick stopped. He could not say it, could not imagine how he could have the sheer folly, nay, the cursed brutality, to come here to twit her with her ignoble birth—of which he must have learned by ignoble means. Every vestige of colour had fled from her face, but she was as calm and still in her beauty as the goddess who presided over the Old Bailey, as calm and still as Pallas Athene herself. Despite all, he could not but admire her.

'Yes,' she said, 'pray continue—I am sure that there is more to come. It would be a pity to waste your journey here, would it not?'

Calm she might appear to be, but her heart was bleeding. Oh, she might deserve reproach for her campaign to catch Adrian, but not from him, never from him—that she could not bear. She could outface the whole world, but not him.

And he must never know that.

'Very well,' he said, for having begun he must go on to the end, however bitter it might be. 'That you are, to put it kindly, nameless.'

He stopped again.

'Say it,' she said. 'That I am illegitimate. Does the word frighten you? It no longer frightens me. Nor did it frighten Adrian when I told him. If I accept him he will take me as I am, illegitimate and fatherless. So, Mr Nicholas Cameron, your errand is a waste of time. Whether I marry Lord Kinloch—or not—the decision is mine to make, not yours, never yours. I will not ask you how you came by this knowledge—but I can guess.'

What to say? That she was honest—more honest than he had dared to hope—and had risked all by confessing all. That Adrian was nobler, or more foolish than he was. That he was a cur beyond belief to arrive in the home where she might consider herself safe and try to blackmail her? Yes. However he might dress up what he had tried to do, blackmail it was.

'I am sorry,' he said. 'I might have known…'

Athene wanted to weep and scream. So he had always thought her a selfish, scheming harpy, and gone was any hope that she had ever nursed that he might see her as she was: young, helpless, alone in a world where her kind had no hope of betterment save through the man that they might marry—as she might marry Adrian.

All he had succeeded in doing was the opposite of what he had intended. She had been ready to refuse Adrian, to assert her better self, but since Nicholas Cameron and the world believed that she had no better self, she would accept Adrian.

'Known what? That I was not the scheming adventuress you thought me? Know this, Mr Nicholas Cameron. Before you came to see me I had made up my mind not to marry your cousin, but you have changed that mind. If I have, with you, the reputation of being little better than the poor women who walk the streets and who sell themselves for gain, then I might as well live up to it. I have nothing more to say to you. You may leave, or not, as you please, but I shall not remain in the room with you any longer. I have my reputation as a future countess to consider.'

By God, she was a prize worth winning, and he, what had he done? In his blind folly he had thrown her away—nay, thrown her into his cousin's arms, for he was sure that she was telling the truth. She was as unlike Flora Laxford as a woman could be.

He made to move towards her, but she shrank away from him, whispering, 'Go, please go. We have nothing more to say to one another.'

Nick hesitated for a moment.

And then left, his world about his ears.

No one could have guessed, from the face Athene presented to society, the misery which consumed her.

What hurt her the most was that not only did Nick think so little of her that he could believe she would deceive Adrian about the circumstances of her birth, but that he must also have set the Runner, Jackson, on her trail. Was that why Jackson had been so urgent in his questioning of her? Did Nick believe that because her birth was dubious then all her actions would be tainted, that he could think she might know more of the Marquis of Sywell's dreadful end than she was telling him?

At least Nick had not taunted her with that, but what he had implied was bad enough.

He had twitted her with Inglesham, though, and perhaps, given the Duke's interest in her, that was not surprising. It was ironic that later in the day she and the Tenisons were due to attend the grand reception which the Duke was giving in his London palace off the Strand—one of the few remaining there.

All the ton were invited, and since this was his first entertainment for nearly fifteen years all the ton had accepted. Adrian was there, and danced attendance on her, his eyes following her everywhere so that he was chaffed by all the young men of his set. Only Nick was absent.

'And why the devil has he cried off?' Adrian complained to a friend. 'Only the devil knows. He was talking about coming only yesterday. He thought he might be given a chance to inspect the Duke's library, Lord knows why he should want to.'

'Supposed to be a grand one,' laughed Freddie Marchmont. 'Odd fellow, Nick, sometimes.'

'Deuced odd all the time lately,' grumbled Adrian, who had not forgiven Nick's lukewarm reception of his proposal to Athene. He thought that she was looking a bit peaky tonight: another problem for him. One might have believed that a girl proposed to by an Earl would look happier and not keep him waiting. For the first time in his pursuit of her Adrian was beginning to have second thoughts.

So, he had not the courage to face me here tonight, was Athene's explanation of Nick's absence, and she was not far wrong. Not only was he ashamed of his recent attempted interference in her affairs, but he was also beginning to tire of his idle life in the capital.

His father had wished him to take part in the Season as a social preparation for a future political life. The Cameron family had the power to send an MP to Parliament, and as the present incumbent was growing old, Mr Anthony Cameron thought that his clever son would make a useful successor. His reason for wanting Nick at Westminster would be so that he could put forward moderate proposals for land reform which would make it unnecessary for the Camerons to follow the Duke of Sutherland's policies in carrying out the Highland Clearances.

Not only did Nick's father wish to avoid the obloquy and hate which would follow such harsh measures, but he felt that he had a duty towards his tenants to try to avoid such a drastic action except as a last desperate resort to save his estates. Nick, having seen the narrow existence of his father's tenants, often felt ashamed of his own luxurious life in society.

When this was added to his unhappiness over Athene it became almost intolerable. He decided to visit his twin sister, who had married a Hampshire squire and was always complaining that she seldom saw him, and then return to London for a short time before going back to Scotland.

Consequently, on arrival at Albany after his disastrous interview with Athene he immediately arranged matters so that he could travel to Hampshire on the morrow, in the hope that a visit there might lighten the burden of misery under which he now laboured.

Whoever would have thought that a woman could affect him so!

Athene was affected too. The Season, which she had begun with such high hopes, had lost all its savour. Whenever she met Adrian he offered her a wounded face. His pride had been damaged by her refusal to accept him immediately. To try to salve his misery, he began to avoid her and to talk to Emma instead—much to Mrs Tenison's delight.

Nick's disappearance also distressed her more than she could have anticipated. Her days became wearisome and her evenings the more so. The only thing which lightened them were the letters from her mother detailing all the serio-comic happenings of the

Steepwood district, including a description of Jackson's visit.

'Apparently,' she wrote, 'I was the only person whom he didn't interview, which makes me either distinguished, or undistinguished, I'm not sure which.'

Athene had a sad chuckle over that, remembering Jackson's quizzing of her. One morning, just before the week she had promised Adrian was over, she received a thicker budget of letters than usual.

'Goodness,' exclaimed Emma, whose own budget that morning was light, 'you are lucky. I don't receive many letters and I do so adore reading them.'

'These are only from mother, and two old friends, one of whom is getting married. I think. Oh, and another, official-looking one. Goodness knows who that is from.' She essayed a mild joke. 'My banker, perhaps.'

Athene didn't open her letters immediately but took them to her room. One of the friends who had written to her was Louise, but, naturally, she hadn't seen fit to tell Emma of that. The official-looking letter she left to the last, even though it had aroused her curiosity.

She opened it carefully, to discover that it was from a firm of solicitors: Hallowes, Bunthorne and Thring. It was short and to the point and left her bewildered.

'Dear Madam,' it said. 'Pursuant to a matter of some urgency which has recently arisen we must ask you, of your goodness, to visit our office tomorrow

at two o'clock of the afternoon, so that this matter
may be resolved immediately.

'We must also urge you to keep this letter, and the
visit, confidential. We assure you that nothing in the
case concerned is to your detriment, and our reputation is such that I am sure that you are aware that you
need have no fear that yours would suffer if you were
to accede to our request...'

What in the world was all that about! If the matter
concerning her was so serious—and so urgent—why
had they not written to her mother? Her mother had
said nothing in this morning's letter which could bear
on this. Should she ignore them and seek Mr
Tenison's advice as to whether she ought to visit 'our
office' when the reason for the visit was cloaked in
mystery?

Why should she ask Mr Tenison? Was not she,
Athene Filmer, well able to determine her own fate?
Had she not, this very week, in some sense or other
seen off both Adrian and his cousin Nick? If she had
been mistaken in her dealings with them, then the
mistake was at least hers and no one else's.

She would go to the lawyers, Hallowes, Bunthorne
and Thring—and of course she had heard of them, as
who in the ton had not? She gave a nervous little
laugh after thinking what pompous names they were.

She wondered what the owners of them were like,
and what they had to do with her. Well, she would
soon find out.

* * *

'I received this letter yesterday,' Athene said, showing it to the porter who sat in a little sentry box in the porch of the lawyers' offices, 'and I am here as requested.'

The porter fetched out a battered notebook and consulted it. 'You are Miss Athene Filmer?'

'Indeed, this letter is proof.'

'Follow me, madam, you are expected.'

The room she was shown into was so grand that Athene stared about her in amazement. The porter motioned her to a chair before disappearing through a pair of double doors, to emerge a few minutes later to usher her into what was obviously the firm's main office.

Inside, a little sharp-faced man who had been sitting at a desk as large as a billiard table rose to greet her with a low bow when the porter announced, 'Miss Filmer to see you, Mr Hallowes.'

'Miss Filmer, I see that you are prompt as to time,' he said, 'and your presence here is indeed a pleasure.'

Athene bowed back. 'I must say, sir, that for me this is rather more a surprise than a pleasure.'

He gave a short laugh at that. 'I was informed that you were a clever young woman. My information was obviously correct. You have kept this meeting confidential, I trust.'

'With a little difficulty, sir. My invention was taxed somewhat by having to find a convincing excuse to leave my employer's home this afternoon, but not so completely that I was unable to do so. I would be pleased to learn from you what this urgent business is which brings me here.'

He laughed a little at that, before saying, 'My dear Miss Filmer, it is not I who have business with you. I am merely an intermediary. I must ask you to accompany me to our private suite where, I assure you, everything will be explained.'

'It seems, sir, that I have no alternative but to obey you, since my curiosity is stronger than my common-sense.'

This elicited another chuckle from him.

'Very good, Miss Filmer, very good, indeed, but have no fear of what you may discover.'

He rose, saying, 'Pray take my arm, Miss Filmer. All will shortly be explained.'

He led her to another pair of double doors, along a short corridor lined with caricatures of legal figures and into a room which was so superbly furnished that it might have been found in the home of a Duke. So it was perhaps not surprising that a Duke should be present in it.

It was the Duke of Inglesham who rose to his feet to bow to them. Mr Hallowes relinquished Athene's arm and said, also bowing low, 'Your Grace, as you requested, Miss Filmer is here to see you. I will leave her with you, since that is your pleasure and your command.'

'Only if Miss Filmer agrees. You may rest assured,' the Duke said to her, bowing again, 'that your presence here is known to no one outside these prem-

ises. Mr Hallowes is aware of the reason why I have
sent for you, and should you, at any time, wish to
terminate our conference you are free to leave this
room—and the premises—immediately. I should
wish, however, that you would do me the honour of
hearing me out.'

Goodness, what in the world could all this be
about? thought the dazed Athene as Mr Hallowes
bowed himself from the room as though he were leaving royalty. When the door had shut behind him the
Duke waved a hand at an armchair. 'Pray be seated,
Miss Filmer. I shall stand, for what I have to say to
you must be said with all due consequence, not from
a man lounging in a chair.'

Since there was nothing else for it, Athene sat
down, but not before saying, 'I cannot help, Your
Grace, but wonder what you have to tell me, rather
than my mother. I am, after all, a single young woman
of little consequence, and it would be more natural
for you to approach me through her.'

'True. Very true. You are, however, a young
woman of great common-sense and presence of mind,
and what you have to say to me when I have finished
speaking will determine whether or not I approach
your mother.'

If, as I am beginning to suspect, thought Athene,
still bewildered, he is about to propose to me, as Nick
Cameron suggested the other day, then it would
surely be expected that he would apply to my mother
first, not last. On the other hand he is a noted eccen-

tric, and this might be just one more demonstration of his oddity.

'If that is so, Your Grace, then I will listen carefully to what you have to say.'

'Excellent,' he murmured, and although what she had just said seemed to have pleased him, he suddenly seemed oddly ill at ease before he began to speak.

'The events of which I am about to tell you occurred before you were born. I was then the heir to a Dukedom and an estate impoverished by my grandfather, who had squandered his enormous fortune on building a great house, and on gambling, drink and women. My father succeeded to a much reduced inheritance. Naturally, as a very young man, this meant little to me. My father was extremely friendly with the Rector of the parish church at Inglesham, and in the year before I went to Oxford I was sent to him to improve my scanty knowledge of Latin and Greek. My tutor had been remiss in educating me in the classics, preferring field sports to indoor bookishness—his phrase.

'The Rector had a pretty daughter of my own age— I was then seventeen, and we became great friends. She joined me in my studies and being with her made them easier for me—I was not about to let a young girl best me, you understand.

'She bested me in another way, for when I first came down from Oxford in the summer vacation I found that she had turned into a rare beauty, such a rare beauty that I immediately lost my heart to her.

I behaved myself, though, while I was at Oxford, telling myself that when my scholastic education there was over I should be able to ask her to be my wife.

'I was such a simpleton that it never occurred to me that there could be any objection to my marrying her. After all, her father was my father's best friend, he came from an old gentry family, impoverished it was true, but the name was one famous in the history of our country and has become more famous since. It was Nelson.

'I shall never forget that last summer when I came down from Oxford for the last time. We roved the woods around Inglesham together, secure in our happiness. Charlotte did once suggest that my father might not completely approve of our marrying, but I could not believe that he would refuse me. One day, when we were alone together—and it was, God forgive me, the only time that it happened—our gentle love-making turned into real passion and we forgot ourselves in fulfilling it.

'Now I knew that, in honour, I must seek my blessing from my father so that we might be married as soon as possible. Imagine my distress and horror when after I had told him of my love he informed me that there could be no question of my marrying a relatively poor young woman, however good her birth. The only thing which could save Inglesham from being lost to the family which had owned it since the Conquest was for me to make a rich marriage—which he was in the process of arranging with the daughter of a London merchant grown rich through the India trade.

'I argued and swore at him. I had been a good son who had always obeyed him without question and yet the first time I had ever asked anything from him he had refused me. Alas, he was adamant. If I did not agree to marry the woman he had chosen for me he would cast me off without a penny. Since the estate was not entailed it would go to a distant cousin and I would be left with only a worthless title when he died.

'In the middle of this my darling's father came to Inglesham Court to tell my father that his daughter was expecting my child. If I had thought that this would weaken my father's resolve, I was mistaken. He was more than ever determined that I should not marry a girl who had allowed me such freedom before marriage. Worse than that, my Charlotte's father agreed with him. We were both to be cast out into the world penniless if we did not give one another up.

'Were we to part, he and my father would fund a small annuity for my Charlotte, and see her settled in another part of the country as the unfortunate widow of the war then beginning, so that she might live a decent and respectable life. I, of course, was to marry the rich citizen's daughter my father had chosen for me. We were not to be allowed to meet again—unless we were so foolish as to try to elope together. Had we met, things might have been different...

'God forgive me, the two men wore me down. I gave up my dearest love without so much as a word of farewell. I had no notion of where she had gone, and I was made to promise that I would not try to find her or the child: I never knew whether it was a boy or a girl. I was well served for my cowardice. My wife was a shrew and we never had a child of our own. I had gained the whole world—for her money restored Inglesham and its estates to their former glory—but I had lost my soul. Had I my time again I would not have done what I did.

'I never knew another happy moment. What my life would have been if I had married Charlotte and abandoned everything I shall never know. What I do know is that to marry for money when one might marry for love is the worst thing anyone can do. The Bible said it once and for all: ''Better is a dinner of herbs where love is, than a stalled ox and hatred therewith.'' I do not blame my wife for our unhappy marriage: I blame myself for agreeing to it.

'When she died I thought to look for your mother, but the trail was cold. Coutts would not give me details of the trust set up for her, if there were one. The Rector and his wife left the parish shortly after Charlotte was sent away, and I had no notion where they went. I had given up hope of ever finding her again until the night I saw you in the ballroom. I could not believe that two women could be so alike and not be related. I made it my business to find out all I could about you, and thanks to mere chance, the chance which rules all our lives, I discovered where your mother lives and that you are indeed my daughter.

'All that remains is to ask your forgiveness.'

Athene, who had been twisting her hands together in anguish as her father's sad tale unrolled, particularly when he had spoken of the folly of marrying for money, and not for love, said, 'From what you have told me you have suffered greatly—which must be punishment enough. My mother suffered, too, and still does. But why have you not told *her* this? Why me?'

'Because I am still a coward. I was, I am, fearful that she might hate me for my desertion of her—for that is what it must have seemed. I was fearful of what she might have told you. To tell you myself seemed to be the best way back for me. You are a clever young woman, compassionate, too. I have seen that pretty child of the Tenisons blossom under your care.'

'A way back,' murmured Athene. 'My mother never uttered a word of reproach about your desertion of her, leaving her to have a love child, and to be the object of malicious rumour. She never told me the name of her lover, and she said that she understood what pressures had been brought to bear on you to desert her. One day, before she was sent away from her home, and all she knew, from the home where she had been kept a prisoner, she packed a bag and tried to go to the byway where she knew that you rode daily in order to speak to you, to ask you to defy the world with her, but my grandfather caught her and stopped her, so she never tried again. He deserves forgiveness—if he still lives, that is. She never told me your name, or her own true one, and I have never met any of her family—which is mine also.'

'We are all sinful and all deserve forgiveness,' said the Duke tiredly. 'But if I were to meet your mother again, do you believe that she would not turn me away?'

'I think not—but would it not be fitting that you risked her doing so?'

'I think that you have your mother's courage and something of the shrewdness which all the Ingleshams are supposed to possess—except for my grandfather, of course. I now know where she lives and in due course I will visit her. The rest lies with God.'

Athene nodded. What her father had confessed to her had struck home. If she were now to marry Adrian was she not about to repeat what he had done and condemn herself to a barren, unhappy life when Adrian was no longer dazzled by her, and his shallowness bored her? The Duke had simply told her in different words what Mr Tenison had said to her on the day when Adrian had come to propose.

Whatever her brave and defiant words to Nick, she

would now refuse Adrian, and tell her father to try his fortune with her mother.

More she could not say or do.

CHAPTER EIGHT

'What in the world is wrong with you, Nick? You are like a bear with a sore head. Even Chudleigh has noticed that you are not your usual cheerful and cynical self, and you know how unobservant he usually is about everything other than the management of the estate and his family.'

Nick frowned. He had been trying not to read the *Morning Post* in case it contained an announcement of Athene and Adrian's coming marriage, when his sister had arrived to disturb his peace.

'Nothing, Lucy, nothing at all.'

His sister sat down opposite to him at the breakfast table, where he sat among the ruins of an insubstantial breakfast. This was simply another sign that something was amiss, since his love of food while remaining thin was a Cameron family joke.

'Don't try to bam me, Nick. It's your sister speaking and I always know when you are not telling the truth. What is it: is a woman troubling you?'

This was another family joke. There had always been a psychic bond between the pair of them. When one was struck, or hurt themselves when either together or apart, the other always cried as well.

Nick shrugged before giving a despairing laugh. 'What a witch you are, Lucy. I might have known that even after a long absence you still have the ability to read my mind. Yes, you're right, it *is* a woman.'

'And is she right for you, Nick? Is that why you are troubled—that she might not be?'

He groaned. 'Yes…no…I don't know. In any case she's going to marry Adrian. He's already proposed to her and he's only waiting for her to say yes.'

Lucy stared at him. 'You mean that he's met someone who didn't immediately fall into his arms? Goodness me, is she very rich, then, that she can afford to turn him down? All that lovely money and a title, too, must surely make up for his lack of brains.'

'That, my love, is the trouble. She's as beautiful as sin, as clever as the devil, as poor as a church mouse, and came to town to snare a rich husband, preferably one with a title. She's made him wait for an answer, one can't imagine why.'

'What I don't understand, Nick, is given all that, why she didn't immediately fall into his arms.' Lucy paused and added somewhat slyly, 'I suppose the cleverness, added to the beauty, is why you are taken with her. Does that have something to do with her making Adrian wait?'

'Yes, and the devil of it is, that on top of that, rich

though Adrian is, he's not as rich as Inglesham, and the *on dit* is that either she's after him, or he's after her. One can only suppose that she's holding Adrian off in order to see whether Inglesham proposes. After all a real live Duke, even if middle-aged, must be the catch of any Season.'

'I see. What I also see is that she must be something remarkable to have you all in such a pother over her.'

'Oh, yes,' said Nick bitterly. 'It's not often that one meets a man's brain in a beautiful woman's body. Everything she says and does is to perfection.'

He nearly added, 'Damn her,' but thought, better not.

'Oh, dear, Nick, you have got it badly, haven't you? What I don't understand is why you didn't propose to her yourself if she's such a nonpareil—if a female can be a nonpareil, that is.'

'I believe they can. But I have antagonised her too much for any proposal from me to succeed, and in the doing I have fallen even more utterly under her spell. We parted at odds and to be truthful we have never been at evens. I know what I feel for her: what I don't know is what she feels for me. I always laughed at fellows who mooned after a particular woman, but I assure you that I am not laughing now.'

'So I see. You suppose her to be mercenary, and after Flora Campbell's betrayal, that irks you. Has this beauty a father or a mother? You say she came to town to husband-hunt. She cannot have done that on her own.'

'No, indeed. She has no family, other than a mother who I gather is something of a recluse, her birth is dubious, and she is a companion to a pretty nonentity. To do her justice, she has caused the nonentity to blossom—another aspect of her damned perfection.'

'Jealousy,' said his sister quietly, coming over and giving him a gentle kiss on his cheek, 'is a very strong emotion when added to frustrated desire and the damage that wretched woman did to you. No wonder you look and sound so unhappy. Shall I order Chudleigh to fetch a barrel for you so that, like Diogenes, you may sit in it and hate all the world?'

'Oh, you are as bad as Pallas Athene. She is full of such learning. I often wonder how poor Chudleigh copes with you—he being so down to earth.'

'Oh, I have my quirks and he has his. Successful marriage consists in accepting one another's oddities with a wry smile and the ability to say, 'Precisely, darling,' in measured tones when one's other self says something mysterious.'

It was Nick's turn to kiss his sister's cheek when he had finished laughing at her sally. 'I had forgotten how much we were one another's other self when we were young. It's a great pity that we live so far apart. You have quite cured me of the megrims. The thing is, that if you ever met her, you would soon be bosom bows with Miss Athene Filmer.'

He was not being entirely truthful by claiming to

be cured, but if his distress over Athene was beginning to trouble his sister then he owed it to her and
her husband to put on a better face which he did for
the rest of his visit. Chudleigh's return from his fields
put an end to their confidences, but not before Lucy
had remarked, 'If you have fallen in love with her,
Nick, then I can safely assume that she must be the
sort of young woman of whom I would thoroughly
approve—husband-hunter or not.'

Telling Adrian that she would not marry him was
even harder than Athene had thought it might be.

He had come to see her when the week was up, his
face shining with eagerness. He had half persuaded
himself that little Miss Emma might be a better bet
as a wife than her clever and beautiful companion,
but when he entered the Tenisons' drawing-room to
receive her decision he was struck all over again by
Athene's classic beauty and her perfect composure.

It was, he thought—struck all poetical for once—
like comparing fine wine with bread and milk, so se-
renely lovely was Athene beside Emma's more ordinary prettiness. The thought of making her his
Countess, of seeing her presented at Court, of having
other men envying him the possession of such a treasure, made him feel quite faint.

It did not occur to him that never once when he
thought of her being his wife were the more earthy
pleasures of marriage a consideration. Athene was to
be a trophy as well as a bed-mate. Oh, he would bed

her, and she would give him his heir, but that was not the main reason for her attracting him so much. He was dimly aware that he lacked the intellect which Nick and some of his friends and relatives possessed, but by marrying Athene he would redress that balance. None of them would have a wife so beautiful, so clever, so poised, so able always to say and to do the right thing.

Alas, it had never occurred to him that she would refuse him—and here she was, doing exactly that.

'But why?' he exclaimed, his honest face troubled. 'I thought that you liked me. I know that I like you, love you, I mean,' he added hastily, dimly aware that a stronger display of affection might suit him better in the dire situation in which he had somehow arrived.

He had thought Athene's plea for delay mere girlish nonsense: after all, girls were supposed to be unpredictable, but that she might turn him down had never entered his head.

'Oh, Adrian, I do like you, very much. But I like you as a friend, not as a possible husband. Oh, I know that you have so much to offer me beyond your own kind self—wealth, position, a title, and a beautiful home. In the end, however, there must be more than that between us for marriage to be a possibility. No— accept that, with the best will in the world, I cannot accept your offer, and let us part as friends.'

'You are sure that you might not reconsider? Would you not like a little more time?'

If Nick had not reproached her, if Mr Tenison had

not asked her to be true to herself, and most of all if her father had not told her of what he had endured because he had not been true to himself, Athene might have given way to spare Adrian the pain which he was obviously feeling. As it was, she could only think of the pain that a loveless marriage on her part might cause them both, and allow that to guide her judgement.

'No,' he suddenly said, reading her beautiful, troubled face correctly. 'I can see that that would not answer. Is there someone else, Athene, someone whom you could accept?'

At least she could answer that truthfully, remembering Nick flinging himself away from her, and her passionate denying response to him.

'No, Adrian, that is, not to say that there might not be someone in the future, but now, no, there is no one.'

'That's all right, then,' he said, relieved to learn that another fellow had not bested him. 'I told no one but Nick that I had offered for you, and I know that he left town without saying anything to anyone about it. I'm sure we both ought to keep mum; you know how odd society is about such things.'

'Yes,' agreed Athene, relieved. She stood to lose the most if it was bandied about that she and Adrian had secretly been discussing marriage and that she had, in effect, jilted him. Mr Tenison had told her that he had said nothing to his wife of Adrian's proposal to her. Mrs Tenison was unaware that Adrian had even visited the house on the fateful day on which he had consulted her husband before making his offer to Athene.

Mournfully Adrian bent over her hand.

'I can only wish you the best in the future,' he said. 'If you should decide to change your decision in the next few days,' he added hopefully, 'be sure to let me know on the instant. You have quite broken my heart, you know.'

He was being so kind in his simple-minded way that Athene felt her eyes fill with tears, but all the same she shook her head.

'No, Adrian, I shall not change my mind. And I wish you all the best, too.'

For good or ill it was over. Athene had refused the opportunity to become everything for which she had hoped and schemed before she had left Steep Ride, and when the door closed behind Adrian she was left with nothing but memories of what might have been.

Life had a nasty habit of going on, Athene discovered, as though the personal drama which had occupied her every moment during the last few weeks had not taken place. The sun rose and set. Balls were given, a boating party on the Thames took place, and the theatre was visited. In short, nothing seemed to have changed.

A few rumours made the rounds to the effect that young Kinloch no longer seemed to be smitten with the Tenisons' poor companion, and had stopped dancing attendance on her. No one was really surprised or interested in why he had. It was, after all, only to be expected, she was scarcely the right sort of *parti* for a titled young man of such great wealth and position.

Adrian flirted with a few girls, found them dull after Athene, and then, on an impulse, seeing the Tenisons and Athene seated alone at one of the greatest receptions of the Season, he went over to them. Yes, Emma *was* a pretty young thing, and since Athene showed no signs of changing her mind there could be little harm in keeping up his friendship with her.

'Oh, we have missed you lately, m'lord,' said Mrs Tenison cheerfully. 'Have you been out of town?'

'Oh, I've been otherwise engaged, madam,' he told her. 'I came to see if Miss Emma would stand up with me in the next dance.'

He purposely avoided looking at Athene—only offering her a distant bow—before walking off with her charge. Mr Tenison, who had already spoken to Athene about her refusal of Adrian, watched them go with a sad expression on his face.

When Athene had told him of her decision in the library, shortly after Adrian had left, he had said, 'I think that you are wise, my dear. You were not at all suited. Had you asked me to advise you, I would have told you that, and not because I think that now he has lost you he will offer for Emma, but because I care for your welfare. I can't oppose the marriage, even if I don't like the prospect of having a son-in-law whom

I can't talk to, but I know that she will be happy with him, happier than you would have been. My one worry is that you may have lost your best chance of marrying well.'

'No,' said Athene, remembering what her father had told her. 'I would not sell my soul in order to contract an essentially loveless marriage—even to gain the whole world—for the price might have been too high. Think only that you are the father I have never had, and that your kindness has made my life pleasant.'

They had parted after that, and now she was condemned, if that was the right word, to watch Adrian turn his attentions to Emma. His heart was not so broken, she thought wryly, that it was not mending itself in double-quick time! If he did intend to marry Emma, though, she wished them both well, even if her refusal of Adrian meant that she would now remain a spinster.

Nick grew increasingly restless in his Hampshire retreat. So restless that his sister's husband said to him over the port, one night at dinner, 'Old fellow, if this young woman you are mooning after is occupying you so much that Lucy is beginning to worry about your health, I suggest that you go back to town and have it out with her.'

So Lucy had told Chudleigh of Athene. Nick said solemnly, 'Does that come from the depths of your knowledge of human nature, Chudleigh?'

'No,' his brother-in-law returned, 'rather of that of the animals which surround us. They are more like us than we care to think. Make her, or break with her, but don't pine away like a ninny-noddy. Action is wanted here, not brooding.'

Nick lifted his glass in a mockery of a toast. 'Splendid,' he said. 'Action it will be—and if she is married, or pledged to be married to Adrian by the time I return, then I shall be off to Rosanna Knight's house on the instant, and bed either her, or her sister! Will that do?'

'Got it bad, hasn't he?' said Tom Chudleigh to his wife while they watched Nick's carriage drive away. 'Good fellow, your brother, but he don't take life easy, does he?'

It was a verdict which Nick was making about himself.

He arrived in London in the pouring rain, and for want of anything else to do visited Jackson's boxing saloon in Bond Street. Nothing much seemed to have changed in the month he had been away. There were the same fellows standing about, or exercising.

He was in the middle of lifting weights when he saw Adrian come in. He was looking singularly pleased with himself and the moment he saw Nick he mouthed something incomprehensible in his direction. Weight-lifting over, he rushed at Nick excitedly.

'Congratulate me, old fellow,' he exclaimed before Nick had so much as got his breath back. 'I'm to be married as soon as the lawyers have done their work, and I want you to stand up with me at the ceremony. I'm to be turned off at Kinloch House—it will hold more wedding guests than the Tenisons *pied à terre* in Chelsea.'

So soon! Athene—as she had promised at their last disastrous meeting—must have accepted Adrian shortly after his own retreat to the country. Everything was over, so he might as well stop mooning about the impossible, get royally drunk, and then bed Rosanna, or perhaps do it the other way round, as he had promised Tom Chudleigh. Before that, though, he had to say something to the beaming Adrian.

'I always believed that Athene would accept you,' he said despairingly. 'I suppose she thought that she'd look less mercenary if she held you off for a little.'

'Athene! Who said anything about Athene? No, it's Emma Tenison I'm marrying, dear little Emma, I can't think why I took so long to realise what a treasure she is.'

Nick gave a short, incredulous laugh. Could Adrian really be telling the truth? Had he, in a few short weeks, gone from adoring one charmer to adoring another?

'Well,' he finally achieved, 'that was a quick change of mind, and no mistake.'

'What's that? I didn't change *my* mind, Athene changed hers and refused me, and a good thing, too. We weren't really suited, you know. She was too clever for me—bound to have been trouble later on.

Whereas, my dear little Emma…' and he offered Nick a smile of such beaming fatuity that Nick could scarcely credit it—or what he had just heard.

'You mean that *she* turned you down?'

'Have you grown cloth ears in the country, old fellow? I've just told you that she refused me. Said that she liked me very much as a good friend, but marriage wasn't on. Said it would be a mistake… What's wrong with you, Nick, I've never known you so slow on the uptake before. Now, you'll forgive me if I toddle off. I'm taking my sweet Emma for a spin in my slow old curricle. I turned the new one over the other day practising for the race to Brighton, but the dear little thing's persuaded me to drop the notion. Said she wants me present at the wedding without a cracked head or a broken arm, and damme, she's right. As it was I sprained my wrist a little, and the curricle's done for!'

In the middle of the shock which Adrian's news about Athene had dealt him, Nick registered the comic fact that 'my sweet Emma' was already taking after her dominant mama and was ordering the so-called head of the family about!

And where was Athene while all this was going on? How did she feel about the rapid desertion of her recent squire, who had claimed to be so besotted by her?

Somehow Nick managed to offer Adrian some coherent congratulations, while mentally deciding that a rendezvous at Rosanna Knight's was not really on the cards now, but one with Athene at the Tenisons most definitely was. He dressed as quickly as he could and drove straight to Chelsea.

The only thing which he had to worry about was whether Athene had turned down Adrian in order to accept Inglesham!

He arrived at the Tenisons wondering what in the world he was going to say to her. To propose on the instant might be seen as being as equally abrupt and surprising as Adrian's immediate transfer of his affections from Athene to Emma—and what a turn-up that was.

He was still turning his tactics over in his mind when the butler, Pears, who had opened the door, informed him that Miss Athene Filmer was no longer in London.

'Not in London,' he echoed witlessly.

'No, sir. She has left us and I believe that she has returned to her home in Northamptonshire.'

'What is it, Pears?' asked Mr Tenison who had watched Nick arrive from an upstairs window and had immediately guessed what his errand might be, but thought it politic not to let Pears be aware of that when he appeared at the front door after an urgent and hasty run downstairs. 'Has Mr Cameron come to call on Miss Emma—or myself?'

'While I am always pleased to see you, sir,' returned Nick, bowing, 'it was really Miss Filmer I was hoping to see.'

'I think, sir,' said Mr Tenison, 'that it would be

better for us not to conduct business on the doorstep. Pray enter. Neither my wife nor my daughter are at home this afternoon, and I would be glad of your company as well as happy to enlighten you as to Miss Filmer's whereabouts.'

He led Nick to the room which served as his library and his study and offered him a glass of Madeira, which Nick, distractedly, took.

'I perhaps ought to explain,' Mr Tenison began, 'that my wife employed Miss Filmer to act as a companion to my daughter because she thought that she would find an older and more experienced one to be too oppressive. Miss Filmer carried out her task excellently, but after your cousin, Lord Kinloch, proposed to Emma, my wife was of the opinion that as she was shortly to be a married woman, Emma no longer needed her services. Accordingly Miss Filmer was asked to resign, which she did, and left Chelsea for her home, Datchet House, in Steep Ride, within the week. I am sure that you will find her there.'

He did not tell Nick of Mrs Tenison's indecent triumph after Adrian had proposed to and been accepted by Emma, nor that he knew of Adrian's proposal to Athene.

'I would have Filmer leave at once,' Mrs Tenison had told her husband. 'I think that she had some notion that she might snare Kinloch for herself, and I don't want her presence here to put a spoke in Emma's wheel.'

Mr Tenison could not assure his wife that she was

unlikely to do any such thing without breaching the confidence which Athene had asked for. He had been compelled to watch helplessly when his wife brusquely and summarily dismissed her.

If Nick thought that the whole business left a sour taste in both their mouths he did not say so. After all, his own conduct towards Athene had scarcely been blameless. He drank Mr Tenison's Madeira, thanked him for his information, chatted a few moments about current news—and left.

But not before Mr Tenison had said to him, 'I trust, Mr Cameron, that when you next see Miss Filmer you will convey my good wishes to her. I was sorry to see her go. She was a good hard-working young woman, and during her stay with us gave my Emma the confidence which she greatly needed and which she will take with her to her marriage to your cousin. May I, at the same time, offer you my best wishes for your own future.'

So the shrewd old fellow had grasped that he had been strongly attracted to Athene, and had let him know in his own inimitable fashion—and had wished him luck into the bargain!

Before she had left London Athene had visited Louise. This was easier than it had ever been before, since Mrs Tenison had relieved her of all her duties. 'I am not in the business of escorting her around the great houses of London so that she might try to catch another suitor now that she has failed with Kinloch,' being her unkind remark to her husband.

Louise heard Athene's news sympathetically. 'You are quite sure that you were wise to refuse Adrian?' being her only comment. 'From all that I hear of him he does not sound at all like my late husband. On the other hand the *on dit* is that he's a bit of an ass.'

'But kind,' agreed Athene. 'No, I have no regrets there. What in the world would I be able to say to him at breakfast after the excitements of the wedding were over!'

'True,' said Louise. 'When do you return to Steepwood, and how shall you bear missing the savour which living in London confers on life?'

'Oh, I have had far too much of that savour lately,' confessed Athene. 'I shall be happy to enjoy the leisurely delights of the country.'

'So you say now, but it might be a different matter when you're there. By the by, what about Kinloch's cousin—Nick something, wasn't it? Did you bid adieu to him as well as to Adrian?'

Athene answered her friend as carelessly and calmly as she could. 'Oh, he left London for the country some little time ago.'

'Did he, indeed? Was this before or after Adrian proposed, or you refused him?'

Athene had forgotten how shrewd Louise was behind her pretty, somewhat feather-headed appearance. 'Oh, my dear,' she finally achieved. 'We had the most tremendous set-to before he disappeared, and I'm sure that I shan't be seeing him again.'

Despite all her brave resolutions Athene's eyes filled with tears, and she could not stifle a sob.

'So, you did care for him. What went wrong?'

'Everything. He thinks me a cold conniving schemer who was after Adrian for his money and his title, and I only found out how strongly I was attracted to him after Adrian had begun to make a leg to me so determinedly and I was responding to him. Had I met him first—but there it was. He offered me nothing but reproaches, and I was equally harsh with him. The worst part of it all is that besides Mr Tenison, he was the only man I could talk to sensibly, and who talked back to me in the same vein—and he had to despise me for what he thought my venality. Oh, Louise, only someone like you knows how hard it is for a poor girl to make a life for herself in this cruel world.'

'Particularly,' said Louise dryly, 'when someone like Mr Nick Cameron, who has only known comfort and riches, can so cruelly judge those who have never owned them.'

'Precisely. Now let us talk of other things. Have you heard anything further about Sywell's death?'

'Nothing. I dare swear that you know more than I do, or that you might do when you are home again. You will write to me as often as you can, won't you? I shall miss you desperately. You are the one bosom bow I have, and as Nick Cameron was the only man to whom you could talk sensibly, so you are the only woman who performs that service for me! I will pray that you meet him again in better circumstances, although I cannot completely like someone who has been so unkind to you.'

The two young women embraced, and parted, Athene to finish packing, and Louise to return to the business of earning a successful living whilst praying that her true identity would remain a secret.

The one thing which sustained Athene on the drive back to Datchet House and Steep Ride and her mother, was that her mother would not be alone in the world as she had been since Athene's departure for London.

Her letter giving the news of her unexpected return arrived on the very morning that she did, and she found her mother waiting for her in the yard at the Angel, which was the post-house in Abbot Quincey. The sight of her drove Nick Cameron and everything which had happened to her since she had left home, out of her head.

'You look pale, my darling,' her mother exclaimed after they had kissed one another. 'Did London air not agree with you?'

'Oh, the journey was tiring, and yes, London is a dirty, smoky place, but very exciting, for all that.'

'Exactly as I remember it on my one short visit. I am surprised, if pleased, to have you home so soon— have the Tenisons not returned? I trust that you parted on good terms.'

'I will tell you everything in due course,' said Athene, who had no wish to begin informing her mother of her strange London odyssey in an inn yard.

'Indeed. Forgive my impatience, but I was a little troubled when I received your letter, and again when I saw you looking so poorly. Pure country air and food will do you the world of good, I'm sure.'

How small Datchet House now looked to one used to London's magnificence, how mean the streets in the villages they drove through, and how tiny the shops! Athene was shocked by her own response to the meagreness of country living. On the other hand the scenery was beautiful, and the water in the Steep River was clear and untainted when they drove by it.

Conversation was slow, too, she found, when neighbours came to call, wanting to know about the excitements of London and the Season. She had told her mother most of what had happened to her there, and while her mother understood why she had refused Adrian, she had grieved at the necessity for it.

'You would have been set up for life,' she sighed. 'Not left, like me, to pine alone in the rural fastnesses of country living.'

'But at what a price, Mother. You would not have had me pay it, I trust.'

'No, indeed. I understand you…but still…'

Athene said nothing of the Duke and his sad confession to her; consequently it was all the more surprising when, one afternoon, there was a knock on the front door, and their little maid being otherwise engaged, Athene answered it herself. Before her, on the doorstep, his handsome face anxious, stood the Duke of Inglesham.

'My dear Athene,' he said, somewhat surprised. 'I had not thought to find you here. I wonder if you would be so good as to ask your mother if she will receive me. I will quite understand if she feels that she cannot.'

'Of course I will receive you,' said Mrs Filmer from behind Athene's back. 'Even the most common criminal deserves a hearing, and you are far from being that.'

She beckoned the Duke into the front parlour where Athene left them alone together: a pair of one-time lovers who had not seen one another for over twenty years.

Jackson had given Nick the Filmers' address in Steep Ride. He could not be sure how Athene would receive him—given the circumstances of their last meeting—but he readied himself for departure, hoping against hope while he did so.

He delayed setting off for a day when Adrian asked him to be sure to attend the reception which he was giving at Drummond House—his first. Mrs Tenison was acting as his hostess for this one occasion and was consequently on such high ropes that it was surprising that she did not float up into the air.

'You can't refuse, old fellow,' he pleaded. 'It'd

look damned odd if you cut line on my very first entertainment of the ton.'

Well, he could always leave early, but before he did so he was leaning against the wall, bored and weary, watching other people enjoying themselves, since London seemed stale to him now that it no longer contained Athene.

He remembered how pleasant it had been to be with her when he was not engaged in reproaching her. Her lively wit had informed all their conversation, and he could well believe Mr Tenison had been speaking the truth when he had said how much he would miss her.

Behind him two men whom he knew by sight had begun talking about the Duke of Inglesham.

'Surprised he isn't here,' said the first. 'Came out of his shell this year, didn't he? Probably gone back into it.'

'Oh, no. Tupman said that the rumour is he's dashed off into the country after one of this Season's beauties.'

'Good God, I thought he'd sworn off women after that shrew he married died. Which one is it he's after now—and why into the country?'

'Oh, his target is supposed to be nothing less than the pretty piece who used to stand behind the Northamptonshire heiress who's marrying our host. She left after Kinloch netted the heiress—not that she's that remarkably well endowed with tin, but she's pretty enough to make a good Countess. The heiress, I mean, not Inglesham's bit of muslin—the Duke surely can't mean to marry her.'

Nick's first instinct was to knock down the bastard who was slandering Athene, his second was to slander her himself by assuming that it *had* been the Duke that she was after.

On the other hand, he thought, when the two men had moved away, I can't necessarily assume that an overheard piece of gossip is true. I shall still go to Steep Ride as soon as possible and discover for myself whether Athene discarded the lesser to marry the greater. Yes, that's it.

Why in the world couldn't he have fallen in love with the dull and proper young woman whom every man of sense was supposed to wish for a wife? Chasing after a clever one might be seen as the act of a fool—or of a clever man! There was another thing to consider, too. It was time, as his sister had said reprovingly to him before he had left the Chudleighs, that he forgot the whole Flora Campbell business, accepted that not all women were like her and found himself a wife.

'And if it's the young thing over whom you've been pining, then I shall be only too happy to call her sister.'

And that was why, two days later, he found himself driving into Abbot Quincey determined to find out, once and for all, if he could start a new life, either without Athene, or best of all, with her.

If she would have him, that was.

* * *

Northamptonshire pleased him more than he had expected. One of Nick's friends had told him that it was dull, but then *his* notion of exciting scenery was the Swiss Alps, and after seeing them everything else must appear dull. He found Abbot Quincey to be a pretty little town, with a post-house, two inns and an alehouse outside which ragged old men sunned themselves in the warmth of late July.

Nick bespoke a room at the post-house when he discovered that Steep Ride did not possess an inn with lodgings. He left his chaise in the yard, his valet in the tap-room, and went for a short walk, turning over several strategies in his head before he drove to Datchet House. He had no notion of what sort of reception he might expect from Athene, but he thought ruefully that, given the cruel way in which he had behaved to her, it might be a harsh one.

He was on his way back to the post-house, whose proprietor had promised him nuncheon, shortly after noon, when he saw a handsome black coach being driven slowly towards him from the direction of Steep Ride. To his dismay, if not his surprise, he saw that it bore the Inglesham arms, decked out in red and gold, on its door, and that inside it was the Duke himself.

So, he—and the gossips—had been right. Athene had refused Adrian in order to hold out for Inglesham, and here he was, come to claim her. Or perhaps he had already claimed her.

Disappointment warring with anger, he was of half a mind to return to the post-house, eat his meal, cancel the rooms and return to London.

Chicken-hearted, he told himself furiously, you are chicken-hearted, and a fool beside. Suppose she has refused the Duke, what then? Would you lose her for nothing? At least I ought to confront her, discover what exactly her plans are, and if she is either the Duke's future wife or mistress, then, and only then, would a return to London not be the act of a coward afraid to confront an unpalatable truth—that I have, for the second time, fallen in hopeless love with a scheming mermaid. Lucy is right. I must face the future and forget the past: it has hung over me long enough.

Despite that brave resolution Nick never knew how he ate his nuncheon—nor could he have told anyone what he had eaten. He drank nothing but water, for he knew that he must keep his wits about him, and he drove to Steep Ride as slowly as he could, for he feared that to drive quickly would result in him speeding like a lunatic.

He had always prided himself on his cool command. He had always laughed at those who had run mad over a woman, and here he was, run mad himself. Whether it was his confused state of mind, a state he had never been in before, or whether time itself was playing tricks with him, he seemed to arrive at Steep Ride almost before he had left Abbot Quincey behind.

As he had been told, the place was little more than

a hamlet with one main street, so that Datchet House was soon found. He came to a stop before it, and alighted. It was modest, little more than a large cottage, with a garden before it full of flowers, and a porch framed in rambling roses before a door with a small glass window above an iron knocker.

Now, he would learn his fate. There was no going back.

Nick lifted the iron knocker and rapped the door twice. He was determined to be neither overbearing, nor timid. A classic calm must be his mode of conduct.

Athene was stitching a kneeler for the little chapel which stood at the end of the village street, where the curate came to preach on Sunday. Her mother, who was engaged in similar work, was talking about the Duke's return to her after they had spent so many years apart.

She was rosy-faced and happy, for once her first shock at the arrival of her lost lover was over she had been able to listen calmly to him when he had informed her why—at long last—he had come to see her.

'I find it difficult to believe,' she was telling Athene, 'that, after all these years, he still remembers me, and those few happy days which we spent together. Can I believe him when he tells me that he has never forgotten me, and that he wishes me to forgive him for having so cruelly deserted me, so that we may marry and give both you and me a name which can rightfully belong to us?'

'I think you can,' said Athene gently—she had said nothing to her mother of the Duke's approach to her before she had left London, for he had asked for that to be confidential, and it was for him to speak of it to her mother and not her.

She wondered how many more secrets she might yet need to keep, beside those of her friend Louise. She had told her mother nothing of her love for Nick and the unhappiness it had brought her because of her original determination to marry money and rank. She had, quite truthfully, simply explained to her mother that once Emma's marriage to Lord Kinloch had been arranged Mrs Tenison had decided that her services were no longer required.

She was sure that her mother would not have approved of her behaviour towards Adrian and Nick, and now that she was back home again she could not approve of it herself. Far better to let her mother enjoy her new-found happiness without troubling her with other people's miseries. The Duke had spent the morning with them discussing arrangements for his marriage to his lost love.

'I shall arrange for a special licence,' he had said, 'and a simple ceremony at the village church. I have had one grand marriage and it did not answer. This time I shall marry for love, not money. Besides, it will delay the gossip which will inevitably follow when I treat Athene as my daughter.'

Her mother had smiled agreement. The last thing which either she or the Duke wanted was to be the centre of all the excitement which a fashionable marriage in London would have inflicted on them.

'I still think that I am going to wake up and find that it is all a dream,' her mother was saying. 'Philip said that he would quite understand if I could not forgive him for deserting me, but I know only too well the kind of pressure which was brought to bear on him. The people I cannot forgive are my father and mother, who kept me from him and then turned me out, although I feel that I must inform them that I am finally to be married to the man I love.'

She gave a sad smile. 'I fear that they will forgive me when they receive my news and learn that I am to be a Duchess after all, but it will be too late for me to forgive them. Had they supported me, my dear Philip's father might have relented.'

It was at this point that there was the knock on the door and the arrival of the little maid to tell them that a Mr Nicholas Cameron had arrived asking if he might be allowed to speak to Miss Athene Filmer.

'Mr Cameron,' said her mother. 'Is that the young gentleman who is Lord Kinloch's cousin, Athene?'

Athene managed a 'Yes.' She had said virtually nothing about Nick to her mother, because every time she tried to talk about him she had the most desperate desire to cry. What in the world was he doing in Steep Ride? What could have occurred back in London to bring him here?

She was silent for so long that her mother said gently, 'Athene, the young man is waiting for an answer. Is there any reason why you do not wish to see him?'

'Yes...no,' choked Athene. Oh, why had she not told her mother the truth? She looked wildly around the pretty little room. She could not speak to him here, not among the memories of her happy childhood. Somewhere neutral would be better.

'Athene...?' prompted her mother a little anxiously. 'If you do not wish to speak to Mr Cameron you must tell him so at once. It is only courteous.'

'Oh, I will speak to him,' said Athene, summoning up all her courage. Supposing he had only come to reproach her again, what then? 'But I would prefer not to do it here. Do you think it possible that I could ask him to take a walk with me? I would feel happier talking to him in the open.'

'Possible,' said the bewildered Mrs Filmer, 'but a little odd. It would be more proper to receive him here...but if that is what you wish...'

'I do wish, and I will explain everything later on, when he has gone,' said Athene wildly. 'Would you be so kind as to ask him in, and talk to him while I fetch my bonnet and shawl?'

Odder and odder, thought her mother, after she had agreed and had watched Athene dash from the room as though her head were on fire. What sort of an ogre could Mr Nicholas Cameron be to inspire such trepidation, such agitation as she had never seen her usually composed daughter betray before?

Her surprise was even greater when the little maid ushered the young gentleman in. True, he was harsher of aspect than most young men were in these degenerate days, and his clothing was not that of a dandy. Nevertheless he had the face and manners of a clever man of the kind whom she thought Athene would enjoy being with.

Nick, for his part, took an immediate liking to Mrs Filmer and the modestly pretty room in which she received him. She was as beautiful as Athene, but, unlike her daughter, was small and gentle with a winning smile and an air of wishing to please and to conciliate. Her clothing, whilst not in the last stare of fashion, was designed to suit a widow who had retired to live in a country village.

'I hope,' he began after he had introduced himself and Mrs Filmer had assured him that Athene would receive him shortly, 'that I have not arrived at an inconvenient time. If so, I will leave and call later.'

He didn't wish to do so in the least, but for some reason, Athene's mother aroused all his protective instincts. He wondered what the unknown father must have been like from whom Athene must have inherited her intellect and her determination.

'Oh, no,' she reassured him. 'My daughter was speaking of taking a walk, and it might be an excellent notion for her to show you the village where we have spent so many years.'

Nick solemnly agreed, and tried to hide his impatience until the door opened and Athene arrived—at last. He was sure that for her own reasons she was delaying seeing him as long as possible.

Although her blue dress, shawl and bonnet were as modest as her mother's turn-out, they suited her. She was a little pale, perhaps, but her manner was as calm as ever. Perhaps it was that which set him wishing that he could take her in his arms and tell her that he loved her. Common-sense, and the memory of Inglesham's carriage, told him that he had no notion of what she had been doing and deciding since he had last seen her a month ago.

He bowed, and came out with, 'Athene, I mean Miss Filmer, you look as well as ever.'

Good God, was that the best that he could do? But the presence of her mother and Athene's frozen propriety—even though she had suggested a *tête à tête* walk for the pair of them—seemed to have ushered him in the direction of the North Pole, too!

'Thank you, Mr Cameron,' she responded coolly, 'you appear to be in the best of health, also. I trust that you left Lord Kinloch and Emma in excellent fettle.'

'Very much so. Preparing for the wedding and hoping that you might be present when it comes off.'

'That might be difficult to arrange,' she said gravely. 'I understand that you wish to speak to me. I believe that our meeting might be a more fruitful one if we undertook it on neutral ground as it were.

I shall, therefore, be happy to show you Steep Ride and its immediate environs.'

Nick bowed again. 'And I shall be happy to see them.'

What a ridiculous conversation, thought all three participants at one and the same time. Athene's inward comment was that an observer might think that they were engaged in writing their own book of etiquette, so proper and grand were they being.

Nick bowed to Mrs Filmer, and made his only completely truthful remark of the afternoon so far by saying, 'Very happy to have met you, Mrs Filmer.'

'And I you,' said Athene's mother. What she was really thinking was, Goodness, what on earth have these two young people been getting up to so that they are unable to speak naturally to one another in front of a third party?

Outside, in the open, watched by a nearby cat and two distant waddling ducks, and no one else at all, Nick took Athene's arm in his and walked her away from Datchet House and towards the wooded country which lay beyond the end of the village street.

She was the first to speak when the rough road degenerated into a track and they were out of sight of possible curious eyes. 'Why are you here, Mr Cameron? What is your purpose in pursuing me?'

He swung her gently around so that she faced him, before forgetting everything he had told himself about decorum, about being gentle with her, to fire at her as though she were the enemy—the memory of seeing

the Duke in his coach informing every word he uttered—'Is it Inglesham, then? Did you refuse Adrian
so that you might marry him? If you object to me
following you here, I suppose that he received a different welcome.'

Dazed, Athene stared at him. She genuinely had no
idea why Nick should reproach her about Inglesham.
She knew that he had said earlier that he suspected
her of dangling after the Duke, but that memory had
been obliterated once she had discovered that
Inglesham was her father.

'Inglesham!' she exclaimed, and then, horror of
horrors, she began to laugh, nervous laughter which
had no mirth in it. 'You think that *Inglesham* has
come here to propose to me? Did you follow him
here, too?'

'No, but I saw him in Abbot Quincey this morning,
coming from Steep Ride. Why, Athene, why?'

His face was as tormented as Athene felt that hers
must be. She suddenly took pity on him—who had
had so little pity for her, but she could not resist teasing him a little...

'Is it your opinion, then, that the conduct of a father
is reprehensible if he takes an interest in his daughter?'

Nick stared at her in astonishment. 'Of course I
agree to that, but what has it got to do with us?'

She gave him her sweetest smile. 'Oh, Nick—' Mr
Cameron had disappeared '—the Duke is not my
suitor. And he never has been. He is my father, the

father of whom I had no knowledge until shortly before you left London for the country. He has come to
Steep Ride, at long last, to marry my mother. I cannot
tell you their story—that is for them to do. You have
tormented yourself for nothing.'

'Inglesham?' Nick stammered at her, all his usual
self-possession deserting him when he grasped what
a monstrous mistake he had made. '*Inglesham* is your
father?'

'I have just informed you so, have I not? As usual
you chose to believe the worst of me. Now leave me
alone and allow me to return home.'

She began to walk briskly up the road away from
him, so that he might not see that her tears were about
to fall, for the self-control on which she had always
prided herself was deserting her—so much so that instead of walking back towards the village she was
rapidly making her way into the woods near Steep
Ride, and not away from them.

Such stupidity, she was raging to herself; he has
turned me into a watering-pot with his folly. He is a
very Othello to think me always in the wrong. First
he was jealous of Adrian, and with some justice, and
now it is the Duke, with none. Next, it will be the
Prince Regent, or the Shah of Persia, or perhaps the
Emperor Alexander himself—even the Angel Gabriel
is not safe.

Nick watched her retreating from him. Inglesham
was her father, not her lover, and he, in his blindness,
had tormented himself and reproached her because he

had not possessed the decency to understand that she had renounced Adrian for the best of motives and not because she was greedy for even greater wealth and position than he possessed.

He had been a fool, once, twice, thrice a fool, and now he was going to lose her, the only woman with whom he had ever been able to talk as freely as he would with one of his fellows. A woman whom he had first lusted after and now loved. To make matters worse, with the Duke's patronage and the dowry he would certainly give her she might have anyone she wanted, anyone at all, and, dammit, the only anyone she ought to want was himself.

He began to run after her, heedless of who might see him, for he must immediately try to repair his jealous folly before he lost her for ever. He caught her up where she stood hesitant, realising that she had gone the wrong way. Nick was panting, not with haste, but with the shock of learning the truth. He could not lose her, nay, he must not lose her.

'Athene,' he said hoarsely, detaining her with a look rather than trying to check her physically, 'Athene, can you ever forgive me? I think that I have been madly in love with you ever since I first met you, so that when you seemed to prefer Adrian to me I was in a ferment of jealousy. I was wrong to reproach you for being mercenary and running after him...'

'No,' said his contrary mistress to this confession. 'No, you were right at the time. At first, I *did* run after him, because he was just the sort of jolly and kind fellow who was lucky enough to possess wealth and a title as well—someone whom I could safely marry without loving him. And then when I got to know *you,* I began to change my mind, and something my father told me made me renounce Adrian because I didn't truly love him and it would be wrong to marry him. But it was too late, wasn't it? You had made up your mind about me.'

Nick thought that she was about to run away from him again.

'No, don't go,' he said hoarsely. 'Forgive me if you can. However badly I have behaved towards you, I have always loved you. There it is, the truth, out at last.'

Before he could stop himself, he took her in his arms: whatever else, he could kiss away the tears which had begun to run down her cheeks.

'Oh, Athene,' he sighed. 'I have dreamed of doing this ever since the first time I first saw you, standing behind young Emma,' and he began to kiss her, gently at first and then with increasing passion.

At first Athene let him hold her, let him kiss her tears away, without responding to him. And then, as his passion grew the greater, hers flowered into life, and when he kissed her on the lips, she returned his kiss so enthusiastically that it was Nick who pulled away with a sigh, fearful of where their mutual transports were leading them.

Transfixed, Athene stood back and stared at him

before saying, 'I thought that you despised me, not loved me. When did this remarkable transformation take place? How, loving me, could you think that I would behave in such a two-faced manner?'

'Jealousy,' he said simply, putting out a hand to stroke her warm cheek. 'And the memory of what happened to me when I first loved a woman whole-heartedly. She deserted me for a richer man shortly before the wedding ceremony, and in my misery and stupidity—for that is what it was—I have been suspicious of all women ever since. To be fair, you must admit that the whole Inglesham business only seemed to make sense if, knowing nothing of his relationship with your mother, one were to assume that he was after you.'

'Well, he was,' said Athene uncontrovertibly, putting her hand over his, 'but not in the manner in which you thought. He had no children by his first wife and he wanted to reclaim the daughter he had lost years ago. Goodness, from the way in which we have all been going on we might have been enacting one of Shakespeare's lesser plays.'

'*The Comedy of Errors,* perhaps,' said Nick, regaining his sense of humour once his jealousy had flown out of the window. 'And now there is nothing left for me to do but ask you if you can forgive me enough to agree to marry me.'

'Could you believe that I am not sure how to answer you? Even if I love you, which I most demonstrably do, will it be possible for me to be happy with

a husband who will run mad if I look at another man?
Dare I take that chance?'

'Could *you* believe that I have learned my lesson
and will trust you in future? My mother once told me
that I was a conceited boy who thought that I knew
the answer to everything. Since I met you I seem to
have had the answer to nothing. You're sure that you
won't regret not marrying Adrian, or possibly someone even grander—someone like your father?'

'No,' said Athene simply. 'I don't want to marry
any man because he is grand. I want to marry someone I love for himself, and that man is you.'

'Is that a yes or a no?'

'Yes, it's a yes. I have to believe that you mean
what you say, and that we can deal as happily together as we have done so often in conversation and
in play whenever we forgot that we were at odds with
one another.'

'That we were at odds was mostly my fault,' he
told her sorrowfully. 'I don't deserve you. I misjudged you, and for that I apologise to my darling
Pallas.'

'There is no need for you to apologise, for I, too,
was at fault from the moment I arrived in London. I
misjudged myself in thinking that I could marry without love—and so I left myself open to be misjudged
by you.'

'Nevertheless,' he said, taking her in his arms
again, 'perhaps this will convince you that my apology comes from the heart.'

This time she responded to his kisses so fiercely from the very beginning, that again, in order to resist temptation, he had after a time to pull himself away with a groan.

'It must be the woods which are affecting us,' he said, looking around him. 'Did you really mean to run into them? Were you looking for your owl for advice, my lovely Pallas? I would have thought that you would have run into safety—not away from it. They are tempting me to do that which must wait for our wedding if we are not to be forsworn in church!'

'I scarcely knew what I was doing when I ran from you,' she said. 'Perhaps the woods were kind for once and lured me into them so that you might follow me where no one could disturb us. The legend says that they are unkind to strangers and those who would desecrate the Abbey, hence the violent deaths of so many of its recent owners. Perhaps they do not see me as a stranger, since I have roved freely in them all my life.'

Nick answered her with a restrained kiss before saying. 'You may be right, but they are dark and stern enough to support any story of death and tragedy. Today, however, they must bear witness to the merry tale of lovers finding themselves at last. I cannot wait to introduce you to my parents and to my dear sister, Lucy. They were fearful that I would never marry, and here I am, caught at last by a very witch who has freed me from the foul enchantments of the past.'

'And Scotland,' said Athene merrily. 'Don't forget

Scotland. You must take me there, for I have never been farther north than Northampton and I can't wait to see "Caledonia, stern and wild...", the land of Sir Walter Scott.'

'I have every intention of taking you there once we are safely married—and that as soon as it can be arranged—we have lost too much time already. And now we must return to Steep Ride in order to show your mother that I meant you no harm. She gave me what my nurse used to call an old-fashioned look when I invaded your parlour—and no wonder, I must have appeared beside myself!'

Hand in hand they walked back to Datchet House, where they found the Duke's carriage still standing outside it as proof that not one, but two pairs of lovers had, in the end, found what all men and women hope for, their other self, with whom they might achieve happiness and fulfilment in the future.

The drama continues!

*Look out for more Regency drama, intrigue,
mischief…and marriage in*

The Steepwood Scandals Volume 5

featuring Counterfeit Earl *by Anne Herries*
& The Captain's Return *by Elizabeth Bailey.*

Available next month, from all good booksellers.

THE STEEPWOOD
Scandals

Regency drama, intrigue, mischief...
and marriage

VOLUME FIVE

Counterfeit Earl by Anne Herries

Scarred after his experiences in the Peninsular War,
Captain Jack Denning feels unable to love. But caught
in a compromising situation with excitement-seeking
Olivia, a proposal is the only option!

The Captain's Return by Elizabeth Bailey

Captain Henry Colton is stunned to find his lost love
living as a widow. Given the way they had parted, in
anger, could he now expect Annabel to let him
back into her life?

On sale 2nd March 2007

*Available at WHSmith, Tesco, ASDA,
and all good bookshops*

A young woman disappears.
A husband is suspected of murder.
Stirring times for all the neighbourhood in

THE STEEPWOOD
Scandals

Volume 5 – March 2007
Counterfeit Earl by Anne Herries
The Captain's Return by Elizabeth Bailey

Volume 6 – April 2007
The Guardian's Dilemma by Gail Whitiker
Lord Exmouth's Intentions by Anne Ashley

Volume 7 – May 2007
Mr Rushford's Honour by Meg Alexander
An Unlikely Suitor by Nicola Cornick

Volume 8 – June 2007
An Inescapable Match by Sylvia Andrew
The Missing Marchioness by Paula Marshall

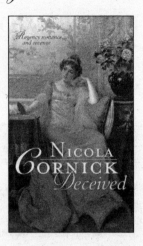

The Regency

LORDS & LADIES
COLLECTION

*Two glittering Regency
love affairs in every book*

MILLS & BOON®

www.millsandboon.co.uk

The *Regency*

LORDS & LADIES
COLLECTION

*Two glittering Regency
love affairs in every book*

MILLS & BOON®

www.millsandboon.co.uk

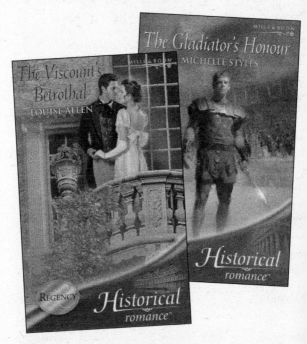

*H*istorical
romance™

HIGH SEAS TO HIGH SOCIETY
by Sophia James

Asher Wellingham, Duke of Carisbrook, was captivated
by her! But who was Lady Emma Seaton? And what
lay behind her refined mask? High-born lady or artful
courtesan, Asher wanted to possess both!

THE COUNTESS BRIDE *by Terri Brisbin*

Catherine de Severin was a penniless orphan with
a shadowed past. She was not a fit bride for a rich,
powerful *comte*. But Geoffrey Dumont cared not, and
would defy anyone – even the King – to marry his
beautiful Cate! Catherine knew she could resist her own
desire…but she had no defence against his passion!

THE TENDERFOOT BRIDE
by Cheryl St John

Linnea McConaughy was not the sturdy widow rancher
Will Tucker expected to manage his household. Instead,
he found himself wanting to protect her and offer her a
home with him… But Linnea wasn't sure if Will could
accept her shameful past – and another man's baby…

On sale 2nd March 2007